Made *for* Us

SAMANTHA
CHASE

WITHDRAWN

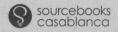

sourcebooks
casablanca

Published by Sourcebooks Casablanca, an imprint of Sourcebooks, Inc.
P.O. Box 4410, Naperville, Illinois 60567-4410
(630) 961-3900
Fax: (630) 961-2168
www.sourcebooks.com

Printed and bound in Canada.
MBP 10 9 8 7 6 5 4 3 2 1

This book is dedicated to my husband and all of the love, support, and patience he's given me.

And none of this would be possible without the amazing team of people I am blessed to have around me. There aren't enough words to say thank you to my editorial team—Deb, Susie, and Eliza. The three of you truly lift me up and inspire me to be more.
You're the best!

Prologue

THE SMELL OF ROSES WAS OVERWHELMING.

Not that the aroma was surprising—there had to be at least fifty oversized arrangements around him, each filled with different colored roses. The funny thing about it was that the flowers were all wrong. Roses had never been his mother's favorite flower; it was just what she had told people because whenever she'd shared her actual favorite flower, people looked at her as if she were a little off.

Daisies. Daisies were her favorite.

Aidan Shaughnessy stood alone at his mother's grave site. Everyone had left hours ago and gone back to the house to eat and to do their best to support the family after losing its matriarch. It was more than Aidan could bear to deal with, so he stayed, all day, alone.

The cemetery was less than a mile from home, so he didn't mind walking back later. Looking down at the freshly laid dirt, he felt both numb and overwhelmed with emotion at the same time. He didn't want her to be alone.

Stuffing his hands into his trouser pockets to try to ward off the chill as the sun started to set, Aidan wondered how he was supposed to move on. His mother was his rock; she was his biggest cheerleader, his toughest critic, and the only person with whom he felt comfortable sharing all of his hopes and dreams. Thinking back to his early teen years, a conversation came to mind.

"Girls are stupid," Aidan said, coming in the back door after school and throwing his backpack on the ground. His mother was in the kitchen washing some fruit, watching him expectantly.

"Are you making an apple pie?" he asked hopefully.

She nodded. *"I know it's your favorite,"* she said with a serene smile as she wiped her hands on her cherry-patterned apron. For a few minutes she said nothing. She waited out her fourteen-year-old, eldest child until he was ready to talk.

"I asked Lisa O'Rourke to go to the homecoming dance and she said yes. Then I got to school today and she told me she didn't want to go with me. Mark King had asked her and since he's captain of the varsity football team, she'd rather go with him." Aidan sat down on one of the stools at the counter, looked up at his mother, and willed the tears he felt threatening to stay put.

"Seems to me you should be celebrating."

He looked at his mom as if she'd lost her mind. *"What? Why would you even say that?"*

She shrugged and began to peel the apples. *"A girl like that? One who would make promises to one boy and then go off with another? Well, good riddance, I say. Plus, let her go off with Mark King. We all know he's the captain of the team only because his uncle is the coach. He's not very good."*

Now it was Aidan's turn to shrug. *"He's not so bad."*

Lillian Shaughnessy carefully placed her paring knife and the apple she was working on down on the counter *and leaned toward her son. "You're going to run circles around him. Mark my words. When you make varsity next year, you are going to make everyone forget Mark King ever existed in that school. And when you graduate high school with a football scholarship and go on to the NFL? Well, you'll look back on this and laugh and be thankful you didn't get tangled up with a girl like Lisa."*

The thought of being in the NFL put a smile on Aidan's face, but it was quickly replaced by a more contemplative look. "But how will I know, Mom? I mean, I thought Lisa was cool. I really thought she liked me. How am I going to know the difference between a girl I can trust and one that…you know…I can't?"

A wide smile crossed Lillian's face. "I'll let you know."

Aidan rolled his eyes. "Mom," he said with a mock whine. "No guy lets his mom pick out his girlfriend. Sheesh!"

"I'm not saying I'm going to pick her out for you," she said diplomatically as she went back to peeling the apples. "I'm just saying I'll be able to help you see if she is the girl for you. If she is someone you want to share your…someday with. If she is worthy of someone as amazing as you, Aidan Shaughnessy."

The two smiled at one another as Lillian finished assembling the pie and Aidan felt a surge of confidence in his future—all because he had the greatest mom right there at his side.

Standing in the middle of the cemetery, Aidan wondered about that future. That conversation had taken place four years ago. As if she had seen into his future, he had made the varsity team the following year and, even now, was in college on a football scholarship. Football was his life. It was supposed to be his future but it wasn't right now. Right now, there didn't seem to be any point in the future.

Why had this happened? Why had his family been destroyed like this? Aidan had no idea how he was supposed to move forward, how any of them were supposed to move forward. This wasn't supposed to happen to the Shaughnessys! They were supposed to be together—always! Looking up at the heavens, Aidan wanted to curse, but his mother had taught him better than that.

"What am I supposed to do, Mom? What are any of us supposed to do?"

The responsibility of raising the kids had all been on Lillian, and everyone knew she loved it. But Aidan's father now had six kids to raise on his own. Aidan had no idea how that was going to work, because while his dad was an amazing man, he was the breadwinner, who worked hard and sometimes long hours.

Aidan thought of each of his siblings—Hugh, Quinn, Riley, Owen, and…Darcy. He felt his heart squeeze in his chest. Darcy was just a baby. She was never going to know her mother. And his mother was never going to get to see her baby girl grow up. Lillian Shaughnessy had wanted a daughter in the worst way after having five boys, and even though there were ten years between Darcy and the youngest boys, twins Riley and Owen, everyone had been thrilled by her pregnancy. A small smile crossed his face even as tears began to fall.

It wasn't fair. None of it.

Once more, Aidan looked to the heavens. "I need you, Mom. We all need you." A small breeze blew, yet

Aidan didn't feel it. "I still have so many questions. You promised to help me with the answers."

Turning, he pulled a rose from one of the many arrangements. Looking at it for a moment, he kissed it and then placed it on top of the grave. With a heavy heart, he began the walk back home.

Alone.

Chapter 1

WHY WERE PEOPLE SO INCOMPETENT? IT WAS A question Aidan Shaughnessy asked himself far too many times a day. How difficult was it to follow instructions? How hard was it to read the damn directions?

"Clearly, it's beyond anyone's comprehension," he muttered to himself as he walked through the model home of the new subdivision his company was working on.

The trim was crooked, the ceiling looked wavy, and the paint job was horrendous. Not only that, but when he reached the master bedroom, he saw the paint colors were completely wrong. Pulling out his phone, Aidan called his assistant and left her a message to get the designer on the job to meet him first thing Monday morning. It was already after seven at night, so Aidan knew no one would be around to clean up the mess now.

With a weary sigh, he shut off all the lights and was locking up the house when his phone rang. Looking at the screen on his smartphone, Aidan felt some of the tension ease from his body.

"Hey, Dad," Aidan said into the phone. "I'm running a little bit behind but I promise to have the pizza there by the time the game starts." He smiled at the thought of having a couple of hours just to unwind and relax with his family. Most men would cringe at spending a Friday night at home with their father and teenage sister, but it was something Aidan looked forward to.

"See that you do," his father said with a chuckle. "Darcy is having a fit that you're not here yet. She's threatening to eat all the brownies herself before you get here!"

That made Aidan laugh because although his seventeen-year-old sister loved to bake, she loved taunting her brothers with her delicious creations even more. "Tell her if she does that, I'll make sure neither of the pizzas have pepperoni. I'll load them with mushrooms and anchovies before I let her take away my dessert!"

Ian Shaughnessy laughed hard. He loved that the age difference between his youngest child and his oldest didn't deter them from bantering with and teasing one another. "Oh, I'll tell her, but be prepared for her wrath if you are one minute late."

"Deal," Aidan said and then called in their order to the local pizzeria.

"Hey, Aidan," Tony said as he answered the phone. "Your usual?"

Shaking his head, Aidan couldn't help but laugh. Small-town living. "Hey, Tony," he said with a smile. "What do you think?"

"Two large pies, one with extra cheese and pepperoni and the other with sausage. Gimme twenty minutes, okay?"

"You got it, Tony. Thanks." Disconnecting, Aidan turned and looked at the house he had just locked up. At least it was beautiful from the outside. Between the stonework, the colors, and the craftsman style, it made for a very appealing home. Aidan had spared no expense on the materials for the model. Everything was top of the line, and he used every upgrade available inside and out to dazzle potential buyers.

Taking a couple of steps back, he admired the landscaping. The grounds looked ready for a *Home and Garden* photo spread. Everything was perfectly manicured, and all the greenery was acclimating to its new soil and cooperating by staying green and in bloom.

If only the inside were up to the same caliber…

"Okay, I have *got* to let that go for tonight," he reminded himself as he walked over to his truck and climbed in. "Dad will have my hide if I spend the night complaining about work."

You would think that at age thirty-four, parental disappointment wouldn't faze a man, but Aidan was different. His father had been through so much in his life, had struggled so much after Aidan's mother had died unexpectedly, that Aidan swore he would never do anything to cause his father any extra grief.

He left that to his siblings.

And they were good at it.

In the years following his mother's death, Aidan had wanted to do more to help his family out. The day after the funeral, Aidan told his father he wanted to quit college and come home, but Ian had put his foot down. Aidan knew his mother wouldn't have wanted him to leave college, but at the time, he'd felt so helpless.

When he blew out his knee in his junior year, it officially ended any dreams of a career in the NFL. But he wasn't disappointed about that now; his life was exactly where it was supposed to be. He had a construction business he had built up all on his own, and he was surrounded—for the most part—by his family.

Some of his brothers had moved away from their small North Carolina town, but Aidan didn't resent them for it. Quite the opposite, he encouraged them to follow their dreams because that was exactly what their mother would have done. With their father preoccupied with raising a teenage girl after a houseful of boys, Aidan had taken it upon himself to be "the encourager" in the family.

Did he date? Sometimes.

Was he looking to settle down? Maybe.

Were there any prospects on the horizon? No.

Maybe he should do something about that, he thought as he drove through town to pick up dinner. The streets were crowded, but that was nothing new. It was Friday night and everyone was out and about. As his truck crept along Main Street with the windows down, Aidan was able to smile and wave to many familiar faces. This was what he did, who he was. But for some reason, tonight it bothered him.

Why wasn't he walking along the street holding hands with a woman? When exactly was the last time he had done that? Searching his memory, he couldn't even remember when. Was it with Amber or Kelly? Hell, he couldn't even remember their names or their faces. That was a surefire clue it had been too long.

"Nothing I can do about it tonight," Aidan muttered and pulled into the last spot in front of the Italian restaurant. There was a line out the door and Aidan was relieved for the side entrance reserved for takeout orders. As he walked in, he was greeted by the same faces he saw in there every Friday night. But by the time Aidan had paid and was walking back out to his truck with the pizzas, he was feeling a little down for some reason.

Aidan had had too long a day to puzzle out the source of this sudden depression, however; for tonight, he vowed to enjoy himself. He loved catching up with what Darcy was up to and hearing about how she was doing in school. And even though Aidan and his dad saw each other on a daily basis because Ian Shaughnessy was in charge of all of the electrical inspections on new construction in the county, Aidan knew his dad always just liked having him around.

Ian was dedicated to his children, and it didn't matter how old they got or how far away they moved: Ian Shaughnessy wanted nothing more than to see his children be happy.

Just as Lillian would have wanted.

Pulling up to his childhood home, Aidan felt a lot of the tension leave his body. This was his haven. No matter what was going on in his life, he still enjoyed coming back here and spending time. Not to mention that right now, the scent of hot pizza was practically making him drool and he had no doubt his little sister was pacing the floor waiting for him to get inside and feed her.

His suspicions were confirmed as soon as he walked through the door.

"It's about time, Aidan!" his sister cried, grabbing the pizza boxes from his hands. "Honestly, a person could die of starvation waiting for you."

"Ex*cuse* me, Duchess," he said with a chuckle, "but some of us have to work for a living. We can't all have food delivered on our every whim."

She rolled her eyes at him as she placed the pizza on the kitchen table. "I would love to have a job, big Brother. But you and Dad and the rest of the Shaughnessy bullies won't let me."

"Bullies?" he asked with a laugh, washing his hands and winking at his father as he walked in from the living room where the pregame bantering was on. "There are Shaughnessy bullies? Why wasn't I told of this?"

"Oh." Darcy swatted his arm playfully. "You're the captain of the bully squad."

"Now we're a squad?"

"Aidan!" she huffed, and plopped down into her seat at the table. "You know darn well you have been the biggest voice in keeping me from getting a job. If you would—"

"Darce, we've been over this before. You don't *need* to work right now. You need to focus on your school-work so you can get into a good college."

Darcy looked from her father to her brother and back again. "A good college? Don't you really mean one that's close to home?" This wasn't a new argument, but Darcy was hoping she'd wear them down eventually.

"There are plenty of colleges close to home," Aidan said evasively, reaching for a slice of the fast-cooling pizza.

"But I don't want to go to any of them."

"Can we please have one meal without an argument?" Ian finally chimed in.

"I'm not arguing, Dad," Darcy countered. "I'm simply stating that there are plenty of great colleges that aren't within a ten-mile radius of our house."

"So in answer to your question, Dad," Aidan said

with a smile, "no. We cannot have one meal without an argument." Normally that was all it took to get Darcy to back down, but tonight she slammed her palms on the table.

"Why won't anyone take this seriously?" she snapped, looking at her father. "Everyone else was allowed to pick where they wanted to go to college. Why can't I?"

"Come on, Darce," Aidan interrupted. "It's been a crappy day. Can't we just enjoy dinner?"

If there was one thing Darcy had learned to perfect in her seventeen years, it was the art of the argument. She had even been on the debate team since her sophomore year, bringing home a trophy or two, and learning some skills that had come in very useful with her siblings. She thought of it as a form of mental self-defense. Unfortunately, she just didn't have it in her tonight. Being the only female in a male-dominated household, there were so many things about her life that didn't seem fair, but she had learned to accept most of them.

Out of her five brothers, she was probably closest to Aidan, even though he was the oldest. He was one of the few siblings who still lived in the area, so she saw him the most and she enjoyed spending time with him. Lately, she could tell something was up with him even though Aidan seemed unwilling to admit it.

Darcy could think of a million reasons why Aidan's day had been crappy. All he did was work and go home alone and spend Friday nights having pizza with her and their father. *Bor-ing*. She wished he'd find someone and go out on a date. Have a social life. She supposed he was good-looking, but if he didn't go out and find a girl soon, he was going to be old and gray and no one was going to want him. Probably not the best time to bring up the old and gray thing.

"Fine," she grumbled. "Why was your day crappy?"

Finishing his slice of pizza, Aidan went to the refrigerator and grabbed himself the one beer he allowed himself every Friday night. "Oh, you know, it's the same old thing. No one reads the instructions on the job site, things aren't getting done the way I want them, my assistant is asking for an assistant. Nothing new."

"Everything was looking good when I was on site on Tuesday," Ian said. "What changed?"

"The paint job is crap, there's some trim that's messed up, and the decorator got all the color tones wrong. I did a walk-through tonight before I left, which is why I was late getting dinner, and I just couldn't believe my eyes. It was as if I had never said a word about anything. I mean, how difficult is it to follow a set of plans?"

"So what are you going to do?" Ian asked, knowing his son was a perfectionist by nature and wouldn't rest until everything was up to his standards.

"I'm bringing in a new painting crew, and I've put a call in to meet the decorator on Monday morning." He shook his head. "Tired of wasting my time."

"Ever think maybe you're looking a little too closely at things?" Darcy asked, and then instantly regretted her comment when her brother aimed an angry glare in her direction.

"I look at things the way they are meant to be looked at," he said defensively. "The craftsmanship I put out there is what makes Shaughnessy Construction stand out. If I relax my standards, then what?"

"Sorry," she mumbled and reached for another slice of pizza.

"Aidan, don't take it out on Darcy. All she's saying is that you have a craftsman's eye. The typical home owner and buyer won't notice the things you see."

"So that makes it right? That makes it okay to just put a crappy product out there? I can't believe you would suggest such a thing."

"I'm not suggesting anything of the sort, Son," Ian said. "I'm just suggesting that you relax a bit." He looked at Darcy slouching in her seat, staring at her plate, then back at Aidan, who looked ready to turn the table upside down. "Who's up for a game of bowling?"

Darcy and Aidan looked up at him incredulously.

"Bowling?" Darcy repeated. "I'm not going to the bowling alley with my dad and brother on a Friday night. Forget about it."

Now it was Ian's turn to roll his eyes. "*Wii* bowling." Ian pulled Darcy out of her seat and then turned to his son. "Don't make me pull you up too. C'mon. Family bowling in the living room. Now. Let's go!"

It was the last thing Aidan wanted to do, but he knew it would make his father happy so he didn't argue. Five minutes later, the three of them were standing in the middle of the living room choosing their order of play. Ten minutes later, it was as if the earlier tension had never even happened.

And that was what was most important to Aidan—his family's happiness.

—∿∿—

Later that night, Aidan sat alone in his apartment. It was late, but his brain wouldn't shut down enough for him to go to sleep. He was restless. His skin felt too tight for his body. And for the life of him, he didn't know what to do about it.

Darcy's comment about being too nitpicky wasn't new, so he wondered if that was really enough to keep him awake. *Meticulous* was a word that was often thrown around when people talked about him. It didn't bother him. Much. Meticulous could be a good thing, if his brothers didn't add "anal-retentive control freak" to it all the damn time.

He rested his head back on the pillow and let out a breath. If he allowed himself to stop being the big brother for a minute and just be a bystander, he could admit Darcy wasn't asking for anything out of the ordinary. He thought she was probably itching to spread her wings. But there was no way in hell he or any of his brothers were going to let her go off to some faraway college on her own. She'd just have to learn to deal with it. But he supposed there were some things they could compromise on.

Looking at the clock on the wall, he saw it was after midnight. He should be tired.

Instead, he grabbed his cell phone and pulled up Hugh's number. Although Aidan couldn't remember where exactly his brother was this month, he knew it was somewhere on the West Coast, and three hours earlier.

"If you're calling me this late on a Friday night, it can't be good," Hugh said as he answered the phone.

Aidan chuckled. "Maybe I just wanted to hear your cheery voice."

"Yeah, right," Hugh said with his own laugh. "Seriously, everything okay? This is late for you."

The comment burned more than it should. He was

responsible, so what? Why did everyone have to make it sound like there was something wrong with him? "It's not that late," Aidan grumbled. "I just…" He paused. "Something's going on with Darcy."

"Oh shit," Hugh muttered. "That is all on you and Dad, Bro. There is no way I'm dealing with a teenage girl. She scares the hell out of me."

This time Aidan's laugh was hearty. "For crying out loud, Hugh, she's a child. And she's our sister!"

"What is it this time?"

"It's mostly the same song and dance but she's getting more…vocal about it. She kind of yelled at me and Dad tonight about the whole college thing."

Hugh sighed loudly. "Listen, Darcy is going to be pissed because, well, she's Darcy. She's a female, and females like to argue. Aidan, look…it's Friday night. I've got a resort filled to capacity—"

"I'm thinking of letting her work for me a couple of days a week after school."

"That's brave, man. Very brave. And she's good with that? I would have thought she'd take issue with having to work with family."

"I haven't mentioned it to her yet. I just thought of it right before I called you. What do you think?"

"Like I said, you're brave."

"Bravery has nothing to do with it. It's just that—"

"She doesn't need to work," Hugh interrupted. "Our sister doesn't want for anything, Aidan. Dad takes care of everything for her. Why can't she just be grateful and…go shopping or something?"

"I agree with you, but maybe she wants to feel like she's contributing."

"To what?"

"To her family," Aidan said. "With all of us moved out, now it's just her and Dad at home."

"And you."

Aidan sighed and pinched the bridge of his nose. "I don't live at home. I have a place of my own and—"

"And you still spend a whole lot of time at home," Hugh said carefully. "It's not a bad thing, Aidan. I think it's great you're close by in case either of them need you, but don't you ever want more?"

How had the subject suddenly turned to him? This wasn't about him; this was about Darcy. Ignoring Hugh's question, Aidan went back to his original train of thought. "If she has a job, maybe it'll pacify her about the whole college thing, and I can still keep an eye on her."

"And working for her brother is going to accomplish that?"

"It's a start."

"Fine. Go ahead and ask her, but do me a favor."

"What?"

"Have someone record it. I want to see her reaction." He laughed for too long before he realized Aidan wasn't. "Look, man, do what you think is best. Let me know what you need from me and I'll do it. You're the responsible one in the family. You always seem to know exactly what to do and what to say to smooth things over. If you think offering Darcy a job with your company is the answer, then do it."

"But…?" Aidan knew there was more.

"But…" Hugh began, "maybe it's time for you to stop smoothing things over for everyone else and start doing something for yourself."

"What are you talking about?"

"Dude, it's midnight on a Friday freaking night and you're on the phone with your *brother*. And that's after you went and had dinner with your father and sister. For God's sake, go out! Go on a date! When was the last time you were even with a woman?"

"None of your damn business," Aidan snapped.

"That long, huh?" Hugh chuckled. "Okay, fine. Don't tell me. I can pretty much guess." He stopped and collected his thoughts. "Just…think about it, okay?"

"About what?"

"And you call me a dumbass," Hugh said with exasperation. "Think about *yourself*, damn it! Think about doing something on a Friday night that isn't family related. Think about going out with a beautiful woman and wining and dining her and spending the night with her nails raking down your damn back."

Aidan hadn't thought about it that way, but he had a feeling he'd be thinking about it a lot tonight. "Fine. I'll think about it."

"Hey, and Aidan?"

"What?" he said grumpily.

"You can call me any damn time you want. Seriously."

A small smile broke on Aidan's face. "Thanks, man. I appreciate it."

"Keep me posted on the whole Darcy situation."

Aidan agreed and they hung up. He was no closer to any decisions on anything. The only thing that had changed was that he suddenly had an itch that needed to be scratched.

Chapter 2

"REASON NUMBER NINE HUNDRED AND FORTY-SEVEN why my life sucks: this job. At least this job today." Zoe Dalton slouched down in her office chair and looked at the pile of messages in front of her. She'd been an interior designer for years, but she'd just moved to the East Coast the month before and working for well-known designer Martha Tate was quickly grating on her nerves.

A flurry of activity outside her door made her look up and her boss appeared, as if Zoe'd conjured her up by force of griping.

"Zoe," Martha said breathlessly as she stepped into the office and sat down at her desk, "I'm going to need you to take over on the Shaughnessy job."

From what Zoe had heard in the previous weeks, the Shaughnessy project was a huge undertaking. There were a lot of houses going up in a brand-new community, and at least half a dozen model homes needed to be decorated. "Why? What happened to Sarah?" Zoe asked.

Martha waved her off. "She went rogue and the client is majorly pissed."

"Went rogue?"

"She ignored the design plans the client requested," Martha said reproachfully. "This was a fairly straight-forward job; everything was clearly specified per Mr. Shaughnessy's directions."

"So I have to go in and do damage control, is that it?"

Her boss nodded. "And…redo everything Sarah did. And make sure the next five houses are done *exactly* as requested."

Seemed like a no-brainer. Zoe shrugged and smiled. "I'm on it."

Martha looked visibly relieved. "Good…good. You have a meeting with Mr. Shaughnessy in an hour. Sarah's collecting all her files, along with all her personal belongings, and you'll have them to go through in a few minutes."

"Her personal belongings?"

"No, just her files. She's fired," Martha said.

Maybe this job *wasn't* a no-brainer. She was going to have to tread very carefully from this point forward.

She nodded and straightened in her seat. "Okay, I'll meet with Mr. Shaughnessy at ten, and then I have an eleven with…"

"Oh, no, no, no, Zoe," Martha interrupted. "You aren't meeting with anyone else today. You'll have to cancel."

"But—"

"You have to give this project one hundred percent of your attention."

"But—"

"You can't expect someone like Aidan Shaughnessy to wait on you and your schedule. I know you haven't been here very long, but the Shaughnessys are a very important family in the community, and this account is huge for us. Sarah can fill you in about them. You're going to need to be available not only to fix Sarah's mistakes but also to make sure absolutely nothing else goes wrong with the rest of the houses. You need to be on this 24-7."

Zoe was not one to raise her voice, but right now it was the only way to get her boss to stop interrupting her. "Hold on!" she said. "I have at least six other active projects I'm working on. I've put a lot of time and effort into developing relationships with these clients. I can't just toss them aside, Martha!"

"Already taken care of," she said dismissively. "I've reassigned all of your projects. If you'll just go through your messages, I'll be sure to pass them on to the designers who are taking them over."

Her head felt ready to explode. Back in Arizona, she'd had her own firm and had been her own boss. Zoe had known there was going to be some compromises when she moved and went to work for someone else, but this was above and beyond what she'd expected. The decision to move had been an emotional one, and she had hoped for a more positive transition than this. This was not something she was willing to take lying down.

"Look, Martha, I'm sure Mr. Shaughnessy is a reasonable businessman," she began diplomatically and was surprised when Martha actually snorted with sarcasm. Zoe raised her eyebrows but continued. "Surely he can understand that while Sarah made a…mistake… we will do everything to rectify it without compromising our other clients." There. That sounded sensible, didn't it?

Leaning forward in her seat, Martha gave Zoe a pitying look. "Zoe, trust me. If it were any other client, I would let you keep your other projects. But this is a… special…case. This is going to demand much more of your time than you think. If, by some miracle, you get things going to the point where I'm not hearing from him several times a week, I'll consider letting you take on other projects again. Until I can be sure of it though, he's your one and only client."

"What if I promise not to let my other projects interfere with the Shaughnessy job?"

Martha shook her head. "Trust me, you can't keep that promise."

Zoe sat back in resignation.

Martha chose her next words carefully. "I'm not trying to scare you or anything, but I want you to go into this meeting today thoroughly prepared."

Zoe shrugged. "I still don't think that—"

"You've had your own business, Zoe, so I know you've had your share of difficult clients, right?"

Zoe nodded.

"And that's why I'm putting you on this job. Think of your most difficult client and multiply by say…ten."

Music of doom began playing in Zoe's head. "Well, I wasn't scared before, but now—"

"We'll talk about this after your meeting." Standing, Martha put an end to the discussion and walked out of the room.

And her day couldn't get any worse. Zoe immediately suspected she was going to hate Aidan Shaughnessy.

The next fifteen minutes were like an out-of-body experience for Zoe. People came and went from her office to get files and messages and collect what they could on her former clients. Zoe felt as if she were watching the whole thing happen in slow motion; it was like she wasn't even there and people were picking over her belongings. And just when she thought the worst was over, Sarah walked in and dropped a massive box on the floor in front of Zoe's desk.

"Good luck with *that* one," she said snidely and walked right back out.

"Sarah! Wait!" Zoe cried, scrambling out from behind her desk to try to catch up. Luckily, Sarah halted in the hallway. "Can I talk to you for a minute? Please?" Zoe could see that her former coworker would as soon spit in her face as talk, but Sarah reluctantly walked back into Zoe's office.

"Thank you," Zoe said, quietly closing the door. She offered Sarah a seat, but the woman continued to stand with her arms crossed, ready to flee. "I know the last thing you want to do is help me with any of this, but could you please just let me know what I'm getting into?" Zoe was practically begging and hoped Sarah would take pity on her.

Sarah relaxed her stance. "I've known Aidan Shaughnessy all my life, and he is an arrogant, condescending jackass. *That's* what you're getting yourself into."

Not quite what she was hoping for, but it was a start. "Okay, I got that part. But what about the job itself? I know there are five houses left and—"

"Six," Sarah corrected. "He's going to make you completely redo that entire first house. I wouldn't be surprised if he's gotten the entire thing stripped down to bare walls already."

Zoe's stomach lurched. She swallowed hard and sat down in her chair. "Okay, six houses. What makes them difficult?"

Sarah finally took a seat. "It's not the houses that make the job difficult, Zoe. It's the man. Just…be careful."

This was getting worse by the minute. "How so?"

"Look, you're new to the area so you're probably not aware of it but…the Shaughnessys are like the Kennedys around here. They've been here forever. There are a lot of them and they're all successful."

"Define successful."

Sarah settled more comfortably in her seat and gave her words some thought. "Let's see… Hugh, the second oldest, owns a bunch of luxury resorts pretty much all over the world. His newest one is in Napa—he bought a vineyard and built a five-star resort on it. It's huge with the celebrity crowd right now. Most of his other resorts are on islands—his next one is going up in Australia, I think—and he does destination weddings and that sort of thing."

"Wow." Zoe was impressed but not to the point of a comparison to the Kennedys.

"Then there's Quinn. I graduated with him. He was a star athlete in high school and we all thought he was going to go play major league baseball, but he took up race car driving. He doesn't do it anymore—one crash too many, I think—and now he has a chain of custom auto body shops up and down the East Coast."

"So they're overachievers," Zoe said conversationally. "So what?"

"It's not just those two." Sarah smirked. "Next we have Riley."

"Wait a minute," Zoe interrupted. "Are you talking about Riley Shaughnessy…*the* Riley Shaughnessy?"

"I am," Sarah said.

"The rock star?" Zoe said, as if it needed clarification.

"Yes. Riley's been singing since he was old enough to talk, but he's very down-to-earth on top of being incredibly talented. No one makes that big a deal of it anymore when he comes home to visit—except the tourists. But to the locals, he's just Riley, and they're protective of him. When he comes home, they do what they can to make sure the tourist fans don't get too out of hand."

"I had no idea this was such a touristy place," Zoe said. In actuality, the thought never occurred to her before she'd decided to relocate. All she knew was she wanted to live on the beach. Growing up in Arizona was all fine and good, but Zoe had dreamed of a time when she could wake up and walk out her back door and put her toes in the sand. Finding the job with Martha had seemed like a godsend.

Until now.

"Okay, so they're a *really* overachieving family," she finally said.

"Still not done," Sarah said. "Did you know that Riley has a twin brother?"

Zoe shook her head, surprised. Everyone knew the rock star, but Zoe had never heard of a twin.

"Owen and Riley are fraternal but they still look a lot alike. I always thought Owen was the sweetest of the bunch by far, but he's also the shyest."

"And what does he do?" Zoe was almost afraid to ask.

"Owen is an astrophysicist. He's absolutely brilliant."

Of course he is, Zoe thought.

"He got picked on a bit because he was so nerdy and quiet compared to his brothers—especially his outgoing twin—but now he goes all over the world teaching at different universities about the sun, the moon, and the stars."

"I'm sure it's more complex than that," Zoe said.

Sarah shrugged. "I have no idea. I hated science while I was in school." She let out a sigh. "And then there's Darcy."

"Oh, you mean there's actually a female in that bunch?" Zoe asked with a laugh.

"The one and only. She's got it the hardest."

"Why?"

"Are you kidding me?" Sarah said. "She's got five older brothers and everyone in this town knows her family, along with everything about her life. She's seventeen years old. How much do you think she gets away with?"

Zoe couldn't relate. She was an only child so she couldn't imagine what it was like having even one over-achieving sibling, let alone five. "I hadn't thought about it that way."

"Plus, there are a lot of people who call her a spoiled brat behind her back. Must be hard on her."

"Poor kid," Zoe said. "What about Aidan? Where does he fall in the lineup?"

"He's the oldest," Sarah said, suddenly tense again. "Maybe that's why he's such a control freak and such a pain in the ass to work with."

"I'm sure he's just—"

Sarah cut her off. "He's a perfectionist and he's totally unreasonable. If you don't follow his instructions to the letter, he goes right over your head. I substituted some perfectly fine paint colors—they were from last year's palette, so they were thirty percent off, and they worked just fine. You'd think he'd be grateful I'd taken the initiative and found a way to save him some money. But no, it's his way or the highway. And all Martha cares about is getting him off her back. And then there's the stuff he won't tell you—like where exactly he wants the sofa or what direction the TV should face—and when you try to figure it out on your own, it'll be all wrong. But he won't even tell you *that* either. Do yourself a favor, Zoe. Brush up on your ESP skills and plan on not getting any sleep. Good luck. You're going to need it."

"I'm so sorry, Sarah." It was the only thing Zoe could think of to say. It was obvious this job had done a number on Sarah. "I really appreciate all of the background."

Sarah nodded and stood. "I need to go. You have a meeting with him in less than half an hour. Do yourself a favor and be early. He hates it when people are late. And by late, I mean on time."

Perfect, Zoe thought apprehensively.

She watched Sarah walk out of her office and then looked at the box on the floor.

"Reason number nine hundred and forty-eight why my life sucks today? Aidan Shaughnessy."

—∽∾—

Okay, that was a lot of information, Zoe kept saying to herself on the drive over. While it was good to have the background information, she wasn't sure how helpful that would be in dealing with the man himself.

After perusing Sarah's project files, Zoe could see what Sarah had done with the colors and finishes on the first model home. It didn't sound so bad, but Zoe wasn't foolish enough to believe it was going to be an easy fix. She had a feeling that paint color was only the tip of the iceberg.

As Zoe had left for her meeting, Martha had warned her that no matter what Mr. Shaughnessy wanted done to that house, she needed to make it right. Zoe wasn't to argue.

Zoe frowned. It wasn't like she argued with clients.

Much.

Her GPS signaled that she had arrived at her destination—ten minutes early, thank you very much—and the sight before her took her breath away. After parking the car, she slowly got out and removed her sunglasses.

"Stunning." The word was a mere whisper from her lips. She'd done her fair share of work with architects, builders, and your everyday home owners, but never before had she seen a home that just drew you in like this one.

The landscaping was immaculate: vivid colors mixed with the perfect amount of greenery. For a moment Zoe would have sworn the plants were fake. Crouching down, she touched the leaves on some of the flowers just to make sure. The lawn felt like some sort of plush carpeting, and she itched to kick off her shoes and feel it on her bare feet. It wasn't as soft as the sand surrounding the beach house she was renting, but this was a pretty close second. She wouldn't mind walking outside to something like this every day.

Maybe someday.

The stonework on the front of the house was perfect, and the color of it complemented the siding beautifully.

All the windows were top of the line and beckoned you to come inside.

But not before stopping on the wraparound porch and maybe spending a few minutes on the swing.

She sighed. She actually stopped and sighed.

The low, white picket fence around the front yard kept it separate from the work sites around it, like an oasis in the middle of a combat zone. Standing in the middle of the lawn, you could almost overlook the chaos going on around it.

Zoe, however, knew the real battleground was inside the house.

Standing, she gave the yard one last smile before walking up to the front door. It was like walking to an execution, and her feet suddenly felt filled with lead. Taking a fortifying breath, she gripped the doorknob and walked inside.

The spacious entryway led into a wide-open floor plan. The floors were real hardwoods—not engineered—and the dark finish shone like polished glass. Zoe looked down to see if she could catch her reflection. She was about to call out and announce her presence, but her decorator instincts took over and she crouched down one more time to run her hands over the floor.

"Like silk," she said softly, loving the feel of the wood beneath her hands.

"That's what I was going for," a deep male voice said from a few feet away.

Aidan had been watching this woman since her arrival. It hadn't been intentional, but he had been in one of the upstairs bedrooms when he saw her car pull up, and had watched in fascination as she inspected the yard. While he felt mildly guilty for causing the other decorator to lose her job, he couldn't help but be intrigued by her replacement. From what he'd observed so far, this woman was somebody who took notice of details. It wasn't hard to see the appreciation in her eyes as she looked at the house.

And he couldn't help but look at *her* with appreciation. The woman before him had fiery-red curly hair and a body with the kind of curves that made a man want to…scratch an itch. *Damn it*. This was so not the time for *that* thought to come to mind. As she straightened before him, he had to admit she was even more stunning up close. Tall. In heels, she was maybe only four inches shorter than him, and that was saying something. Most women didn't come close to his six-foot-two-inch height.

Aidan's mouth went dry when he caught sight of the greenest eyes he had ever seen. She smiled and held out her hand in greeting. "Mr. Shaughnessy, hello," she said, her voice just a bit husky. "I'm Zoe Dalton."

For a moment, Aidan couldn't speak. He reached out and took her hand in his, fully intending to give her a businesslike handshake, but as soon as he felt her soft skin, he pretty much forgot his own name.

You really have been without a woman for too long, he admonished himself. "Miss Dalton," he murmured, forcing himself to focus. He shook her hand a little too roughly and released it as if she'd burned him.

Zoe was equally speechless. Why had no one mentioned that this man was the sexiest thing on two legs? His rock star brother may have been nominated as one of the sexiest men alive, but Riley had nothing on his older brother. Dark hair, blue eyes, and hands rough enough that Zoe wanted to feel them all over her. It was rare for a man to make Zoe feel small and delicate, but Aidan succeeded—he was built like a linebacker.

Zoe fanned herself briefly as Aidan turned and walked away.

And the view was just as spectacular from behind.

She almost groaned.

Her gaze was lingering on how fine he looked in those faded jeans when he cleared his throat. "I want you to look around this house, Miss Dalton, and tell me everything you see that's wrong."

She swallowed hard and stepped forward. "Everything?"

Aidan turned to face her, crossing his large arms over his chest. "I want you to start at the front door and walk through the entire house."

There was the potential here for things to go south very quickly. Beyond what she'd read in Sarah's files, Zoe wasn't familiar with his work, so she didn't want to risk offending him, but Martha did tell her to do *whatever* Mr. Shaughnessy wanted done without argument. With a brief nod of her head, Zoe placed her soft leather briefcase on the granite countertop, pulled out her tablet, and began to type furiously, creating her own document on the house.

Walking to the front door, she stepped out onto the porch and swung the door closed before opening it again. "The door sticks a little," she began as she walked back inside. "There's some paint on the hardware on both the interior and exterior sides." She closed the door and looked around the entryway. Stepping to the right, she opened a closet door and looked inside. "There should be electrical in here. It's a deep closet, so I'm pretty sure people would appreciate having a light inside." She closed that door and noticed that Aidan hadn't moved from his spot in the living area.

Pretending not to be bothered by him watching her like that, she stopped and made some notes on her tablet. There was a fabulous cubby unit across from the closet. It had coat hooks and plenty of compartments to house baskets and all kinds of decorative items. She ran her hand over the built-in bench and frowned. "This needs to be sanded down more and another coat of paint added." Turning to face him, she said, "Chances are, a home owner would cover this area with a cushion, but that doesn't mean it shouldn't be smooth."

If she wasn't mistaken, he actually smirked.

Next to the entryway closet, she found a half bathroom and turned on the light inside. Unimpressive. "The paint is sloppy in there. It's not plumb either. The dark paint on the walls against the white ceiling accentuates that. There's a wave going on in there that almost makes me seasick."

Zoe crossed the entryway and opened the door to the two-car garage. She took a quick peek around and shut the door before turning back to Aidan. "There's a crack in the concrete floor by the electrical box. Sometimes concrete does that, but if you're going to patch it, make sure it doesn't look like a patch."

The smirk broadened slightly.

Zoe typed a couple more notes and walked into the living area until she was standing about three feet away from Aidan. She met his eyes briefly before turning around and facing the entryway from a new angle. With a tilt of her head she stopped and frowned. "It's out of plumb on the garage side of the entryway. If you stand here, you can see the curve in the wall." She didn't wait to see if he'd look; she had a feeling he was already well aware of all the problems.

Doing a slow three-sixty turn, she stopped and typed, then faced the living area. "The color is wrong in here." Lifting her head, she looked directly at him. "Granted, I don't know what color you were going for, but this is too yellow. You can see those beautiful, dark chocolate-colored cabinets in the kitchen from here. Between those and the dark floors, the walls are all wrong."

"Tell me why," he said deeply.

"You've got some amazing colors going between the floors, the cabinets, and the stone in the fireplace. This color on the walls doesn't do any of it justice. It's a yellowish beige, and it's boring. You want something that is going to complement everything that you've done. You want a color that people are going to walk in here and go *wow*." Looking around again, Zoe shrugged. "This doesn't inspire. This is the weekend-warrior-handyman special."

As soon as the words were out of her mouth, Zoe regretted them. Maybe he liked that yellow. Maybe he'd chosen it and it was the one color Sarah hadn't substituted. Why couldn't she just keep it professional? She'd never had trouble focusing with any of her *other* clients.

She turned and looked at him and noticed that the smirk was gone. He looked pissed. Okay, there were two ways she could play this. She could immediately apologize and grovel a bit, or she could move on and hope she was just blowing it out of proportion.

"I think we can do something better with the furniture." *And option two it is!* "The sectional is fine, but we can jazz it up once we change the colors in here." Moving to the kitchen, she went on for about five minutes about the things she saw that weren't quite right— brush strokes in the paint, crooked glass tile in the backsplash—and decided to stop there. His silence was killing her. She typed a few last notes on her tablet before putting it down and leaning against the countertop.

"Do I pass?" she asked.

"Excuse me?"

"I take it that this is a test to determine if I can see that the problem is in the details. Let me assure you, Mr. Shaughnessy, that I do. I have a real problem with craftsmen who rush through a job and put out shoddy work. I think the home owner deserves a house that has been put together perfectly. And as for the finishes and decorating," she said as she stood a bit taller, "we want potential buyers to come in here and not only want to buy this house, but to want their own to look as perfect as the model. If not better." She paused and shrugged. "Not that it will be possible because the model will be perfect on steroids." *There*, Zoe thought, *he can't be pissed at me if he knows that I'm a perfectionist too.*

He quirked a dark brow at her. As much as Aidan hated to admit it, he was impressed. And he wasn't impressed easily. Zoe Dalton had not only seen everything he'd wanted her to see, but she had even picked up on an issue or two that had escaped him.

Not an easy thing to do.

Aidan continued to stand there and look at her, so Zoe figured she'd better nudge him along. "Are we ready to hit the upstairs? I have a list of problems with that staircase."

And in that moment, Aidan Shaughnessy thought he just might have met his match.

———

Driving back to the office, Zoe had no idea if she had won Aidan Shaughnessy over or just signed her own termination papers. As they'd walked through the rest of the model home, Zoe had continued to do the bulk of the talking. Not that she didn't enjoy the strong and silent type, but in this particular case, it would have been nice of him to offer some input. She was trying her best to represent the firm, and it was hard to tell if he was going to keep them on when he said next to nothing.

When they were done with the house, Aidan had walked her to the door, thanked her for her time, and effectively let her know they were done by shutting the door in her face. Okay, that hurt; she couldn't deny it.

Now she had to go back to the office and explain to Martha that she had no idea if she'd saved the account or lost it for them. "Damn it," she muttered as she pulled into the parking lot of Tate Interiors. "I am so screwed." Why, oh, why hadn't she just kept her mouth shut? Sure, he had asked her to pick out what was wrong with the house, but maybe she could have just toned it down a bit. After all, a lot of the issues had nothing to do with Sarah and everything to do with the guys on Aidan's payroll. So she was essentially insulting his company to his face.

She was so going to be fired.

Thoughts of what she could do right now to smooth things over with Martha raced through her mind. Maybe she could run to Starbucks and pick up Martha's favorite latte and a muffin. Martha liked muffins, didn't she?

Screwed. Totally screwed.

Sitting in her car, baking in the hot August sun, probably wasn't the smartest thing to do, but the thought of climbing out and walking into the office without knowing what was going to happen wasn't appealing either. What if Aidan had already called Martha? How many times a day can someone do the execution walk?

Shoving her car door open, she answered her own question. "At least twice."

There was a moment of uncertainty when she considered leaving her briefcase and purse in the car. After all, if she was going to be fired, it would make for less stuff to carry out. But after a few minutes, Zoe decided to stand tall and walk inside as if she had just had the greatest client meeting of her life.

"Just be positive, just be positive, just be positive," she chanted softly as she crossed the parking lot, walked into the lobby, and waved to Sheila the receptionist. Just a few more feet and she'd be at her office and…

"Martha wants to see you, Zoe," Sheila said pleasantly.

So close, she thought. Turning, she plastered a fake smile on her face and thanked Sheila for letting her know. Sure, she could pretend she hadn't heard Sheila and gain a few minutes of peace and quiet before Martha came looking for her, but that was petty and childish and…

"There you are, Zoe!" Martha called out from across the office.

Again, so close.

The desire to drop her head and drag her feet all the way to Martha's office was strong, but Zoe knew it would gain her no sympathy in this situation. It was time to be a big girl and face the music.

And then find the radio playing that music and smash it over Aidan Shaughnessy's head.

Zoe braced herself and stepped into Martha's office. "You wanted to see me?"

"Shut the door, please."

Not a good sign.

Zoe did as she was told, then turned and sat down where Martha gestured.

"How did the meeting go with Mr. Shaughnessy?"

Zoe felt like a deer in the headlights for a moment and quickly did her best to mask it. "I think it went well."

Martha nodded. "Did the two of you discuss what needed to be changed?"

That was one way of putting it. "We did a full tour of the house, and all of the issues were pointed out."

Eyes narrowing, Martha studied her until Zoe started to squirm. "Hmmm…and how did you feel by the end of the meeting? Is this something you can handle?"

Unable to speak, Zoe simply nodded.

Martha sat back in her leather chair and frowned. "Well, honestly, Zoe, I thought you'd have more to say about the whole thing. I mean, Aidan Shaughnessy called here after you left."

Zoe cringed. She opened her mouth to start her lengthy apology, but in typical fashion, Martha waved her off.

"He made me promise that you aren't going to handle anything but his houses until the project is complete, and all you can do is nod?"

"Wait…*what*? He wants me to do the job?" It would have been nice if he had mentioned that to her rather than making her sweat it out.

"Well, of course he does. Didn't he tell you that before you left?"

Sarah's tip about ESP came back to Zoe, and she felt the urge to find Aidan and strangle him. It was one thing to pull that kind of nonsense after she'd become familiar with his methods—she'd had plenty of practice from decoding Martha's demands—but she was not okay with it right out of the gate. Not cool.

If he wanted to work with her even after she had pretty much ripped his house apart, though, Zoe figured she must have done something right.

"You're looking pretty fierce, Zoe," Martha said quizzically. "I thought you'd be pleased."

Putting her attention back on her boss, Zoe tried to relax. She'd deal with Mr. Aidan Shaughnessy later. "I am pleased. I'm just surprised he called you already," Zoe said, even though it was the decision, not the phone call, that surprised her. Aidan Shaughnessy was full of surprises, it seemed.

Martha waved her off. "He's just like that. We've worked with Mr. Shaughnessy on small projects in the past, but this is a huge opportunity for the firm. After the way things went down with Sarah, I'm glad you were able to salvage the situation."

"Did you think he was going to fire the firm over it?"

"No," Martha said, but she didn't sound too confident.

"I've been doing this for a long time. The biggest obstacle to overcome is doing so many houses for one client. We need to keep it fresh and new and exciting and make sure we're not just cloning the first house. Do you know what I mean?"

"Absolutely. I haven't had the opportunity to look over the specs of the rest of the models, but I'll get on that tonight so I can be prepared."

"There's a lot riding on this project, Zoe. I chose you because you understand what that's like. I know you and your firm were highly respected back in Arizona. It's going to be nice not to have to babysit you."

Zoe wasn't so sure. After all, they might still have the job, but she was certain it was going to take a little while for everyone to settle in and get comfortable working together.

And reading each other's minds.

Oh good Lord, Zoe thought for a moment, *good thing it doesn't go both ways*. The things going on in her mind when she'd gotten her first look at Aidan were less than professional.

I have got *to stop thinking about that*, she told herself.

"I appreciate your confidence in me, Martha. I won't let you down."

Her boss visibly relaxed. "Okay, well, I have the schedule that Mr. Shaughnessy emailed over."

He already sent over a schedule? Zoe thought. "I'll check it out when I get into my office."

"No worries. I've already printed out a copy for you so you can get started *right away*." She handed it to Zoe almost reluctantly.

It took less than a minute for Zoe to realize why.

"Is he crazy?" she cried. "This schedule is impossible! There is no way to get everything done in that time frame!" When Martha chuckled, Zoe looked up at her. "What? What's so funny?"

"You'll understand once you get to know Mr. Shaughnessy. He's a bit of a…"

"Tyrant? Control freak?" Zoe supplied. *Sexy distraction?*

"I was going to say enigma. Everyone may chafe under the way he handles things, but they put up with it because his methods produce spectacular results. He gets things done when no one else can."

That was easy for Martha to say, but it didn't do a thing to make Zoe feel any better about working with him or his ridiculous schedule. With a smile and a promise to keep Martha up-to-date, Zoe took her things to her office and shut the door.

"Enigma, my ass," she muttered. "Just another way of saying that he's difficult."

Chapter 3

IT WAS AFTER SEVEN WHEN ZOE FINALLY LEFT THE office, but she was considering going by the Shaughnessy model home one more time for inspiration. It would require only a minor detour, and then she promised to reward herself for a hard day's work with some takeout for dinner.

"Minor detour" proved to be a bit of an understatement however. The sun was still shining as Zoe slowly drove along the main street through town, and she was still not yet accustomed to all of the tourist traffic. Droves of people were milling about, looking as if they'd just left the sand and surf. Zoe felt a pang of envy. She had purposely rented a house right on the beach, yet she hadn't had much time to enjoy it since moving in. And from the look of Aidan Shaughnessy's schedule, she wouldn't be enjoying it anytime soon.

Up ahead she could barely make out the sign indicating the entrance to the Shaughnessy community. But it wasn't tourist traffic blocking her way; it was construction vehicles.

What in the world?

Slowing down, Zoe carefully maneuvered her car through the numerous large trucks and found a spot to pull over. Climbing out of the car, she saw a steady stream of workers going in and out of the house. A loud, booming voice yelling orders immediately brought her attention to the man standing on the front lawn.

Aidan.

Maybe it wasn't the best time for her to be here, but if she was going to work with him and try to keep on schedule, it only made sense for her to find out exactly what was going on. She opened the small, white picket gate, which seemed pointless considering the construction team had ripped out most of the fencing for easier access to the house. Still, she was trying to go for the more civilized approach as she entered the yard.

As if sensing her arrival, Aidan turned and looked right at her. "Miss Dalton," he said casually, although his voice told her that he was somewhat taken aback by her sudden appearance on the site. "Did we have an appointment?"

"Apparently we have several," she said briskly. She tried to hide it with a smile, but Aidan's knowing smirk told her otherwise.

"So Martha gave you the schedule."

Zoe nodded. "I would have appreciated you just going over it with me while I was here earlier. Obviously you already had it written up and ready to go." He shrugged and went back to talking to one of the contractors, and Zoe had to count to ten to keep calm. "I don't mean to be rude here, but what's going on?"

"Excuse me a minute," Aidan said to the worker before turning back to Zoe. "What does it look like, Miss Dalton?"

Oh, so it was going to be like that, was it? "It looks like you're tearing apart a perfectly beautiful house!" she said, a tad loudly. Numerous people stopped moving, but as soon as Aidan turned and looked at them, they went back to work. "I know we talked about some of the issues on the *inside* of the house, and I've gone over your schedule, but this seems extreme."

Aidan was taken aback. Was she arguing with him? No one argued with him. Well, except for his family. On his job sites, however, no one dared. Folding his arms across his chest, he scowled at her. He waited for her to apologize, or at least squirm, but she didn't. She held her ground. *Score one to Zoe*.

"The mess your former colleague made put me behind schedule. This kind of action is needed to move forward and still be able to reveal the models on time."

Keeping her earlier opinions about a lot of the problems not actually being Sarah's fault to herself, Zoe gave a mild shrug. "I suppose. But…if I could…maybe make a suggestion?" The stormy look in his eyes almost stopped her. Almost. "Okay, I can see why you have the drywall guys here and why you're taking care of all of those issues, but the rest of it can wait. We can still use most of the furniture, if not all of it, with some creative decorating."

"You said it didn't work," he reminded her.

"No," she said, "I said we could do better. That can be accomplished without going through the hassle of replacing everything. Here. Come with me." She started walking toward the front steps, but Aidan reached out to stop her. She looked at him quizzically.

"You can't go in there."

"Why not?"

"They're taking down drywall. You're hardly dressed for a construction zone." And she looked sexy as hell. How was he supposed to concentrate on the job at hand?

Zoe looked down at her black pencil skirt and heels and knew her outfit wasn't ideal for navigating the debris littering the ground, but she'd walked through worse. "So I'll put on a hard hat. I'll be fine. I want to show you what I have in mind, and hopefully it will put your mind at ease on at least part of the project."

"How about a compromise?" he said before she had gone two steps. The last thing he wanted was for her to break an ankle on his construction site. "I promise to leave the furniture alone for tonight if we can go over it first thing tomorrow morning."

"But I'm here now."

"And you'll be here tomorrow," he reminded.

"Yes, but my way, I can sleep in beyond five a.m."

A sudden image of Zoe in bed snapped to Aidan's mind and his throat went dry. So. Not. The. Time. "Is my schedule going to be a problem for you? The early hours?"

She rolled her eyes. "Seriously? No, the early hours aren't going to be an issue. I was merely suggesting that because I'm here right now, I can get some of the things on your list crossed off and put you *ahead* of schedule." For a minute, she thought she had him.

He shook his head. "It's not on my schedule for tonight, and I have enough to deal with. We'll meet tomorrow morning as planned. But I'll leave the furniture alone for tonight." And then he turned back to the drywall worker who had been standing there the entire time waiting on Aidan's next set of orders.

He had dismissed her.

Again.

And she didn't like it.

Muttering under her breath about inconsiderate people, Zoe walked away with her head held high and even managed to walk out the gate without slamming it. When she got back to her car, she cursed her rotten luck.

Flat tire.

"Seriously?" she murmured and crouched down to look at the tire. It had been fine when she'd left the office. Looking around the street, she saw construction debris—dirt clods, rocks, bits of drywall that still had screws in it—strewn all over the road. "Damn it."

Grumbling, she pulled her phone out of her purse and scrolled through her contacts until she found the number for the auto club. Having just moved to the area only a month before, she didn't have a mechanic yet.

"You are caller number eight in the queue. Please hold," the automated voice rambled on.

"Of course I am." She sighed as she leaned against the car and waited.

And waited. And waited.

The automated voice bumped her up to number six, so she figured she still had a while to wait. A quick glance at her watch showed that it was now almost eight o'clock. Dinner was slowly becoming a thing of the past. If she was lucky, she'd find a cup of yogurt at home.

If she ever *got* home.

"What are you doing?"

Zoe didn't have to look up to know Aidan was coming her way. "Flat tire. I'm on hold with the auto club."

Aidan looked around the road, and even though the sun was starting to go down, it was obvious what had happened. Without another word to Zoe, he stalked back toward the house and began barking orders to get the street cleaned up.

It *was* impressive; Zoe watched in amazement as workmen instantaneously began scurrying around and sweeping up the street. It would have been more impressive, however, if that had happened *before* the damage was done to her car.

"You are caller number five…"

"Aces," she muttered and saw Aidan heading back her way. He stood there looking at her expectantly. "I'm on hold." Her intention was to look away and dismiss him just as he had done to her several times today, but then he took the phone out of her hands and disconnected the call.

"*Hey!*" Zoe exclaimed indignantly.

Still without responding to her whatsoever, Aidan pulled out his own phone and made a call. "What's your address?" he asked when he turned around to her. The shocked look on her face was almost enough to make him smile. She stood defiantly with her arms crossed over her chest. "My brother has an auto body shop here in town," he explained. "They're going to come and replace the tire. But it's going to take a while. They'll bring it to your house when they're done."

"And what am I supposed to do in the meantime, walk home?" The correct response to his statement was probably *thank you,* but she didn't like his high-handed attitude. She was independent and knew how to take care of herself. She didn't need or expect anyone to swoop in to save her. Especially not Aidan. The last thing she needed was for him to see her as incompetent.

"I'll take you home."

Zoe considered his words, and her lips twitched into an unexpected smile. "That's not on your schedule." She was more surprised when his mouth twitched in response.

"I made sure to include some time for…things beyond my control."

She laughed out loud at that one. "Is that what this is? A flat tire merits your use of extra time, but my desire to get ahead of schedule doesn't?"

He shrugged. "What's your address?" he asked again. Zoe rattled it off and he repeated it into the phone and hung up. "I can't give you an accurate time frame, but you'll have it back tonight."

"You'll have to tell me where to find them so I can stop by tomorrow and pay them." It was an expense she hadn't counted on, but it had to be done.

"This happened on my job site and because my guys were careless. I'll take care of it."

There was that tone again. "I'm more than capable of paying for a new tire," she said defensively.

"I'm sure you are," he said, squaring off with her. "But that's not in question here. You work for me, your car got damaged on my job site, and it wasn't your fault."

"Technically, I'm not on the clock." She stepped forward until they were almost toe-to-toe. "So it's my own fault that it happened. I saw all the trucks here in the street and I came through anyway. Therefore, my responsibility."

Aidan studied her for a moment. "Are you always this argumentative?"

"Yup." She tilted her head and studied him right back. "Are you sorry you decided to keep me on to do this job?"

He threw his head back and laughed, unable to remember a time when anyone had bantered with him quite like this. It was refreshing. "Not yet." That seemed to satisfy Zoe. "Give me five minutes and we'll be on our way."

"Sounds good." She watched him turn and walk away and then called out to him. Aidan turned around. "Thank you," she said simply and was rewarded with one of his rare, authentic smiles.

True to his word, five minutes later, they were climbing into his pickup and pulling away from the work zone. "Will they be all right without a supervisor?" Zoe asked.

"I've got three of them there to make sure nothing gets missed."

Turning to look at him, she was certain that she'd misheard him. "Three?" He nodded. "Then…then why were you there too? Don't you trust them?"

"I like to be there to make sure everyone knows exactly what needs to be done and what I expect of them. I'll go back and check on them later just to keep them on their toes."

"You know that they're probably going to be there all night, right?"

Aidan turned to her and nodded. "Then they should have done it right the first time. All of my crews know that. If it isn't done right the first time, then they have to come back, when I say it's convenient, and fix it to my exact specifications. Trust me, these guys will make sure every house that goes up in that community from now on will be perfect."

"Wow," she said, turning away from him. "That's… that's just…wow."

"What?" Brows furrowed, he wondered at her comment.

"So basically these guys are working for free tonight, is that what you're saying?"

"I don't know about for free—they're subcontractors. If they want to pay these guys for being incompetent, that's on them. I, however, will not be footing the bill."

So many things were on the tip of Zoe's tongue, but she kept them to herself. No need to cause an argument. In another ten minutes, she'd be at her door and saying good-bye to him. Surely they could go that long without arguing. Maybe.

"Have you eaten dinner?" he asked casually.

"As a matter of fact I haven't. I had planned on grabbing some takeout and going home. You know, before the whole tire thing."

Aidan nodded and turned in the parking lot of the local pizzeria. He parked his truck in front and climbed out, walking around to open Zoe's door. "This place has the best Italian in town." Once Zoe's feet hit the ground, Aidan turned and walked toward the entrance.

Zoe stood there for a moment, a little shell-shocked. He hadn't asked if she wanted to eat with him or if she even liked pizza!

"Um…what if I don't eat Italian?" she said, arms crossed.

So much for going ten minutes without arguing.

Aidan turned and looked at her as if she had grown

a second head. "What do you mean? Everyone eats Italian food."

Zoe shrugged. "What if I don't?" She tried to keep a straight face and not giggle at the indecision on Aidan's face. He clearly didn't know what to do with people not just immediately going along with everything he said.

Taking a step toward her, he said, "We can grab something else if you'd like."

Ah, there it was. He was actually taking a moment to think about someone else's feelings. She considered him for a moment, then walked by him to the restaurant entrance.

"What are you doing?" he asked.

"I actually love Italian food. But I prefer being asked first if I'd like to have dinner someplace, or with someone." Before he could respond, Zoe went through the door and up to the hostess, who led her to a corner booth. Aidan joined her, his expression guarded.

"So that was…what? You were teaching me a lesson?" he asked as he sat down.

Picking up the menu, Zoe simply shrugged. "It would have been nice if you'd actually asked me what I'd like to eat rather than just making the decision for me."

Aidan was stumped. What was the big deal? He was hungry, she was hungry, and neither of them had eaten dinner. They were passing the pizza place, end of story. Aidan wondered why he didn't just take her home and get something to eat on his own. Trying to get this woman to soften toward him was starting to feel like more trouble than it was worth. Not that he cared what this woman in her sexy pencil skirts thought about him. No, sir.

Zoe's face was mostly hidden by the menu, but he saw her sparkling eyes peek at him briefly, and he could see her shoulders shaking.

She was laughing at him? Seriously?

"What is so damn funny?" he demanded.

"You have a lousy poker face," she said, putting down the menu. "You looked like your head was about to explode."

Nailed it in one. "Okay, fine. You had your fun. If you didn't want to eat with me, you should have just said so."

"Um…when? You pulled in the parking lot and climbed out of the truck without asking if I wanted to stop."

Aidan looked up at the ceiling and then back at Zoe. "Do you want to eat or not?"

"That depends," she said sweetly.

"On?"

"Are we going to share in conversation, or are you going to be all bossy and dominate the whole thing?"

If Aidan didn't know any better, he'd swear that Zoe had talked to his family, or at least Darcy. Doing his best to relax, he picked up his menu to give himself something else to look at besides her distracting eyes, distracting hands, distracting everything. "We can talk about whatever you want." His teeth were clenched so tightly, he was sure he'd broken a molar. He'd dealt with quite a few difficult clients in his line of work with no problems. Why did this woman make him so damn uncomfortable?

"If you weren't grinding your teeth when you said it, I would have believed you."

That was it. He was done. She was fired. He'd find

another design firm because nothing was worth all of this aggravation. Slamming his menu down, he went to slide out of the booth when the waitress came over. "Hey, Aidan! This is a surprise. We normally only see you back there at the takeout counter. It's nice to see you sitting inside for a change."

Aidan had known Tammy Wilson since high school. He was totally trapped. "It's good to see you, Tammy. How's Richie doing?" Casually, he slid back into the booth and did his best to ignore Zoe's satisfied smirk.

"Working like a fiend, as usual," she said as she placed two glasses of water and a basket of bread on the table. "The tourists don't make it easy for him. I think he's given out an entire year's worth of speeding tickets in the last week alone."

Aidan smiled. "Hopefully that means he'll let me go with a warning next time I'm rushing through town."

"Oh, stop. You don't rush anywhere, and Richie wouldn't dare give you a ticket." She winked at him and then suddenly seemed to realize Zoe was a woman she didn't recognize. Her eyes went wide and then she looked from Zoe to Aidan and back again. "So…um, hi. I'm Tammy."

"Hi, Tammy, I'm Zoe Dalton. I'm working for Martha Tate, doing the model homes for the new Shaughnessy community. I moved to town about a month ago."

"I knew I hadn't seen you in here before," Tammy said with a smile. "Welcome to the area. What can I get the two of you to eat?"

"We'll have—" Aidan started.

"Actually, I haven't had a chance to look at the menu yet, Tammy. Can you give me a few minutes?"

"Absolutely. Take your time." She smiled at Zoe and then at Aidan. "You should try something new too, Aidan. We happen to make more than pizza and spaghetti and meatballs." She winked at Zoe and walked away.

He actually felt himself blush. Picking up his menu, he noticed that Zoe was studying hers with a serene smile on her face. "Enjoying yourself?" he asked.

Without looking up, she nodded. "More than I thought possible. You're really quite entertaining to be around. This whole adventure has allowed me to learn so much more about you."

"Like what?"

Zoe found what she wanted to order and then placed the menu down and looked at Aidan. "For starters, you like to have control of every situation. You clearly don't think anyone can make a decision for themselves and that whatever you decide is better. You don't like to try new things." Pausing, she reached for her water and took a sip. "How am I doing?"

Nailed it in one. Again. A change of subject was definitely in order.

"So what are you ordering?" he asked with a huff. Geez, when had he become this controlling, predictable guy? Everyone seemed to see it but him. What was wrong with liking some order in his life? Or with wanting to help people make their decisions? When had it become wrong to just stick to the things he liked without it being a federal case?

Despite how fun it was to push his buttons, Zoe thought she had pushed enough for one night. "I think I'm going to have the caprese salad."

"And?"

"And what? That's it. I'm having the salad. What's wrong with that? I mean, I know it's not as original as pizza or spaghetti, but…" She trailed off teasingly.

"Nothing. It's fine," he said with mock nonchalance. He continued to peruse the menu, trying to come up with something, anything, besides pizza or spaghetti. Maybe Italian hadn't been such a great idea.

"Out with it, Shaughnessy," she said with exasperation.

"It seems to me I had to sit here and get razzed for my lack of originality and then you go and expect to get away with just ordering a salad? How is that fair?" he said, stalling. If Zoe weren't so distracting, maybe he'd be able to make a simple decision about what to order for dinner.

"Maybe a caprese salad is out of the ordinary for me," she teased and was relieved to see a hint of a smile on Aidan's face.

"Or maybe you're one of those women who don't eat when she's out on a date." As soon as the word "date" was out of his mouth, Aidan realized what he had said. Zoe's eyes went wide for a second before she recovered.

Two can play at the change-of-subject game, she thought. "Okay then, what are you ordering?"

"I am going to go with the lasagna with meat sauce." And he was quite proud of himself too.

"Way to be different," she mumbled.

"Now what?" Seriously, he was ready to order a strong alcoholic drink because this woman was killing him. And it wasn't even a Friday.

"So basically you're skipping the spaghetti and

meatballs to order a differently shaped pasta with chopped-up meatballs."

Well, when she said it, it did sound ridiculous. "Okay, how about this? I'll let you order for me…"

"Really?" she asked, her voice almost giddy.

"But…"

"Damn it, you're going to ruin this, aren't you?"

"But I get to order for you."

Interesting. Zoe considered it and knew she was safe. Carbs and pasta were her weaknesses, and she pretty much wanted one of everything on the menu, so she couldn't go wrong. "Okay, fine. Deal." Reaching across the table, she held out her hand to shake on it. As soon as Aidan's hand touched hers, she felt it. That zing or zap or whatever it was that people said happened when you were attracted to someone. *How did* that *happen?* she thought. She quickly pulled her hand back and rubbed her palm on her leg. "Just…just no pasta with meat sauce."

"Why not?"

"I don't want you trying to steal a taste."

So many things raced through Aidan's mind at that moment, he thought his head might *actually* explode. If he was going to steal a taste of anything, it wasn't going to be of her dinner.

"Deal."

—⁓—

"So what did you do?" Aidan asked with a hearty laugh.

"What do you think? I said 'no thank you' and got the hell out of there!" They both sat back in their seats and laughed some more. "I mean, when he asked during our initial phone interview how open-minded I was, I thought he was talking about colors and design and that sort of thing. I didn't think that he'd…"

"Want you to work naked?"

Zoe shook her head and blushed furiously. "Okay, that was my worst client experience. Now it's your turn."

"I don't think I can top that," he said as he reached for his soda and took a drink.

"I didn't say top it. I just said worst. Come on. Spill it."

Aidan looked at Zoe and for a moment was simply in awe of her beauty. She was laughing and smiling and teasing and…everything. Clearing his throat, he did his best to get back to the conversation. "Okay, it was one of my first big renovation jobs. I had been doing some minor carpentry work for about a year and was ready to branch out. So this guy calls me and I go out to the house and meet with him and his wife. He takes me outside, to where they have a detached two-story, two-car garage, and he wants me to convert the upstairs to a man cave."

Zoe quirked a brow at him. "A man cave? That's what you're going with? What's so weird about a man cave?"

He held up a finger to stop her. "Ah, I haven't finished yet." Zoe nodded, and he leaned his elbows on the table and got comfortable. "So we go inside and his wife goes back to the house. We're talking about what he wants in the space and it all seems pretty straightforward—a bar, big-screen TV, bookcases, new bathroom, yadda, yadda, yadda. So I'm taking measurements and writing my notes, and he asks me if I do any excavation work."

"For a man cave? On the second story?" Zoe leaned forward, clearly intrigued.

Nodding, Aidan said, "Weird, right? So I tell him it depends on the project and if we have plumbing issues and whatnot, and he interrupts me and says, 'No, I'm thinking like a tunnel.' I still wasn't sure what he was getting at, so I turned to him and was like 'Dude, what do you need a tunnel for?' And he's like 'I want to be able to sneak my girlfriend in and out of here without my wife seeing her.'"

"No!"

Aidan smiled and continued to nod. "Yes! And he was totally serious!"

"So he wanted you to build like a walking tunnel from the back of the garage to where?"

"The property was heavily wooded behind the garage. They owned about an acre back there, and he only wanted a crawl-space tunnel from the back of the garage out to the property where she could park her car without being seen."

"And he expected her to crawl for an acre?"

"Apparently so."

Zoe leaned back in her seat and crossed her arms. "Well, that's just all kinds of wrong. What did you do?"

"Honestly? I wanted no part of it. I told him I could do the renovations on the garage and do the man cave thing, but he'd have to find somebody else for the tunnel."

"So you did it? You did the man cave for him?"

He shrugged. "Sure. Why not?"

"Because he was a freak!" she said with a laugh. "And you were just helping him stay freaky!"

"The way I see it, he was a freak no matter what I did or didn't do. I just knew where to draw the line."

Zoe reached for her drink and finished the last of it. "When did people get this way?"

"What way?"

"Freaky. What happened to normal people?"

He chuckled. "They're still out there. They're just harder to find."

They sat in companionable silence for a moment until Tammy came over. "Well, you two, I hate to say it, but we're getting ready to close."

They both looked at her like she was crazy. "You close early on Mondays?" Aidan asked.

Tammy laughed. "Um…no. We close at eleven, just like we do every night."

Aidan looked down at his watch, his eyes going wide. "Well, damn." From the looks of it, Zoe hadn't realized the time either. "Sorry, Tammy. We didn't mean to hold you up." Fumbling for his wallet, he promptly paid the check.

"No worries," she said with a wink and walked away.

They each quickly scrambled from the booth. "Okay…wow. I had no idea it was so late," Zoe said as she straightened her skirt and fidgeted with her hair. "Um…do you think we can check on my car? Maybe it's ready and we can just pick it up while we're here in town and then you won't have to drive me home."

For a moment he was stumped. They were having a good time—or at least he *thought* they were having a good time—and now she was looking to get rid of him. "Yeah, sure. I'll call over and see what's up." Taking his phone from his pocket, he walked ahead of Zoe out of the restaurant.

She joined him and looked at him expectantly. "I couldn't get anyone on the line," he apologized. "I'm sure it's no big deal, and for all we know, your car could be waiting for you at home."

Zoe climbed back into Aidan's truck and directed him to her house. When they pulled into her driveway, she noticed the look on Aidan's face. "What? What's the matter?"

"You live on the beach."

"Uh…yeah. Why? What's wrong with that?"

Shaking his head to clear it, Aidan turned and looked at her. "What? Oh…it's nothing. I just didn't realize you had a house that was, you know, *right* on the beach."

"It's only a rental. I could never afford to actually own one of these houses, but for the time being, it's mine. I've dreamed of my own beach house for as long as I can remember." Opening the car door, she climbed down and looked up at the sky. It was a beautiful night, positively filled with stars. She sensed more than heard Aidan's approach. Closing her eyes and inhaling deeply, she said, "I love the sounds and the smells of the beach. Don't you?"

He couldn't have spoken if he wanted to. There she stood with her head thrown back, her eyes closed, looking like some sort of ethereal being in the moonlight. His mouth went dry and his throat tightened. It was considerably inappropriate for him to be entertaining the idea of kissing her, but right now that was all he wanted.

Slowly, Zoe opened her eyes and turned to look at him. "I'm not normally up this late, but now that I am, I'm going to take advantage of it and do something I've been dying to do since I moved here."

Aidan said the first thing that came to his mind. "You're not going in the ocean at this hour." His words were deep and harsh and fierce. He stepped in close to Zoe and gripped her by the shoulders. "Do you know how dangerous that is?"

Tilting her head slightly, she looked at him curiously. "I was going to say I was going to walk on the beach barefoot."

He immediately released her and took a step back with a nervous chuckle. "Oh. Okay." *Smooth, Aidan. Real smooth.* "Well, you shouldn't do that alone either, not at this time of night."

"I live right here, Aidan. I don't think it's a big deal to walk around the back of my house." She watched him carefully. "You could walk with me for a while. If that would make you feel better."

Well, since it was *her* suggestion…

"Yeah, sure. Whatever." He was going for casual, but it came out sounding on the grumpy side. Hoping that Zoe hadn't noticed, he started walking toward the sand. Looking over his shoulder, he asked, "Are you coming?"

She stood there for a moment, trying to get a grip on who exactly Aidan Shaughnessy was. Earlier today he had been a complete ogre, someone she was dreading working with. But now? Now he seemed like a really decent man who cared about other people and maybe just didn't know how to express that without coming off as being bossy.

Or grouchy.

Aidan was standing in the sand, and Zoe noticed he'd left his shoes and socks on the stairs that led to her deck. Kicking off the heels that had been the bane of her existence for the entire day, she dropped her purse on the step and then caught up to him.

It was the perfect night—the moon, the stars, the sound of the waves crashing on the shore, and the sand between her toes. She almost let out an orgasmic moan at the feel of it. Why it made her so happy, Zoe couldn't say. All she knew was that relocating her life was totally worth it for this feeling alone.

"So…you like walking on the beach?" Aidan finally asked as they strolled closer to the shore.

Aidan's fumbling attempts at small talk made Zoe smile. "I do. And I've been so busy since the move with getting settled and work and life that I just haven't made the time to come out here and do it. I'll stand on the deck and watch the waves…" She stopped and sighed. "I just don't seem to make the time to do what I want the most."

He could totally relate. Oh man, could he relate. Hadn't he just had the same realization Friday night? There were things he wanted, things he needed, and he kept letting life dictate how he spent his time. And it was never for anything fun.

"Can I ask you something?" Zoe said, stopping in the sand.

Aidan turned to look at her. "Sure." It came out more as a strangled croak than a word, and he quickly coughed to make it look like there was a reason for him to sound that way.

"Am I crazy?"

Loaded question, he thought. "In what way?"

"I've made work my entire life. I love what I do, but what kind of person moves to a house on the beach and then doesn't take the time to walk down a dozen steps to put their feet in the sand? I mean, how lame is that?"

"It's not lame," he said quietly. "And you're not crazy." Zoe kept looking at him to continue. "I've lived here my whole life and I can't remember the last time I came to the beach. Now *that's* crazy."

"Well, the weather has been beautiful for the last month, and I'm just hoping it will stay that way so we'll have plenty more opportunities." Turning, she looked out at the ocean and sighed with pleasure. "If I could, I'd sit out here all night and listen to this."

He nodded. "I had forgotten how peaceful it can be."

A yawn escaped before she could stop it. "But unfortunately, it's been a long day and I've got an early meeting in the morning." She smirked, but was glad when he didn't seem to take offense. They had avoided talking about the model home project all night, and she certainly didn't want to start now.

"What kind of imperious jerk would do such a thing?" he teased and couldn't help but join in Zoe's laughter. It was a pretty great moment, in his mind.

It was broken a moment later when headlights flashed by in front of Zoe's house. "That must be my car," she said as she looked toward the house. Taking a step away, she was about to head back up the beach when Aidan reached out a hand to stop her. Zoe looked at him and felt the same disappointment she saw on his face. Truth be known, she wasn't really ready for the night to end. If it weren't for the fact that they had a job to do in the morning, she would probably stay outside and talk with him until the sun came up.

"I had a really good time tonight, Aidan," she said softly. "Thank you for dinner. And for getting my tire fixed. I really appreciate it."

"It was my pleasure," he said gruffly. His fingers were gently wrapped around her wrist; she could move away any time she wanted to, but Aidan hoped she wouldn't. He knew it was late. He knew he should go.

He knew he wanted to kiss her.

But he also knew he couldn't, not only because she was going to be working for him, but also because it was too soon. They'd just met that afternoon, and Aidan wasn't the type of guy who liked to rush things. He didn't want anyone to get the wrong idea.

Very carefully, he pulled his hand away, his fingers gently grazing the inside of Zoe's wrist, and he felt her shiver. Their eyes met and held, and he had to force himself to look away. "Come on. Let me walk you back to the house."

Zoe looked over her shoulder and saw that whoever dropped off her car was already gone. "It's just right there, Aidan. You don't have to."

"Not up for discussion," he said as he came to stand beside her. They fell into step with one another until they reached the back steps to her house. A typical beach house, it was up on stilts and there were about a dozen steps up to the deck. Aidan sat on one of the steps and put his shoes and socks back on, and Zoe picked up her purse. "Good night, Zoe. I'll see you in the morning."

Zoe watched him walk away and contemplated

standing there until he pulled out of the driveway. But she had a feeling he'd sit in the car until she went inside.

Climbing the stairs, she pulled her keys from her purse and went to unlock the door. By the time she was inside, Aidan had pulled away.

Normally, she was someone who enjoyed solitude. Except for right now. For a brief moment there, she had thought Aidan was going to kiss her.

And she was going to let him.

Stepping away from the window, she sighed happily. For the first time in what seemed like forever, she was actually excited about going to work tomorrow.

Chapter 4

FOR ONCE, ZOE DIDN'T MIND BEING UP EARLY. AFTER the time she'd spent with Aidan, she was anxious to meet with him and start working together on the model home project. She decided that Aidan was just a little misunderstood. He wasn't really a pain in the butt to work with like she had been warned—on the contrary. Working with him might be challenging, but Zoe found that prospect exciting.

She was dressed more casually today, since she knew he had torn the model home apart the previous night. It was better to be prepared for flying dust and debris and dress down rather than show up dressed like she had yesterday and not be able to get anything done. Climbing into her car, which now sported four new tires, she smoothed her black slacks, righted her green sleeveless sweater, wiggled her toes in her ballet flats, and got on her way.

Unable to help herself, she sang, way off-key, to the songs on the radio and had a silly grin on her face. She felt good, happy even. Who would have thought, after the way their meeting had initially gone yesterday, she and Aidan would have hit it off so well? He could be charming and sweet and downright funny when he wanted to be. She supposed she understood why he didn't show that side around the job site; the workmen would take advantage of that in a heartbeat. Still, she knew she certainly wouldn't do that, and started to speed up to get to the site faster.

As she turned onto the street, the first thing she noticed was that the road was immaculate. That was a good sign. It looked brand-new compared to the state it was in the previous night, and she was pleasantly surprised.

Parking her car, Zoe also saw there weren't nearly as many trucks on this particular site as there had been last night. Another good sign. Climbing out of her car, she grabbed her briefcase and shut the door. For all of the workmen who had been here and walked all over the front yard, it still managed to look pristine. Even the white picket fence was completely back in place. So far, everything was looking up.

"You're late, Miss Dalton."

Zoe turned to where Aidan was standing on the front porch of the house. Actually, she was five minutes early, but there was something in his tone that kept her from arguing the point.

The high-handed jackass of yesterday was back.

It was like dealing with Jekyll and Hyde. Well, if he was going to be that way, so was she.

"Forgive me. I was just taking mental notes on how the front yard looks completely put back together after all of the crews coming and going last night." She kept her tone clipped and professional. Walking through the front gate and closing it behind her, she walked up the front steps and into the house without so much as a greeting to Aidan.

When he joined her, she was standing at the granite kitchen island with her sketch pad, pencils, and tablet waiting. She was going to make damn sure this house would be the most spectacular showcase she'd ever done.

"As you can see, the drywall has been repaired so that every room in this house is plumb." Aidan looked up and caught her curt nod. "Painters will be coming in later today to start repainting." He pulled a sheet of paper from his briefcase and placed it down on the counter. "Here is the list of all the colors that I want used."

Zoe picked it up and scanned it before putting it back down and grabbing a pen to make some notes. A minute later, she slid it back to him. "I'd like you to sign and date this, please."

He shot her a look. "Excuse me?"

"I'd like you to sign and date this piece of paper," she repeated dryly.

"What for?"

"I want to make sure you remember that *you* chose these colors—without my input—so if the colors go up on the walls and you aren't satisfied with them, you take full responsibility for it. I will not bear the burden of your wrath for things I had no hand in."

"*Burden of my wrath*," he deadpanned. "Seriously?"

Crossing her arms across her chest, Zoe gave him a level stare. "You have a reputation. We'll leave it at that."

He snatched up the paper and signed where she had indicated and then slid it back across the counter to her. "Anything else?"

"That depends on the next piece of paper you give me."

He sighed—loudly—and raked a hand through his hair. "Is there some sort of problem here? I mean, you understand that I'm the boss and that you're working for me, right? The only reason you're here is because your firm screwed up."

If he had slapped her, she wouldn't have felt this bad. Relaxing her arms at her sides, Zoe cleared her throat and picked up her tablet. "What time are the painters coming?"

He went over the schedule for the day with her. Together they walked through the house, and this time it was Aidan who did most of the talking while Zoe took notes. An hour later, when they were done, he gave her his business card with his cell phone number on it, in case she had any questions about the house, and left.

"Well, that was totally awful," she said, sighing after she heard his truck pull away. She tossed his business card in the bottom of her briefcase and vowed that unless the house was on fire, she wasn't going to call him. Pulling out her paint chart, Zoe quickly began going through it to find all of Aidan's selections. She had a lot to do, and with the paint samples in hand, she could move forward with accessorizing and redoing everything Sarah had done.

A glance at her watch showed that it was still early, so she gathered her things and walked out to her car. There was plenty of time to go through the showroom back at the office and do some online shopping in the comfort of her own space. She'd come back and meet with the painters later to make sure they had all the correct colors.

She *prayed* they'd have the right colors.

It was too early in the job for her to have to do battle with Aidan Shaughnessy…again.

She'd worked at a feverish pace to stay on schedule, completely consumed with the need to make everything perfect on this job. By the end of the day, Zoe was exhausted, and she looked it. Martha happened to walk by her office and did a double take. "Good grief, Zoe, it's only been a day. Surely it's not all that bad!"

Slouching in her seat, Zoe combed her mass of curly hair away from her face with her fingers and tugged as if to pull it out. "The man is infuriating. I'm second-, third-, and even fourth-guessing every single item I pick out for this house. It's…it's…"

"Maddening?"

Zoe nodded. Pulling up a chair, Martha sat and looked at Zoe with a reassuring smile. "You have to be confident in what you're doing. I think men like Aidan Shaughnessy feed on other people's weaknesses. If you go in there with confidence and present what you've done, he's not going to give you a hard time."

"Are we sure about that?" Zoe asked. "Because it seems to me that I could get every single item he handpicked for this place and he'd still find a problem with something."

Martha chuckled. "I know it seems that way, but things just got off to a rough start. You're going to go in there and fix it and make it right. How can he have a problem with that?"

Letting out a breath, Zoe sat back up in her chair. "Okay, you're right. I know you're right. I let him get under my skin and I should know better. Sorry."

"You have nothing to apologize for. I think it's great

that you want to make this work so badly, but don't make yourself crazy," Martha said with a laugh. "I knew you were the perfect person for this job. It'll get easier. I promise."

"I hope you're right, Martha." Zoe knew she wasn't but was too tired to argue about it. With a quick wave and a smile, Martha left.

Zoe looked at her watch and saw it was almost six. There was no way she was staying any longer and no way she was going to stop by the model home on her way through town.

While her computer was shutting down, she pulled the schedule from her pile of paperwork to see what was planned for tomorrow. Earlier when she had spoken to the paint foreman, Charlie, he hadn't been opposed to Zoe lending a hand. And that was exactly what she was going to do.

Making a mental note to dress in jeans and an old shirt tomorrow, she gathered up all of her paperwork and closed up her office. With the hectic schedule that day, she hadn't had a spare minute to herself. Knowing that there still wasn't much to eat back at her place, it meant another night of takeout.

She'd starve before she ate Italian again.

Okay, maybe not *starve,* but it would be a long time until she willingly went out for Italian again. Except Friday night was pizza night, and now she knew where to get good pizza.

"I despise myself," she muttered as she climbed into her car. "I am too weak and my love of carbs is too strong!"

In the end, Zoe went for Chinese and drove home,

wishing she had a convertible. The sun was still out, so she ate her dinner out on her deck and listened to the waves crashing on the shore. Then she went for a long barefoot walk along the shore until the sun began to set. It was the perfect night.

Even if she was alone.

———✦———

"What the hell do you think you're doing?"

Oh good. Aidan's here, Zoe thought to herself from her perch on the six-foot ladder. "I'm painting."

"I can see that," he said with a huff of frustration. "What I want to know is why. I have an entire paint crew here for this. Painting isn't part of your job!"

Ignoring his temper tantrum, Zoe continued to cut in the paint at the ceiling line.

"Get down from that ladder, Zoe. I'm not kidding."

"No can do," she said lightly. "We're on a schedule here. Dark red is tricky to work with, and while I'm sure Charlie himself is capable, his crew of college students is better suited to spraying the easier, more neutral colors in the rest of the house. Much better for their skill level. I'd rather handle this myself."

"What do you know about painting?" Aidan was completely ticked that Zoe wasn't listening to him and staying put on the ladder. If she didn't step down soon, he'd bring her down himself.

"I used to paint every house that I decorated back in Arizona when I was starting out. It cut the costs and I'm good at it." Most people found it to be tedious, but she had always found it relaxing.

"But it's not your job. You're here to—"

"Fix what my firm screwed up?" She threw his own words back at him and only wished she could have seen the look on his face.

"Zoe, please come down," he said in a deep voice, nearly a growl.

"If I don't finish cutting this in with the brush at the trim line and get the rest of the wall rolled out, the colors won't match. It's important to follow through quickly." She brushed her way to the corner before leaning back and making sure there were no brush strokes or streaks. Only then did she start to climb down from the ladder.

Aidan watched her movements. She was wearing a snug pair of jeans that hugged her curves perfectly. He hadn't noticed just how nice of a bottom she had until now. The skirt hadn't done her justice. But here and now in jeans, her figure practically had him salivating.

But that wasn't all.

The black tank top fit like a second skin. Her hair was up in a ponytail high on her head, leaving her neck completely exposed. There was a paint smudge on her cheek that his fingers itched to wipe away.

Focus, he reminded himself. This was his company and he had a job to do. Maybe the lines had gotten a little blurred the other night with Zoe, but he knew better than to indulge in that again. He couldn't get involved with her. They were colleagues of sorts, and anything beyond that would be unprofessional.

And it sucked.

"And just what are you wearing?"

"Oh, for the love of it," Zoe muttered and bent down to grab her bottle of water. "There isn't a dress code in our contract. I checked."

"Very funny. Are you aware that you are working in a house with about two dozen men?"

Keeping her back to him, Zoe downed half her water bottle before she responded. "Is there a point to this line of questioning because I've got a wall to paint—pronto."

Looking around at the one wall Zoe had already completed, Aidan had to admit she'd done a damn-near perfect job. "Well, I still haven't gotten to see how this new crew is doing, and now I won't because you interfered," he said, even as she put more paint on the roller and began painting the next wall.

"Look, Mr. Shaughnessy," Zoe said. "You're a businessman who knows the importance of getting the job done right and on schedule. I needed to make sure this room was going to get done right the first time. There isn't a whole lot for me to do until all of the painting is done, so I'm helping to speed up the process. I've been informed that I'm not allowed to have any other clients while I'm on this job, so that means I'm going to jump in where I'm needed to keep us on track." Looking over her shoulder, she glared at him. "Do you have a problem with that?"

Right now Aidan had about a dozen problems with that, but none of them were rational.

"We're not insured for you to be painting."

Zoe's painting didn't even falter. "That's the stupidest thing I've ever heard."

"You could fall off the ladder."

"I could also fall off a ladder while hanging drapes, a picture, or placing decorative items up in high places. Nice try." Turning to face him, she dipped the roller back in the paint and expertly removed the excess. "You should be thanking me. Some of those guys don't even know how to properly use a roller. They just spray it on. All. The. Time. Now that's all fine and good for an inventory home that you just want white walls in, but there is no way they can spray this red paint. It needs to be rolled out carefully, and it needs to be done several times. Trust me. In the time it will take me to get this room painted three times, they'll have the rest of the house almost done. Okay?"

He knew she was talking to him, but Aidan's attention was suddenly honed in on Zoe—more specifically, her breasts. Right there, in the middle of Zoe's tank top, splashed across her magnificent breasts, was a daisy.

His mom's favorite flower.

His eyes moved up to meet Zoe's furious gaze. *Crap*, now she probably thought he was just some pervert staring at her breasts, but right now it was that damn daisy that had him transfixed. Forcing himself to look away, he murmured an apology and fled the room.

"Well, that was odd," Zoe grumbled and turned to finish painting the wall. It was a good thing he had the sense to leave the room because she'd felt like taking the paint pole and smacking Aidan on the side of the head. He had the nerve to lecture *her* efforts to stay on top of *his* stupid schedule, and then instead of listening to her, he was standing there staring at her breasts the entire time! *Jerk*.

Suddenly energized with indignation, Zoe didn't take long to get the room finished. Afterward, she carefully took the paint tray and walked outside with a sense of accomplishment.

"I've got that, Miss Zoe," the paint foreman said as he jogged over to her from the adjacent lot.

"Thanks, Charlie."

He took the tray from her and yelled for one of his crew to come over and get it cleaned up. "I just saw the room and I have to tell you, I'm impressed. I've been doing this a long time, and red is not an easy color to work with."

She blushed at his praise. "Like I told you yesterday, I enjoy painting. And while I think it looks pretty good right now, the truth will be known tomorrow when it's dry and Mr. Shaughnessy comes and inspects it." She couldn't help but make a face as she said it and smiled when Charlie laughed. "Every person here could say that it looks great, but until Mr. Shaughnessy says it passes inspection, it's anyone's guess."

"Ain't that the truth. This is the first job we're doing for him, but the interview process I went through with him told me he's a pretty high-maintenance guy."

"That's the understatement of the year." They shared a laugh and Zoe found that she felt comfortable with Charlie. He was no more than a couple of years older than her, certainly no older than Aidan.

"So you've worked for him before?" Charlie asked.

Zoe shook her head. "I only took over on Monday because another decorator at the firm messed up."

"Damn. So they took her off the job and put you on it?"

She shook her head again. "She was fired over it."

He cursed under his breath and then immediately apologized for being crude. "That seems pretty harsh."

"I'm sort of walking on eggshells too. I don't want to mess anything up."

"That's why you wanted to take on that room yourself?" he asked and Zoe nodded. "I can't say that I blame you. My guys are good, but most of them don't have a lot of experience, which is why we do a lot of spraying. That's fairly easy. Doing brushing and rolling takes a lot more skill and patience."

"I find it therapeutic," she said with a chuckle and Charlie joined her.

"I'm sorry, are we all on a coffee break?" Aidan asked, walking up to them.

Zoe wanted to roll her eyes. After his bizarre behavior earlier, she had thought maybe he wouldn't come back again today. And even if he did come back, she'd hoped he'd leave her to her work in peace. No such luck. Charlie started to apologize, but Zoe stepped in to save him.

"I just finished painting and was bringing my supplies out to get cleaned up. Charlie's guys are taking care of that for me. He was just complimenting my work."

Aidan eyed the man with a hint of anger. Was he going to ask her out for drinks or something after work too? *How can any man resist Zoe,* Aidan thought, *all charming and sweet, and in those snug jeans and tight tank top…*

He had to get a grip. He was making himself crazy. Aidan turned back to Zoe. "The room's complete?"

She nodded. "I'll tackle the trim tomorrow if it needs it. I was just going back in to pick up drop cloths and get the ladder out of there. I don't want anyone else to go in there and risk bumping into the wall or anything."

"I'll take care of it," Aidan said and turned toward the house.

Zoe gave Charlie a nervous parting smile and chased after Aidan. "I just said that I didn't want anyone else in there, didn't I?"

"It's my damn house and I don't see why I can't go in there."

"Are you even listening to yourself?" she snapped and was surprised when Aidan stopped in his tracks and turned to look at her. "You put me on this job and I have done everything that you asked. No, wait. I've done *more* than what you've asked, and I don't appreciate you undermining me and ignoring my requests."

Pinching the bridge of his nose, Aidan silently counted to ten. Zoe waited. He knew she was right. If it were anyone else, he wouldn't be cleaning up their mess, but it bothered him to think of Zoe doing this kind of manual labor all by herself. It wasn't his fault his parents had raised him to be old-fashioned. In his mind, there were still traditional roles for men and women.

"I'll make you a deal," he finally said.

She eyed him warily. "I'm listening."

"I'll let you finish cleaning up in there today, if—"

"You'll *let* me do my job? Oh, the joy," she interrupted.

"*If* you promise that you aren't going to do anymore painting."

She crossed her arms and stood there defiantly. *If he didn't think I could paint a room without killing myself on the ladder, why did he hire me?* Zoe thought. It was on the tip of her tongue to argue about it, but Aidan had already ticked her off enough for one day. "Fine," she finally said. "No more painting." Besides, she'd already finished what she wanted to do herself anyway.

"That includes the trim. If it needs to be touched up, Charlie's crew can handle it. Or, if you'd prefer, I'll ask Charlie to do it personally. Deal?"

"Deal."

Aidan visibly relaxed. "Thank you."

"I haven't had a chance to look at the rest of the house, but it looks like they're getting ready to call it a day too," Zoe said. "Maybe you should check on them, and you and I can go over my room tomorrow. Okay?"

Nodding, Aidan quickly walked away.

Zoe had to wonder at his odd behavior today. And yesterday. And the day before. What made Aidan Shaughnessy tick? She *thought* she'd gotten a good glimpse of the man while they were at dinner the other night, but standing there now, watching him walk away, she realized that she had merely scratched the surface.

For the next two weeks, Aidan and Zoe managed to steer clear of one another. A truce of sorts had been formed when Zoe had met with Aidan the following day, and he had sincerely complimented her paint job. The trim did not need to be retouched, which was a relief for both of them, and when Zoe took out her file to show Aidan some of her planned accessory purchases, he didn't argue.

After that meeting though, if Zoe did happen to see Aidan, it was from a distance. He was busy elsewhere now that construction on the rest of the houses in the community had started. That was fine with Zoe.

On some level, it still bothered her that she had been so wrong about him. For a brief moment she had been hopeful…but she supposed that everyone had been right after all. Aidan Shaughnessy was a difficult man, and there wasn't anything she could do to change him. It wasn't her job.

By the end of that second week though, she felt really good about everything she had accomplished. She assumed that Aidan was pleased—or at least found it acceptable—because he hadn't made any comments or placed any calls to Martha to complain. She considered that a victory.

Looking forward to the weekend, Zoe drove away from the site a little later than she had planned that evening and went in search of the Italian restaurant where Aidan had taken her. She had decided against it the previous Friday on principle, but her need for pizza was just too great.

The thought of sitting out on her deck and enjoying her dinner made her smile. Zoe did have to thank Aidan for one thing: his insistence that she not work with any other clients while she was working for him meant she was actually able to go home at night and relax. She walked on the beach every night and had finally begun to feel a peace in her life that she hadn't felt in a while.

Not since she'd lost her mother to breast cancer.

Sometimes, on her nightly walks, she would talk to her mother. It didn't matter if other people were around because it made her feel better to talk to the woman who had raised her alone and left her far too soon, six months ago. Zoe didn't like to talk about it with anyone; even Martha and her coworkers were unaware of the real reason Zoe had chosen to move across the country. It was private.

Her mother had never seen the ocean—it was an unfulfilled dream of hers. In her entire life, she had never left Arizona. It hadn't been a conscious decision; life had just worked out that way. But on the wall in her mother's bedroom had been a beautiful painting of a beach at sunset. Toward the end of her mother's illness, they had lain in bed together and looked at it, her mother talking about how much she had wished she could have seen such a beautiful view in person. Maybe that was why Zoe was so obsessed with it. So on her walks, she would tell her mother about how soft the sand felt or what the ocean breeze smelled like. It made her feel better, almost as if they were experiencing this new life together.

Zoe pulled into the pizzeria parking lot and marveled at the crowd. There was a line out the door; there was probably a long wait for a table. But then she noticed a side entrance marked "Takeout Orders." Zoe grumbled to herself for not thinking ahead, but it wasn't like she had someone to rush home to.

Joining the crowd inside the designated area, Zoe waited her turn to get to the counter and was surprised to be greeted again by Tammy, her waitress from the night she had come here with Aidan.

Tammy recognized her immediately and greeted her with a smile. "Hey, Zoe! How are you?"

"Fine, Tammy, thanks. And you?"

"Oh, you know, living the dream." She winked at Zoe and got out her pad. "Are you here to pick up Aidan's order, or getting something for yourself?"

Aidan's order? Awkward…

"Um…something for myself," Zoe said. Placing

her order for a small pizza with everything on it, she paid and thanked Tammy before taking a seat to wait for her dinner. Wracking her brain, she tried to remember if Aidan had still been on-site when she'd left. She couldn't be sure. She hoped at least she'd be gone before he arrived.

"Hey, Aidan!" a man behind the counter said as Aidan walked in the door. "We're running behind tonight. Give me about ten minutes, okay?"

Zoe did her best to hide behind the crowd and not look his way. If she got up now, he'd totally see her. But she could hear him talking with some of the other patrons, and with any luck, by the time her order was ready, she'd be able to grab her food and escape unnoticed. Taking out her cell phone, she started a game of solitaire to keep her eyes from wandering around the room. Someone sat down beside her and every girly part of her body went on high alert.

"Hey, Zoe," Aidan said softly.

She took a minute to compose herself and moved a couple of virtual cards before looking up, careful to keep her expression neutral. "Aidan."

It was the most they had spoken to each other all week.

"How are you doing?" he asked. Zoe knew he was just trying to make conversation, perhaps trying to smooth over some of the awkwardness, but she wasn't interested. He was the one who'd created the tension and the awkwardness between them in the first place, so let him deal with it.

Tammy called her name for her order, and she jumped out of her seat as if it were on fire. Without acknowledging Aidan, she walked up to the counter and thanked Tammy as she grabbed her box and walked out. It almost seemed too easy. Too…simple.

"Zoe!"

So close. Stubbornness was something she'd been born with, so she continued to walk to her car and proceeded to unlock the door and put the pizza on the passenger seat. But then Aidan called out to her again before she could get in the car. There was nothing she had to say to him and she was off the clock, so she simply stood next to her car and waited.

"Are you all right?" he asked when he stopped in front of her.

Zoe shrugged. "Of course. Why?"

Aidan stuck his hands in his pockets and suddenly regretted following her out. It was obvious she didn't want to talk to him, and that was the way he thought he wanted it, but seeing her sitting there in the restaurant had reminded him of their first night together. Well, not *together* together. Hell, this was why he hadn't wanted to be around her for two weeks. She just made him feel so completely disarmed. But that first night, they had both been so happy, carefree.

Zoe didn't look happy and carefree right now. She looked guarded.

And pissed.

At him.

Clearing his throat, he shifted his weight and scrambled for something to say. "The house is looking good. I like the pieces you chose for the home office space."

While she might have taken a moment to bask in the

glow of his compliment, Zoe reminded herself of their positions—employer and employee.

"Thank you. If you'll excuse me, my dinner is getting cold." Turning toward her car, she was surprised when Aidan's hand gently wrapped around her upper arm and spun her around. Her eyes blazed with fury. "Take your hands off me please." Her words had the desired effect, and he not only released her but he also took a step back.

"Look," he began cautiously, "I just wanted to say… I'm sorry." She crossed her arms over her chest. "I was a complete ass last week after we had dinner. I didn't know what to expect the next morning, and I really did have a good time with you and…" He threw up his hands and gave a helpless shrug. "I'd never done anything like that before."

"Had dinner with another person?" she asked, cocking an eyebrow.

Aidan couldn't help the sour look he gave her. "Cute. No, that's not what I meant. I've never…socialized… with the people who work for me. And—"

Zoe cut him off. "It's fine. Don't worry about it. It was just dinner, Aidan. That's all. I know you have to be a certain way on the job site. If the workers get the impression that you're a pushover or that you're their pal, they'll take advantage and slack off. I get it. You don't have to take it to such extremes, though. You can be tough but fair without being such a jerk. If you had just talked to me like a normal person, this all could have been avoided."

It was everything that should have made him happy to hear and yet it didn't. Just dinner? Was that really all she thought? Was he the only one who felt anything between them? Looking at her blank expression, Aidan suspected he was. And now he felt like a fool.

And then out of nowhere, a scene played out in his mind.

"How am I going to know the difference between a girl I can trust and one…you know…I can't?"

A wide smile crossed his mother's face. "I'll let you know."

He hadn't thought about that conversation with his mother in years. The daisy on Zoe's shirt last week had freaked him out because it just seemed like too much of a coincidence. He felt a connection to her that he'd never felt with another woman. He enjoyed talking with her, bantering with her. Hell, he even liked arguing with her. He liked the way her green eyes darkened when she was angry and how her ivory complexion flushed when she was nervous.

In all the years since that conversation with his mother, Lillian had been fairly discreet about passing along her opinions of the girls he dated. She never came right out and said she liked or disliked any of them, but he knew her well enough to catch on that she didn't think any of them were right for him.

And she had been right.

He wished he could talk to her just one more time.

It was hard, but he had to force himself to look away from Zoe's face because he had a feeling she probably thought he was crazy.

And that freaked him out too.

Zoe had her keychain dangling from her fingertips, awkwardly fiddling with the keys as she waited for him to say something. A sparkle of red caught Aidan's eye.

When he looked closer he saw that it was a pair of crystal cherries.

That can't be a coincidence, he thought and quickly snuck a peek at the sky. Was that what was going on here? He shook his head to clear it. No. That was impossible. Feeling spooked, Aidan took another step away from Zoe. "Well…um…I better go and grab my order. My father and sister are probably wondering where I am."

She simply nodded.

"So…um…have a good weekend," he said as he continued to walk backward toward the restaurant.

"You too," she said softly and turned to climb into her car.

Standing in the doorway, Aidan watched Zoe drive away and had to wonder what in the world was happening to him.

———

It wasn't until Darcy had left the dinner table with her phone in hand—making plans to see a movie with friends—that Aidan finally decided to approach the subject with his father.

"Can I ask you something?" he began cautiously as the two of them worked together to clear the table.

"Sure," Ian said. "Anything."

"Do you ever…I mean, have you ever, you know, felt Mom around since she died?"

Ian stopped dead in his tracks. "What are you talking about?"

Damn it, Aidan thought. Maybe he should have just kept this all to himself and slowly gone insane on his own. "You know what, it's nothing. Never mind. Forget I even brought it up." He quickly disposed of the pizza boxes and poured out the remainder of his beer because, clearly, the alcohol was not helping the conversation.

Standing back, Ian watched his son move nervously around the kitchen. The kitchen was completely clean and yet Aidan continued to walk around, wiping down surfaces and straightening magnets on the refrigerator.

Ian's eyes narrowed. Aidan had never been one to talk about himself or ask for help when he needed it. He supposed it came from the sense of responsibility Aidan had, being the oldest and all. But right now, Ian would bet every penny he had that something had knocked Aidan off balance. Ian was just about to ask him about it when Darcy came bouncing back into the room.

"Okay, so Julie's mom is going to pick me up and drop us off at the movies. We're going to the nine o'clock in town. Then we're going to grab ice cream afterward and I'll be home at midnight. Is that okay?"

She was pushing her luck, Ian thought to himself, but he'd let it slide for tonight. Tonight he needed some time alone with Aidan to see what was going on. "That's fine, Darce. Just promise to give me a call if you're going to be later than midnight." He watched his daughter spin with delight.

Rushing over, Darcy planted a loud kiss on his cheek. "Thanks, Dad!" And then she ran from the room.

Ian didn't want to start a conversation that had the potential to get interrupted when Darcy got picked up, so he bided his time until then. He talked to Aidan about sports scores, his conversation with Owen earlier in the day, and the possibility of Owen coming to town for a couple of weeks after the New Year.

For the first time ever, Ian was impatient for Darcy's ride to arrive. Even though they spent a lot of time together, he and Aidan tended to stick to family matters and work. Aidan wasn't the type to talk about himself or any personal problems.

"Darce!" he called out when he heard the sound of a car horn coming from the driveway. "Your chariot awaits!"

As predicted, she tore through the house like a tiny tornado. She hugged them both good-bye and let the door slam shut behind her.

"She's a force of nature." Ian sighed. A smile crossed his face as he went to sit down in the living room. But it slowly faded as he took in Aidan sitting on the sofa looking positively miserable.

"What's going on, Son?"

Aidan looked up. "What are you talking about?"

Ian simply leveled a glance at his son. No words were necessary.

"Okay, fine. It's just that, I come home here and… sometimes it's like Mom never left. Everything is still exactly the same. I can look in every room and remember everything about her. But outside? I never felt… I never sensed her presence, I guess, until recently."

"Okay," Ian said simply, wondering where Aidan was going with this. "And did that bother you?"

He shrugged. "I don't know." He scrubbed a hand across his face. "It's…it's kind of embarrassing."

Now Ian shrugged. "Might make you feel better to talk about it."

Aidan had his doubts but figured if anyone could help him, it was his father. Shifting in his seat, Aidan told him about the long-ago conversation between him and his mother. "She always helped, Dad, right until the end. And now? Now…I've met someone and…she's amazing. She's sexy and beautiful and she challenges me and infuriates me and she makes me laugh."

"Those are all good things, Aidan, but I don't understand what this has to do with your mother."

Aidan leaned forward, his elbows on his knees. "What was Mom's favorite flower?"

"Daisies," Ian said with a smile. "She said they were very happy flowers."

"Maybe it's common, maybe it's not, but…I never noticed daisies where any other woman was concerned. I mean, how often do you see a grown woman wearing clothes with daisies on them?"

"That's an odd question," Ian said, considering it. "Not very often, I suppose. But that doesn't mean it's unusual."

"Zoe had a shirt with a big daisy on the front of it the other day," Aidan said miserably. "I took one look at it and damn near had a panic attack."

"It's just a flower, Aidan. And for that matter, it was just a shirt. It's not a big deal, Son."

"Okay, then there were the cherries."

"Cherries?"

Aidan nodded. "During that same conversation with Mom, she was wearing the apron with the cherries on it. Do you remember it?"

"Of course I do. Your sister wears it when she bakes."

"Tonight, I ran into Zoe at the pizza place. We

were talking out by her car, and I look down and her keychain is a pair of red crystal cherries. It can't be a coincidence!"

Ian wanted to hug his son, but he had a feeling that Aidan wouldn't find the comfort in it that he would. "Aidan, while yes, those things are reminders of your mother, I don't think that they're actual *signs* from your mother."

"So you're telling me that you've never had anything happen that can't be explained? Never stumbled across something that just made you think of Mom?"

"Well, I didn't say that, but—"

"Dad, I know it sounds crazy, but I don't know if I can just blow it off as a coincidence. Every time I find myself struggling with my feelings for Zoe, I see something on her that reminds me of Mom. Whenever it happens, I hear Mom's voice, reminding me that she'd help me." It was important for Aidan to convince him. "Dad, I don't know whether I'm having these thoughts because Zoe reminds me of Mom, or because I'm losing my mind."

Unable to help himself, Ian reached out and pulled his son into his embrace. He held him tight for a solid minute before straightening. "If you believe that your mother is trying to tell you that Zoe is the woman for you, then I think you should follow your heart." Emotions clogged his voice. "All she ever wanted was for you to be happy. She would never steer you wrong."

"I just miss her so much sometimes," Aidan said softly.

"Me too."

And then Aidan did something he hadn't done in sixteen years.

He cried.

Chapter 5

A WEEK LATER, ZOE SAT WITH RAPT ATTENTION AS SHE watched the evening news.

"As of right now, this is a tropical storm, but it's slated to pick up intensity in the next couple of days. If things go as predicted on our models, we'll hit a category-one-hurricane status on Monday as it approaches the East Coast. It is expected to make landfall on the central Carolina coast."

"Of course it is," she murmured as she continued to listen to the report.

"We'll keep you posted on evacuations and hurricane preparedness as we go through the weekend."

Shutting off the television, Zoe looked out at the beach. She could see the difference in the waves and the sky since yesterday, and part of her was scared but the other part couldn't help but be fascinated.

On the screen was a brief list of things that coastal residents should know and do, like making sure to fill their cars with gas and having IDs that listed their addresses, in the event of an evacuation. A category-one hurricane did not necessarily mean evacuation, but should she have a plan?

Standing, she walked out on her back deck and noticed that the crowds had thinned out, but that wasn't unusual for a stormy day. There were some television crews taping their reports farther down the shore, but as far as she could tell, life was staying pretty close to normal, and if that was going to be the case, Zoe figured she'd hit the supermarket and stock up on snacks and comfort food and hunker down to wait out the storm. It could be exciting to watch Mother Nature unleash her fury on the beach.

She looked at the clock and saw it was only eight. There was plenty of time to do a little shopping and be home in time to…well, nothing. It was another Friday night, and she had nothing to do.

Lame. Very lame.

Thirty minutes later, Zoe stood in the produce section wondering how her comfort food plan had completely crumbled. Obviously people took these hurricane predictions seriously because there seemed to be a thousand people in the store. Zoe was shoulder to shoulder with a group of people picking over the last of the apples.

Deciding that fruit and vegetables were highly overrated, Zoe thought a change of strategy was in order. While these people were busy buying healthy stuff, Zoe made a beeline for the bakery. Finding slim pickings there as well, she finally had success in the cookie aisle. Loading the basket with all of her favorites, she then hit the remainder of the staples—bread, milk, meat, and eggs.

The checkout lines seemed to go on forever, and it didn't make sense to be choosy about which one she joined. Stopping at the back of a line, she looked around in amazement. She'd never dealt with anything like this—the frenzy, the flutter of activity.

"Oh, Zoe dear, how are you?"

Turning her head, Zoe noticed her neighbor, Mrs.

Maddox, in the line behind her. "Oh, hi, Mrs. M. I thought I'd get in some shopping before the storm. Guess we got here just in time, huh?" she asked with a chuckle.

Julia Maddox was in her seventies and had lived on the coast her entire life. With her children grown, now it was just her and her husband, Fred, here. "I never understood the reasoning behind it and yet I can't seem to help myself," she replied. "Our pantry is always fully stocked, but as soon as I hear a storm warning, I find the need to come to the store and buy more. Fred doesn't even question it anymore. He simply gets in the car and waits."

Zoe smiled and looked down at the items in her cart. "Well, my pantry isn't very well stocked and since the shelves here are nearly wiped out, there wasn't much to choose from. But I think I have enough to satisfy me in the junk food department."

"You're always welcome to come and sit out the storm with us. We've been through enough of these that we rarely leave. Sometimes the predictions are worse than the reality." She sighed and leaned a little on her cart. "After a while you learn that it's okay to stay put and just stay inside."

"I bet you've seen some amazing storms."

Julia nodded. "Mother Nature sure is something. There's something oddly soothing watching a storm blow through." She chuckled. "My daughter Beth doesn't necessarily agree, but she's learned to not argue with us."

"Does she live nearby?"

"She's about two hours inland. I spoke to her earlier

and she's already chomping at the bit to get us to drive in to her, but I put her off." She shook her head. "I think it's too soon to start packing up. Besides that, Baron doesn't like long car rides. Poor thing gets carsick."

Baron was the Maddoxes' beloved miniature American Eskimo dog. Every morning, Zoe watched Julia walk up and down the beach with the dog. "That's not good. Poor boy. So you think you and Mr. M. are going to stay put?"

Again Julia nodded. "My Freddy loves to watch the Weather Channel. He doesn't think this storm is going to amount to much of anything. So," she began and motioned to the food in her cart, "I'll bake some cookies, make a nice stew, and make sure that my Baron has enough food and puppy pads just in case he can't go out."

Zoe frowned. "I thought you said you didn't think it was going to be that bad?"

"Well, bad enough to evacuate, no. Bad enough that I'm not going to want to walk around outside, yes." She chuckled. "I'm getting a little too old to be walking around in the wind and the rain. And Baron is a mama's boy and he prefers that I walk him." She shook her head and laughed. "That makes Fred very happy!"

"I'll bet," Zoe said, joining in the laughter. The line was moving quickly and before she knew it, she was loading her groceries onto the belt. She turned and looked at Julia. "Do you think there's anything else I need to do to be prepared?"

Julia looked at the food Zoe was unloading. "I think you're going to be fine with the food. You might want to tape the windows," she said with a shrug. "Sometimes we do; sometimes we don't. If you'd like, I'll send Fred over tomorrow to take a look at things."

"That would be wonderful. Thank you so much," she said as she sagged with relief. "It's my first hurricane."

Julia smiled. "A good storm can be exciting, that's for sure. But living on the coast, it can get tiresome…fast."

"What do you mean?"

She shrugged again. "If it's an active hurricane season, it's not unusual to find yourself standing in line like this more and more often. It can get expensive."

"Because of the damage?"

"Because of the food shopping!" Julia laughed. "Fred says he's the most well fed during an active storm season."

Zoe couldn't help but laugh with her. Her food was all on the belt and currently being rung up. She helped the cashier bag everything up, paid, and wished both Julia and the cashier a good night.

By the time she got home, it was nearing eleven and she was exhausted. Once the groceries were all put away, she changed into a pair of yoga pants and an oversized sweatshirt and walked down to the beach. The wind was pretty powerful and the waves were bigger than anything she'd ever seen before.

"I wish you could feel this, Mom," she said quietly, looking up at the starless sky. "The wind feels amazing and the waves look and sound pretty fierce." She stood and let the wind whip around her. She thought about her conversation with her neighbor and looked at the houses that lined the beach. There hadn't been time for her to meet a lot of people, but she vowed to change that. Back in Arizona, she'd known everyone in her small town and had had a wonderful support system around her, even in her darkest times.

But the home that had once been her comfort now only carried painful memories. Everywhere she turned reminded her of her mother. The decision to move hadn't been easy, but Zoe had needed a change. The only thing she knew was that she wanted to live on the coast; it didn't matter which one. Some online job hunting eventually brought her to North Carolina and even now, with the threat of somewhat dangerous weather, she wasn't sorry about being there instead of back west.

"I'm sorry about that too, Mom," she said with a heavy sigh. "I'm not there. I haven't been to visit you and you have to know that it kills me. I know we discussed this a long time ago and this is where you wanted me to be but…I feel like I'm not being a very good daughter. I'm here, living my life, and you're…" She swallowed hard. "You're all by yourself."

She couldn't have said another word even if she wanted to. Her heart was too heavy.

Zoe's walk down the shore and back was shorter than normal because the wind was whipping and it really was getting late. Back at the house, she locked up and closed the blinds and got ready for bed. There was a level of restlessness she couldn't quite put her finger on. Maybe it was the impending storm. Or maybe it was Aidan. She hadn't allowed herself to think about him. Much. She knew that dating a coworker or client was never a good decision, but she would have considered it for him.

And she had a feeling she would have really liked it.

The rest of the weekend was like nothing Zoe had ever experienced before. While a lot of her neighbors had packed up and taken off for parts farther inland, there were a few who were taping up their windows and standing their ground. The property management company had called and gone through a list of things she would need to do to prepare the house, but they would send someone out to board up the windows for her if she was going to leave.

She had agreed to tape up the windows after letting them know that for the moment, she was staying put. The woman she had spoken to had tried to convince her to leave, but Zoe wasn't ready to concede just yet. Shrugging it off, Zoe went about cooking her comfort foods, walking on the beach while the tide was out a bit, and talking with the locals about bygone storms. Everyone had a story to tell; some were fairly tame while others scared her. The thought of jumping in her car and finding a hotel was starting to become more and more attractive.

"No, no, no," she admonished herself, while walking on the beach on Sunday afternoon. "You can stick it out. It's not going to be that bad and you're going to be fine."

"Excuse me, miss?" Zoe looked over her shoulder to see a police officer walking toward her carrying a tablet in his hand. "Good afternoon, I'm Officer Robert Hannigan. I'm checking on residents to see who is staying and who is leaving. Is this your house here?" He motioned toward hers and she nodded. He typed into his tablet. "Are you leaving today or tomorrow?"

"Um…no. I'm planning on staying." She had meant to say it with confidence, but the stern look he was giving her instilled some concern.

"You do realize that by deciding to stay, you are putting yourself at risk?"

Zoe nodded.

"If the storm worsens and something happens, emergency operations may be delayed in getting to you, do you understand?"

Again, she nodded.

He studied her for a long minute. "This must be your first summer here because I don't remember meeting you before, Miss...?"

"Dalton," she said. "Zoe Dalton."

"You're renting, right?"

"Yes."

"Have you ever experienced a hurricane on the coast, Miss Dalton?"

"No," she said. "I've lived in Arizona my entire life. I only just moved here a little over two months ago, and I really don't want to have pack up and leave again so soon. I've been talking to the locals and they've told me what to expect. I'm not going into this unprepared. I'm going to tape up the windows and I have batteries and flashlights and bottled water. I've gone over all of the preparedness paperwork."

He nodded. "Uh-huh." He tucked the tablet under his arm. "Can I offer you a bit of advice?"

"Sure."

"Evacuate. Leave now. I know you don't understand this because you've never experienced it, but storms of this magnitude can be unpredictable. You don't want to take a chance at being stranded or worse."

"I think I can handle it."

"Miss Dalton, I can't force you to leave, but just

consider… These houses are built on stilts. They're all old and were built at a time when there were fewer guidelines. You need to think of your safety. You may not find a hotel room tomorrow. You should go now and wait until the storm passes before coming back."

"Officer Hannigan, I'm sure you mean well and that you're only doing your job, but I really don't want to pack up and leave. I feel one hundred percent safe here. Really. I appreciate your concern and I respect the work that you're doing. Honestly. But I'm going to stay."

He considered her again for a long minute until Zoe started to squirm. He was quite intimidating—over six feet tall and just…huge. She had a feeling he could fling her over his shoulder and force her to evacuate.

"Okay," he finally said. "If you'll just sign here." He took out the tablet and pulled up a signature screen for her to sign with her finger. "This states that you've opted to stay and not evacuate even under the suggestion of local law enforcement." He indicated where she needed to sign. Taking the tablet back from her, he then clicked to another screen. "If you don't mind, we also need some personal information—full name, phone number, employer—that sort of thing."

Unperturbed, she gave him the information and he nodded when he typed in her employer. "Ah, you work for Martha Tate," he said with recognition.

"You know Martha?" Zoe asked.

"She and my mother are good friends. They grew up together. Small town and all that. Are you working on anything local?"

"Yup, the Shaughnessy job," she said, figuring he must be familiar with the huge project, small town and all. But she was still somewhat surprised when he started to laugh. "What? What's so funny about that?"

"I'm sorry," he said with amiable mirth. "Aidan's a good man—known him my entire life—but I know what a royal pain in the…rear"—he cleared his throat—"he is to work for. You must be pretty tough if Martha wanted you to take on that job."

Zoe suddenly had a new respect for Officer Hannigan. "Well, thank you."

He shook his head. "Yup. Aidan's a control freak. But he gets the job done…" He trailed off and smiled.

"Exactly!" Zoe said with a huge grin. "I'm glad I'm not the only one to think that!"

"Trust me. You're not."

The wind whipped up and Zoe shivered. "I really do appreciate you stopping by to check on me, Officer Hannigan." She held out her hand to shake his.

"Please, call me Bobby. Now that I know you're working for Aidan, I can see why a hurricane doesn't seem like such a big deal. Be safe though!"

They laughed and he wished her luck before walking down the beach to the next house. Zoe watched him go and wondered if Officer Hannigan was single, not that she felt any kind of zing of attraction to him—not like she had with Aidan. But still, if she was going to live in the area, she figured she'd have to start dating eventually.

Too bad the only one she wanted to date was a stubborn Irishman by the name of Aidan Shaughnessy.

———

"What the hell do you think you're doing?"

It was late Monday morning, but since businesses were

closed due to the impending storm, Zoe was standing on the beach, wrapped up in an oversized sweater, watching the waves crash and looking up at the clouds swirling in the sky. She didn't even bother to turn around. "You're going to have to start thinking of some other way to start your conversations, Aidan. That one's getting old."

He stepped in front of her, his face full of fury. "I'm serious, Zoe. Why didn't you leave like everyone else?"

"Look around, Aidan," she said loudly. The wind and the waves were nearly deafening. "Plenty of my neighbors have stayed. I'm not going anywhere."

"Like hell you're not. Get your things and let's go," he demanded.

"I can't go, Aidan," she said. She looked at him defiantly for a minute. His blue eyes were nearly black and he looked damn intimidating, but her hair kept whipping around her face. It was hard to look tough and defiant with hair in your mouth. "Why are you even here? Why aren't you tucked away in a safe zone?"

"Because Bobby Hannigan came around to check on the construction site and told me that my fearless decorator was braving out the storm! I thought he was joking." Well, first Bobby had mentioned how hot she was and then mentioned she wasn't going to leave the beach. Aidan wasn't sure which one had pissed him off more. "I didn't think you'd be crazy enough to stay here and wait to get hurt," Aidan said angrily.

"God, do you hear yourself? You're not responsible for me, Aidan, and I'd be careful about who you go around and call crazy."

"Okay, that was out of line, I admit it. Now will you please pack up so we can get out of here?"

"No. No *we* can't. You can. But I'm not." Ignoring him, Zoe turned and walked in the opposite direction of her house. The air felt thick and heavy, and even though no rain had begun to fall, she knew it was only a matter of time. She had hoped to be safely inside before that happened.

He got in front of her before she was more than a dozen feet away. "I'm asking you nicely," he said and even did his best not to clench his teeth. "You're going to take a direct hit here, Zoe. I'm not saying this to make you do things my way; I'm telling you this because I'm concerned for your safety!"

"I know. I saw the updated storm predictions this morning." She looked around a bit before facing him again. "I was planning on leaving, but my neighbors—Julia and Fred—their dog got away when they were loading the car. They weren't going to leave either but I guess their daughter convinced them. She lives a couple of hours inland, so it helped that they had somewhere welcoming to go. They're old and Fred was anxious to get on the road and Julia was near hysterical that Baron had gotten away. I promised her I'd find him and keep him with me. I can't leave until I do that."

"You're not serious, are you?"

Zoe nodded. "That dog means the world to Julia, Aidan. She was crying as Fred drove away. I can't just leave. Not yet. I'm sure he'll come back to the house. I just have to keep looking for him, wait him out a bit."

"Zoe, it's not your responsibility. You need to leave now with everyone else. Please."

Her green eyes gazed at him, full of indecision. "I made a promise, Aidan. Don't tell me you wouldn't do the same thing. If it were you who promised a friend, a neighbor, or a family member that you'd do something, wouldn't you see it through?"

His answer was a muttered curse as he turned his head and began scanning the beach. "Okay, what kind of dog are we looking for?"

It was like a huge weight had been taken off of her shoulders, and she reached out and hugged him before she knew it. "Thank you. Thank you, Aidan." Pulling back, Zoe looked around the beach. "Okay, he's an American Eskimo. He's kind of small, maybe fifteen pounds, all white. His name is Baron."

They walked together toward the Maddoxes' home, taking turns calling the dog's name. Zoe's tone was worried while Aidan's was more annoyed. The wind was really whipping now, and the air seemed electro-charged. It was like nothing Zoe had ever experienced in Arizona, and it was a little scary too. They came around the side of the house, and Aidan looked at Zoe. "This is ridiculous," he finally said. "What if he's hiding? I mean, how long do you plan to stay out here looking for him?"

"I hadn't really thought about it. I didn't think he'd stay away long. Mrs. M. said he's never done something like this before."

"Figures," Aidan muttered.

Zoe stopped in her tracks. "Look, I appreciate you helping me but there's no plan here, no schedule. I didn't expect something like this to happen. I promise, once Baron is found, I'll leave. You can go and do… whatever it is you had planned on doing. You don't have to stay. I don't want to keep you from getting home."

Aidan stopped and reached for her, turning her toward him. "Are you really going to leave, or are you just saying that so I'll let it go?"

Zoe shrugged. "Honestly? I don't know. Even if I left, Aidan, where would I go? There probably isn't an available hotel room within fifty miles of here. And with the traffic backing up the roads, the storm will be here before I could even get to one." It pained her to have to admit that, but there was no point in arguing anymore.

"Look, please go inside and pack up whatever you need. I do have someplace to go and we can get there without taking most of the evacuation routes. I'll keep looking for the dog. Please, Zoe."

She looked over her shoulder at the ocean and sighed. So much for her big adventure. "Fine," she said quietly and stepped around him and walked up the stairs. He followed closely behind her. "Give me a few minutes to get my things together. But I'm not leaving without Baron."

He didn't argue but quickly took off at a jog down the beach, calling the dog's name as Zoe made her way back to her house. Once on her deck, she stopped and turned and looked out at the deserted beach. She hated the thought of leaving but knew it was for the best. Walking into the house, she called the property management company back and told them of her decision to leave. They promised to send someone over to board up the windows for her. With that taken care of, she quickly threw a couple changes of clothes into a bag and placed it by the door before heading back outside and scanning the beach for Aidan.

Her knees weakened and she almost sobbed with relief when she spotted him jogging her way—with

Baron running beside him. "Thank God," she whispered and made her way down the stairs to meet them. "You found him!" Unable to help herself, she threw her arms around Aidan and hugged him fiercely before taking a step back and crouching down to give Baron a scratch behind the ears. "You really had me scared, boy. No more running away for you!"

Aidan nodded. "He was just strolling back toward the house without a care in the world," he said with a grimace in the dog's direction. Still, he bent down to rub his furry little head. He was relieved they'd found the dog too. And now they could get going. "Are you packed?"

"Yes. Sort of."

"Sort of? What does that mean?"

"I've put a bag together with my personal stuff but there're a few other things I'd like to take."

"What can I do to help you?"

"I've got a ton of food in the refrigerator. I cooked a bunch just in case I lost power. There's a cooler in the pantry. Also, the Maddoxes gave me a bag full of dog food for Baron, and there's a leash and some dog toys too. You can help me, if you don't mind."

With Aidan's help, they got everything in Zoe's house squared away. She locked the door and sighed with resignation. Aidan went to put everything in his truck and Zoe stopped him.

"I can follow you in my car."

He shook his head. "No. There's too much traffic out there and there's a chance we'll get separated."

"Aidan, if things happen here like they're predicting, my car could get washed away. I can't leave it here!"

He huffed with frustration. "Okay, fine. Let's take

it to the job site and leave it there, but we have to leave now!"

It wasn't the time to fight with him. He loaded her bags and the dog into his truck, and Zoe followed him in her car on the short drive to the subdivision. Traffic in town was light for once, but only because most everyone was already on the main highways leading out of town. At the construction site, he directed her where to park her car, clear of any real danger. She locked it up and climbed into his truck.

"You might have mentioned the fact that the dog doesn't like to ride in cars," he said as she settled in beside him.

"Sorry. Mrs. M. mentioned it, but it kind of slipped my mind. Did he get sick?"

Aidan's eyes went wide. "No. Not yet. Why? Is that what's going to happen?"

"I have no idea. She just said that he gets sick on long car rides. I have no idea how he'll be with us. Are we going far?"

"I have a house I'm building about thirty minutes from here. I finished up the in-law apartment over the garage and it comes in handy for this kind of an emergency."

"How often does this happen?"

"The Atlantic hurricane season goes from June to November. We get hit with a handful of hurricanes and tropical storms every year. They always evacuate the coast." He looked at her pointedly. She ignored him. "My place is farther inland, so I don't use the apartment very often, but when I need to, it saves me from having to find a hotel room when the rest of the population is looking for one."

"Is it near your family?"

He shook his head. Using his Bluetooth, he quickly made a call. "Hey, it's me," he said. "Are you guys going to be okay?" He paused and listened. "No, something's come up. I'm going to the apartment… Do you have everything? Do you need to come with me? I can turn around and pick you up… Are you sure?"

Zoe figured he was talking to his family and felt bad that he wasn't with them because he had come looking for her.

"Okay. I'll check in with you tomorrow morning if we have power. Please be careful." He said good-bye and hung up, never once looking in Zoe's direction.

"Is everything okay?" she finally asked.

"What? Oh…yeah. They're fine."

"Okay. Good." She paused for a minute before her curiosity got the better of her. "Who exactly are we talking about?"

"My father and sister. They're nowhere near the evacuation zone, but I still worry. There are a lot of trees on the property, and I'm always afraid that something's going to happen in one of these storms. I keep telling my father to cut some of them down, but he won't listen."

"Sounds like someone I know," Zoe muttered.

Aidan lips twitched, but he didn't say anything, focusing on the road. The wind was pulling at the truck, and Aidan had a white-knuckled grip on the steering wheel as they made their way through just about every side street and back road in the area. Baron whined every time they turned.

He felt a little bit guilty about not being with his father and Darcy. He knew they were going to be fine.

They always were. The most they'd get was some heavy wind and rain, maybe lose a tree limb or two. In some of the more severe storms, they'd lost power for a couple of days, but his father had a generator.

But still… This was the first time that he wasn't weathering out the storm with them.

"I'm sorry that you aren't with them. You really didn't need to come after me. I'm sure everything would've been—"

"It's okay," he said.

She opted to focus on soothing the dog for the remainder of the drive.

They pulled off the main road and drove down a long dirt driveway that opened onto a large piece of property with a house on it. Zoe gaped at the house and then at Aidan. "This is your apartment?"

He chuckled. "No. That's the house. Behind it is a two-story garage. There's an apartment over it."

Zoe turned back to the house, completely captivated by it. The afternoon sky was darkened with storm clouds, but it was still light enough to appreciate the view. It was a beautiful house, similar to the others that Aidan's company was building, using really fine materials and obviously a skillful architect.

They pulled up in front of the garage and parked. It wasn't until they were walking up the steps that Zoe asked, "So how are you able to come and go from this space? Is the house empty?"

"Yes."

He didn't elaborate. Rain was just beginning to fall though, so she decided to let the subject drop while they moved all of their things inside. Aidan worked quickly to get all of the perishables put away and placed Zoe's suitcase in the one bedroom. Baron paced around nervously for a few minutes before settling in on the chair in the corner.

Sensing that Aidan wanted to work alone, Zoe stood back and inspected the place. It wasn't big, but it was a functional space—living room, dining room, and kitchen all in one, plus a bedroom and full bathroom. *Perfect for a single person*, she thought. He hadn't done much in the decorating department, but she didn't really think he would have, since it wasn't a permanent living space for him. She wondered what his permanent living space did look like. He was such a stickler on his sites— would his own home be as nice and carefully decorated? Or was he a little more human after all, one who lived sparsely, like a typical bachelor?

When Aidan finally ran out of things to do, including setting up some paper for the dog, a dish of water and dog food on the kitchen floor, and putting the doggy toys next to the chair that Baron had obviously adopted, he stood a safe distance away from Zoe. Being alone with her here was making him nervous. Maybe it was because of the conversation he had had with his father, or maybe it was that he knew the effect she had on him. Getting her safely away from the coast was most important—he just hadn't thought through what would actually happen once he convinced her to leave with him.

Liar.

Okay, maybe he had *some* thoughts on the subject. In most of them, she hadn't argued with him—she'd thanked him like a hero and then begged him to kiss her. He shook his head in disgust. *These are not the thoughts of a rational man*, he chided himself. There was no way out of this situation, at least not until the storm was over. But she was safe, and they'd get through it.

Maybe.

Zoe let out a big sigh and finally allowed herself to move into the space. "So…now what?"

"What do you mean?"

"Well, it seems to me like we've trekked far enough away from the actual coast that you feel safe, but really…is this it? So far this is just a rainstorm to me."

"Haven't you been watching the news?" he asked. "The storm cell is huge."

"Of course. Nothing else has been on the TV all weekend long. There was even a documentary on hurricanes."

"So you must be an expert now, huh?" he said with a smirk.

"Obviously." She smirked back and plopped down on the couch. "Now let me see… A hurricane is a powerful storm system with a large low-pressure center that produces intense winds and heavy rainfall." Looking at him, she smiled when he gave her a thumbs-up.

"Anything else?" he asked with a chuckle.

"Well, I learned that hurricanes form over a large mass of warm ocean water during the warmer months." She smiled. "How's that for expert?"

"Very good. You can be the new channel five weather girl," he teased and went to grab them both something to drink. This was what he wanted, the easiness between them, the camaraderie they'd had that first night at dinner.

"Laugh if you will, but this is all brand-spanking-new to me. I've never lived anywhere but Arizona, and we don't have hurricanes there." Pausing, she thought for a minute and then shrugged. "For the most part, the worst thing we ever had to deal with weather-wise was the heat. We'd get some storms with heavy lightning, but other than that, the weather was fairly tame. I'm fascinated by this. I had hoped to watch it all unfold on the beach, but you went and ruined that for me." The pout couldn't be helped.

Aidan thought it was adorable. "My apologies for ruining your death wish." He sat down beside her and dared to take one of her hands in his. "How about this… if the storm weakens and it turns out there was no reason to evacuate, you get to tell me 'I told you so.'"

First she had to ignore the feeling of her hand surrounded by his, which was no easy feat. It had her entire body tingling. Then she decided to have a little fun with him. She shook her head. "Not good enough."

"Not good enough?" he repeated. "Come on, everyone likes to be able to tell someone 'I told you so.' I know from experience that you've been dying to say that to me about several things at the model home."

"Oh, and I will when the entire project is complete. I'm keeping a running tally of all of them."

"Hey, come on, there aren't that many," he said in mock self-defense.

"By the time this project is over there will be."

"Okay. Fine. Whatever. So you want something more than an 'I told you so.'" He considered some possibilities but didn't think that sharing the ones he had in mind would help the situation at all. "What if—"

"Wait! I got it!" she interrupted and pulled her hand from his. Baron let out a playful bark at her loud tone.

"If, when this is all over, there is no damage to the area and it's obvious that it was pointless for me to leave, I get to do the next model home completely on my own with no input from you."

"Hmm…uncertainty over your safety, or you running amok in my models… No way. That is not a fair trade," he said, but he was actually having fun with this.

"It is too a fair trade!" she said with a laugh. "You just came and swooped in and demanded that I do what you say like you usually do. I should get to do the same thing to you!"

"Not on an entire house!" he argued good-naturedly and reached out to scratch Baron's head when he barked again.

"Okay, then a room," she countered.

"Fine. A bathroom."

"Really? A bathroom? Why not give me the hall closet to work with?" Rolling her eyes, she continued. "I get to have free rein to do…the master bedroom."

Aidan almost groaned. He was already fighting some pretty serious attraction to her and just hearing the word *bedroom* come from her mouth was wreaking havoc on his senses. The thought of carrying her into the bedroom only a few feet away and kissing her for the first time… running his hands through that glorious mane of red curls… He felt himself breaking out in a sweat.

Zoe couldn't figure out what was happening. One minute they were joking and laughing and now Aidan looked…off. "Hey," she said, trying to snap him out of his stupor. "Are you all right?"

He shook his head to clear it. They were stuck here together, and even though he wanted Zoe—craved her—he still wasn't sure it was the right thing to do. Despite everything he felt, at the end of the day, he and Zoe worked together and he really didn't want to do anything that would interfere with his business. He'd worked so long and so hard to make it what it was.

Why does it have to interfere? a little voice inside of him asked. Good question. He supposed if they were to agree to…whatever it was they had between them, and wanted to explore it, they could agree to keep work and their private relationship separate. He didn't think Zoe was the kind of person who would make crazy demands on his time or do anything harmful to his business. He respected her as a designer and decorator; heck, he'd signed her on to handle the decorating of six of his model homes. That said something, didn't it?

"Aidan?" she said again.

"What? Oh, yeah. Sorry. My mind wandered for a minute."

"Are you sure? You looked kinda weird there for a second."

Weird? That certainly wasn't what a guy wanted to hear when he was thinking about potentially seducing someone.

"No, really. I'm fine. I just started thinking about the job site. We've got houses in various stages of construction and, like you said before, wind and rain can cause a lot of damage. We've secured all of the supplies as best as we can but…you just never know."

His mind had wandered, of that there was no doubt, but Zoe didn't think it had anything to do with the security of the job site. Bottom line was, he didn't trust her enough to let her do what she was daring him to.

"I think you were trying to think of a way to get out of letting me have control over that room."

"No. Seriously, I—"

"Yeah, yeah, yeah." She waved him off. "The rain could stop right now, the sun could start shining, and the storm could blow back out to sea and you would still hope to get by with just an 'I told you so.'" She shrugged and stood. "Whatever. No big deal." Walking into the kitchen, she started pulling open cabinets. It shouldn't be a big deal, but it was. She wanted Aidan to trust her, and not just because of some silly game or bet, but because he recognized her talent and ability.

And maybe because he liked her as more than just a decorator.

That he liked her as a woman.

Now it sucked because she was essentially stuck with him until the storm was through and she was going to have deal with the fact that it was all one-sided. She admired Aidan as a businessman. She was in awe of his skills as a craftsman.

And she was totally attracted to him as a man.

Well…crap.

"Where are the Oreos?" she muttered as she continued to search for her snacks.

She never heard him approach, but suddenly Aidan was right behind her—so close she could feel the heat of his body—as he reached up above her, opened the cabinet, and pulled the cookies down from the top shelf.

Zoe looked over her shoulder and glared. "Seriously? You were hiding my own cookies on me? That's just wrong."

Realizing how close they were, Aidan took a step

back and gave her a lopsided grin. "I forgot to buy any." He shrugged. "I thought maybe you wouldn't miss them."

"Did you not notice that I bought the double-stuffed ones? And a gallon of milk?" Zoe couldn't help but laugh at the fact that they were even having this conversation. "Believe me, I know the importance of junk food during a storm."

"I thought you said you've never been through a hurricane?" Distracting Zoe with the question, Aidan opened the package and took a stack of the cookies for himself.

"There are other storms besides hurricanes and… *hey!*" Doing her best to snatch the cookies back, she lunged for him but Aidan quickly sidestepped out of her way. "Okay, fine. You want to play it that way? I bet you've got some stuff here that you're territorial over." She began furiously scanning the contents of the cabinets and pantry when she hit the jackpot. Crinkling the bag in her hands, Zoe watched as Aidan's eyes went wide.

"You wouldn't," he said carefully, taking slow, measured steps toward her.

Zoe crinkled the bag a bit more.

"Okay, I was wrong to try to hide the cookies," he said.

"And then start eating them without asking?"

He nodded. "And for eating them without asking." Aidan continued to stalk her as Zoe walked around the apartment. For a minute he wasn't sure who was stalking whom. "I promise I won't eat any more of them. Just…put the bag down."

"I bet there's dip somewhere too," she said with a mischievous grin. "Like some really good onion dip."

"Zoe…" he warned.

"Because you cannot have these ridged potato chips without dip." Making her way back to the refrigerator, she opened the door while keeping one eye on Aidan. Reaching in, she pulled out the container. "Extra large. Hmm…probably the perfect amount for this family-sized bag."

"There's plenty enough for us to share. You've had your fun and I've apologized."

"It was lacking sincerity," she said sweetly as she closed the refrigerator door. "I think that in order to balance things out here, I should get the chips and dip for myself."

"But I only took six cookies!"

"*Six?* I thought you only took three!"

Uh-oh. "Then I should get points for honesty." Flashing her a boyish grin, he took a step closer and his grin broadened when she didn't take a step away. "I don't see why we can't share."

"I'm not the one who was hiding the cookies," she said with her own grin and waited to see if he'd come any closer.

He did.

"Well then, let's agree to share. But you can help yourself to the chips first. Deal?"

Before he knew it, Zoe's hand was in his and he was pulling her up against him. Her green eyes went wide and her lips parted in surprise. It would have been so easy to just lean down and touch her, kiss her, claim her. Zoe moved just that last inch and she was pressed up against him and Aidan felt everything in him harden.

Everything.

"Zoe," he whispered.

A sudden crack from outside the house made them jump apart.

"What was that?" she said, rushing to the window to see where the sound had come from.

Aidan moved to another window and took a look around. It was hard to tell with such a limited view. "It was probably a tree limb."

"Oh. Well, that's not so bad, right?"

Stepping away from the window, he looked at her and shook his head. "That just tells me that the winds are picking up. The trees are all far enough away from the house and the garage that they shouldn't have hit anything. If that's what made that sound, then not only have the winds snapped a tree, but also things are moving and becoming projectiles." His voice was solemn.

"Should we board the windows or tape them or something?" Zoe asked nervously, stepping away from her spot. This was all suddenly becoming very real. Watching things on the news or talking about it was very different from the reality of being in the middle of it. She was no meteorologist, but projectile objects were definitely not a good sign. Without conscious thought, Zoe stepped into the middle of the room—away from the windows—and began twisting her hands nervously.

"I don't think we'll be able to with the way things are going. I didn't plan for that, so I don't have enough plywood; plus there's no way for me to safely be up on a ladder in this."

"Is this normal? You know, things flying around like that?"

Distractedly, Aidan was looking out the window as he said, "It can be an indication of a tornado." As soon as the words were out of his mouth, he could have kicked himself. Scrambling to recover, he turned to Zoe and said, "We'll just have to hope for the best."

"Hope for the best? *Hope for the best?* You pulled me out of my home to go to a safer spot, Aidan! How is this safer? Now there's the possibility of tornados and trees crashing on top of us! There weren't any trees on the beach or anything that could become airborne like that! And now I'm stuck here having to worry about tree limbs flying through the windows or the roof!" Zoe was seriously freaking out at this point, and she didn't even know why. Something about the tension between her and Aidan was making her even more jittery than the storm. And at this moment, the storm was making her pretty anxious.

"Zoe, you need to calm down. One limb falling doesn't mean they're all going to come through the windows or the walls." He tried to sound calm and soothing, but it didn't appear to be working. He felt as keyed up as she seemed. He didn't know whether he was coming or going with this woman.

"But you can't be sure, can you? You can't stand there and tell me with any amount of certainty that we're any safer here than I was at my house! Dammit, Aidan, I at least felt more at ease at home. Why couldn't you have just left me alone?" Zoe could feel herself losing it—it was all just too much at the moment. She should have stayed in her rental house after they found Baron.

She should have insisted that Aidan leave without her. Then he could have been with his family. This was just a mess.

"You weren't safer on the beach!" he yelled back, unable to believe that not five minutes ago he was about to kiss her and now they were arguing again. "You may not want to believe this, but there are times when I actually *do* know what I'm talking about and do know more about something than you! This apartment is a hell of a lot safer than being on the damn coast in the direct line of a hurricane!"

Tears began to well in her eyes and Zoe cursed them. She hated that he was right. She hated that she was stuck here. But more than anything else, she hated the fact that he had the ability to make her cry, even indirectly.

She felt scared and trapped, and there was nothing she could do about it. It took every ounce of strength to fortify herself and get her heart rate under control again. She had to prove that she was strong.

"You know what, Aidan? It doesn't matter what happens because you'll find a way to make it seem like no one knows what's best except for you." Her voice shook as she spoke but at least she kept the tears from falling.

He, too, was trying to be calm. "I have lived here my entire life. I've lived through dozens of these storms, and I know what to expect. Please. I don't want you to freak out. Let's just sit and try to calm down. Okay?"

"If it's all the same to you, I think I'll go lie down. My suitcase is in the bedroom so I'm guessing I'm going to use the bedroom and you're sleeping on the couch?"

If Aidan didn't know better, he'd swear there was some sort of taunt or dare in that statement, but he'd let her be for now. If having some time alone made her calm down and feel better, he'd gladly let her have as much time as she needed. Rather than speaking and risking upsetting her even more, he simply nodded.

Zoe barely acknowledged the motion as she turned on her heels, walked to the bedroom, and slammed the door.

The sound of the door slamming was louder than the damn tree limb hitting the house. Baron jumped up with a whine and tucked his tail between his legs. With a curse, Aidan put the chips, dip, and cookies away, picked up the dog, and sat down with him on the couch.

As strange as it seemed, Aidan was thankful for the company. "I know exactly how you feel, boy," he said softly as he patted Baron on the head. The dog settled closer and soon had his head resting in Aidan's lap. "It seems like I can't catch a break with her. Even when I'm doing the right thing, I'm wrong."

Baron looked up at him with woeful eyes, as if he completely understood what Aidan was saying.

"You've got it easy. She was happy to see you. You know I'm going to keep you safe, right? Why can't Zoe see that?" He sighed and raked a hand through his hair. "If I could control the weather, I would. I don't know what it is that she expects from me."

Baron put his head back down and promptly closed his eyes, seemingly done with this conversation.

It was going to be a long night.

<hr />

Three hours later, Aidan was ready to climb the walls. The storm was raging far worse than he had expected.

He had no cell phone reception but luckily he had power and TV. It boggled his mind, but he was thankful nonetheless.

He and Baron had bonded, anyway. They'd sat there in mournful silence watching the storm on the TV, occasionally alternating to watch ESPN and tune in to the sports events on the West Coast. Before he realized what he was doing, Aidan was talking to the animal again.

"Well, buddy, what do you think, huh? It's not so bad here. Sound of the rain on the roof, nice and cozy inside. Why do women make everything so complicated?" He rubbed behind Baron's ears, and the dog seemed to go into sort of a blissful trance. The dog was doing okay, at least. He was paper trained, so Aidan hadn't had to take him outside, and the dog was pretty well behaved. He was small enough that he fit on the furniture, and the couch was beginning to take on a layer of white fur, but Aidan had to admit the pup was pretty good company. Not a close second to hanging out in close quarters with Zoe, but Aidan had obviously blown that for the moment.

He figured it might do well for them to have dinner, something hot, before they lost power. He had a generator too, for such an emergency, but he still felt it might be nice for them to have full power to prepare a meal.

Looking at the closed bedroom door, he contemplated knocking and asking Zoe if she wanted him to bring her something to eat or if she might want to join him in the small dining room. From what he'd gathered from all of her outbursts today, the fact that he didn't ask her things and simply told her what was going on was a sore spot. He made a note of that and would try to be careful to not do it again in the future.

Zoe had mentioned she'd done some cooking just in case she lost power, so Aidan supposed that would be the smartest way for them to go, eat what was readily available just in case they lost power in the middle of cooking. He was just about to stand and go knock on the door when the news report suddenly regained his attention.

The reporter was standing on the beach. And not just any beach—Zoe's beach. "Zoe!" he called out and was mildly annoyed that she didn't answer. There was the possibility she had fallen asleep, but he was beginning to feel uneasy with the direction of the report.

"No one expected the storm to make landfall with this much strength," the reporter continued, barely able to form words while trying to avoid being blown away. Aidan had to wonder what kind of idiot made someone risk their life for a weather report.

Or what kind of idiot took the assignment.

"Authorities tell us that most of the residents chose to evacuate, many at the last minute. But as you can see behind me, no one can doubt that they made the right decision."

Everything in Aidan went cold and numb.

Behind the reporter was Zoe's house.

It had collapsed into the ocean.

Chapter 6

AIDAN DIDN'T KNOW WHAT TO DO. MAYBE HE WAS seeing things. Maybe it was some sort of mistake. Maybe he was having a bad dream. The footage showed the actual collapse of the house, and with each loop of footage, he felt more and more ill.

How was he supposed to break the news to Zoe? If she was freaked out earlier over a tree limb cracking, what was she going to do when she saw her house falling into the ocean?

"Okay, get a grip," he admonished himself. "This has to be done. You need to be the strong one." *I'm always the strong one.* "Just go and knock on the door and ask her to come out here. She can watch the news report herself and then you can figure out what she needs." Looking down at the dog, which was pacing with him, Aidan wished that Baron had some answers.

The pep talk did little to calm his fears. He knocked on the bedroom door and called Zoe's name. She didn't answer. Either she was being stubborn or she really was sleeping. Deciding that he couldn't wait, he cracked open the door and peeked inside... There she was, sound asleep.

Aidan walked over to the bed and cursed the fact that he was going to have to disturb her and give her such devastating news. Maybe he should wait? After all, there was nothing they could do about it now. On the bed, Zoe stirred, and he knew that if their roles were reversed, he'd want to know.

He sat down beside her and placed a hand on her shoulder. She felt so much smaller than he imagined. Delicate. Whispering her name, he gently shook her shoulder. Zoe slowly opened her eyes and at first she seemed pleased to see him, but then she must have remembered their earlier argument because in an instant she looked annoyed. "What are you doing in here?" she asked groggily.

Taking a steadying breath, he made sure to keep his voice soft and calm. "I need you to come out to the living room with me. There's something I think you need to see."

For a minute she thought about defying him, but there was something in Aidan's eyes that warned her this was something important. Forcing herself to sit up, she pushed her hair away from her face. "What is it? What's happened?"

Oh God, he thought. He didn't want to be the one to have to tell her. "Just…trust me. Please." Standing up, Aidan held out a hand for her. "Please, sweetheart."

Zoe's heart began to race. This was bad. This was so, so bad, and if Aidan was afraid to tell her, it just scared her even more. Taking his hand, she rose from the bed and followed him into the living room. Baron sat regally beside the couch like a furry little soldier, and if Zoe wasn't mistaken, it was as if he knew something she didn't. Aidan led her to the sofa and motioned for her to watch the TV. After five minutes, she turned to him. "What am I watching for?"

"I'm sure they'll play it again in a minute," he said grimly.

Zoe reached for his hand and clutched it in both of hers. "Aidan, please. You're scaring me. What's happened?"

He swallowed hard. "A few minutes ago they showed footage from the beach. Your beach."

"How can you be sure? I'm sure in this mess the entire coast looks the same."

Aidan knew Zoe had no idea how much he wanted that to be the case. He was just about to say that when the report came up. All he could do was point to the screen and wait.

She gasped as her hands flew over her mouth at the sight of her house collapsing. *This can't be happening. This can't be happening. This can't be happening.* Her stomach roiled and she thought she was going to be sick. Everything in her wanted to turn to Aidan and confirm what she was seeing, but she couldn't tear her eyes away from the screen. Slowly, Zoe began to rock, everything in her churning and trembling.

Aidan had never felt so helpless in all his life. Very cautiously, he reached out and placed a hand on Zoe's knee. He whispered her name. "Hey. Are you okay?"

Zoe turned to him with disbelief. "Aidan, my whole life just crashed into the ocean! Everything I own is gone! I'm homeless! Ohmigod, what am I going to do?" She jumped up from the couch and looked down at him as tears began to fall.

"Okay," he said calmly, slowly rising to his feet.

He did his best to be the voice of reason. That was his job. It was what he always did. "I know you're upset and I wasn't sure what the right thing to do was—do I wake you up and show you what happened or do I wait? I thought you had the right to know."

Her eyes went wide and then a rage like she had never known came unleashed. In the last six months she had lost her mother, moved across the country and away from the only home she had ever known, and now her new home was in the Atlantic. All of which she screamed at Aidan. "You're damn right I had the right to know!" She began to pace the room furiously. "I don't deserve this. I don't deserve to keep having so many horrendous things happen to me!"

She was getting hysterical and Aidan knew from dealing with his sister that it was important to try to reel her in. "I know this is bad, Zoe, I do. But you have to thank God that you weren't home when it happened. This could have been so much worse." For a minute, he really thought it had worked, that his words had gotten through to her and calmed her down.

What sounded suspiciously like a low growl came out of Zoe's mouth before she came at him.

"Oh my God. My personal belongings, Aidan! My clothes, jewelry, photos…" And that's when it hit her. It was like losing her mother all over again.

"Zoe…I'm sorry." He felt completely helpless. There didn't seem to be anything he could say that would make her feel any better. He reached out to touch her, to maybe pull her into his embrace, but she moved away as if she repulsed him.

"I just…I need to be alone." Turning away from him, Zoe walked to the window and watched the storm raging outside.

"I know things look bad right now," Aidan said from across the room, "but they're going to get better. I know we can't replace everything, Zoe, but we can try."

She just stood with her back to him, looking out the window and shaking her head. "I don't think so, Aidan. I don't want your help."

Aidan considered himself to be a reasonable man. He was the one in the family to whom everybody turned when they had a problem, and for the most part, he knew exactly how to help them. Granted, this particular situation was definitely out of the ordinary, but it certainly wasn't his fault. He'd saved her life, dammit! Not that he was expecting a thank-you or anything right now, but in the grand scheme of things, he was the good guy in this scenario and he had hit his limit at this point! He knew she was upset—hell, she was more than entitled to be upset. And he could have handled a little animosity thrown his way but not this, not all of this.

"Well, that's just too damn bad because you're going to take it! Right now, I'm all you have, Zoe. Now I'm sorry this happened, but I'm not sorry that I came and made you leave this morning. You'd be dead right now, sweetheart. Have you thought about that?"

That silenced her for a minute. Taking a calming breath, she looked at him. "I can't keep starting over, Aidan. It's not fair. I can't keep losing everything and then be expected to just pick up and be all right and ready to start over. I'm done."

"No, you're not," he said, his voice softening. "It's overwhelming right now, but it's going to get better."

Zoe stormed across the room until she was standing right in front of him. "What do you know, Aidan? You have your family with your successful and brilliant siblings; you have people you're connected to who love you. You have no idea what it's like to lose everything!

So don't you dare stand here and try to sound like you understand what I'm talking about or what I'm feeling because you don't. You can't!"

"Really? What…you think you're the only person in the world who's ever lost someone? Well, news flash, Zoe, everyone has dealt with loss! You think I don't understand what you're feeling? You're wrong. My entire world collapsed around me when I was eighteen. My mother was killed by a drunk driver while driving home in a storm. I was away at school and I thought my whole life was ahead of me. I was going to play in the NFL and be a football superstar! And then in an instant, everything changed."

Zoe hadn't known about his mother. Only today had he even mentioned his father. In all of the talk about his family that she had heard, no one had bothered to tell her that his mother had been killed.

"I wanted to drop out of school," he said harshly. "I didn't know how I was supposed to go on. My father pushed and insisted that I go back. Told me how proud my mother was of the man I was becoming and that I should continue to do that for her. So I did it. I didn't want to but I went back. Two years later, I blew out my knee and that was the end of my football career. And I lost everything *again*. So you know what? Don't you *dare* stand there on your damn soapbox and lecture me, sweetheart. I've not only been there before, but I live with the sadness and the disappointment and the devastation of knowing that I'm never going to see her again every damn day."

"Aidan…I…" She reached out to him but he turned and walked away. There really wasn't anyplace for him to go because the apartment wasn't very big, so he simply walked out into the storm, with Baron right behind him.

"Great," she muttered, still staring at the door. "For those keeping count, I've lost my mother, my house, *and* the dog. Fan-freaking-tastic."

〜〜

Zoe had no idea how long she had been lying on the bed curled up in a fetal position and staring at the wall. Everything was gone. She focused on a spot on the wall and did her best not to blink because if she closed her eyes for even a second, she could see her house collapsing into the ocean. She had clearly seen that the houses around hers looked pretty battered and broken too, but knowing her misery had company somehow wasn't very comforting.

Aidan was right; she *was* lucky to be alive. If he hadn't come for her, she certainly would have died. And she should have shown him a little gratitude. While everything certainly looked grim right now, there was no way she was ready to just give up. That wasn't the kind of person she was and that wasn't the person her mother raised her to be. She just wasn't used to leaning on anyone else, and it was scary to think about leaning on Aidan.

Even though he'd offered.

And where was he? He had walked out into the horrific storm. She hadn't heard the truck start up, but she might not have been able to with all the rain and wind. How far could he have gone? Just thinking about it made her feel ill. What a mess.

There was no way to take back the things they'd said.

Sure, in time maybe they'd each forget, or pretend to forget, but it was never going to be completely gone. Why was it that they seemed to bring out the worst in each other? How was it possible to go from laughing and joking one minute to screaming and yelling the next? They were a volatile combination, and Zoe knew that was the last thing she needed in her life right now.

She'd never thought she was the type of woman who'd crave someone to comfort her and take care of her. While she knew the importance of being independent, that didn't mean it wouldn't be nice to have a man swoop in and take care of some of her problems once in a while.

Like how Aidan swooped in and saved your life today? Or took you out to dinner when you had a flat tire...that he paid for.

Maybe.

Well, it's not like Aidan's actions weren't first and foremost about his need to control things, she thought. *Right?*

And damn if that didn't hurt.

In the time she had been living in North Carolina, Zoe had met plenty of men. Unfortunately, the only one who really captivated her attention and made her want to just simply purr in pure female appreciation was Aidan Shaughnessy. And in all of their interactions, just when he'd seemed interested, he'd pulled away.

Or maybe she was just seeing things that weren't really there.

Too bad there weren't such things like possible-future-relationship-material goggles or something. She'd definitely invest in a pair of those.

For the life of her, she couldn't figure out what was wrong with her that kept…repelling…Aidan. Zoe knew she wasn't Miss America material, but she certainly wasn't the kind of woman men kept pushing away! Great. It was just her luck that she finally found a guy she was interested in and he had to be the one pulling back.

Rising from the bed as the windows began to shake with the force of the wind, Zoe padded over to the bathroom and grimaced at her reflection. "Yup, keep looking like this and the whole male population will push you away," she muttered. Her hair was tangled and her makeup was streaked from crying. She was a mess. Add to that the cropped yoga pants and the plain white T-shirt and she cringed. "Thank God for my pedicure," she said as she looked down and wiggled her toes. "At least my feet are pretty."

Doing a quick scrub of her face, she decided against redoing her makeup. What was the point? It wasn't as if she were able to hold Aidan's interest even when she was wearing some. She tried to tame the mass of curls on her head but after a few minutes, she just gave up.

Stepping out of the bathroom, she had a decision to make—crawl back in bed or go in search of food. The sound of her stomach growling made the decision for her.

She was going in search of the damn chips and dip now that she had the chance.

They still had power and the TV was still on—muted, but on—and without looking at it, she shut it off. There was no way she could risk seeing the footage of her house again. It was too much too soon.

Walking to the kitchen, she changed gears and opted for something with a little more substance, pulling out the container of potato soup she had made earlier. It seemed like a hearty, storm-related comfort food to have. Going through the cabinets, she pulled out a pot, transferred the soup into it, and placed it on the stove over low heat. Quickly washing out the container, she rummaged around and found the rest of the things she used to garnish the soup—bacon, sour cream, and cheese.

Another strong gust of wind rattled the windows, and Zoe shivered and wondered where exactly Aidan was. He had been gone a long time. A quick look at the clock showed that it had been over two hours since he'd walked out. Zoe wanted him to come back, to know that he was safe—and decided to make a bowl for him for whenever he came back.

Which would hopefully be soon.

As if conjuring him up in her mind, she gasped at the sound of the door closing and turned to see him standing in the doorway. He was soaked. His hair was slicked back and his jeans and T-shirt clung to him like a second skin. Zoe's mouth went dry at the sight. In her mind, she instantly conjured up images of peeling those clothes off of him—some with her teeth—and taking him back to the bedroom to warm him up.

Damn, maybe I need to go stand in the rain to cool off.

Neither said a word; they simply stood and stared at one another, unsure what to say or how to act.

Rather than continuing to stand there in what was soon to be a puddle of her own drool, she cleared her throat. "Um…I just started heating up some soup for us to eat. It's cream of potato. I don't know if you like that sort of thing or not, but I've also got some chili, some stew… I can whip up some sandwiches if you'd prefer or—"

"Zoe," he said, his voice raw and deep. She paused and looked up at him. "The soup is fine. I'm just going to go change."

"Oh. Okay." Thank God he finally stopped her from yammering on. She normally only babbled like that when she was nervous, and she had never experienced that with Aidan, not even at their first meeting. But suddenly everything seemed different. Strained. It was tempting to turn the television back on just so she could find out how much longer they were going to be dealing with the storm.

But she was too scared to do it.

In the meantime, she busied herself with rubbing a dishtowel over Baron, who had come in right behind Aidan, all dripping fur and muddy paws. She put out a fresh bowl of water for him and topped off his kibble dish. Then she turned back to the soup. It was late afternoon, so…was this lunch or dinner? Technically, they'd skipped lunch, so she guessed they'd call it an early dinner. The lights began to flicker and she hoped the electricity would stay on, at least through their meal. She didn't want to contemplate passing the time with Aidan in the dark.

Turning off the burner, she prepared two bowls of soup and placed the bacon in the microwave to heat it up. Within minutes, Zoe had everything on the table and was waiting for Aidan. Wait…should she wait for him? Should she just start eating? Unfortunately, her mother had raised her with good manners, so no matter how loud her stomach was growling and protesting, she decided to wait.

"Sorry that took so long," Aidan said not two minutes later when he stepped out of the bedroom. "Wet jeans don't really cooperate when you want them to." His words were light and easy, as if they hadn't screamed at each other earlier.

"No problem." If he could be cool and casual, so could she. "I just finished putting everything out." They sat down and ate in silence for the first five minutes before Zoe decided there was no way she could go through the remainder of the storm acting like two polite strangers. "It sounds like it's getting worse out there."

He nodded. "I was working down in the garage and had the radio on. It seems like despite how fast this storm came at us, it's suddenly stalled. The current forecast said it's staying over us well into tomorrow."

That was so not the news she was hoping for. "Is that normal?"

"No. Most of the storms I've seen came and went over the course of maybe up to twelve hours from start to finish. I don't ever remember one just stalling out over the area."

"Great," she muttered.

"Well, the good news, if there is any, is that it's starting to weaken. We're going to be bombarded with wind and rain and there will definitely be flooding—"

"I thought you said this was good news," she interrupted.

"If it had stayed over this area with the intensity that it hit with, there would be a lot more widespread damage. Now, hopefully, it won't be as bad."

Right, she thought miserably. So maybe not *every-one's* house will be floating in the Atlantic, only hers. But saying that wasn't going to help the situation, and she really did want to get through the rest of this storm at least on speaking terms with Aidan.

"What were you working on?" she asked instead. "You were gone a long time."

"The generator. I was making sure everything was hooked up and in good shape. I haven't used it in a while."

"So what is it good for…like a couple of lights? The refrigerator?" She looked at him and gave him a helpless smile. "I have no idea how much power those things give off."

"Such a girl," he said with an easy grin and leaned back in his chair. "Thank you for the soup. It was delicious."

"You're welcome. Now tell me what I need to expect. I packed up a bunch of candles and some flashlights in my suitcase. Should I get them out?"

He shook his head. "Not necessary. The generator will go on automatically if the power goes out. It's not one of those loud ones that runs on gasoline. This is much easier, and don't worry, it powers everything. You'll hardly notice a difference."

"Oh." The sigh escaped before she could help it.

"What? What's the matter?"

"Nothing," she said quickly as she stood up and began to clear the dishes. There was no way she was going to admit that she might have preferred a couple of hours of candlelight to his superefficient generator. He'd think she was an idiot, probably more so than he already did.

Turning to get the rest of the things from the table, Zoe let out a small squeak when she found Aidan standing directly in front of her. "Geez, Aidan," she said breathlessly. "You scared the hell out of me." Just in case he needed clarification for that scream. *Smooth, Zoe.* Doing her best to step around him, she got flustered when he kept blocking her every move. "What?!" she finally yelped.

For one long moment, Aidan could only stare at her. Her face was devoid of makeup, and if anything, she looked more beautiful than he'd ever seen her. Her eyes were brighter, and even though he knew she'd been crying, and with good reason, the sight of her simply took his breath away.

She whispered his name and it snapped him out of his trance.

He had meant to ask how she was doing; his sole intention for getting up and approaching her had been to make sure she was okay. But now?

"You are so damn beautiful," he said softly, slowly lifting his hand and skimming his fingers along the soft skin on her face. Her eyes slowly closed and her lips parted on a sigh. His other hand came up and caressed her other cheek. He marveled at the softness of her skin and smiled at the faint line of freckles that went across her nose, things that were lost to him when he was forced to keep his distance.

Time seemed to stand still, and it didn't matter that a storm was raging outside or that they had been fighting with one another for weeks. The only thing that mattered right now was Zoe. It would have been so easy to just lean forward, to press his lips to hers, but Aidan had never been one for going the easy route.

Zoe opened her eyes and almost melted. Aidan's gaze, so deep, so blue, was focused on her with a passionate intensity she had never seen before. His hands, hands roughened from years of work, touched her with infinite gentleness. They traced her cheeks, then her chin, and slowly skimmed down the column of her throat; her entire body cried out for the same attention.

She wanted more and she needed to know that Aidan was aware of what he was doing, that he wasn't going to pull away. Reaching up, she placed her hands on his and stilled his movements. "What are we doing?" she whispered. The smile he gave her in return finished the job of melting whatever parts of her were holding out.

"If you have to ask, then maybe I'm not doing it right." Leaning his head down toward hers, Aidan stopped when there was barely a breath between them, his lips almost touching hers. "I've wanted to do this since I first saw you touching the flowers outside the model home."

Zoe laughed softly, unable to help herself. She removed her hands from his and slowly looped her arms around his neck. "You wanted to invade my personal space and talk to me?"

He chuckled and rested his forehead against hers. "Yes. That's exactly what I wanted to do. And now that I've done it, I guess I can walk away."

"Take one step and I may have to kill you," she said with another laugh of her own as she did her best to pull him closer.

And then it wasn't funny anymore. It was very serious. It was everything. Aidan cupped Zoe's face in his hands and pressed his lips to hers. He felt her sigh and relax against him, and it felt like everything he had ever wanted and like nothing he had ever known. Her lips were soft and pliant under his and for the first time in his life, Aidan didn't take. He didn't plunder. He gave, and he savored.

It was a kiss of exploration and for now, it was enough. They each enjoyed the sensation of discovery. Aidan's hands traveled up into Zoe's hair; he loved the fullness, the texture. He particularly loved the sounds coming from her as he gently anchored his hands into it. Tilting his head slightly, he finally allowed his tongue to trace the fullness of her bottom lip.

God, she was sweet. With a small whimper, she clutched him closer and then opened her lips to let him in. Aidan groaned with the first contact of his tongue against hers. It was slow, sweet, and erotic. Why had he never appreciated the wonder of kissing? Sex could be good and satisfying, but this? This feeling of being pressed together and simply building up to the next thing was almost more satisfying than any sexual experience he had ever had.

Maybe it was just the thought of what it would be like to make love to Zoe, or maybe it was just Zoe herself. His hands left her hair and skimmed back down over her cheeks, her throat, her shoulders. They slowly grazed the swell of her breasts before grasping her hips. He felt dizzy; his legs felt weak. Were they really still standing in the middle of the kitchen? The sofa was only ten feet away, but that would require moving and moving would force his lips to leave hers.

Not something he was willing to do at the moment. Or anytime soon.

Moving his hands from her hips, he reached around

and boldly cupped her rear. And lifted. Zoe gasped against his mouth but as soon as he placed her on the countertop, she was the one who dove back into the kiss.

This is better, Aidan thought. He moved in close and smiled against her mouth when she wrapped her legs around his hips. *Yes.* Slow was good, but moving things forward was even better. With his hands still on her bottom, he pulled her snugly against him. If she didn't argue with him grabbing her and putting her on the counter, he figured Zoe probably wasn't going to complain about the erection that was now firmly pressing against her.

He was right.

Zoe hummed her approval of the new position and the proof that Aidan was attracted to her. *Oh my.* She'd known he'd be a good kisser, known his hands would feel amazing on her body. And now that she'd had a small sampling of what the man was capable of, she wanted more.

Her entire body was aching for more—more of what they were doing and more of him in general. Zoe was more turned on than she expected. What would happen if she were to turn the tables on Aidan and become the aggressor? Did his need for control go all the way to the bedroom?

Dare she try to find out?

She didn't need to. As if reading her mind, Aidan slowly moved his lips away from hers, across her cheek, and down her jawline, to the pulse beating in her neck. "I could stand here and kiss you all night. But I'd much rather move this to the bedroom…and kiss you in other places."

She almost purred.

"I'm a big fan of other places," Zoe said with a sigh as her head fell back. Aidan's mouth and tongue were doing wicked things along her throat, and she wanted him to have full access.

Aidan couldn't help but chuckle slightly against her. He couldn't remember a time he'd been so turned on and filled with humor at the same time. It was a good feeling, a really good feeling.

And it was about to get a whole lot better.

"It's good that we're on the same page," he whispered between heated kisses. He couldn't get enough of kissing her, touching her, breathing her. It was sensory overload. As much as he wanted to move things to the bedroom, he couldn't make himself stop what he was doing.

"Aidan?" Zoe pulled her lips from his and reached up to cup his face. "Either take me to the bedroom or take me right here, right now." She was curious to see his response to having someone else calling the shots. One dark brow arched back at her. She mimicked the expression.

And then without a word, he lifted her up and flung her over his shoulder. Zoe let out a yelp of surprise and then she simply laughed with glee. Aidan took her to the bedroom and kicked the door shut before she had a chance to catch her breath.

The small lamp on the bedside table flickered off and then came back on a minute later. "So the power really won't go out?" Zoe asked quietly as she snuggled closer to Aidan, a sleepy smile on her face.

He shook his head. "Nope. The generator will make sure we're okay."

"Oh." She sighed sadly.

Aidan tucked a finger under her chin and gently forced her to look at him. "That's the second time you've responded that way. What's wrong with that?"

With a shrug, she said, "It's just…well…there's something romantic about being stuck in a storm with nothing but candlelight."

"Zoe, it would be ninety degrees in here if the power went out. Now it doesn't have to be. The generator is powerful enough to run the air-conditioning and all of the appliances. We won't miss any of our modern conveniences. We're lucky. Not everyone has one of these."

The chuckle escaped before she could help it. "You're such a guy."

"You didn't seem to mind that a few minutes ago."

She elbowed him in the ribs.

"What? What did I say?"

"I talk about how romantic the candlelight would be and your response was about the practicality of a generator."

"And?"

"And…you completely missed the point."

"So you'd rather be all sweaty right now? Is that what you're telling me?"

Sighing dramatically, Zoe moved out of his arms and sat up to look at him. "Why can't I have both the convenience of the air-conditioning while having some candles lit around the room?"

"Because there's nothing wrong with the lights," he said.

"Are you being deliberately obtuse, or do you really not get this?"

The words were no sooner out of her mouth than Aidan pulled her down and pinned her beneath him. He silenced any further questions, for the time being, with a kiss. They'd just made love more than once and yet he was hungry for her again. She instantly melted beneath him as her arms came around him and her hands snaked up into his hair.

It was quickly becoming one of Aidan's favorite positions to be in.

Actually, any position that had his body pressed up against Zoe and her hands on him was his favorite position.

She sighed his name against his lips—another favorite—and Aidan would have lit as many candles as she wanted if it meant keeping her happy and satisfied and in this bed with him.

The storm continued to rage outside. Every once in a while they heard the windows rattle or tree branches snapping off in the distance, but they were safe and secure in their own little world and it seemed as though nothing could touch them. Aidan was perfectly content to be cut off from the outside world. It wasn't often that he allowed himself to get to this point of no contact. Actually, he couldn't remember the last time he hadn't been glued to his cell phone, making sure no one needed him. He was finding that there was something to be said for letting everyone else handle life's problems.

The only problem he worried about was never wanting to leave this apartment again. The storm would end eventually and real life would invade on the peace they had found. Their little slice of seclusion would soon be taken away.

Slowly Zoe's legs came up and locked around his hips.

For now, long live the storm…

———

It was after two in the morning when Aidan walked out into the kitchen to grab something to drink, check on Baron, and see if he could find a weather update on the TV. The remote was poised in his hand when Zoe stepped out of the bedroom wearing one of his shirts.

The weather report was the last thing on his mind.

She walked over to him with a small, sleepy smile on her lips, took the glass of water from Aidan's hands, and took a sip. "What are you doing out here?" she asked quietly.

"Same as you. I was thirsty. Then I thought I'd see if I could catch a weather update." He studied her beautiful face and felt his chest tighten. "It's still too crazy outside to let Baron out, but he doesn't seem to mind." He pointed to the dog sleeping peacefully in his makeshift bed in the corner of the room.

With a nod, Zoe took him by the hand and led him to the sofa to sit down. She still didn't want to see the video footage of her house again, but the reality of it was sinking in. Aidan tucked her in close beside him but didn't turn the television on. She turned to him questioningly.

"Tell me what brought you here to North Carolina," he said softly.

They had talked about so much that first night that Zoe was a little surprised to realize they hadn't really talked about this. "I was born and raised in Somerton. It's a pretty small town and for most of my life, I had no desire to be anyplace else." Shifting slightly, Zoe rested her head on Aidan's shoulder. "Then my mom got sick. It was all…so fast. One day she came home from work and told me she didn't feel very well and the next, she was diagnosed with breast cancer."

Aidan went very still beside her. There wasn't anything he could possibly say to that. There were no words he could utter that could possibly offer her the comfort he knew she needed.

He knew that feeling well.

"Maybe if she had gone to the doctor more often or if she'd done a self-exam, they might have found it sooner. But by the time they finally diagnosed it, it was stage four." Taking a moment, Zoe forced herself not to cry. "She made me promise to go out and live, to make sure that I took the time to see and do all of the things I always wanted to see and do." She shrugged. "I guess she realized there were a lot of things she had put off in her life because she thought she'd have more time."

"So you wanted to see the ocean," he said, remembering their conversation from that first night.

She nodded. "I felt like I owed that to her. It was one of her dreams and she didn't live long enough to see it for herself." She took a moment to calm her emotions and steady her voice. "After the funeral I was just so numb, like I couldn't believe it was happening. It seemed like everyone in town was there for me and yet I'd never felt so alone. It had always been just the two of us. I never knew my father, and my mom was a late-in-life baby so my grandparents had passed away when I was a teenager. I was well and truly alone."

A lump formed in Aidan's throat because he remembered all of the people who had crammed into his house after his mother's funeral. Everyone was there to offer their condolences and help, but even in a crowd of people, he had felt alone.

"How long did it take you to decide to move?"

"I knew before she died. She made me make plans and she wanted to hear about them; she said it made her feel better about leaving me if she knew that I had a plan to get out of Somerton and explore the country."

"Why North Carolina?" He was happy she was here with him, but he wanted to keep her talking and hopefully move on to a lighter topic so that she wouldn't be so sad.

"The West Coast held little appeal to me. Plus it was out of my budget. I had my own decorating firm in Somerton; it was small but it was mine. I knew I'd have to let it go and find another firm to work for, at least for a while, so I did a national search on one of those job finder sites and found Tate Interiors. Mom would help me look over the job listings and when we read Martha's, we both just knew that it was exactly what I needed."

Aidan kissed the top of her head. "I'm glad you're here."

It was quite possibly the nicest thing he had ever said to her. Wrapping her arms around his middle, Zoe hugged him lightly. "Thank you." They sat for several minutes in silence. "Tell me about your mother."

Aidan didn't talk about his mother, not with anyone.

It hurt too damn much. Hell, he had only mentioned her to his father out of desperation. But with Zoe, it felt like the right thing to do. "She was incredible."

Zoe smiled against his chest.

"She had six kids and yet she managed to make each one of us feel special; even if we were all in the same room together, she just had a way of looking at you and letting you know that everything you said was important to her."

"That couldn't have been easy."

He shook his head. "I don't imagine so." He felt that lump form in his throat again and he forced it away. "We used to have the best conversations. I always felt we had a better connection because I was the oldest, but I'm sure if you talked to any of my siblings, they'd tell you they felt the same way. There wasn't anything I couldn't talk to her about. No matter how ridiculous it was, she gave you her full attention."

"She sounds amazing."

"She was. I wish we'd had more time together. I wish she could have seen all that I've accomplished, what we've all accomplished."

"She does. You have to believe that."

"Sometimes I do." He wasn't ready to share with her his thoughts on that subject. "I was away at college when she died. It was a tropical storm, late October. She never should have been out in it. Darcy was a baby and had an ear infection. My father was working late and she needed to run out to pick up a prescription. If I'd been home, I would have gone. Hugh could have gone; he was old enough and he had a license, but he was grounded for something and they had taken his driving privileges away. Looking back it seems ridiculous, but there it is."

"Aidan…" Zoe could tell this was hard for him and didn't want him to continue or to relive such a painful memory.

"They told us she died on impact," he said flatly. "The drunk driver who hit her walked away with barely a scratch. Between the force with which he hit her and the force of the storm, she never saw it coming. At least that's what I have to tell myself."

"Oh, Aidan…" She hugged him fiercely. His arms came around her and they clung to each other for a long time.

Chapter 7

"THAT'S A GOOD LOOK ON YOU, RED," AIDAN SAID AS he came strolling out of the bedroom in nothing but a pair of well-worn jeans.

Zoe looked down at herself and chuckled. All she had on was one of his T-shirts. She hadn't even bothered with her panties. Looking over her shoulder at him, she winked. "You think so?"

He nodded as he stalked toward her, standing in the kitchen. "Oh yeah. As a matter of fact, I think you should stay in that all day."

Doing her best to pretend she was considering her options, she squealed with delight when he came up behind her and scooped her up in his arms. She swatted playfully at his shoulders. "As much as I love this caveman thing that you've got going on, I'm starving. One bowl of potato soup a day is not enough for me."

"And water. You had some water last night too."

She rolled her eyes. "Seriously, put me down." Aidan maneuvered her in his arms until all she could do was slowly slide down his body. She nearly purred with delight at the feel of him against her. "You fight dirty, Shaughnessy."

"I never claimed otherwise," he said gruffly and leaned down and kissed her.

As much as Zoe was growing addicted to the feel of his mouth on hers, her growling stomach was her first priority. Quickly stepping away from him, she went in search of food to make for breakfast. But Aidan quickly stepped in front of her.

"Aidan…"

"You made the soup yesterday, so let me make you breakfast."

Well, she thought to herself, *that has a nice sound to it*. "Okay," she said and smiled up at him. "But what can I do to help?"

With his hands on her shoulders, he gently moved her out of his way. "Not a thing. Sit at the table and… talk to me."

She eyed him suspiciously. "You don't mean dirty talk, do you?"

Aidan's laugh was loud and hearty. "You have a dirty mind, you know that? No, I didn't mean dirty talk. I just wanted you close to me to keep me company."

"Oh." She blushed furiously. "Well, that I can do." Before she sat down, she walked over and gave Baron some attention as she refilled his food and water bowls. Then, smoothing the T-shirt down over her bottom, Zoe took a seat and watched as Aidan made his way around the kitchen. In no time, he pulled out bacon and eggs and bread. He looked completely at ease and sexy as hell. "So you cook, huh?"

"I enjoy eating too much to live on fast food and frozen entrées. Besides, I'd go broke fast if I had to live like that." They shared a laugh as he placed the bacon in the pan and moved it around until it started to sizzle. "Actually, my mother believed it was important that we all learn to cook. As the oldest, I got the most of her attention in the kitchen. Even now, when the holidays come around and we want something that was her specialty, my father and I make it together."

"Does he enjoy cooking too?"

Aidan shook his head. "Actually, none of us particularly enjoy it, but we know how to do it. Dad had to get a crash course in how to cook. When my mother died, he had five kids living at home, including an infant. There was no way he could survive without knowing how to cook. There was the casserole brigade that came around for a while after my mom died, but eventually we had to learn to fend for ourselves. Whenever I came home on school breaks, we'd cook together. Hugh and Quinn would help out too, but Riley and Owen were still too young."

"I can't even imagine what that's like, you know, having so many siblings. It was always just me and Mom. I don't even have any cousins that I can think of." Sighing, Zoe rested her chin in her hands and watched as Aidan continued to move about the kitchen with ease. Baron came up beside her and settled by her feet.

"When I was younger, I used to wish that I were an only child." He chuckled and shook his head at the thought. "There was never any privacy. And because I was the oldest, I always had to help somebody."

"Yeah, but I bet you're all really close," she said wistfully.

"We are," he said with a smile.

Zoe quietly pondered that and watched Aidan expertly flip the bacon, begin scrambling the eggs, and put bread into the toaster. Unable to sit still any longer, she walked over to the refrigerator, pulled out the orange juice, and put it on the table before getting glasses and silverware. They worked together completely in sync until Aidan put their plates on the table.

"Thank you," Zoe said as she looked at the heaping plate of food. She was thankful that Aidan already knew she wasn't the kind of woman who ate like a bird. The portion in front of her was exactly what she had been hoping for.

Taking a forkful of food, Aidan contemplated what he wanted to say. Actually, he knew exactly what he wanted to say, but worried about upsetting Zoe.

"You're scaring your breakfast," Zoe teased. "That tells me you're thinking about something. Please tell me it's not work."

Putting his fork down, he sighed. "Yes and no," he said carefully and then looked up and met her gaze. "If there's damage to the construction site or to the surrounding area, we'll have to suspend our normal schedule. The amount of time will depend on the extent of the damage that we're dealing with so I want you to be prepared for that."

Nibbling on her bacon, Zoe nodded. "I suppose I can work on the plans for the remaining houses in the meantime."

"Does Martha have any other projects you can work on?"

She shrugged. "I have no idea what she has available. Martha told me you requested that I not work with anyone else while working with you. I had to give up the rest of my clients."

He actually felt bad about that now. "If we have to suspend the job for a couple of weeks and you can find a short-term project to work on, I wouldn't be opposed to it."

"Okay." As she looked at him though, Zoe could tell that there was still something else. "Now tell me what's really going on, Aidan."

How did she read him so well? Was he that transparent?

"Have you given any thought to what you're going to do…you know, about a place to live?"

Her stomach clenched at the thought of it, but not as bad as it had earlier. "The phones are still down," she began. "I tried making some calls this morning but couldn't get through to anyone. I'm hoping between the management people and my insurance that I'll have someplace to live without too much of a gap in time. In the meantime, I plan on finding a hotel room." The casual shrug was meant to look as if it weren't a big deal, but inside, the thought of living in a hotel was not appealing at all. "I'll probably have to reorganize my schedule for a longer commute because I'm sure it's going to be somewhat impossible to find a room near here. Wherever it is, as long as it doesn't float away, I'll be fine."

Aidan placed one of his hands over hers for comfort. He knew she was trying to sound like she had it all together, but he also knew that it had to be difficult for her. "You can stay here if you'd like."

Zoe's head snapped up and her surprised gaze met his. "What?"

"I mean…I don't use this place much. It's not like… I'm not saying that we're going to move in together." His words rushed out so fast that he was almost tripping over his own tongue. "So…really…you'd have the place to yourself. It's still a bit of a commute, but you wouldn't have to live out of a hotel room. You'd have a kitchen and privacy and—"

"Aidan," she interrupted, "it's okay. It's very generous of you, but I'll be fine in a hotel. I'm hoping that it won't be something that I'll have to deal with indefinitely."

"But you don't have to." He was completely baffled at her refusal. "Wouldn't you rather have someplace with more creature comforts than a hotel room?"

"I suppose. But really, as much as I appreciate the offer, I prefer to take care of it myself." Quickly shoveling some eggs into her mouth, Zoe hoped Aidan would take the hint and let the subject drop.

"And how exactly are you planning on doing that?"

Okay, maybe not.

"For starters, I plan on being on the phone with the management company just as soon as we can get a call to go through."

"I hate to break it to you, but chances are they're going to be overwhelmed with the number of properties that must have been damaged by this storm."

"Yes, that's a possibility, but I'm guessing that mine is the only one in the ocean. That would make me a priority."

"You would hope," he muttered.

Dropping her fork, she glared at him. "Look, I'd think that you of all people would understand this. You don't like other people telling you what to do or how to run your life. Neither do I. But I've never had my home wash away in a storm and I'm trying to handle it the best way I can!"

He didn't like the way her voice shook, and he reached over and squeezed her hand again. "Okay, you're right.

I've never dealt with anything like this either. All I'm saying is that…maybe you can stay here, make your calls, and just…chill until you have a new place to live. You said it yourself—I'm sure that it's going to be hard to find a hotel room right away between the tourists and the evacuations."

Zoe made a noncommittal noise.

Aidan could understand her pride. If their roles were reversed, he didn't doubt that he'd react the exact same way. He recognized the hint of defeat in Zoe's eyes, the sense of disappointment that things were beyond her control.

"At least you'd know that you had a roof over your head and a place to spread out while you got things in order. What do you say?"

Everything inside of her wanted to say that she didn't need the help, that she was going to be just fine on her own like she always was, but instead, she allowed herself to admit the truth. She needed him.

"Thank you."

There was no phone service.

The cable was still out.

The rain and the wind continued.

And yet neither Aidan nor Zoe seemed to notice. After they finished their breakfast and cleaned up the kitchen, Aidan had an overwhelming need to comfort her.

Standing back, he watched as she washed the pans and dried them and then washed and dried her hands. His hunter green T-shirt looked good on her. It hugged her curves—curves that he had kissed every inch of and wanted to again.

They had made love several times last night, and each time was more passionate than the time before; each time there was a desperation to please and be pleased. Slowly stepping up behind her, Aidan gently placed his hand on her hips, bowed his head to her shoulder, and simply breathed her in. Zoe relaxed against him. His mouth wandered from her shoulder to her throat, where he softly kissed her.

In the middle of the kitchen, in the middle of the storm, they were able to communicate without words. He'd carried her to bed before in a way that was fun and playful, but this time he wanted to show her another side of himself.

Carefully, he turned her around and then took both of her hands in his. Walking backward, he led her back to the bedroom, his eyes never leaving hers. For once she didn't argue, didn't have a sassy retort. She knew him. Somehow this woman was able to see inside of him and know his thoughts almost as well as he knew them himself.

Zoe closed the bedroom door behind them and when they stopped beside the bed, Aidan reached down, took the hem of the shirt in his hands, and slowly slipped it off over her head. The glorious mane of red hair fell across her shoulders as he dropped the shirt to the floor. He wanted to tell her she was beautiful. He wanted to say she was sexy as hell and his every fantasy come to life.

But the words were too small. They weren't enough.

Aidan Shaughnessy was a man of action. Stepping

in close, he cupped her face in his hands and he kissed her. Kissed her slowly. Tenderly. Thoroughly. He kissed her until she sighed and melted against him and then he kissed her until she was gasping for breath. Moving as though their steps were choreographed, they changed positions until he was able to guide her down to the bed, her head on the pillows, her body soft and pliant beneath him.

And still he didn't speak.

Stepping back from the bed, he slowly removed his own clothes before coming down beside her. His hands were like a mere whisper against her skin. He loved watching the way she reacted to his touch. The soft gasps and sighs and purrs were the sexiest sounds he had ever heard. It was fascinating to watch the play of emotion on her face and the way that her lips moved with silent words. She didn't need to speak. Aidan already knew what she was asking for.

They moved together as if they'd been lovers for years. And even though every touch was a discovery and every movement was a new beginning, there was no need to rush, no need to move things along to the next level. If it were possible, he'd keep them here, locked in this one moment in time for as long as humanly possible.

All he wanted to do was give to Zoe rather than take—something maybe no one else ever had done.

He wanted to cherish her.

And maybe…just maybe…he wanted to love her.

───◦∞◦───

Zoe didn't think it was possible to feel so thoroughly exhausted and fully invigorated at the same time. As the next morning gave way to the afternoon, she had never felt more alive.

Even as she lay blissfully in Aidan's arms.

She didn't think she'd be able to move again after the way they had made love the day before. Never before had a man touched her the way Aidan had. The day had completely gotten away from them, and when she had fallen asleep from the sheer exhaustion of it all, she realized she had never been happier.

"I think I may be delirious," he said, his voice rough like gravel.

"Why?"

"I think I'm seeing sunlight coming through the windows."

She chuckled. "You're not delirious. That actually *is* the sun. The storm is finally over. If you listen closely, you can hear the birds chirping too."

Aidan wasn't too sure about that; the only thing he could hear right now was his heart pounding from what he and Zoe had just done.

Again.

He didn't think he'd ever get enough of making love with her. If anything, her response to him was so incredible, so terrifyingly beautiful, it just spurred him on to want to please her more.

He was definitely getting in deep here. Now that the storm was over and reality was waiting for them on the other side of the door, he wasn't sure how they were going to move forward from this spot—this one perfect spot.

"I wonder if the phones are working yet," she said quietly. Lifting up her head, Zoe saw that it was after two in the afternoon. "We probably should get up and see what needs our immediate attention." As if on cue, Baron barked from the other side of the door.

"I'm guessing the dog, for starters."

Sitting up, Zoe looked over her shoulder at him.

He couldn't speak. Her hair was a tangled mess, her lips were red and swollen, and she had a sleepy, sexy look about her that made him want to pull her back down beside him and say that the rest of the world could just go away because he had everything he needed right here.

"I'm kinda sorry the storm is over," she said.

"Why is that?"

"You never did let me light the candles."

Rolling his eyes, he pulled her back down playfully and kissed her thoroughly on the lips. "Hurricanes are not the time for candlelight," he said when he finally let her up. "They are a fire hazard and completely unnecessary when you have a generator."

Zoe stood and walked toward the bathroom. "Ugh! For once can you not be so damn practical?" There was laughter in her voice as she said it, but her frustration was definitely there.

Yeah, she certainly wasn't the first person to point that out to him. He didn't see the point in doing impractical things for fun. That didn't necessarily make him a bad guy, did it?

The next thing he knew, he heard the shower running and knew Zoe would be stepping beneath the spray any second. The caveman instinct was back and he wanted to go in there with her and have her again. Unfortunately, his practical side prevailed and he decided it was time to go take a look outside.

Reluctantly, he rose from the bed and pulled on a pair of jeans and grabbed a T-shirt. Out in the living room, he motioned for Baron to follow. He opened the front door, stepped out onto his entryway, and looked at the property. Some trees were down, but they were on the edge of the property and weren't a threat to anything. The main house and the garage didn't seem to have any obvious issues, nor did his truck.

Baron was dancing around at his feet and Aidan figured now would be a good time to let the dog actually go outside rather than here in the apartment. Again. Together they walked down the stairs and Aidan stood back and let the dog do his business. For a moment he wondered if the dog would wander off like he had the day of the storm, but Baron trotted back over and looked up at Aidan for approval.

"Good boy," he said, kneeling to pat his soft little head and rub him a little behind his ears. Maybe someday, when he was more settled, he and Zoe could get a little dog like this one. He shook his head—where had *that* crazy thought come from? It was probably just as well the storm was over and he could get some space away from Zoe. She was getting under his skin, and he really had to keep his head on straight. He patted Baron one more time, stood up, and led him back up the stairs.

Back inside, he saw Zoe wrapped in a towel, walking back into the bedroom.

"We've got phone service!" she called out.

"That's great!" He chuckled at her enthusiasm.

"As soon as I'm dressed, I am going to have my phone glued to my ear for the rest of the day!"

"Don't forget, not everyone may have returned to

work or have access to their office or even have phone service," he warned. "I don't want you to get your hopes up."

At that moment Zoe came waltzing into the room fully dressed and walked right by him with a serene smile on her face. "You are not going to ruin this for me," she sang. "I'm going to make my calls and some progress and you, Captain Negativo, will have to deal with me doing the 'I told you so' dance."

"Is it a naked dance?" he asked, waggling his eyebrows. "Because I can completely get on board with that."

"Such a guy," she muttered and reached for her phone.

Aidan left her to her business while he took his turn in the shower. He was anxious to go back to the construction site, but he wasn't going to leave without making sure that Zoe was all right.

He was just stepping under the shower when he heard his phone ring, so he hoped that whoever it was could wait fifteen minutes. The hot spray felt heavenly and he had a feeling he was going to have a long day. Well, what was left of the day.

Once he was out and dry and dressed, he walked back into the living room and heard Zoe talking to someone he assumed was her landlord. Part of him wanted to take the phone from her and talk to the person himself—demand that they find a place for Zoe immediately and reimburse her for all of the things she had lost—but he knew that was being unreasonable. In the short amount of time they had known one another, Aidan had learned that one of the things that made her craziest was when he took control away from her, so he resisted the urge. There was an order that things needed to be done in, and this was something that Zoe had to handle herself.

Grabbing a can of soda from the refrigerator, he contemplated where he needed to begin. Did he stand here and wait for Zoe to be done with her calls? Did he put a call in to one of his foremen and see if anyone had been out to the site? That seemed liked the perfect place to start and it would guarantee him a way of having at least a clue of what he was going to be walking into.

He picked his own phone up from the kitchen counter and remembered his missed call. Running his finger across the screen, he saw that the call was from Darcy. She was probably just seeing if he had service on his phone again, he thought, and wanted to give him an update. Darcy felt the need to let everyone know exactly what was going on at all times. Hitting the voice mail button, Aidan leaned against the counter and listened.

And froze. Everything inside of him went numb right before he felt like he was going to be sick. Hitting the delete button, he ran across the room for his shoes, quickly slid them on, and found his keys.

Zoe noticed Aidan's frantic movements as she was hanging up the phone. "Aidan? Are you all right? What's wrong?"

"I have to go," he said distractedly.

"Why? What happened?" She immediately stood and went in search of her own shoes, fully intending to go with him.

"I...I can't... I have to go." He was searching for something else but couldn't seem to remember what it was.

"Aidan, you're scaring me. Who was on the phone?"

But he was already at the door and stepping out. He turned and looked at her briefly, his eyes barely reaching hers. "Zoe…I'm…I'm sorry."

And then he was gone.

———————

For a full minute Zoe was too stunned to speak. Who was on the phone? She was scared and worried for him. One minute they were both fine, relaxed, and seemingly taking care of business, and now he'd left her there without a car or any indication of when he'd be back!

"Okay, deep breaths," she said to herself. "Maybe there was a family emergency." While that seemed like the most logical explanation, it would have been nice if Aidan had just said that as he was sprinting out the door, instead of just offering a mumbled apology. Who did that?

While it wasn't an ideal situation, Zoe knew she had more than enough to keep her busy until Aidan came back. She had a list of phone calls to make and had to start figuring out how to regroup from all of the things that had happened thanks to the storm. Baron seemed as surprised as Zoe when Aidan stormed out— he was standing by the door whining, so Zoe went over, picked him up, and brought him to sit on the sofa with her. At least he would keep her company while she waited for Aidan.

The next call she had to make was to the management company to see if they could give her another house on the beach, with a reasonable rent, and right away.

She wasn't holding out much hope on that one. After

all, she was probably not going to be the only person in need of a new home. But it wouldn't hurt to ask.

And she did still have this apartment to stay in—thanks to Aidan.

When they had arrived here two days ago, Zoe felt the apartment was small. Aidan was a force to be reckoned with and he was larger than life—at least to her. Over the past two days, they had been too consumed with the present and in enjoying one another to think about much else.

Now, with him gone, the apartment felt bigger but emptier. She took a minute to let the woman in her simply relive every look, every touch, every amazing moment they had shared.

When Aidan had arrived at her house and demanded that she leave, there had been no realistic possibility of things progressing romantically with him. Far from it. As usual, he had been bossy and demanding and had made her mad. That was who they had become, who she had become comfortable with. And when they continued to argue after their arrival here, Zoe had simply resigned herself to being attracted to a man who ticked her off and who wasn't attracted to her.

Boy, had she been wrong on that one.

From the moment Aidan had first kissed her, she had been lost. The man kissed better than her every fantasy, and the way he touched her and made love to her still had her body tingling. She had imagined Aidan would be just as controlling in the bedroom as he was everywhere else, but she had been mistaken in that as well. Never before in her life had a man done so much to ensure her pleasure.

Looking toward the door longingly, she wished he were here right now. If he were, she would do whatever she could to reciprocate all of the ways that Aidan had put her first, pleasured her on so many levels. There was time for that later, she supposed, but it still would have been nice to be able to do it right now.

"Not a bad way to procrastinate," she said, reaching for the phone again.

Two hours later, her head was pounding and her stomach was growling, but she'd made some progress. Thanks to her landlord and the management company, claims were already in the works on the house, which made it easier dealing with her own insurance company. It wasn't going to be a quick process, but there was no doubt that she'd be receiving some sort of compensation. While it would be impossible to replace her personal items, at least she'd have the money to replace her clothes and furnishings and electronics.

As expected, no one could promise her a place to live right away. Living in this in-law apartment was far from hardship, however. The commute to work was longer than from her old place, but it wasn't impossible. That reminded her she needed to put a call in to Martha. Looking at her watch, Zoe wondered why Aidan hadn't called her. She hoped he was all right and that his family was okay.

Checking some items off her list, Zoe pulled up Martha's cell phone number. She knew her boss wouldn't be in the office this soon and figured her cell was the most logical place to start.

"Hey, Martha, it's Zoe!" she said when her boss answered.

"Zoe! You're the first to call in. How are you? How did you do with your first hurricane?"

As much as it pained Zoe to have to repeat the story again, she spent the next fifteen minutes telling Martha all about the house and her losses, but left out the fact that Aidan was the one who had convinced her to leave. She simply said that a friend had come and talked her into it.

"Well, it's lucky for you that you did!" Martha cried. "Oh, Zoe, I…I don't even know what to say! I can't even imagine what you're going through. If you need some time off—"

"No, no, no," she protested. "I don't need anything like that. Let me know when you're ready to open the office again. Do you have any idea when that might be?"

"Not before tomorrow," Martha said, "and maybe not until the day after. We have to see how much storm damage there is. I'll give you a call as soon as I know, okay?"

They hung up, and Zoe realized that she had nothing to do but wait. There was still a ton of food in the house so she made herself a sandwich and stared at her phone like it was a ticking time bomb. The urge to call Aidan was nearly overwhelming. The only thing stopping her was that she didn't know if he'd be annoyed if she called him. Maybe he'd feel like she was checking up on him, which she was, and then think that she was one of those smothering girlfriends.

Wait, was she even his girlfriend? What exactly were they? They hadn't talked about their relationship at all, and now Zoe had to sit and wonder whether these last two days were just about killing time or if they were actually going to continue with it. Well, damn. That took some of the afterglow away. What if all Aidan had been doing was killing time there with her?

Sitting back down at the kitchen table, Zoe started to think back through their conversations. He had been rather quick to make it clear that if she stayed here temporarily, that it wouldn't be with him. She groaned at the memory. "And there I was so blinded by the glow of a few good orgasms that I didn't even notice how adamant he was on that or bother to question it. Idiot."

With her appetite gone, she tossed her sandwich out and went and grabbed some ibuprofen to help with the headache that was threatening. She was restless and unsure of what to do with herself. She hadn't really left the apartment in days. Maybe that was contributing to her overall ill feeling. Looking over at Baron, she decided that maybe a walk would do them both some good. Grabbing his leash, she called him over and couldn't help but smile when he enthusiastically pranced over. "Obviously you're not feeling the same level of desertion that I'm feeling," she said as she attached the leash and straightened. "For a while there, I thought you had completely written me off."

Baron barked.

Zoe couldn't help but laugh. "It's good to see that we're still friends." Opening the door, she already felt a little bit lighter. The fresh air, the sunshine…it was having the desired effect.

They walked the property and then down to the end of the block and back before Zoe was ready to be back inside. She realized midwalk that she hadn't brought her phone and now she was obsessing about whether she had missed any calls—like from the management company, Martha, or Aidan.

As they were walking up the driveway, something caught Zoe's eye. As they got closer, Zoe noticed something shiny lying near a puddle.

Aidan's phone.

Now what? She picked it up and straightened and looked around—as if the answer to why his phone was in a puddle or why Aidan wasn't here yet was suddenly going to appear. A curse of frustration crossed her lips before she could stop it. There went any chance of caving and getting him on the phone. Hopefully by now, he would have realized his phone was missing and maybe he would borrow one and call to check in.

Back at the apartment, she took care of Baron first with a fresh bowl of water before reaching for her phone.

Nothing.

"Well, damn." She sighed and tried to go over her mental checklist of anything she might have missed while making her calls earlier. Unfortunately, she was brutally efficient and had covered all her bases, which should have made her feel good.

But right now she'd kill for something productive to do.

Her loose ends were getting tied up. Insurance claims were filed, and for the most part, she had enough money in savings to tide her over until she received her insurance money. Honestly, things could have been a lot worse. Crossing item after item off her list, Zoe felt more at peace than she had just a few short hours ago.

Except for where Aidan was concerned.

She had a bad feeling about things with Aidan.

Something wasn't right. Why hadn't he called her yet? If he was looking to escape and put some distance between the two of them, she wanted to think he'd at least be open and honest with her about it and not just run out the door. If it was a family emergency, Zoe wanted to believe he would have told her. The fact that he had run out the door and left her here just seemed…off. What in the world could have been said to make Aidan react that way?

There were no answers—at least none that were coming to her at the moment.

Chapter 8

No one was answering the phones at Aidan's office. Zoe had tried several times, and it continued to go directly to voice mail.

Which was full.

And he didn't call from someone else's phone either.

And he didn't come back to the apartment.

By seven the following morning, Zoe was ready to kill him.

Of course that would require being able to leave this apartment and find her way back to town! Though it was early, the walls were already beginning to close in on her. Armed with her morning cup of coffee, she called for Baron to follow her and made her way down the stairs and watched the dog run around the yard. The sun was shining off the open mailbox, and the temperature was near perfect. Hell, there was even a gentle breeze blowing. Was there any sign of Aidan? No.

"Son of a *bitch*," she muttered as her frustration level hit a breaking point. Knowing it was time for her to take action, she called out to Baron. Storming back into the house, Zoe had an idea—if Aidan wouldn't answer his phone, maybe she could find someone else who might know where he was. Pulling her phone back out, she Google searched Aidan's address. His place in town back by the beach came up but nothing else. Then she searched other Shaughnessys in the area and came up with an address and phone number for an Ian Shaughnessy. She remembered all of the names Sarah had gone through, and this one didn't ring a bell, but she was making the call either way.

By now it was almost eight o'clock, but Zoe didn't care about the early hour. She cared about getting back to town, getting her car, and getting on with her life. She would feel bad if something heinous happened to someone in Aidan's family, but right now, in this moment, she was ready to do something heinous to him!

A female answered the phone. "Hello?" She sounded like she had just been woken up and Zoe almost felt bad. Almost.

"Yes, hello, I'm looking for Aidan Shaughnessy. Is he there by chance?"

"Who is this?" the girl asked hesitantly.

"Um…my name is Zoe. Zoe Dalton. I've been trying to get in touch with Aidan."

A loud yawn was the only response.

"Look, do I even have the right number? Do you even know who I'm talking about?" She felt like a complete idiot when she might not be talking to the right person.

"Yeah, I know who you're talking about. Aidan's my brother." Another yawn. "I haven't seen him since yesterday afternoon. He hasn't called here either."

Zoe at least knew why that was, but she cursed out loud and then covered her mouth. She remembered Sarah saying that the sister was in her teens, but that didn't mean she needed to hear Zoe's frustration.

"Is there something you needed him for?"

Where did Zoe even begin? "Um…yeah, but…it's kind of personal."

"Really?" The sleepy voice suddenly seemed very interested.

"So…there's no other way to reach him?"

"He could be at his apartment. Not the one here in town, the one farther inland."

"No, he's not here," Zoe said and then instantly wanted to take the words back.

"You're at the apartment? Seriously?" Now it went from interest to excitement.

Dammit, dammit, dammit! "Okay, look. Your brother let me stay here because I was living in a house on the beach. He told me it wasn't safe, and it turned out he was right because the damn house fell into the ocean. So now I'm here and my car is there… Well, it's at the construction site, and I have no way of getting back to it!" Zoe blurted it all out without taking a breath.

"Wow! That was your house? We saw it on the news!"

"Great," Zoe muttered. "Okay, look…who am I talking to exactly?"

"Oh, hey. I'm Darcy. Aidan's sister."

"Yeah, I got that part. So you have no idea where Aidan is?"

"Nope."

"Is he okay?"

"Not really. He kind of freaked out yesterday, and now no one's heard from him. That happens sometimes. It's not just you… You know, in case you were wondering."

She was, but that still didn't help anything. "Is everyone else all right?"

"What do you mean?"

"Well…" Damn, this so wasn't the way Zoe wanted

to find out what was going on. "He just sort of ran out of here yesterday after listening to his voice mail. He didn't tell me anything so I've been sitting here hoping and praying that no one had gotten hurt in the storm. I know I don't know any of you, but I just wanted to make sure everyone was safe."

"Aw…you're so sweet," Darcy said. "We're all fine. Aidan's going to be fine too. He's just…well, I don't know how to explain it. Let's just say that you need to give him a few days and then he should be back to his old self."

Zoe didn't have that kind of time to sit around and wait. "Okay," she began calmly. "I can appreciate that you either don't *want* to tell me, a total stranger, what's going on with your brother or you can't or…whatever. Can you please just let Aidan know that I'm leaving and heading home?"

"I thought your house was in the ocean. Where are you going home to?"

This girl could try the patience of a saint, Zoe thought. "I'm going to make other arrangements," she said, deciding that two could play at this being vague game.

"Oh, okay. Did Aidan ask you to leave?"

"What? No. He said that I could stay as long as I need to."

"Then why are you leaving?"

Zoe pinched the bridge of her nose and counted to ten. Wasn't this girl too old for so many questions? Wasn't this a game reserved for toddlers? "Like I said, I have to make other arrangements. Plus, I need to get back into town to get my car and get my life back on track. Could you just let him know? Please?"

"Oh, sure," Darcy said. "Do you want me to have Aidan call you? You know, when I see him?"

"No. No, that's fine. I'm sure I'll see him eventually."

"Right. Okay. Well, sorry about your house, Zoe," Darcy said, and Zoe appreciated the sincerity in her voice.

"Thanks. And I'm glad you and your family are all okay."

"Yeah, we're fine. For the most part," she said with a laugh. "Good luck with your new place and maybe I'll see you around sometime."

"That sounds good. Thanks, Darcy." Zoe hung up and sighed. She still didn't have any answers to her questions about Aidan. Although apparently, he just wasn't big on answering anyone about anything.

Actually, that made her feel better and less singled out.

"Okay, focus," she said to herself as she dialed Martha's number. Martha answered on the first ring, and Zoe sagged with relief. Surely Martha could help her find somewhere to stay, even just temporarily. Heck, Martha knew everyone—surely she'd pull a favor for Zoe.

"Hi, Martha, um, I'm sorry to bother you, but things aren't working out here and I'm going to need to find a new place to rent right away. I was hoping to stay here for a while temporarily, but I just can't."

"Surely your friend isn't just going to throw you out!" Martha sounded mortified at the very thought.

"Oh, no. It's not that. I just think I should go. I don't suppose you know of any available places, do you?"

"You know, it's funny you should mention that,"

Martha said with a hint of excitement. "It's not as nice as your place at the beach, but my daughter does have a cute little studio apartment over her coffee shop in town. It's about twenty minutes south of where you were living, but it's only a block away from the beach. I just talked to her today and fortunately they didn't sustain any damages. I can see if it's still available, if you'd like."

"Oh, Martha! That would be amazing! Do you really think she'd be open to that?"

"When I tell her that it's for you, I'm sure she'll be fine with it. She used to live up there before she moved into her fiancé's place. She's been ready to rent it out for about three months, she's just been lazy about finding a tenant. Let me just call her and make sure. I'll call you right back, okay?"

"Thank you so much for this." Emotion began to clog Zoe's throat. "You have no idea how much this means to me."

"Oh please. It is the least that I can do. I'm just sorry for all that you lost."

"Most of it is replaceable."

They hung up with Martha promising to call back or to have her daughter call her, and Zoe felt the first real bubble of hope. She couldn't believe she might be able to start rebuilding her life so soon! Aidan would probably be annoyed that she was already planning on leaving, but hopefully he'd understand her need to reclaim her life a bit. Surely he wouldn't fault her for that, right?

Her phone rang and she was thankful to see it was Martha's number.

"So? Was she interested in letting me rent the

studio?" Not the greatest greeting ever, but she was suddenly feeling anxious.

"Absolutely!" Martha said. "When do you want to come and see it?"

Would right now *seem too desperate?* "Well, to tell you the truth, I would love to see it right away, but…" Zoe cringed. "Um, I'm sure I'll be able to pick up my car tomorrow… How about we say I'll swing by the coffee shop tomorrow around eleven. Will that work?"

"That sounds just fine. Are you sure you don't need me to come and get you?"

"No, I'm…fine," Zoe hedged. Aidan had to come back eventually. "You're too kind, Martha. Thank you." It was amazing that the woman whom Zoe had found to be exhausting and pretty tough to be around was the one coming to her rescue.

"Call me tomorrow. By then we should know what we're looking at work-wise. I'm taking today to call clients and get the roundup of where everyone else is with storm cleanup."

"Thank you." Relief flooded her. "I'll talk to you tomorrow then." They hung up and Zoe sagged in her seat.

―――

The next morning Zoe held her phone in her hand and did her best to will it to ring. Of course it didn't, but she was beginning to go a little stir-crazy. She wanted to give Aidan the benefit of the doubt—after all, he had lost his phone in a puddle—but there was no excuse for why he hadn't used *another* phone to call her.

It was beyond inconsiderate.

She could sit and pout about it, but that was getting old and she knew it was time to move forward and make arrangements to get to her car and get on with her life. Placing the phone down, she stood and then jumped when Baron let out a very loud bark. A dog barking wasn't anything to freak out about, but the dog had been a fairly quiet companion for days. What could have him barking now?

Just then the door opened and Aidan walked in. Zoe wasn't sure if she should run into his arms or run him over on her way out the door.

"Zoe," he said quietly, looking like he hadn't slept in days.

"Aidan."

As soon as the door was closed behind him, Aidan stood rooted to the spot, his hands tucked into his pockets. Baron jumped happily at his feet, but Aidan kept his focus on Zoe. "How are you?"

A million snarky retorts were on the tip of her tongue, but she held them. "Honestly? I'm a little confused. Where have you been?"

"I…" he began weakly. "I had something I had to do."

Her eyes went wide at the less-than-informative reply. "Seriously? That's it? Care to share what that was?"

"No."

The urge to scream was so great that she had to take a step back and get herself together. And they were already standing pretty far apart. "That's not acceptable, Aidan."

He slowly swiped a hand across his face before moving into the space. "It's all I've got." Without another word, he walked over to the refrigerator and grabbed the orange juice and poured himself a glass.

She was speechless. Did he honestly believe that it was okay to walk away and leave her here—for days!—without an explanation? Without a phone call? Zoe was aware of the fact that she wasn't the most compassionate person, but this defied reason. After too long of a silence, she finally spoke. "I thought we'd moved beyond this," she began cautiously. "I thought we had finally started talking and confiding in one another. There's nothing you can't tell me, Aidan."

He stared at her for so long and so hard that Zoe began to squirm. "Not this," he said flatly and placed his glass in the sink.

"So that's it then?" she said, but most of the fight had gone out of her faster than air out of a balloon. She knew when to argue and when to pull back and when to simply throw in the towel. Yelling, screaming, and pitching a fit weren't going to work here. She wasn't sure how she knew it, but she did. In that instant, the old Zoe was back. She should have known better than to put her hopes on anyone. The only one who was going to take of her was herself.

And damn if that didn't hurt.

"I'll get my things together. Could you take me to my car?"

"What? You're leaving? I thought you were going to stay here."

A shrug and a sad laugh were her only response as she turned to walk toward the bedroom.

"Zoe? What's going on? I thought we agreed on this."

Her throat felt tight and she could feel the tears

starting to well in her eyes. "And I thought we had transitioned from the whole employer-employee thing to something more. Clearly we were both wrong."

He sighed loudly. "It's not like that, dammit! And where are you going to go? There's no way you could've found a hotel room, not within a fifty-mile radius. It's a mess out there."

"Well, I guess you'd know that better than me, being that you've been out driving around," she threw over her shoulder as she walked to the bedroom, but there was little fire in her words. Just weariness.

She was tired.

So very, very tired. And disappointed. In Aidan. Herself. And the whole situation.

With the kind of efficiency she normally prided herself on, she collected her things and in less than ten minutes, had the entire bedroom suite looking as if it hadn't been lived in. Next she moved back out to the kitchen and collected all of her food and put everything back into her cooler and moved it over to the door. She was about to get Baron's things together, but when she looked up, Aidan was already doing it.

And there it was.

He wasn't going to fight with her or demand that she stay. For once Aidan Shaughnessy wasn't going to argue with her, wasn't going to demand that things go his way.

It was a hollow victory.

—◊—

The drive back into town was almost painful. Aidan did his best to keep his eyes on the road and not look over at Zoe, but all he had to show for it were eyes that hurt.

She was talking softly on the phone to someone—he couldn't be sure, but from the little he was able to hear it sounded like it was Baron's owners. No doubt she was making arrangements to get the dog back to them.

And for some ridiculous reason, that bothered him. He'd never had a pet, but after spending those days in the apartment with the damn dog, Aidan found that he liked it, had actually thought about getting a dog with Zoe, and now, in a matter of minutes, he was going to lose them both.

How could she want to leave? He had offered her everything she needed. Why wasn't it enough? This was why he didn't get involved in relationships—they were impossible to understand.

He knew Zoe was going to be upset with him when he got back, but he had seriously hoped that they had reached a point in their relationship where she would be able to accept that he wasn't able to talk about certain things. He was entitled to his privacy, wasn't he? He almost snorted at the thought because, clearly, he wasn't. The fact that they were in the car proved it.

Behind them in the backseat, Baron was panting loudly and pacing back and forth on the seat. Aidan wanted to say something to try to calm him down, but he didn't want to be the first one to break the silence.

Childish.

He wasn't proud of it, but right now it was oddly satisfying to think he could last longer at keeping his mouth shut.

He just wished his brain would shut up too.

The thing was…he knew keeping this issue to himself and not telling Zoe what had happened meant he

was going to lose her. Who was he kidding? He was
going to lose her anyway.

He had just moved up the expiration date.

Aidan knew he was a good son, a good brother, and
a good businessman. But relationships? He shook his
head. That was something he had never excelled at. He
would've tried with Zoe. Hell, he *wanted* to try with
Zoe. But it just wasn't meant to be.

Dammit.

So now what? It wasn't as if they were never going to
see one another again. For all intents and purposes, she
still worked for him. He couldn't fire her—that would
be unprofessional. He couldn't ask her to quit either.
He cursed under his breath. This was why he didn't
get involved with people he worked with. Too many
damn complications!

Before he knew it, they were turning into the subdivision and he was pulling up behind her car. He was about
to say he was glad there wasn't any damage to it, but
Zoe was already opening the door and climbing out.

Everything inside of Aidan screamed for him to stop
her. To apologize. To make her understand. But he
couldn't. This was all for the best. In time, he'd get used
to seeing her without wanting her, needing her.

Touching her.

A low growl came out of him as he climbed down
from the truck and helped her move the luggage and
cooler to her car. While Zoe got everything situated,
Aidan got Baron. As if sensing his mood, the dog let out
a small whine when Aidan took hold of his leash and
helped him down.

"You're a good boy," he said softly, crouching in

front of the dog. "But do yourself a favor and listen to Zoe until your owners come and get you. And even then, make sure you don't run off again." The dog looked up at him with sad eyes. "I know, buddy." He scratched him behind the ear and looked up to find Zoe standing beside him. She held out her hand for the leash and he handed it to her. Whether it was intentional or not, he touched her hand and everything in him went on alert. Aidan looked up at her, but Zoe was watching Baron.

"Thanks for the ride," she said quietly and turned and walked away.

"Zoe?"

She stopped but didn't turn around. "What?"

Dammit. He needed to see her face, needed her to see that this wasn't easy for him. "I'll…I'll call Martha when we're ready for you to resume work here on the homes."

With nothing more than a nod, she walked to her car and helped Baron in. Aidan stood rooted to the spot until she drove away and her car was out of sight.

~~~

Zoe's head was spinning as she drove away, battling the tears she refused to let fall. Anger. Sadness. Disappointment. Those were the words that just kept a steady chant in her head.

Stupid chant. Why couldn't she let her brain think of pleasant things like…rainbows, sunshine, unicorns. Unicorns? "Great. Now I think I need to be a twelve-year-old to be happy. This is what my life has come to." She snorted with disgust and then looked at Baron through her rearview mirror. "You've got it easy, Baron.

You know you have people who love you and who take care of you. Be sure you appreciate them."

He barked.

"Lucky dog," she muttered and then chuckled at the play on words. "We're going to meet your mommy and daddy in a little while; then you'll be all set. At least one of us will be." Rolling her eyes, Zoe focused fully on the road in front of her. "And now I'm talking to a dog."

With at least an hour to kill before meeting up with the Maddoxes, Zoe took her time driving through town and seeing what kind of damage the storm had left behind. It seemed as though no one had been spared, but luckily most people had gotten away with fallen branches and minor issues.

"I guess only the lucky ones get their houses tossed in the ocean."

There was a ton of activity going on everywhere she looked, and as much as she wanted to keep driving around, she knew she was probably just getting in the way of vehicles that really needed to be on the street. With nothing left to do, she drove to her office to meet up with Martha.

She parked the car and looked at Baron with indecision. "I don't know if Martha's going to want you wandering around the office, boy. But I'm also afraid to leave alone in the car for too long." Deciding that the worst Martha could do was ask her to take the dog back out, Zoe reached for Baron's leash and helped him from the car. She didn't get more than a few feet when Martha came walking across the parking lot toward her. "Hey, Martha! I know I'm a little early but I didn't have much else to do."

"Not a problem. I was ready to get out of here for a little while. I've been on the phone all morning with clients with storm damage." She gave a dramatic shudder. "I didn't drink enough coffee to handle it all. So really, you're saving me."

That made Zoe laugh. "How so?"

"The apartment is over my daughter's coffee shop. Two birds, one stone."

"Ah. Again, I know it's early, but I told the Maddoxes to meet me there at the shop to pick up the dog. I don't want to monopolize your entire day."

"Nonsense. Like I said, there's only so much I can do there right now too. Plus, now I can grab a blueberry scone and have a little extra time with my daughter."

In that instant, Zoe missed her mother fiercely. "I promise to bring those to you every morning since I'll be living right above the shop," she said to distract herself.

"Oh, that would be lovely."

They pulled up to the shop a few minutes later and Zoe found herself smiling. She hadn't been this far south before, but it was just as quaint as the beachside part of town where she had been living. Sure the sand wasn't right outside her door, but right now, that wasn't a bad thing. Climbing out of the car, she could still smell and hear the ocean, so that was definitely good enough.

As she looked up and down the street, a smile crossed her face when Baron barked excitedly. She spotted the Maddoxes and kept a firm grip on Baron's leash so he wouldn't take off. As soon as they were close enough, she let go and watched the joyful reunion.

"Honestly, Zoe, you're an angel," Fred Maddox said

as he hugged her. "Julia was beside herself the last few days and she couldn't wait to get here and see our boy."

Julia was crouched down and hugging Baron and nearly weeping with happiness. "I'm with Fred, Zoe. I don't know what we would have done without you. Thank you for taking such good care of Baron. I know he can be difficult."

"He was a sweetheart," she reassured. "No trouble at all."

"It's nice of you to say," Julia replied. "With all the kids grown and moved away, he's all we have. He's part of the family." She gave the dog another squeeze before straightening and walking over to hug Zoe. "And so are you."

"Oh…Mrs. M.," Zoe began, but the emotion clogging her throat stopped her from saying more.

"Come on, Julia," Fred finally said. "Let me have a chance to give my boy a good head scratch."

It was sweet, Zoe thought, to see how much the dog meant to them. Maybe that was something she should do—get a pet. As soon as the thought entered her mind, she dismissed it. Didn't she have enough to deal with without adding puppy training to it? "It was my pleasure, Mr. M. He's a good boy."

They talked for a few more minutes, but Zoe was anxious to see the apartment and the Maddoxes were just as anxious to get back to their daughter's house. They'd be staying there until repairs could be done on their house. Zoe admired their spirit—Mrs. M. was teasing Mr. M. that she was finally going to change the wallpaper, and he was taking it all in good humor. Zoe promised to call them when she got settled in, and they both thanked her at least a dozen more times before walking away. She sighed happily and was surprised when Martha walked over and hugged her.

"What was that for?" she asked curiously.

"You're a good girl, Zoe. Not many people would have stayed behind to look for another family's pet. I just wanted you to know that."

"Thank you," she said quietly. Feeling herself about to become overwhelmed with emotion, she took a deep breath and reached for the door of the coffee shop. "Shall we?"

"I hope you're not going to be disappointed," Martha said as they walked inside. "You had an entire house before, and this is really just a one-room space."

"Please, Mom, try not to oversell the place!" A woman in her late twenties came out from behind the counter and hugged Martha. "Stick to decorating and not selling real estate, okay?" She turned and faced Zoe, her hand outstretched. "Hi, I'm Lisa. I'm so sorry about your place, but hopefully you'll like the apartment."

Lisa seemed fun and personable, and Zoe liked her immediately. "Thanks," she said, shaking Lisa's hand. "And really, I'm not going to argue with having a place to move into so soon after losing the house. I couldn't believe my luck when Martha told me you had a place available. Do you have any other applicants?"

Both mother and daughter laughed. "Applicants?" Lisa repeated with humorous disbelief. "Zoe, I've been putting off renting this place out just because I'm sentimental about it. When Mom called and told me about you—she's always bragging about you and the work that you do—I knew I had procrastinated for a reason."

Reaching into her apron pocket, Lisa pulled out a set of keys. "Seriously, if you like the place, it's yours—effective immediately."

"Really? Wow…I…I don't even know what to say." Zoe looked from Lisa to Martha and back again. "What about a deposit? How much are you looking for rent?"

"Don't worry about a deposit. If you're anything like my mother, you'll probably make the place a thousand times more fabulous than it already is. And as for rent… honestly…why don't you go upstairs and look at it and we'll talk money when you come down?"

Zoe was about to protest, but customers walked in at the same time Martha began to lead her out. "Don't worry about the rent. I'm sure Lisa's not going to ask for much," Martha said dismissively as they walked around to the side of the building to a doorway and quickly changed the subject. "There's plenty of light out here, so you don't have to worry about that. Lisa lived here for five years without any problems. There are always police cars patrolling the area, so it's very safe." Once inside, they walked up a set of stairs to the second floor, which led to another doorway. Martha opened the door and let Zoe walk in first.

It was only one room but what a room it was! Zoe walked in slowly and already could imagine herself living there, and if Lisa would let her paint, she could really make the place special. The ceilings were high with exposed beams, and the floors were hardwood. There was a kitchen nook that would be absolutely fabulous if Lisa could just afford to put in granite countertops, and as she walked around touching everything, she knew the space was perfect for her. The furniture was nothing special, but Zoe could add her own touches to the place to really make it nice.

The windows at the front of the room looked out over the town, past which you could see the beach. "That's some view," she said over her shoulder to Martha. "I think it's fabulous."

Martha walked toward the back of the room and opened a door and motioned for Zoe to walk in. The bathroom was large, with utilitarian fixtures, but Zoe thought she could make it cuter by changing the cabinet pulls, and adding colorful towels and a shower curtain. If it were hers, she'd make it spa quality, but that was too much to expect. Martha was clearly delighted that Zoe liked the place. "But…you'll want to pull yourself out of there for this last space."

"You mean there's more? Where?" They stepped out of the bathroom and in the opposite corner of the room was another doorway, minus a door. Zoe followed Martha and found a set of stairs leading up. "Is this what I think it is?"

Martha grinned. "If you're thinking of a rooftop entertainment space, then you're right!"

Up on the roof, there was a covered seating area that Zoe could just picture with beautiful wicker furniture, a stainless-steel barbecue, and a separate dining area. Her fingers itched to spruce the place up. Maybe her insurance money would allow for some luxuries like that. She couldn't believe she'd lucked into such a nice place, just like that. She turned to Martha. "So Lisa moved in with her fiancé, and I can move in here right away?"

"Absolutely," Martha said with a serene smile. "I'm hoping for a wedding in the spring for them and grandbabies not long after." She sighed happily. "So what do you think, Zoe? Will this work for you?"

"Are you kidding me? I just hope I can afford it!" She said it with a laugh, but there was a large amount of truth in that statement. Her house on the beach had been older and in need of a lot of work, but Zoe had chosen it because of the location and the cheap rent. She didn't want to insult Lisa by offering something too low or pass out from sticker shock if Lisa threw out a high monthly rate.

"Zoe, trust me. You can afford this place."

She only wished she had Martha's confidence. They walked back down to the coffee shop, and Martha discreetly walked away to get herself some coffee and a scone and to leave Zoe and Lisa to talk. "So? What did you think of it?"

"I love it!" They laughed and then Zoe turned serious. "It really is nice and I can see just how I would decorate it. What do the utilities usually run on average?" That seemed like a reasonable place to start.

"Utilities are included," Lisa said immediately.

"Oh, okay. Great. So...um...what were you looking to get rent-wise?"

Lisa hesitated and then said, "You know what, Zoe, I'm actually kind of hoping I can make a deal with you. The place is nice enough, but I think if it was upgraded, with some really nice features added to the kitchen and bathroom, I'd be able to get a lot more rent in a few years. If you'd be willing to trade your decorating skills for some of the monthly rent amount, and live in the place while it's upgraded, I think we can really help each other."

She named an amount and if Zoe had been drinking

anything, she would have spit it out across the room. "You're not serious, right? I mean, you can get four or five times that amount!"

Lisa reached across the table and placed her hand on top of Zoe's. "Listen, my mother adores you and she doesn't like many people. Knowing that you work for her, I asked her if it would be okay for me to ask you this, and she said it wouldn't be a problem because she only does commercial decorating and I know you had your own business before. I didn't inherit my mom's decorating skills, and I know the place could be so much more valuable if I got it done right. I'll pay for the materials, of course, and your fees will be part of a barter deal for the rent. I love that place. It was my first apartment, and it's where I started my business and met my fiancé. It's a good place with a lot of good memories. This could be really good for both of us. What do you think?"

Tears sprang to Zoe's eyes. "I don't even know what to say."

"Say that you'll take it and that you'll make it totally fabulous and then invite me over to have some wine on the roof once in a while."

"Deal!" They stood and hugged and that's when Martha joined them. "I can't thank you, either of you, enough."

"Nonsense," Martha said. "No thanks necessary. We're happy to help." Lisa waved and excused herself to go help another round of customers.

Zoe stood there for a moment and for the first time in days felt a tiny hint of hope.

Hours later, Zoe had to wonder how she had gotten to this point in her life. So much drama in such a short amount of time, and she still felt relatively sane.

Martha had said her good-byes and Zoe got into her car and drove away.

It only made sense to drive by where her house used to stand and see if there was any way to retrieve any of her belongings. Her heart lurched at the site of the fallen house. The police were there as well as insurance people, the landlord, and the property management people. Parking her car a safe distance away, she approached the group hesitantly. They all recognized her, including Officer Hannigan, and together they did what they could to recover some of her things.

An hour later she walked away pretty well empty-handed. Almost everything was a loss. She hated the look of pity in their eyes, and even though she knew she had someplace to go, another home to go to, this small chapter of her life was over.

It wasn't until she was driving away that the first tear fell.

"It's not fair," she muttered, fiercely wiping the tears away as she drove. "All I wanted was a chance to start my life over. Why did it have to be *my* house that fell? Everyone else got to go home while I have all my personal items littering the Atlantic coast!" She knew she was being unreasonable and babyish. Lots of people didn't get to go home—their houses had water damage, and missing roofs, and broken windows. There were lots of people in a similar boat. In fact, she knew deep in her heart that she was a lucky one, but it sure didn't feel like it when she was touching the splintered wood and digging through debris to find shattered pieces of her life. She had hoped that watching the video loop on the television would have prepared her better, but clearly she was wrong.

"I should move to a damn mountain next time," she said and then snorted. "Probably get a once-in-a-lifetime avalanche to wipe me out." Didn't things like this come in threes? She'd already lost her mother, now she'd lost her home. Did losing Aidan count as the third? Was her run of bad luck finally over?

"It is if I say it is," she finally said as she drove on toward her new apartment. "It's time to prove that the universe can't keep me down." With that thought in mind, she drove to the nearest Walmart, almost twenty miles away, and did her best to bargain shop and replace some of the obvious necessities of life.

"Now I know what Santa Claus must feel like." Heaving the large bags into the trunk of her car, Zoe contemplated her next stop. Climbing into the car, she pulled out her phone and went to her notes application to look at what was on the list she had made earlier. "Sheets and blankets? Check. Dishes, glasses, and silverware? Check. Towels? Check. Feeling completely exhausted? Check."

The next stop was for food. A quick check of her finances told her she was okay to restock a new pantry, and even though she felt like she could sleep for a week, she pushed the shopping cart up and down each aisle to get the necessities.

Thank God there were leftovers in her cooler so she wouldn't have to actually cook tonight.

There were some familiar faces at the supermarket, and Zoe did her best to be polite and social and even to downplay the trauma of losing her house. People were extremely generous in their offerings of everything from food and furniture to funds to help her get back on her feet. She was overwhelmed by the way the community wanted to help her out, especially considering she was so new to the area.

It kind of reminded her of home and the way everyone embraced her after her mother had died. It was both comforting and enough to make her cry. Again.

By the time she was able to load the groceries in her car, she was ready to drop. Her limbs felt as if they were full of lead and any kind of movement was about as appealing as going on a mountain climb, which let's face it, she *was* once she got back to the coffee shop. That flight of stairs up to the second floor with everything she had to transport was going to be like climbing Everest.

"Think of how you won't have to go to the gym for a week after this," she said with forced cheerfulness. And then that little devil that seemed to enjoy sitting on her shoulder every once in a while reminded her that she hadn't been to the gym in a year. Great. Nothing like a snarky conscience to make her day complete.

It took four trips, but she finally had the last of the packages up in the apartment. Once she closed the door, Zoe looked around and sighed. There were bags and boxes on every surface, and the overall feel was chaos. There were linens to wash, cabinets to organize, and food to put away. None of which was appealing at the moment.

So she did the only thing one could possibly do in a situation like this—she opened up the carton of ice cream she'd purchased, made a plan of attack, and vowed to keep moving forward.

With that determination in mind, the transition to living in the new apartment went much smoother. By the end of the following day, it felt like she'd always lived there. While that should have been comforting, there was a part of her that wondered if there was something wrong with her. After all, what kind of person goes through so many upheavals in a three-month time span and just keeps going with the flow? Wasn't she about due for some sort of breakdown or pity party?

"Maybe I'm emotionally stunted," she said to herself Friday afternoon while sitting at her desk at the office. Martha had given her a couple of consultations and small jobs to fill the time until the Shaughnessy site was back on schedule. Not that she minded the break; the more time away from Aidan meant more time for her to come to grips with what was and what could have been.

"Hey, Zoe," Martha said, popping her head into her office Friday afternoon. "I was wondering if you had the catalog for the lighting company that we use in Charlotte. I can't seem to find it anywhere."

"Damn it," Zoe muttered and then looked up apologetically at Martha. "Sorry. I think I left it at the Shaughnessy site before the storm. Can we order another one, or do you need it right away?" *Please say order… please say order…*

"I tried calling them directly to order another catalog, but they're closed for the weekend already. Would you mind going over to the Shaughnessy site and getting it and just bringing it in on Monday?"

Like she had a choice? Zoe kind of owed Martha forever. She could handle picking up one little catalog, right? "Sure. No problem." *Liar, liar, liar!* "I think I'm pretty much done for today, so if it's all right with you, I'll head over there and hopefully find it where I left it."

"I really appreciate it, Zoe. I thought we had more than one around here but I guess not."

"No big deal." So. Many. Lies. "I'll bring it with me Monday morning, along with your coffee and blueberry scone. How does that sound?"

"Like it's not a bad way to start off a Monday."

They walked out of Zoe's office together and it was a good distraction—a good temporary distraction. Once in her car, Zoe went into a full-blown panic attack. What if Aidan was on-site? What if he came over to talk to her? What if he acted as if nothing had happened? What if he kissed her? Nausea rolled through her and she broke out in a cold sweat.

"Okay, first of all, no kissing. I will put my foot down on the kissing," she said calmly as she willed her heart rate to slow down. "He hasn't called or tried to reach out so he does *not* get to kiss me." Oh, but she really wanted him to. "Just go in, get the damn catalog, and get out. Don't give him the chance to engage in conversation. Be professional. Be confident." And with one last deep breath she added, "Just don't be…" What? "Disappointed when it turns out that he was just killing time."

It all sounded fine and well—like she was a woman with a plan. The closer she got to the job site, however, it all became random noise in her head. All of her confident affirmations from moments ago were suddenly sounding a lot like "Just be nice to him because he's clearly going through something" and "Ask him if he'd like to join you for dinner." Turning in to the community, Zoe snorted at herself. "Get a grip."

That suddenly became very easy to do because Aidan's car was nowhere in sight. After her initial wave of relief, Zoe realized it still didn't seem right. With everything going on in the aftermath of the storm, why wasn't Aidan around? Of course there was always the possibility he was in another part of the subdivision. And if that was the case, she wanted to grab her catalog and go as fast as possible.

But what if he'd gone MIA again? What if whatever it was that had pulled him away from her was keeping him away from the job site too? She shook her head and pushed the thought aside. "Not my problem."

She parked in front of the model home she had worked on and quickly went inside and looked around. Judging by the construction sounds she heard from the second floor, she'd have to redo some of that space. The last place she'd had the catalog was in the kitchen, but after scanning all of the surfaces and inside the cabinets and drawers, she came up empty. With no other choice, she had to go to the construction trailer Aidan had set up to house his mobile office.

Zoe walked across the lot and climbed the three steps that took her inside the trailer. She took a look around, hoping to find Aidan's assistant or someone to help her.

"Oh my God! You're Zoe, right?"

Turning, Zoe spotted a teenage girl sitting behind

a desk. She had long black hair and big blue eyes—unmistakably related to the man Zoe had been hoping to avoid. "You must be Darcy," she said with a smile and was surprised when the girl came out from the around the desk and hugged her. "What are you doing here?"

"Oh, Aidan hired me to work here a couple of hours a week after school. I had been bugging him about wanting a job, but he and my dad thought that I didn't need one. So I just kept hounding them until they caved."

All Zoe could do was nod.

"So what are you doing here?" Darcy asked. "I thought they had put a hold on the deco stuff."

"They did. But I left some stuff here and now I can't find it."

"What kind of stuff?"

"A lighting catalog, actually. My boss needs it, and the last place I had it was the kitchen in the model. You haven't seen it by chance, have you?"

"Lighting, huh? Actually—"

"Darcy! C'mon, let's go! I don't have all day!" a loud male voice boomed from outside the trailer.

Zoe looked at Darcy expectantly.

"That's Quinn. Another brother." She rolled her eyes. "My dad got held up at a job site and I need to get home and get dinner started and do my homework. Blah, blah, blah."

"If you have to go, I can just—"

"It's not like the world will come to an end if I don't get my homework done on a Friday. I mean, who does homework on a Friday night?"

"Well, I suppose—"

"It's like they don't understand that I'm seventeen and not a little kid anymore. They need to accept that I'm almost an adult and they can't control my every waking move. I just wish that—"

The door slammed open. "Darce, seriously, I've got to get going."

Zoe stared at the man standing in the doorway. It was obvious he was a Shaughnessy: same dark hair and blue eyes, and he was just as muscular as Aidan, but not as tall. It was predictable that the entire family would be good-looking. She just hoped they all weren't as inconsiderate as the eldest.

"Quinn, this is Zoe. Zoe, this is my brother Quinn. He used to race cars. Now he does custom auto body stuff and makes really old cars look new again."

Quinn walked in and shook Zoe's hand. "Nice to meet you."

"Same here," she said before turning to Darcy. "So… about that catalog?"

"What? Oh, right. Yeah, I found it out there and brought it in here so nothing would happen to it. I put it in the drawer. It looked important."

"Thanks. My boss will be very happy that I didn't lose it. She needs it for a client."

"No problem. Can I come and watch you work when you're back on-site? I've always wanted to see what a decorator does."

She looked so hopeful and her voice was full of excitement, how could Zoe refuse? "Of course. I'm just waiting to hear from my boss on what date I'm supposed to be back here."

"Darce," Quinn said with a little more impatience.

"I've got to get back to the shop." He was about to say more when his phone rang. Turning his back on his sister and Zoe, he answered and listened. "Oh, hey, Anna. What's up?" He paused. "Are you kidding me? When?"

Darcy leaned in close to Zoe. "Anna is Quinn's best friend. We all think that he should go out with her, but he just doesn't see it. He says she's just a friend, but I think they'd be a cool couple."

Zoe had no idea how to respond to that. They stood together and listened to Quinn's side of the conversation, and although he was speaking quietly, Zoe could have sworn she heard him say her name. Darcy elbowed her in the ribs and she had no idea why.

"I bet that has to do with Aidan," Darcy whispered.

Zoe wanted to ask why but just then Quinn turned around, looking flustered.

"Uh…Zoe?" he began nervously and then looked at his sister. "Darce, why don't you get your stuff together and go put it out in my truck? I'll be out in a minute."

She rolled her eyes. "Right. Like I'm not going to want to hear what you just found out about Aidan?! Forget it. Spill!"

"You are spooky. You know that, right?" he said to his sister and then turned his attention back on Zoe. "Look, my dad was supposed to pick up Darcy but he got held up at a job so he asked me to take her home. I've got to get back to my shop." He paused and raked a hand through his hair. "I just found out from a friend—"

"Who should be his girlfriend," Darcy interrupted and stuck out her tongue when her brother glared at her.

"—that she ran into Aidan at the convenience store, and he's planning to go out to the house by the woods that got really worked over by the storm. He's planning to do a bunch of repairs up there by himself. No one else has seen him or talked to him in a couple of days. She said someone needs to go out there to check on him and make sure he's all right. She would go herself, but she has to get back to work."

"Oh, well…I can take Darcy home," Zoe said helpfully. "Really, I don't mind at all."

Quinn shook his head. "While I appreciate the offer, I think it might be better if you went and saw about Aidan."

"Me? Why?"

Indecision was written all over Quinn's face. He glared one more time, and Darcy finally took the hint and collected her books and sweater and walked out the door with a mumbled good-bye to Zoe. Quinn waited for the door to close before he spoke again. "Look, I know we just met and you don't know me but…Anna said Aidan's a bit of a mess and he's mentioned your name more than once."

"Mine? How do you know it's me? I'm not the only Zoe in the city, I'm sure." It sounded lame to her own ears.

And the look that Quinn gave her showed that he thought the same thing. "So you're telling me you're not the same Zoe who stayed at the apartment with Aidan during the storm?"

"How do you know about that?"

"Please, Darcy doesn't keep anything to herself," he said with a chuckle. "I can understand if you don't want to get involved. I mean, I have no idea what your relationship is with my brother. But right now, I owe it to my father to get Darcy home safely and I have a business to get back to. We've all been worried about Aidan, and I just thought…you know…maybe you could help out."

Geez, guilt much? Reluctantly, she agreed. Quinn grabbed Zoe in a bear hug and thanked her. "Don't thank me yet," she said. "I haven't done anything."

Quinn walked to the door and turned to wink at her. "Trust me, you are a lifesaver and I have a feeling you are the best person for the job."

And with that, he was gone.

Chapter 9

IT DIDN'T TAKE LONG TO FIND HIM. ONCE QUINN AND Darcy left, Zoe had walked around through the construction site and asked one of the foremen if he'd seen Aidan. On the far end of the property was a house that had sustained a lot of damage. As she walked over to it, all she could think was *What have I gotten myself into?*

This so wasn't her problem and it had nothing to do with her, really. Why hadn't she just said no? Let his family deal with him because they'd know what to do. If there was one thing Zoe hated, it was the element of surprise. There was nothing worse than walking into a situation and having no idea what to expect.

Hated. It.

For a brief moment when she reached the house, she seriously contemplated just leaving again. No one would know. It wasn't like she was ever going to see Quinn Shaughnessy again, and as for Darcy…well…she was a kid and Zoe couldn't even think about what she'd say to her if she saw her again.

"I am so going to have to take a class on learning how to say no," she muttered as she climbed the front steps and reached for the door. "Why not just put a tattoo on my forehead that says *sucker*?"

She wasn't more than two feet inside when she heard Aidan's muttered curse coming from the second floor. Taking a deep breath, she began slowly climbing the stairs, wondering the entire time what she was supposed to say to him. After all, she still had no idea why he had left her the way he had.

She spotted him in the master bedroom and almost gasped at his appearance. He hadn't shaved; he looked exhausted and…hell, right now he almost looked like a man without hope. He was in a pair of ripped, faded jeans and a stained T-shirt. She'd never seen him like this. He supervised on the site; he didn't do the manual labor anymore. It was completely out of character for him. Stopping in the doorway, she leaned on the frame and waited for him to acknowledge her presence.

And waited.

And waited.

She cleared her throat and dropped her purse down on the floor, which seemed to snap Aidan out of his stupor.

"What are you doing here?" he grumbled.

"I could ask you the same thing."

"I asked you first," he said belligerently as he reached for the hammer in his tool belt. Zoe stepped forward and pulled it out of his grasp and placed it on the worktable behind her. "*Hey!*"

"You have guys who do this sort of thing," she said simply. "So why don't you tell me what's going on?"

Aidan glared at her. "In case you haven't noticed, there's a lot of work to be done around here. We had a lot of damage from the storm, so I'm helping out. Sometimes I do that. And what do you care? You left."

Zoe's eyes went wide. "*Me?* What are you talking about?"

"I got the message, Zoe, believe me. I offered you a place to stay, and you chose to go somewhere else.

You don't want my help, you said so yourself," he said defensively and crossed his arms over his chest like a child.

She almost dove across the room at him to shake some sense into him. Instead, she took a deep breath and forced herself to pause before speaking. "Aidan, you're the one who left. You took off without a word, scaring me half to death, and I was alone and stranded. I didn't even have my own car. That was the jerkiest behavior I've ever seen. I don't know what it was all about, but you're a fine one to accuse me of leaving. Surely you can understand that I felt I needed to get myself a place to stay. I didn't feel I could count on you, Aidan, with that kind of behavior. Maybe other people—like your family—think it's normal, but from where I come from, it's not."

"I told you to stay," he said. "I told you that you could stay there while you got your stuff worked out."

Taking a step back, she studied him. "It turns out I got it worked out faster than I thought. Aidan, are we really going to argue about who left whom?"

He just stood there glaring at her, but she had to admit he looked like hell. His face was haggard, his eyes were shadowed—whatever had been going on, this was taking a toll.

"C'mon, Aidan," she finally said. "You look exhausted. I think you need to go home." If their history was anything to go by, Zoe was expecting an argument from him. Much to her surprise, he unhooked his tool belt and let it drop to the floor.

Taking one of his hands in hers, she led him out of the room, down the stairs, and out the door. Once outside she let go of his hand just in case anyone saw them and was surprised when he reached for her and took it back. Together, they walked in silence back to Zoe's car.

"Do you need to talk to any of the guys before you leave?" she asked.

Aidan shook his head. "Everyone knows what they need to do. I was just back there because I needed something to do by myself."

They climbed into her car and she heard him sigh wearily. Zoe looked at him—really looked at him—and knew whatever he was dealing with was hitting him hard.

That left her two options—she could take him home and hope he'd wake up tomorrow in a better frame of mind, or she could talk to him now. Starting the car, she got the AC going and then turned back to him. "What's going on, Aidan? What happened?" His head was back against the headrest, his eyes closed, and for a minute, Zoe didn't think he was going to answer her.

"I didn't go to the cemetery."

What? "Okay. When?"

"The day after the storm."

Seriously, what? "Do you want to go now? I can take you there if you want."

Aidan turned his head and looked at Zoe with a look of utter devastation on his face. "It was seventeen years ago that she died. Every year we all go to the cemetery together. I didn't go this year. I forgot. I freaking *forgot!*" His voice rose and then was softer when he continued. "I've never missed a year. Never. I wasn't thinking about the date or what day it was because I was busy fu—"

"I'd be real careful with what you say next," Zoe warned.

"I was with *you*," he said angrily. "I forgot about something that was really important because I was too busy…*playing*…around with you."

"You're kidding, right?"

He glared at her through eyes he could barely keep open. "What?"

"I mean, you are not seriously going to blame this on me, are you?"

"Didn't you just hear what I said?" he asked.

It took every ounce of self-control she possessed not to haul off and slap him. Instead, she twisted in her seat to get a clear look at him. "You said that every year you all go to the cemetery, right?"

Aidan nodded.

"And in the seventeen years your mother has been gone, has anyone ever missed a year?"

"Well, yeah, but…"

"Uh-uh…just answer the question. Yes or no?"

"Yes," he said through clenched teeth. "Riley has missed a couple due to touring conflicts, and Hugh missed it twice because of travel delays but…"

"Okay. Did anyone get on their case for not being there?"

"No, but—"

She held up a hand to cut him off. "Did anyone give you any grief for not being there or is this all self-inflicted grief?"

"No," he said begrudgingly. "Actually, it was just my dad, Darcy, Quinn, and Anna this year."

"And why was that?"

"Let it go, Zoe."

"I'm just trying to understand, Aidan," she said. "There was a storm, an act of nature that was beyond your control. Have you gone to the cemetery since then?"

"No."

"Why not?"

"Because…because…I should have been there with everyone else. I…I let her down."

And in that moment, Zoe's heart completely broke for him. Without a word, she faced forward and pulled out of the parking spot. She drove quietly through town until she came to the spot she was looking for. When she parked and turned the car off, Aidan turned to look at her.

"What are we doing at the florist?"

"We're going to the cemetery. I thought you might want to bring flowers."

He looked at her with disbelief. "I'm not going to the cemetery, Zoe. I can't."

She chose to ignore him as she climbed out of the car and walked into the florist. If he wanted to behave like a child, then she'd just have to take matters into her own hands.

There were dozens of bouquets and arrangements to choose from, and Zoe had no idea what kind of flowers Mrs. Shaughnessy had favored, so she went with a bouquet of flowers that she liked. While the florist was putting it together for her, she asked about where the cemetery was. She wasn't foolish enough to believe there was only one, but she had to have some information just in case Aidan wasn't forthcoming with telling her.

Once she paid, she walked back out to the car and handed Aidan the bouquet as she climbed in. His eyes opened and he looked at the flowers and then at her as if he'd seen a ghost. "What? What did I do?" she asked, feeling freaked out by the look on his face.

"Why…why did you get these?"

"Because we're going to the cemetery—like it or not—and I think it would be nice to bring your mother flowers."

He shook his head and sat up straighter in his seat. "No. I don't mean why did you… I mean…why these particular flowers?"

"Because they're cheery."

"It's a cemetery, Zoe."

"All the more reason to bring something cheery. Besides, daisies are my favorite." She started the car and looked at him expectantly. "The florist told me there are two cemeteries close to here. We can rely on me driving aimlessly or you can tell me which one to go to. Your choice."

"You're not going to let this go, are you?"

She shook her head. "Absolutely not."

Aidan gave Zoe the directions and then sat back in his seat but not before he put the bouquet of flowers on the console between them, dropping them there as if they'd burned him. They drove in relative silence; he offered directions when she wasn't sure where to go, but other than that, he sat back and stewed at her high-handedness. "I'm not getting out of the car when we get there," he finally said.

"Okay." She shrugged. "Suit yourself."

"Don't you get it, Zoe? This isn't going to work. I

don't care if you drive me there. You can't fix this!" His voice rose again along with his frustration.

Zoe knew what he was doing. He figured he would try to insult her and yell at her and pretty much tick her off until she just gave up. What he didn't count on, and clearly didn't remember, was that she had a stubborn streak of her own.

They pulled up to the gate a few minutes later and there was a guard shack at the entrance where she was able to ask exact directions to Lillian Shaughnessy's plot. As they drove down the single paved lane through the cemetery, Zoe didn't dare glance in Aidan's direction. When she stopped at the row the guard had directed her to, she put the car in park and sighed. "Are you going to take the flowers to your mother?"

He sat silently beside her.

"Fine." Taking her keys and the flowers, Zoe exited the car and walked determinedly down the row until she came to the Shaughnessy plot. There were a few wilting flowers in the canister there, and tears sprang to her eyes as she read *Beloved wife and mother*. Taking the flowers out, she replaced them with the new ones and then stood back and bowed her head.

"I know you don't know me, Mrs. Shaughnessy. I'm Zoe." She paused and took a breath. "I'm a friend of Aidan's. He's devastated that he missed coming here with everyone. I don't have to tell you how stubborn he is or how he's beating himself up over it. I know you understand and I'm sure you've forgiven him, but he can't seem to forgive himself. I don't know if there's a way for you to let him know it's all right, but if you could, I know he'd feel a lot better."

Emotions began to clog her throat as she thought about all the times she had wished for a sign from her own mother and never received one. "The thing is, I understand how he feels. You see, my mom's in heaven too. She's buried back in Arizona and even though I haven't been gone long, I still feel guilty that I'm not there to bring her flowers. Not that there's been a specific occasion to, but I just think it would be nice to bring her flowers…just because. Anyway, maybe you wouldn't mind sharing these daisies with her. She loves them." Pausing, she wiped away the tears that had begun to fall.

"He misses you so much. They all do. I just think that Aidan still doesn't know how to handle his grief. And that just tells me you were an amazing woman. I wish we could've met. You raised some amazing children." She did a final sweep of her tears. "He really is sorry for not being here with the rest of the family. It was kind of my fault; he was protecting me from the hurricane. He saved my life, actually. He's still beating himself up over it though." Zoe looked toward her car and smiled sadly. "He's an honorable man. I'm sure you already know that, but I just wanted to let you know that others know it too."

She walked slowly back to the car and climbed in without a word. It wasn't until they were completely out of the cemetery and back out on the main road that she finally asked Aidan for directions to his place. He gave them to her, his voice void of emotion. That was all right with her. She was pretty mentally drained herself.

Fifteen minutes later, she pulled into the driveway of a small house about three blocks in from the beach. The sun was still out and it was barely dinnertime. Without asking him, Zoe got out of the car and followed Aidan to the door and waited as he unlocked it and then followed him inside. The house was dark and it looked like he hadn't been home in a while.

"Are you going to be okay?" she asked quietly, looking up into his eyes and almost melting at the intensity with which he was looking at her.

"Why are you here?" he asked. The gravelly tone to his voice was back.

"I told you. I was worried about you."

His dark eyes bored into hers as he stepped in closer until they were touching from chest to toes. He closed the gap by resting his forehead against hers. "Why are you still here?"

Zoe took a steadying breath. Everything inside of her wanted to wrap Aidan up in her arms and just hold him. This wasn't the polished and in-control businessman she had come to know; this was a man struggling with his demons, and she wanted to be the one to take care of him. "I wanted to make sure you were all right."

"If I said I was, would you leave?" His tone was more vulnerable than harsh.

"Would you want me to?" She had no idea where he was leading with this, but after everything he had put her through, she wanted him to make himself clear.

For a long time, he simply stared at her. "No," he finally said, his voice barely audible. "I don't want you to go."

A small smile played at Zoe's lips. "Then I'm not going anywhere."

That seemed to please him because his whole body

sagged with relief as he sighed. He turned on one small lamp and then walked into what she assumed to be his bedroom. Unsure what to do, she followed and when she stood in the doorway, she was mesmerized as he pulled his shirt over his head.

Then he kicked off his shoes and pulled off his socks before reaching for his belt and pulling it off.

She made herself comfortable leaning against the door frame.

His large hands went to the button on his jeans as his eyes locked with hers. Slowly he lowered the zipper and tugged the jeans from his body, leaving him standing there in only a pair of black boxer briefs.

God bless the creator of boxer briefs, she thought to herself.

It would be so easy, she thought, to just walk over to him and act as if he hadn't been gone for days, that he hadn't pulled a disappearing act that had pretty much devastated her. She could just walk over to him, kiss him, strip down, and crawl onto the bed with him. As a matter of fact, Zoe looked at Aidan and then the bed and then back again. His face was unreadable.

Slowly, Aidan began to walk toward her. Did she want to do this right now? He looked like he hadn't slept since she'd last seen him so when he was practically toe-to-toe with her, she spoke before he could. "Why don't you grab a shower and get some sleep? You look like you're ready to drop."

Reaching out, he skimmed a hand down her cheek. "Are you going to leave again?"

"I thought we covered this already," she said softly as she lifted a hand to cover his and held it against her skin. "I'll see if there's anything here that I can make for dinner. This way you can eat and then get some sleep. All right?"

He looked like he wanted to argue, but his eyes were slowly drifting closed and Zoe could tell that he wasn't going to stay awake long, no matter what he thought. "Okay," he finally said. Stepping around her, he walked out of the room and across the hall to the bathroom and shut the door. Zoe almost sagged against the wall with relief. Never in her life had her self-control been tested like it just was. From the moment she'd met him, Zoe had felt a connection to Aidan. Since their time together during the hurricane, she knew what it was like to be with him, to make love with him, and how good it could be. She knew the feel of him, the taste of him, and how incredibly sexy he was.

Even slightly haggard from punishing himself, he was still the most irresistible man she had ever seen. A part of her was tempted to strip down and join him in the shower right now.

She looked across the hall as she heard the shower turn on; it wasn't hard to picture Aidan standing underneath the spray. She could imagine the water rushing down his body and the way he would look as he took the soap and completely lathered himself up from head to toe.

Her mouth went dry.

A loud moan came from the other side of the door and Zoe had to wonder if it was a moan of pleasure or pain. He hadn't looked physically injured, but he also didn't look like he'd had an easy time of it. She stood motionless, filled with indecision. The nurturer in Zoe insisted that Aidan needed a shower, a good meal, and a good night's sleep.

But the woman in her, who just heard another moan, started to kick off her sandals. "Dinner," she hissed at herself. "You're supposed to be making dinner." As much as it pained her, she picked up her sandals and started to walk down the hallway toward the kitchen—and then stopped and looked back at the closed bathroom door.

What if he was too tired to stand up? She didn't know with any certainty what he'd been doing for the last couple of days. What if he couldn't stay awake in there? There was a real possibility of Aidan hurting himself. So really, what was more important—making a lousy dinner with whatever he had in the pantry or making sure that the man didn't drown?

"Safety first. That's the motto, isn't it?" Spinning around, Zoe dropped her sandals, walked back toward the bathroom, and paused outside the door. "Aidan?" she called out with a light knock.

No answer.

"Aidan, are you okay?" Another light knock.

The only answer was another moan.

Hmm…that could be taken a couple of ways. She was just about to knock again when she heard him say her name. Opening the door, she stepped into the steamy room and closed it behind her. "Are you all right?"

"No," he said weakly from behind the curtain.

Everything inside of her began to panic. "Okay. What can I do? What do you need?" Zoe's mind raced. Aidan didn't answer so she stepped closer to the shower curtain. "Aidan?"

Before she knew it, the curtain was pulled back and Aidan was reaching for her and pulling her, fully clothed, under the hot spray with him. "You," he said as he pulled her close and lowered his lips toward her. "I just need you."

———∞∞———

Aidan awoke later that night feeling human again for the first time in days. The main reason for that was the woman asleep in his arms. *Zoe*. Without conscious thought, he pulled her a bit more snugly against himself and smiled.

Zoe hummed softly in her sleep and snuggled closer to him as if she were ready to climb inside. It was a good feeling. He didn't deserve her; he wouldn't be surprised if she woke up right now and cursed him to hell and back.

Too late. He'd already been there.

But she was here. She was warm and naked in his arms, in his bed, and it was as if the world had righted itself again. His decision to pull her into the shower earlier had been impulsive, and Aidan had actually expected Zoe to put up more of a fight. Instead, she had kissed him as if her life depended on it and stripped her shirt off. The sight of her half-naked and soaking wet was enough to bring him to his knees.

Literally.

There were a million reasons why he should have been asleep right then.

And only one why he wasn't.

And it was her soft breath on his chest that made him ache for her all over again.

Unable to help himself, Aidan placed a soft kiss on top of Zoe's head and breathed in the scent of her. He jumped slightly when she slowly raised her head.

"Aidan?" she whispered sleepily.

"Were you expecting someone else?" he teased and gently eased her head back down to his shoulder.

"What are you doing awake? You need to sleep," she said around her own yawn.

"I woke up a while ago and was just lying here thinking about what an amazing woman you are."

"Me?"

He nodded and kissed her head again. "Can I ask you something?"

"Sure."

"Why did you go to the cemetery?"

"Because…" *Did he not remember? Typical.* "You talked about how it upset you that you missed going with your family. I thought it would be a good thing for you to go."

"No, I get that, but…even when you knew I didn't want to go, that I wasn't going to get out of the car, and I know you realized that long before we got there, you still went. Why?" There was no condemnation or accusations in his questions; he was genuinely curious.

Zoe sighed beside him. "When I lost my mom six months ago, I promised myself I'd go to the cemetery as often as I could. I'd go and I'd sit, sometimes for hours, and just tell her about my week. Then life got hectic and crazy and I was planning the move and selling my business and I went less and less. And now I'm here. And I can't go to her cemetery."

Her voice was sad and Aidan felt like an even bigger

jerk for making her talk about this. "I'm sorry," he said quietly. "I shouldn't have brought it up. I just…"

Lifting her head again, Zoe looked at him. It was still somewhat dark in the room; the only light came from a light down the hall. "It's okay. I think this is something we need to talk about."

Aidan nodded and once again adjusted their positions until she was back down beside him. "I'm sorry I interrupted," he said and felt her smile against his shoulder, which she then promptly kissed.

"Well, anyway, I knew what you were feeling because there have been many times, especially since the move, that I would sit and beat myself up because I was so far away and couldn't visit her." She paused for a minute. "I kind of knew you weren't going to get out of the car, but I secretly hoped once we got there that you would."

"I should have," he said and then cursed. "What kind of son doesn't get out of the car to put flowers on his mother's grave?"

"One who still grieves so strongly that he's overwhelmed by it," she said simply, and Aidan realized she really seemed to understand him in a way that no one, not even his family, did. "And it's okay, Aidan. I've gone for grief counseling and I've read dozens of books on the subject. Going there, that's for us—the living. Our loved ones aren't really in that place. That's where they're buried, yes, but their spirits are elsewhere. Your mother knows you love her, and whether you go to the cemetery every day or every week or for every holiday and anniversary, that's for you. And you need to be okay with it."

"I don't know how to move on beyond the guilt," he admitted, and his voice cracked with emotion.

Zoe shifted so that she was on her stomach and facing him. "Do you talk to her?"

"What?"

"Do you talk to her? You know, when you go to the cemetery or just when you're alone?"

"Uh…no. That's crazy."

She chuckled. "Actually, it's not. And it helps."

"I don't see how."

Rolling her eyes, Zoe moved again to try to get comfortable. "Before the storm, I used to walk along the beach and talk to my mom. She had always wanted to see the ocean and feel the sand, and when I first moved here, I would walk along the shore and tell her what I was seeing and what I was feeling. It made me feel closer to her."

"Was anyone around? Because I've got to tell you, if I saw someone walking alone on the beach talking to themselves, I'd think they were crazy."

Playfully she pinched his side. "I'm being serious here."

"So am I," he said with a hint of defensiveness. Aidan turned and moved the pillows behind him and sat up. "Okay, I used to talk to her a lot right after she died, but…it wasn't like she could respond. So I just…stopped."

"Did it make you feel better when you used to do it?"

Aidan had to think about that for a minute and then he nodded. "I guess it did."

"So then why did you stop? If it made you feel better, why not keep doing it?"

This was so not the conversation he wanted to be having right now. But he was the one who'd brought it up; he figured he had to follow through. "I was home on break from college about a year after she'd died. I was pissed off and overwhelmed and basically exhausted from helping my father out with my siblings, and I walked out of the house and out to the garden in the yard and just started…talking to her. I was sort of ranting about how it wasn't fair that she wasn't here any longer and that I missed her. My brother Hugh came out and heard me and started ragging on me, saying I needed to man up and quit whining like a girl. I never talked to her again after that."

"Well, that's just sad," she said quietly and sat up beside him, tugging the sheet with her to keep her covered. "I know I can't really empathize what it's like to have a sibling respond like that because I'm an only child, but I probably would have reacted the same way." She turned and looked at him. "I'm so sorry, Aidan."

"What did you say? You know, when you put the flowers at her grave? I could see that you were talking, but…" He shrugged. "I couldn't imagine what you could possibly have said to my mom."

"I talked to her about you and how you were beating yourself up over missing the anniversary and for not being there with everyone. Then I told her what an amazing man you had grown into, a man whom she would be proud of."

The lump in Aidan's throat was big enough to choke him. "Really? You really said that?"

Zoe nodded. "Then I talked to her about my mom and how maybe she could share the flowers with her since I couldn't take them to her in Arizona."

Tears began to form in Zoe's eyes and even in the dim light, the sight of them was enough to cause Aidan's heart to ache. Wrapping an arm around her, he gently maneuvered them until they were lying down again. Slowly, he lowered his head to hers and kissed her—softly, sweetly. He had been right earlier; Zoe Dalton was an amazing woman, one he didn't deserve.

But one he wasn't willing to let go of just yet.

"I know I behaved badly and I'm sorry," he said gravely, staring down into her beautiful face. "I didn't take your feelings into consideration. My family is used to this kind of behavior from me and you're not."

"I'm not going to lie to you, Aidan, you hurt me. And on top of that, I was angry and…confused. And even though you think your family is used to it, that doesn't mean they're not concerned about you."

"But that's different. It's like that with family. But that's no excuse. I never should have left you the way I did. You didn't deserve that. I'm sorry, Zoe, really, really sorry. Do you forgive me?"

Aidan held his breath. It was important to him not only to say the words out loud to her, but to actually hear her say she had forgiven him.

"Aidan," she began seriously, "it would have been very easy for me to go and check on you at the site when your brother asked me to, even if I didn't forgive you for what you did and what you put me through."

"Zoe…"

She held up a hand to stop him. "But I never would have stayed, never would have made love with you if I hadn't already forgiven you. I was scared for you and I had no idea where I even was and had no way to leave."

"But you did," he said, and this time there was a hint of accusation.

"What was I supposed to do, Aidan?" she asked gently, clearly not wanting to fight with him. "I couldn't reach you on the phone and I had a life and a job to get back to. I couldn't stay at your apartment indefinitely."

"I wanted you to stay," he said quietly.

"I'm not going to apologize for that," she said firmly. "I can't. I took care of the things I needed to take care of with the house and the insurance company, but I still had to go back to work, Aidan. I had to move forward. And…we never discussed what had happened between us. You offered me a place to stay, but you also made it very clear you weren't staying with me. And then you left. From my point of view, I didn't know if what happened was just…a way to pass the time."

Aidan had her pinned beneath him in the blink of an eye. "Never," he said fiercely. "It was never like that. God, is that the kind of man you think I am?"

Zoe's eyes were wide at first but then she seemed to relax. "I didn't know what to think. I don't want to think you would do something like that. I know it wasn't like that for me." She swallowed hard, her gaze never leaving his. "I wanted to be with you. I *still* want to be with you."

Aidan felt as if a great weight had been lifted from him. Somewhere deep inside of him, while he had been running and hiding, he had feared that not only had he let his mother down, but that he had lost Zoe in the process as well before he ever even had a chance to really know her. Hearing her declaration filled him with a renewed sense of hope.

"That's a good thing because I'm not just killing time here either, Zoe. I wanted you from the first moment I laid eyes on you. Every time I look at you, I feel myself struggling with my self-control."

A slow smile spread across her face. "You do?"

He nodded. "That first day in the model home? I wanted you. When we walked through the house, every room we went into I pictured which surface I wanted to take you on." He smiled at her gasp of surprise. "And when we went to dinner that night and walked on the beach afterward? All I wanted to do was throw you over my shoulder and march into your house and make you mine."

"And instead you slammed the door in my face."

"I'm sorry! I thought I was doing the right thing, by keeping distance I mean. I don't ever get involved with a coworker. It's just a rule of mine, but the more I got to know you, the more time we spent together, the more I wanted you and it damn near killed me to not be near you every time you were on the job site."

She reached up and skimmed her hand down his cheek and then around to rake up through his hair. "I didn't know. I had no idea. I didn't even think you were interested in me."

"Sweetheart, you were all I could think of. Day and night. I didn't take you to the apartment before the storm with the intention of seducing you. My intentions were purely honorable. But once you were there, and I knew we were going to be there for at least a couple of days, I knew I had been torturing myself for nothing. There was no way I could keep my distance from you." He chuckled. "Actually, I didn't think you were interested in me."

"Seriously? I all but threw myself at you more than once. How could you not know?"

He shrugged. "I'm a little slow with these things. But now I know what I want."

"You do?"

He nodded and leaned his forehead against hers. "Yeah, I do. I want to spend time with you, Zoe. I want to spend time talking with you, working with you, laughing with you, and making love with you. I'm not interested in killing time. I want to make the most of the time we spend together. What do you say?"

She gave him a sassy grin. "Hmm…I don't know. That almost sounds too good. Are you sure you can put up with me for all of that?"

Now he genuinely laughed. "Yeah, I think I can handle it, and just in case you doubt me, let me prove it to you."

And he did, repeatedly, well until the sun came up. And then they both fell asleep with very satisfied smiles on their faces.

Chapter 10

"SO THE NEW CARPET IS GOING TO BE INSTALLED ON Thursday and the furniture will be delivered on Friday." Zoe looked at her notes and added a couple of comments to them. "If we can get the painters in there on Wednesday and have them close by on Thursday just in case the carpet installers mess anything up, we should be okay."

They'd been back on the job site for a week. Zoe was thrilled that things had been going smoothly—both on the job and off. They weren't joined at the hip and Aidan seemed to be more at peace with himself, for the most part. He was back to being on-site as a supervisor, and it looked as if everything was back on track work-wise.

They had spent almost every night together, alternating between his place and hers, but there were certain nights that Aidan spent with his family, and Zoe was very careful not to encroach on that time. She had seen Darcy in the office almost every day, and although the teenager was constantly inviting her to dinner, Zoe made sure to keep a safe distance. She didn't want Aidan to feel like she was pushing herself on his family time. And if not seeing him one or two nights a week so that he could have that time with them without her there was what he needed, Zoe was more than willing to go along with it.

When Aidan continued to walk around the second-floor rooms of the model home without commenting,

Zoe continued to speak. "I know this is taking longer than you originally planned, but the storm put everyone behind. If you want, I can try to push things up for Monday and Tuesday. I can't guarantee they'll do it, but I'll make the calls if you'd like."

Still no response.

It wasn't anything new; when Aidan was in work mode, it was sometimes hard to get him to respond to things. It was even harder to get him to respond when he wasn't getting his way. Looking at him now, Zoe realized he wasn't happy about the current schedule. Taking her phone from her satchel, she was about to tell him she'd make the calls right now, but she would have been speaking to his retreating back as he walked down the stairs.

"Um…Aidan?" she called after him but—surprise, surprise—no response. Zoe knew she should get used to this kind of behavior, but sometimes it was just irritating.

Walking back into the master bedroom, in which a leak in the roof had just been repaired, Zoe scrolled through her contacts on her phone until she found the number for the carpet installer. She ran through her list of reasons, or the way she would most likely have to beg, to convince them to install earlier. She was just about to tap the screen to dial when she heard a distinct *click* behind her. Turning, she saw Aidan standing against the closed door.

A small smile played at her lips. "Did you forget something?" she asked coyly.

Shaking his head, Aidan slowly stepped closer to her into the room. "No. I haven't forgotten anything."

Zoe stood still, more than willing to make him come

to her. "Are you sure? Because I seem to recall watching you walk down the stairs a few minutes ago. Why would you come back?"

A deep, masculine chuckle was his first response, but he waited until he was standing directly in front of her before saying a word. "Do you remember the first time we walked through this house together?"

A small shiver of excitement tingled down her spine. "As a matter of fact, I do."

"Do you know what I was thinking when we walked through this room?" he asked as he leaned forward so that his lips were hovering right next to her ear.

Zoe had to lock her knees together and keep from purring at the feel of his breath against her skin. "That the colors were all wrong?" she teased.

Banding one arm slowly around her waist, Aidan pulled her up against him. "I was thinking of how much I wanted to lay you down on this massive bed and strip away everything you had on, except for those killer heels, and make love to you."

His voice was a deep rumble against her ear, and Zoe shivered with delight at his words. Turning her head slightly until their lips were almost touching, she said, "Why didn't you?" Aidan was about to respond when she continued. "Or maybe the better question is, why aren't you doing it now?"

It was all the encouragement he needed. In one swift move, he scooped Zoe up in his arms and strode across the room to the bed. The sheets and blankets had all been stripped away due to the renovations, and that suited them both just fine. He didn't seem to be in a rush, and while normally that was something she appreciated, right now she was mildly concerned about them being in the model home.

As if reading her mind, Aidan said, "I sent everyone home and bolted the front door. No one's coming in."

Winding her arms around him, Zoe pulled him down on top of her, luxuriating in the feel of him and the weight of his body on top of her. He kissed her deeply, thoroughly, and left her breathless.

"Not that I'm complaining," she said as he worked his way from her jawline down to the slender column of her throat, "but what brought this on?"

Lifting his head, he responded, "Weeks of fantasizing about it," and then immediately went back to teasing and tormenting her.

Zoe raked her hands through his hair, holding him to her, and was almost ready to burst with joy. There were so many things she loved about Aidan, but his recent burst of spontaneity was probably at the top of her list. He might not believe in romantic gestures—they never went dancing and he'd never sent her flowers—but he never ceased to surprise her.

His hands and lips were seemingly everywhere, and it was hard to keep from stripping off her own clothes and begging him to hurry up. The man was thorough if nothing else. "Aidan," she whispered, anxious to get to the good stuff.

He chuckled against her throat. "So impatient," he murmured. "You know that just makes me want to keep you here like this that much longer, right?"

The man was killing her. Feeling just a bit wicked, Zoe twisted beneath him and whispered several naughty suggestions in his ear, things she promised to do to him if he got undressed, and almost burst out laughing when he nearly jumped off the bed immediately. In the blink of an eye, he was down to his briefs.

Sitting up, Zoe unbuttoned her blouse and threw it to the floor on top of the pile Aidan had created. She stood and shimmied out of her skirt and bra. With nothing left but her panties and stilettos, Aidan put a hand over hers to stop her.

"Leave the shoes," he said thickly.

Those were the last words he was able to speak for quite some time.

They were getting dressed when Aidan remembered there was something he had wanted to talk to Zoe about.

He had just gotten distracted.

It wasn't anything new; just being in the same room with her was enough to distract him from anything he was doing. It was an odd feeling. One minute he was fine and completely in control and the next he'd catch a glimpse of her and all he could think was that he wanted to be near her—talking to her, hearing her laugh, touching her. He wasn't used to feeling like this, especially not while on the job. This was why he had always stayed away from workplace entanglements. But then again, there'd never been anyone to tempt him the way she did.

"Believe it or not, I did have something I wanted to talk to you about," he said as he finished putting his belt back on.

Zoe was fixing her hair in the mirror mounted above the dresser. "About next week's schedule?"

He shook his head. "No." He cleared his throat and

nervously shifted from one foot to another. "I was um…
I was wondering if you had plans tonight?"

She looked at him from their reflection in the mirror
and shook her head. "I was just going to grab some takeout and do laundry. Why?"

For most people, Friday night was date night, but for
Aidan, it was the night he spent with his family. It had
never bothered him before and Zoe didn't make a big
deal out of it, but it was suddenly a big thing to him
and he felt that maybe it was time for a change. "I was
wondering if you wanted to come with me to my father's
for dinner." He looked away and pretended to wipe dust
from his pants. "It's no big deal. It's just pizza. We just
hang out and talk. Darcy'll be there, and it's normally
a good time to catch up on what she's doing in school.
She makes killer brownies." He nervously cleared his
throat again. "Sometimes we watch a movie or play
video games, but…"

The next time he looked up, she was standing directly
in front of him. "I would be honored to have dinner with
your family, Aidan."

He gently pulled Zoe into his embrace. "It's not
exactly a traditional way to spend a Friday night. I
should take you to dinner or out someplace."

Smiling, she leaned forward and kissed him on the
cheek. "You *are* taking me to dinner, at your father's
house. And you know I love pizza."

Pulling back, Aidan looked at her with wonder.
"You deserve more than that," he said gruffly. "I know
I should do more than that for you and that things aren't
ideal right now with the job and the long hours and—"

"Hey," she interrupted softly. "I'm not complaining."

Reaching up, he cupped her cheek and kissed her gently on the lips. "I promise to make it up to you. You deserve more than a quickie on a model home bed and then pizza and video games with my family."

She laughed sweetly. "Aidan Shaughnessy, you worry too much." Slipping from his embrace, she walked over to the bed, picked up her satchel and tablet, and checked for her keys. "I don't know about you, but I'm starving. Please tell me that one of those pizzas is going to have pepperoni on it."

Taking one of her hands in his, he led her from the room and rolled his eyes. "I think you're going to fit in perfectly tonight. Just try to eat fast. Darcy is kind of possessive of her pizza. Particularly the pepperoni."

"Good to know."

Outside they agreed to take their own cars, and Zoe promised to stay right behind him even though she had GPS. Aidan climbed into his truck and started driving. It didn't take long for his mind to begin to race. He'd never done this—never brought a woman home for a Friday night dinner.

To be honest, he'd never wanted to. It was only Zoe.

It was a good thing he had spoken to his father about her before or he was certain there'd have been an awkward moment or two when they arrived. Maybe he should call and give him a heads-up before they arrived.

Taking his phone out, he first called in their dinner order and then called home. "Hey, Dad," he said when his father answered.

"Are you on your way?"

"I just called the order in and—"

"Well, darn," Ian said.

"What's the matter?"

"I meant to call you earlier but things just got away from me."

"What's going on? Are you okay? Is it Darcy?"

"No, no, no…everyone's fine. There's just more of us tonight."

Crap. "Who's there?"

"Owen surprised us. He's heading to South Carolina for some seminar and on his way through, he stopped at the shop and saw Quinn, who was on the phone with Anna, and…well, before you know it, we've got a houseful for dinner."

Aidan cursed under his breath. This was not the way he wanted the night to go. It was one thing to slowly introduce Zoe to his family. His father and Darcy were fairly harmless and bordered on boring, but throw in his brothers and Anna? Now there were going to be a lot of questions he wasn't sure he was ready to answer.

"Are you all right? Do you think it's too late to add to the order? I can call in a second one if you'd like."

"No, it's not that, Dad. It's just… Damn it…I was calling to let you know I was bringing Zoe to dinner tonight."

"Well, that's great! I can't wait to meet her. Your sister has been talking about her nonstop since they met. She'll be thrilled to know you're bringing Zoe tonight."

"Dad," Aidan began patiently, "inviting Zoe tonight was a big decision for me. I was expecting a quiet evening with you and Darcy. Maybe some bowling on the Wii. But now…"

"Oh stop. You worry too much. Owen can barely speak to anyone of the opposite sex and if Quinn gets out

of line, Anna will smack him in the head." Ian chuckled.
"I wish he'd wake up and realize she's the one for him.
We're all getting tired of waiting."

"What are you talking about?" How had he lost track
of the conversation already?

"Never mind. Call and order a couple more pizzas.
Quinn's bringing the beer and Darcy has already
whipped up about a hundred cookies. I think we'll
be fine."

"I don't know…maybe…"

Ian sighed loudly. "Aidan, I am getting too old to
have to lecture you. You're a grown man. I think it's
wonderful that you are bringing Zoe over. You have
a big family, and if you're serious about this woman,
then she's going to have to meet them sooner or later.
No one is going to do anything crazy. From what your
sister tells me, Zoe's already met Quinn, and as for
Owen…like I said, if he says more than two words
in front of Zoe I'll be surprised. Now stop second-
guessing yourself, make the call and order those extra
pies, and come home."

It wasn't often that his father got stern with him, so
Aidan knew better than to argue. "Yes, sir," he said
before hanging up and making the call for the extra
food. When they stopped to pick it up, Aidan decided
he'd explain the situation to Zoe and let her decide if
she was still willing to go with him. Maybe she didn't
want to feel like she was on display for so many people.

He could only hope.

A few minutes later, Zoe parked next to him and
climbed out of her car with a smile. "Are we allowed
to count this as the place where we had our first date?"

Aidan felt like she was teasing him and pulled her in close and kissed her soundly. "No."

"Wait…what? Why not?"

"We weren't dating then. It doesn't count."

"But you totally wanted to date me," she goaded. "Admit it."

They walked slowly toward the takeout entrance as Aidan shook his head. "I said I wanted to get you naked. It's completely different." She elbowed him in the ribs as they walked through the door.

"And they say chivalry is dead," Zoe deadpanned.

The line was as long as it usually was and people waved to him just like they always did, but their gazes lingered when they noticed Aidan with his arm around Zoe's waist. There were so many wide-eyed stares that Aidan was tempted to stand on the counter and announce to the masses that yes, he had a date. Which reminded him…

"Listen," he began quietly, his head turning toward hers. "I called my father on the way here just to let him know I was bringing you to dinner and he told me that we're going to have a houseful joining us."

Zoe looked at him quizzically. "Why? Because you're bringing someone with you?"

He explained about Owen and the trip into town just as his father had explained it to him. "I had no idea there were going to be so many people there. If you aren't comfortable with it, we can try this again next week."

"Are you uninviting me?"

"What? No. No…I just wasn't sure if you actually wanted to be bombarded with Shaughnessys. As it is, Darcy practically trails behind you wherever you go. I just didn't want you to be uncomfortable, that's all."

She reached up and cupped his cheek and smiled. "Well, aren't you sweet?" Standing on tiptoes, she kissed him on the cheek and didn't care how many people were staring. "It can't be much worse than what we're experiencing right now, right?" She casually motioned to the people around them. "Now I know what the animals in the zoo must feel like."

Aidan pulled her even closer and kissed her temple. "Yeah, that's my fault. I don't date much so this is an oddity. Sorry."

Pulling back, Zoe looked at him. "Hmm…an oddity, huh? Not sure how I feel about that."

Aidan knew she was kidding but it still made him feel uncomfortable. He didn't like being the center of attention. While he knew they were going to walk out of here in five minutes and be away from inquiring eyes, what was it going to be like when they got to his father's house? What kind of crazy, awkward questions or stories were going to get around?

"Oh, stop worrying," Zoe whispered beside him. "Let them look. We're just here getting pizza like everyone else."

He shrugged and was saved from saying anything else when his name was called for his order. Quickly paying and avoiding eye contact, he ushered Zoe out the door and back to their vehicles. Placing the pizzas in the truck, he walked over to Zoe's car and waited for her to roll down her window. "Last chance? I won't blame you for wanting to run."

"Are we just meeting?" she asked and laughed when Aidan looked at her funny. "I would think that by now you would know how much I love a challenge, and what you, dear Aidan, have done here with all of your worrying and warnings is presented a challenge. I'm excited to meet more of your family."

"You won't feel that way after about thirty minutes," he said grimly.

"Nonsense. I've already dealt with Quinn and he's positively charming, and Darcy and I are practically BFFs. I can't imagine that your father is going to be scary or that your brother Owen is going to be a problem. He's the scientist, right?"

Aidan nodded. "He's scary smart. If anything, you'll walk away after talking to him wondering how it is that you even get up and dress yourself. It's actually kind of intimidating sometimes, and he doesn't even realize it."

"Then I'll be sure to steer the conversation away from science," she said with a wink and a grin.

"Good luck with that. Owen only knows how to talk about science."

"Aidan?"

"Yeah?"

"You're on the verge of babbling. Get in the truck and let's get to your dad's before our dinner gets cold, okay?"

He nodded and walked back to his truck like it was the green mile. With a sigh of resignation, he got in, started it up, and headed for home.

And hoped that he wasn't making a big mistake.

———

"So then he tries to mop up all of the soap suds, but the washing machine just kept spewing more out!" Quinn was saying as he laughed hysterically.

"Actually," Owen interrupted, "it was more than soap suds. You see, although soap bubbles are traditionally made from soap, most bubble solutions consist of detergent in water. Glycerin is often added as an ingredient. Detergents form bubbles in much the same way as soap, but detergents will form bubbles even in tap water, which contains ions that could prevent soap bubble formation. Soap contains a carboxylate group that reacts with calcium and magnesium ions, while detergents lack that functional group. Glycerin, $C^3H^5(OH)^3$, extends the life of a bubble by forming weakening hydrogen bonds with water, slowing down its evaporation." He paused and looked around the table and then down at his hands. "Sorry."

Rather than being irritated by his little brother's interruption, Quinn just slapped him on the back with a smile. "What would any conversation be without some science thrown in, right? Never too old to learn something."

Owen reached for his pizza and began to eat.

"So anyway, Zoe, Dad had to replace the floor in the laundry room and all of the trim and drywall! It was a complete gut job!" He laughed even harder. "I guess laundry just isn't your thing, Bro!"

Aidan glared at him. "I was twelve, for starters, and it was a one-time thing and I do laundry just fine now. And after that, I seem to remember I had to do that load of laundry because you peed your pants!"

"Hey!" Quinn snapped, wiping tears of mirth from his eyes. "That was only because Hugh scared the crap out of me by hiding in my closet." He shifted in his seat as his face flamed a bit. "He was cashing in on the fact that we had watched *The Shining* the night before and I was scared to death of everything."

"Whatever, dude. The point is that you peed your pants. And I had to wash them." Aidan held up his hands and everyone started to laugh, except Quinn. "Not so fun when the joke's on you, is it?" he said to his brother.

"Yeah, whatever," Quinn said as he crossed his arms across his chest and pouted.

Anna sat beside him and placed a hand on his arm. "Stop being such a baby. You were the one who brought it up." Before he could answer, she placed another slice of pizza on his plate and got up to grab him another beer. She sat back down and handed it to him before turning to Zoe. "So how's the job going? Is everything back on track?"

Zoe gave a rundown of what was going on and what she was thinking of for the second house. "If you'd like, I've got some mock-ups on my tablet. We can go inside and look at them," she suggested.

"That sounds great. Let the guys do the dishes." Anna laughed as she stood and ruffled Quinn's hair and walked away.

Darcy quickly followed.

Zoe found her purse, pulled her tablet out, and pulled up her file on the next model home. The three of them sat on the sofa in the living room and talked about fabrics and colors and furniture selections.

"I love the curtains you chose for the master bedroom," Anna said. "I wish I had a room like that. Zoe, I know you work for Martha Tate, but I can't really afford Martha's company. Do you ever do small jobs on the side?"

"Absolutely! Martha only does commercial decorating, and she's totally supportive of me doing residential work on the side. I can come over and help you sometime if you'd like."

Anna reached over and squeezed one of Zoe's hands. "I would love that! I am so not good with decorating. I go for the basics—solids, no patterns. I completely lack imagination."

"I'm sure that's not true. And seriously, I would love to come over and help you. You tell me what your budget is, and we can make it happen." They began to chat among themselves about colors and patterns when Darcy interrupted.

"Would you be willing to look at my room, Zoe?" she asked quietly.

Both women stopped talking and turned to her. "What's the matter with your room, Darce?" Anna asked.

The girl shrugged. "It's just… It's the same stuff Dad bought for my room when I was, like, six years old. He refuses to take me shopping to do anything with it. He says that it's not necessary." She looked at Zoe and Anna, her eyes huge. "But it is! So can you? Will you come upstairs and help me?"

Zoe looked at Darcy and then turned to Anna, who shrugged, before returning her attention to Darcy. "Of course I'll help you. C'mon, let's go and have a look."

Back in the dining room, all eyes were on Aidan. "What? What's everyone looking at?"

Quinn smirked and then looked at Owen and then his father and then back to Aidan. "So…I take it that everything worked out when I sent Zoe to come and get you at the site the other day?"

Aidan rolled his eyes at his brother's ridiculous question and tone. "Yes."

"I guess that means I can take the credit for you getting your head out of your ass and returning to the land of the living."

"Shut up."

"I'm just saying it's about time you started dating. We were all getting concerned," Quinn said, clearly trying to goad his brother again.

"There's nothing wrong with being single," Owen said, placing his pizza back on his plate. "Forty-four percent of adult Americans are single, according to U.S. Census figures. This means that there are over one hundred million unattached people out there."

Quinn chuckled. "Impressive. You were one in one hundred million, Aidan."

"However"—Owen raised his hand slightly to get the attention back—"statistically, the odds on finding someone favor the male population: There are eighty-six unmarried men for every one hundred unmarried women, although in some regions the gender ratio favors women, especially out west. Paradise, Nevada, a suburb ten miles from Las Vegas, has one hundred and eighteen unmarried men for every one hundred unmarried women. Other cities where females have the advantage include Austin, Texas; Fort Lauderdale, Florida; Tempe, Arizona; and Sunnyvale and Santa Ana, California." He cleared his throat. "All warm and sunny places."

"Maybe you need to move?" Quinn said with a grin. "You know, leave the nest. Run away from home."

Reaching for a beer, Aidan refused to be baited and instead turned his attention to his other brother. The normally quiet one. "So where's the seminar at, Owen?"

"Oh…um…Charleston. It was sort of a last-minute

thing. Their speaker became ill—some sort of stomach bug that really has the potential to be gone within the next twenty-four hours, but the coordinators panicked and wanted to make sure they had someone lined up who could actually…you know, speak… without vomiting."

Aidan and Quinn looked at each other and each made a face. "There's a visual for you," Quinn said.

"So does that mean there's a chance that you're going there for nothing?" Aidan asked.

Owen shook his head. "No, I'm definitely speaking. They asked the other scientist to leave and are currently decontaminating the banquet room to make sure no one else contracts what he had."

"Sounds a little drastic," Aidan said, taking a sip of his own beer.

"About as drastic as disappearing for a few days because you're upset?" Quinn said daringly.

"All right, let's get this over with," Aidan said, slamming his hands down on the table.

"Boys," Ian said in a tone they all knew meant business. "Enough's enough. Aidan's allowed to do what he wants. He's a grown man."

"That's bullshit," Quinn said, suddenly angry. "He runs off, gets everyone worried, and then we all have to just act like nothing's wrong? Uh-uh. I'm done with that." He faced his brother. "You scared the hell out of everyone. We all get that you were upset, man. We do. But you're getting too old for this running away shit."

Aidan's first instinct was to argue, but unfortunately, his brother was right. "I know," he said quietly. "It was… It was everything combined. I felt…guilty.

I never missed an anniversary. Ever. And I missed it because I was with someone. I didn't know how to handle it."

"Aidan," Quinn said even though his father was about to speak, "cut yourself some slack. It was one time in seventeen years. Hell, you're the only one who goes to the cemetery as much as Dad. Mom's not going to be mad because you missed this one time. You're human. It's about time you accepted that."

"What the hell's that supposed to mean?"

"It means you walk around here like you have to be perfect, and you're not! It's damn exhausting watching you put on this martyr act. You've been here for all of us, even when it wasn't what you wanted. You've sacrificed everything for this family; hell, you're practically like a second father to all of us. Don't you think it's time you put yourself first? You've got a beautiful woman who clearly is into you, God knows why, and you should be enjoying your time with her."

Aidan glared at his brother. He didn't like the lascivious way he said that last sentence. "Zoe is none of your concern."

"Jesus," Quinn muttered, "that's what you took away from that? Seriously? I'm happy for you, Aidan! We all are! Stop trying to be the goddamn parent around here and just be yourself!"

"I'm not—" Aidan began but his father immediately cut him off.

"Your brother's right, Aidan. And I'm largely to blame."

"What are you talking about? You're not to blame for anything."

Ian shook his head. "You were so strong and you seemed to be able to come home here and make everything…work. I was overwhelmed and devastated and could barely function most days. And then you'd come home from school and suddenly everyone was behaving and things were getting done around here. I relied on you, maybe too much, and now I see I've monopolized your time. We all have." He looked at his son sadly. "You have a life, Aidan, but you're not really living. I've watched you tonight with Zoe and that's when it hit me—I haven't seen you genuinely smile in a long time. She makes you smile. You shouldn't be here tonight. It's a Friday night and you should be taking that lovely woman out on a date, not having pizza with your family."

"I enjoy having pizza with my family," Aidan said defensively. "And whether or not I'm dating anyone, I'm still going to want to spend time with you…all of you."

Ian shook his head. "No one's saying you can't. All I'm saying is that it's okay for things to change, Son. It's okay if you don't come for pizza every Friday night. It's okay for you to do something for yourself first."

Aidan wasn't sure how this had all come up but he wasn't happy about it. He didn't want anyone telling him how to live his life or that all of a sudden, his life was bothering everyone. There was nothing wrong with him or the way he cared for all of them.

He was thinking of a retort when Zoe, Anna, and Darcy walked back into the room, all talking excitedly about decorating something. Sitting back, Aidan watched the interaction and felt a trickle of unease. The dynamics were changing—Darcy was getting older, obviously everyone had a problem with his role in the family, and now there was Zoe. Maybe bringing her here tonight was a mistake. Maybe he wasn't ready for it. Maybe...

"Zoe's going to make me some new curtains for my room," Darcy said as she sat down. "She has the fabric already and we took measurements. Is that okay, Dad? Can we do it?"

Ian smiled at his only daughter. "As long as you didn't badger her into doing it, Darce, and she lets us pay her at her usual rates for her services. I'm sure Zoe has plenty to do with her job already."

"Oh, I don't mind, Mr. Shaughnessy. I'll tell you what, for Darcy's room, I'm going to give you the family rate—if you'll cover the materials, the labor's free. Making curtains is a breeze. We've got a great machine at the office that I can use. Martha won't mind me using it. I lost mine in the storm."

"Aidan told us about that, Zoe. I sure am sorry for your loss. That must have been hard."

She nodded. "It was more of a shock than anything. In my wildest dreams, I never thought I'd experience anything like that. But I'm very fortunate because Aidan convinced me to leave when I had planned on staying. If I had been home," she said and her voice cracked with emotion, "well, let's just say I'm glad he didn't let me be stubborn. And then my boss found me a great place to live. So really, I'm very lucky." Reaching down low, she grabbed Aidan's hand under the table and squeezed it so that no one else could see.

"Not many people could go through what you did

and call themselves lucky," Ian said. "But I think that just speaks for the kind of woman you are. And if you're sure you don't mind helping Darcy…"

"It's my pleasure. Sometimes it's nice to just do a project for fun rather than for work."

"Don't forget about me!" Anna said excitedly. "I'm completely ready for a makeover, and I hired you first!"

"What's the matter with you?" Quinn demanded, looking angrily at Anna. "There's not a damn thing wrong with you! Why do you need a makeover?"

Anna blushed furiously. "My *house*, Quinn. I'm looking to do some kind of face-lift on the house. Everything in it is just so…bland. I looked at some of the rooms Zoe's done and asked if she could help me do something like that at my house."

"Oh," Quinn said quietly.

"Anyway," Anna said cheerily, although the smile didn't reach her eyes. "I'm looking forward to it. Who doesn't enjoy being surrounded by pretty things?" She looked at Zoe. "Like I told you, when I bought the house, my brother Bobby was living with me. So I used that as an excuse to keep things less girly. But now I want candles and maybe a nice sound system built into the wall." Her eyes were big and hopeful.

Zoe smiled at her encouragingly. "You do too have good ideas. I love the idea of making it a romantic retreat." Then she stopped for a minute and thought about what Anna had said. "Have I met your brother? He's not by chance a police officer?"

Anna nodded. "Bobby Hannigan is indeed my brother. He mentioned that he met you so I was thrilled when I finally got to do the same." She turned and grinned at Aidan. "Anyway, now that he's got a place of his own, I want things to be more…feminine and romantic, you know?"

"Why does it need to be romantic?" Quinn interrupted. "What's gotten into you, Anna?"

Anna looked at him blandly and then turned to Zoe. "The Shaughnessys aren't the most romantic bunch, are they?"

Zoe almost agreed, but one look at Aidan and she knew that she couldn't. "I'm not so sure about that," she responded simply.

Beside her, Aidan stood. "Well, this has been fun," he said, forcing a smile. "But all this talk about romance and dating has reminded me that it's time for us to go." Gently, he tugged Zoe to her feet.

She looked at the people sitting around the table. "Thank you for sharing your Friday night with me," she said to everyone. "This was wonderful."

"And you're going to come back, right?" Darcy asked anxiously. "You're going to work on my curtains, right? And maybe help me with the rest of my room?"

Zoe smiled at the girl. "Absolutely. As a matter of fact, I'm going to try to have the curtains done for you next week, and I'm going to look around for some accessories that will match. Maybe some pillows or a lamp or something. How does that sound?" Darcy didn't answer. Instead she jumped up and hugged Zoe. Zoe looked at Darcy and then to Aidan and smiled before wrapping her arms around her. "Don't get too excited just yet. I may make terrible curtains."

Darcy pulled back and smiled. "That's not even possible." Then she turned serious. "Thank you, Zoe. Thank you for taking the time to hang out with me and help me with my room. I really appreciate it." She hugged Zoe again fiercely before running from the room.

Everyone was stunned silent for a minute until Aidan spoke. "Okay, then." He walked over and hugged his father and shook Quinn's hand. Then he hugged Anna and walked over to Owen. "Knock 'em dead at the conference, Bro," he said before hugging him. Owen pulled back and looked at him oddly. "It means good luck."

"Oh," Owen said and then turned shyly to Zoe, not meeting her eyes. "It was very nice to meet you, Zoe."

"You too, Owen. I hope to see you again."

After Zoe had said her good-byes to everyone, she and Aidan left the house and walked out to their cars. They stopped next to Zoe's car and Aidan turned her to face him. "Thank you for not running screaming from the house."

She swatted at him playfully. "Oh stop. It wasn't that bad. They're all very sweet."

He rolled his eyes. "Were we at the same table?"

"You're very lucky to have them. I think it was a wonderful night."

"Oh yeah?" he asked with a sexy grin. "I think I can do better than that."

Now it was her turn to grin. "Really? Better than wonderful?" She shook her head. "I don't know if that's possible."

"That sounds like a challenge," he said, closing the small gap between them until his forehead rested against hers and he could feel her from chest to toes.

"What did you have in mind? Candlelight? Soft music?"

He pulled back and chuckled. "What is it with you women and the music and candlelight? What is the big deal?"

"Ugh…Anna was right. You Shaughnessys are hopeless!" she said with a laugh.

"So just because I don't understand the big deal about a bunch of candles and music, I'm hopeless?" Zoe nodded. "Tell you what…let's go back to my place and I'll show you how romantic I can be without those things."

"Hmm…" she said softly, gently pulling him back to her. "I think I'm willing to take that chance."

"I was hoping you'd say that," he murmured against her lips, loving the feel of her under his hands and the taste of her against his lips. She was quickly becoming an addiction. And he wasn't sure what to make of it, but he knew he wasn't ready—might never be ready—to let her go. He'd think about that later.

"Do you have any plans for tomorrow?" he asked, still holding back from kissing her and taking what he wanted.

"That depends," she said, angling her head in encouragement.

"On?"

"On how well you sweep me off my feet tonight." Her eyes met his and her tone was light and teasing.

"Sweetheart, I'm tempted to leave one of our cars here and sweep you up right now," he said gruffly. "Hell, if I could, I wouldn't wait to get you back to my place. I'd have my way with you right here, right now." He sighed roughly. "But I'm not big into audiences."

"That's good because…neither am I."

"How about this…we each get into our cars and drive to my place, and then I promise to pick this right up again and sweep you up in my arms and not let you out of them."

"Oh…I really like that plan. But I'm gonna need something to hold me over until we get there. That ten-minute drive is going to seem like an eternity."

And Aidan knew it to be true. He cupped her nape in his hand and hauled her up against him and kissed her as he'd been wanting to for what seemed like forever. Her lips opened under his and his tongue plundered. His entire body tightened as she clutched his shirt and matched his passion. It was heady, erotic, and if he didn't put an end to it right now, they'd be giving the entire neighborhood a show.

Reluctantly he pulled back. "Ten minutes," he said breathlessly.

"I'll race you," she said and ran for her car, laughing the entire way.

Aidan could only stand there and smile. It was a good feeling.

Chapter 11

Zoe couldn't quite put her finger on it, but something had been bothering Aidan since the night she'd gone to dinner with his family.

For several weeks they'd been moving along, seemingly happy. She thought about that night after they'd raced back to his apartment, and the memory of the things they'd done to each other still made her blush. Physically, they were fine. But every time Zoe interacted with his family, she could tell it made him uncomfortable.

As promised, she had made the curtains for Darcy, and that next Friday night, Aidan brought her to dinner with him and she and Darcy spent a good portion of the night working on her room.

"You're spoiling her," he had said when he saw all the packages Zoe had with her that night.

"Oh, hush. She's outgrown her room and all she's asking for are a couple of things to bring it up-to-date."

"Seems like a waste of money to me," he had grumbled.

Then she'd had lunch with Anna at the pub that she worked at and didn't mention it to him. Of course when he and Quinn showed up, thanks to Anna telling Quinn of their plans, Aidan had seemed annoyed that she was there.

She'd confronted him on it later that night when he'd

come over for dinner. "Was there something wrong with me having lunch with Anna today?"

"No. Why?"

"Your attitude during lunch said otherwise."

"What are you talking about? What attitude?"

Zoe rolled her eyes. "Aidan, you pretty much growled through every conversation that we all had and you barely said two words to me."

"I just don't understand why you didn't mention you were having lunch with her, that's all."

Hands on hips, she turned to him. "Oh, and you tell me about every little thing that you do when we're not together?"

"That's not the same," he said dismissively. "Most of the time we're not together, I'm working. I'm not off having lunch with *your* friends or family."

That comment was like a smack in the face. She held it together and was tempted to remind him that she had no family for him to dine with, but decided that it was not a fight worth having. "Is that what you want me to do? Tell you what I'm doing every minute of the day and maybe get your permission before I do anything?"

"That's not what I'm saying, Zoe. It just…it took me by surprise, that's all. I'll admit that I handled it badly. What more do you want from me?"

That was the million-dollar question. Zoe loved spending time with Aidan, loved talking with him and working with him, and their nights together were just about perfect; but for all of that, she could tell he was still holding a part of himself back and she didn't know why. She was smart enough to know that Aidan truly cared about her. But there was this invisible line in the sand that was tripping them up, and Zoe just wished she knew what it was.

She and Anna had been spending more and more time together, and Zoe was really coming to trust her. As she pulled up in front of Anna's house, Zoe decided she had to put it all out there and ask Anna what she thought was wrong.

Aidan was aware that Zoe was going to Anna's today to help her with her house. While he wasn't overjoyed about it, he told her to have fun.

Progress.

Anna was bouncing on her toes outside her house when Zoe pulled up. "I am so excited about this! You have no idea how much I have been dreaming of doing this and just never put the effort in! You're a lifesaver!"

"Let me get my red cape out of the way and then we can get started!" Zoe teased as she climbed out of the car and popped the trunk. Inside she had fabrics and paint samples and her trusty toolbox to take measurements. Anna walked over and helped her with everything and then they headed toward the house. "I know you're going to want it all done today, but remember that these things take time."

"I know, I know…it's my own fault for waiting so long. I never should have let Bobby's living here affect the way I did anything, but—"

"Nothing wrong with that. Luckily you don't have to keep it that way." Zoe put her things down once they were inside Anna's house, and she began to look around. It was a two-bedroom bungalow with an open floor plan but it definitely lacked any imagination.

"You hate it," Anna said from beside her. "It's okay. You can say it."

"I don't hate it, but there is so much we can do here." She turned to Anna with a big grin. "I'm kind of excited! And it won't even take a lot of work."

"Seriously? I was imagining we were going to have to rip everything apart and start from scratch."

Zoe shook her head. "If you're up for it, we'll paint all the walls to freshen and brighten it up in here and we'll do new window treatments. You'll be amazed what we can do with some slipcovers and pillows and accessories. You won't need to buy new furniture or anything—unless you want to."

"Whew! That's a relief. I know I said I want a make-over, but my budget isn't quite on board yet."

"No worries. We can take our time with it and this way you can let me know when you want to move forward."

Anna relaxed beside her. "See? Lifesaver."

They sat down and started going through colors for the walls and options for slipcovers when Zoe finally felt she could broach the subject of Aidan. "Can I ask you something?"

"Of course," Anna said with a nod.

"I kind of get the feeling that Aidan isn't thrilled about me being around his family."

"Did he say that?"

Zoe shook her head. "No, it's nothing he's come right out and said. It's more like…"

"Like the day he and Quinn joined us for lunch?"

"Exactly! It's like he tolerates it, but he's not happy about it and I don't know why. I don't think I've been overbearing or that I'm someone who shouldn't be allowed around other people, but he is clearly uncomfortable with the whole thing. I know you've known him for a long time and I hate to bring it up, but…I'm kind of floundering here and don't know what to do."

Anna sat back and thought about it for a minute. "Okay, if I had to venture a guess, I would say that Aidan is having a hard time with the change in the dynamics."

"How?"

"Aidan's the oldest and he takes that role seriously. They all know they can count on him for everything. I kind of feel bad for him sometimes because it's like no one lets him have a life of his own. They turn to him the same way they turn to Ian." She shifted to get more comfortable. "Don't get me wrong, Aidan's never complained, but I think he got comfortable being the guy everyone turns to."

"How has that changed?"

Anna grinned. "His brothers are all sort of ribbing him because he has a girlfriend. I told Quinn to knock it off because it's not like they're kids. They all think that it's great, but Aidan's never been serious with anyone. And he's *never* brought anyone home with him. So really, this is new territory for all of them."

"I didn't ask to come home with him," Zoe said with a hint of exasperation. "He invited me!"

"Oh, I didn't mean for you to get upset," Anna said quickly, placing her hand on Zoe's. "Okay, here's something that you need to know about the Shaughnessys— they don't do well with change."

"How is that even possible? I mean, from what I've heard, one brother is a rock star, another has a string of five-star resorts… How do they do those things if they don't handle change?"

Anna frowned. "It's not so much change like you're thinking in regard to Hugh and Riley. They may travel a lot, but believe me when I tell you they micromanage the things around them so that some things *don't* change." She laughed. "Riley makes sure all of his dressing rooms look the same by sending a decorator in before each show to set everything up."

"Seriously?" Anna nodded. "Okay, wow. That's… different. And kinda diva-ish."

"And Hugh makes sure that every suite he claims for himself at each resort is done exactly the same. It doesn't matter what the theme is of the resort, his suites are all the same."

"Wow."

"Exactly. I know you're new to the area and to the family but…the house? Ian's house? They haven't redecorated it, like, ever." Zoe's eyes went wide. "It's true. That house looks almost identical to the way it did the day Mrs. Shaughnessy died."

"That's…" Zoe had no words.

"It's weird. You can say it. I mean, there have been small changes over the years—a new couch when the old one wore out, some paint to freshen up, but for the most part? It's the same. I don't see how any of them can move on when their home base, so to speak, is stuck in a time warp."

"I have some of my mom's things in storage," Zoe said after a minute. "I like having it and eventually I'll find a place for it, but when she died, I couldn't stay in the house that we lived in. It made me too sad."

"I think it would have been a good thing for them to move, but poor Ian was struggling with dealing with six kids, including a baby. So many people rallied around them and lent a hand where they could, but I think it would have been too hard to move that many kids after all they had lost. At the time, there was comfort in staying in that house. But now? I think it would be a good thing for them to either rehab the place or move. It's too big for Ian to live in alone."

"Darcy's still home," Zoe said.

"For now. They're pushing her to go to a local college, but she's dying to branch out and be someplace where everyone doesn't know her, her family, and the fact that she lost her mom. It's been hard on her."

"Okay, so all that being said, what do I do, Anna? How do I try to get Aidan to relax?"

A sad smile crossed Anna's face. "I don't know that you can. Besides not being romantics or very open to change, the Shaughnessys are as stubborn as mules."

"Great." Zoe sighed. "How can I make something work if it seems to be impossible?"

"I don't think it's impossible, Zoe. I just think that it's going to take a lot of time and patience. Are you willing to stick it out for the long haul?"

Was she? While everything else between her and Aidan had been going smoothly, they didn't talk about the future or about where they saw themselves, say, six months from now. Zoe wasn't one to push and she wasn't the clingy type, but now that Anna brought it up, where did she see the two of them going? Was Aidan *the one*? Did she want to stick around to see him overcome whatever this issue was?

"You're thinking pretty hard over there," Anna said softly. "I hope I didn't scare you off."

Zoe shook her head. "No, but you did give me a lot to think about."

"I guess it's my turn to ask if I can ask you something."

"Of course."

"Do you love him?"

Anna's tone was so serious, as was the expression on her face, and for a moment, Zoe felt herself panic.

"I don't know," she finally said honestly. "I mean, I've never really been in love before. I know what I feel for Aidan is strong, and when I'm not with him, I miss him." Even just thinking about him now had her heart lurching. "When we're together, I don't want to think about being apart. I don't mind the nights when I'm alone, but that's only because we spend most nights together, so it's good to have a little break from time to time. And even when he's being an ass when we're around his family, I still would rather be there with him than by myself. And…"

"I hate to tell you this, Zoe, but it sounds like you're in love."

"No."

"Uh…yeah."

"*No*," she said more forcibly.

"'Fraid so, my friend," Anna said as a smile spread across her face.

Zoe jumped to her feet. "But…but…" She looked down to where Anna was still sitting. "How did this happen?" Now the panic began to set in.

"I really can't answer that for you, but I'd like to think that it was a 'first sight' kind of thing. Aidan's pretty decisive, and I can't imagine him ever being around you and not being in love with you. I just can't," she said giddily.

"Wait…whoa…we just said that I'm the one in love with him. No one said Aidan was in love with me. The man pretty much shuts down every time I'm around his family. Does that sound like someone who's in love?"

"Normally, no," Anna said as she stood up and walked into the kitchen to grab them something to drink. "But we're not dealing with your average person. We're dealing with a Shaughnessy."

Zoe took the glass from Anna's hand. "And what does that mean exactly?"

"It means they're not used to having anyone else there. Sure, there have been people who have helped out after Mrs. Shaughnessy's death, but…they don't let people in. Not really."

"You're in," Zoe reminded.

A shadow crossed Anna's face. "Yeah, well, that's only because I was there…before. Quinn and I? We've always been friends. My parents live next door to Ian and because Quinn and I are the same age, we just gravitated toward one another when we were younger."

"And now?" Zoe asked, suddenly remembering Darcy's words about Anna and Quinn.

Anna sighed. "Now…it's habit. We've always been friends. We're always going to be…friends."

"Is that what you want?"

"It doesn't really matter," she said sadly. "It's what we are." She paused and then shook herself out of her funk. "But we're not talking about me or Quinn. We're talking about you and Aidan."

Zoe let it drop. "So what do I do?"

"Maybe you need to talk to him about it. You know, sort of bring it up before the next family get-together so you can make him aware of the fact that you're noticing the problem."

"Hmm…maybe. Knowing Aidan, he'll tell me that I'm imagining things or that I'm crazy."

"That does sound like him," Anna said with a wink. "Honestly, Zoe, I wish I knew what to tell you. In all the years I've known them, you're the first one any of them has brought home."

"You can't be serious. There are five men in that family—five *attractive* men. I'm sure they've had girl-friends before me!" she said, filled with disbelief.

"Always casual, never serious. I'm telling you, the girls in town used to go crazy trying to figure out ways to get invited into the Shaughnessy home. It was almost like a rite of passage, only none of us passed."

"You did."

Anna shrugged. "It wasn't the same. I was there because I was a neighbor and a friend. If it wasn't for that, I never would have made it up the driveway."

"That's a bit extreme, don't you think?"

"If you don't believe me, ask Darcy. Ask her how many girls her brothers have brought home."

It didn't seem possible, Zoe thought to herself, but she definitely intended to find out. "Okay, I'm all Shaughnessy'd out. Let's get back to you and the fabulous transformation we're going to make to your home." Bending over, she picked up her fabric swatches and began moving around the room. "Ready?"

Anna let out a squeal of joy. "You know it! Let's do this!"

Zoe sat quietly next to Aidan while they waited for their pizza order the following Friday. "You're awful quiet tonight," he said softly. "Are you okay?"

Bringing up what she and Anna had talked about had been on her mind all week, but every time she'd felt like she was ready, she'd chickened out. Now here she was, fewer than thirty minutes away from the middle of a situation she knew Aidan wasn't comfortable with, and she didn't know what to do.

Pull off the Band-Aid.

"You know, if you want to go have dinner with your family…without me…I'm fine with that. You know that, right?"

"You don't want to have dinner with us?"

She shook her head quickly. "No, no…it's not that at all. I'm just saying that…I don't want you to feel…obligated."

"Zoe, you've lost me here. What's going on?"

A small sigh escaped her lips and she looked around the crowded restaurant. This was so not the place she wanted to have this conversation. "You know what? It's nothing. Forget I said anything."

Aidan reached out and took one of her hands in his. "Uh-uh. Something's on your mind. Tell me."

Looking over at him, she felt her heart actually hurt. He was so handsome and he was probably one of the best people she knew and if it wasn't for this one issue, he'd be damn near perfect. Why was she rocking the boat? He said her name softly again and she caved. "Okay, don't take this the wrong way but…I get the feeling that you're not really comfortable with me hanging out with your family."

She waited a minute and was relieved when the sky didn't fall.

He stared at her. Hard. "If this is still about the lunch thing with Quinn and Anna, I've already apologized. I admit that I handled that badly and all but—"

"It's not just the lunch thing," she said quietly and let her eyes meet his. "Aidan, when we're alone, just the two of us, you're relaxed and happy and you smile. When we're together with your family? You're tense and short-tempered and you never smile. That's not a coincidence."

"Maybe it's them and not you."

She made a face at him. "Really?" There was no way to mask the sarcasm. "All I've heard from everyone who knows you is that you're all very close and how much you all get along. They all talk about you like you walk on water. But you're telling me you never laugh and smile with them? Ever?"

He scrubbed a hand over his face and sighed. "It's just…different. It's like I've been this one guy for so long and now all of a sudden, I'm different. They're all looking at me differently and I feel different and…it's weird."

"Why are you feeling different? I don't understand why you're trying to be someone you're not," she said sadly as she squeezed his hand. "I think you're pretty amazing just the way you are. I don't want you to be somebody else."

"Easy for you to say," he mumbled.

"Aidan, I worked with you before I got involved with you. I know you. I saw the good, the bad, *and* the ugly in you and yet I still got involved with you. You can be yourself with me and your family."

He shook his head. "You don't understand. I'm the

one everyone comes to. I'm the go-to guy whenever any of my siblings has a problem. Hell, even my father relies on me for a lot. And now they're all tiptoeing around me because they don't want to bother me or interrupt our time together. It's… It bothers me. I'm used to things a certain way and now everyone's changing it without even talking to me about it."

"Okay, so set them straight. Tell them you're still the go-to guy. Tell them they can still call and talk to you. I'm not an ogre, Aidan. I'm not going to get upset because you care about your family."

His name was called, signifying that their order was ready. He looked at her as he stood. "We'll talk about this later, okay?"

As he turned to walk toward the counter, Zoe stood and reached for his hand and turned him around. "That's fine but I want you to *promise* me that you will try to relax at dinner." His only response was a curt nod.

It was just the four of them tonight—Zoe, Aidan, Darcy, and Ian. Zoe tried not to focus on Aidan too much as she sat and listened to Darcy chatter on and on about how much she loved the way her "new" room looked. Zoe was glad to help, and truthfully, it hadn't taken a lot of time. She wished the males in this family would cut Darcy some slack and understand that a girl was definitely different from a boy.

They were almost finished eating, Ian and Aidan arguing over the last slice, when Darcy cleared her throat. "So I got an application for UC Berkeley." All conversation stopped. "And one for USC."

Ian dropped the slice of pizza. "Darcy, we've been over this a thousand times. There are plenty of great colleges right here. You're not going to California."

"Why not?" she snapped. "Why is it that Aidan got to go to Michigan for college? And Hugh went to Massachusetts? And Quinn… Well, he didn't go to college but he was down in Florida doing his races. You let Riley travel all over the world and Owen…Owen's gone to so many colleges that I've lost count and none of them were local! Why don't I get to choose where I want to go?"

"Darce," Aidan interrupted, "we have company. Now is not the time."

"Zoe doesn't care!" she cried. "She's practically family." Then, turning to Zoe she asked, "Do you think it's fair that all of the men in this family were allowed to go do whatever they wanted and I'm forced to stay here?"

All eyes were on Zoe, and she knew this was not a discussion for her. "I think that you really need to talk about this with your dad, Darcy," she said uncomfortably, knowing full well if she had her choice, she'd be siding with the girl one hundred percent.

Darcy looked like someone had slapped her as tears formed in her eyes. "I can't believe you're siding with them," she said quietly, rising from the table.

"Darcy," Zoe said quickly, "I know you're frustrated and I get it, I really do, but this is between you and your dad. It's not my place—"

"I'm completely outnumbered here! None of them understand how much they're stifling me! I'm tired of the double standard! I'm tired of not being allowed to live my life!"

"That's enough, Darcy," Ian said firmly. "We'll talk about this later."

"Zoe, please! Talk to them! Make them see how they're killing me!" she cried before running from the room.

Both Shaughnessy men sat back in their chairs and sighed. "I'm sorry you had to witness that," Ian said. "She's hell-bent on going out of state."

"Can I ask…why…you're so against it?" Zoe asked hesitantly.

"You're joking, right?" Aidan snapped. "She's a young girl with no knowledge of how the world really is and you think we should just send her off to another state by herself?"

"And whose fault is it that she has no knowledge of how the world really is? There's protecting her, Aidan, and then there's just doing her a disservice. At some point, she's going to leave home. She's not going to live here forever. Wouldn't you feel better if she knew how to handle herself, protect herself, and take care of herself?"

"There are a lot of crazy people out there—"

"And I get that," she interrupted. "But there are crazy people going to the local colleges too. Just because she's going to school close to home now doesn't mean the people are any less crazy or strange or mean than they are in another state."

"But…" he mumbled.

"You can't protect her from everything, and if you keep trying to hold her here in this little box you've made for her, she's going to rebel in a big way. I've seen it happen, Aidan."

"You don't know what you're talking about," he spat and stood. "And besides that, it's really none of your damn business."

"Actually, it kind of is," she retorted, standing so that she was in his face. "Having *been* a teenage girl, I know *exactly* what I'm talking about! More than you, probably! And I've been coming here for dinner for a month now, and I see Darcy almost every day at the construction site. She's not just your little sister; she's become a friend and someone I care about."

"She's a child, Zoe! You're too old to be her friend!"

"Aidan…" Ian warned but was swiftly ignored.

"Now you're going to tell me who I can and can't be friends with?" She was appalled. "News flash, you don't get to call the shots for everyone about everything. I get that you take your job as the oldest here in the family seriously and that's great, but there comes a time when you have to let people go; they're entitled to make decisions for themselves. They're even entitled to make mistakes for themselves."

He shook his head furiously. "No. Why should they have to make mistakes? What's the point in it when there is obviously a right way for things to get done?"

"God, do you even hear yourself? You're not perfect, Aidan!" she yelled. "You make mistakes too, no matter how much you think otherwise. You're making one right now. Keep going like this and she's going to hate you and want nothing to do with you. Is that what you want?"

He went to walk around her, but she reached out and grabbed his arm and stopped him. "Is it?"

Aidan yanked his arm free. "She can hate me all

she wants, but I'm not letting her go off into the world where no one is around to help her." His words were said through clenched teeth.

"I don't believe that's your decision to make," Ian said, coming to his feet. "I know we've talked about this before, Aidan, and we've always been on the same page, but ultimately, the decision is mine to make. Darcy is my daughter and I'll handle this." He lowered his head and shook it sadly. "I didn't realize how much I put on you over the years. It wasn't your responsibility to play the second parent, and yet I can see now it's exactly what I let happen."

He sank back down in his chair and ran a hand through his graying hair. As he looked up at his son, all of his sadness and disappointment in himself shone through. "I'm so sorry, Aidan. I'm so sorry that you felt you had to carry the burden of taking care of all of us. You deserve to have a life of your own, one where you're not obligated to…come and have dinner every Friday night or that you don't go out and date because your family commands so much of your time. Your mother would hate me for doing that to you."

"Hey," Aidan said calmly, kneeling next to his father's chair. "It's not like that. I wanted to help. You never asked; I jumped in where I was needed, just like I was raised to do. Mom taught me to take care of people. It's what I do. You didn't force it on me."

Ian shook his head. "Maybe not, but I certainly didn't pay attention to how much you were missing out on by running interference around here."

"Dad…"

"It's a Friday night and you've got a beautiful woman

with you. You should be out dancing or having a romantic dinner, not sitting here arguing with your father and sister." He reached out and put a hand on Aidan's shoulder. "You know I love spending time with you, Aidan. And you have been nothing but a blessing to me since the day you were born. But it's time for you to have a life of your own."

"I have a life, Dad," Aidan protested. "And my life is fine."

Ian shook his head. "It's not, but it will be." Coming to his feet, he looked around the room and smiled at Zoe. "This is our last Friday night pizza fest."

"What? Why?" Aidan asked, confusion written all over his face.

"Because you should be out with Zoe. Darcy should be out with her friends."

"And what about you? What are you going to do?"

Ian shrugged. "I don't know, but it's about time that I learned how to do some things for myself. Maybe I'll join a bowling league or go out with some friends or something. They've been asking for about ten years now, so maybe I'll give them a shock and finally show up."

"No need to do anything drastic," Aidan said lightly. "What about Darcy? What are you going to do?"

"Honestly, I don't know, and that's okay. I don't have to have the answers right now. Maybe there's a compromise in there somewhere, but I'm never going to know if I keep letting you handle it for me."

"I don't think I'm handling everything, Dad. I want to help. I need—"

"To be a son and a brother and stop trying to be

everyone's father," Ian said as he pulled his son in for a hug. "Go take this pretty lady out for a moonlit stroll or something. I'll handle the cleanup…and your sister."

Zoe stood back and watched as Aidan clearly struggled with this turn of events. She knew this was not the way he wanted things, and if what Anna had said was any indication, the change was not going to go smoothly.

Without a word, Aidan walked out of the kitchen and picked up his keys and cell phone by the front door. He stood there waiting for her. Zoe smiled at Ian and walked over and hugged him. "I'm sorry. I didn't mean to have it turn into all of this."

Ian shook his head. "I think you did us a favor. Aidan may not see it that way right now, but believe me when I say I'm thankful for you, Zoe. Don't let him make you think otherwise."

Easier said than done, she thought. She could already see the walls going up and knew there would be no moonlit stroll anytime soon, if ever. "Take care of yourself, Ian," Zoe said softly and forced herself not to cry. "Thank you for welcoming me into your home. I've enjoyed our dinners together."

He studied her for a moment. "I don't like the way that sounds," he said quietly, knowingly. "That sounds suspiciously like a good-bye."

Zoe forced a small smile to her face. "It's not a good-bye, but I think you and I both know Aidan is not happy right now and I'm going to bear the brunt of some of it. It just may be a while before we see each other again." Leaning in, she kissed his cheek, then walked over to Aidan and picked up her purse.

They silently walked out of the house and to their

cars. Earlier they had discussed going to Zoe's place after dinner. As much as she hated the thought of hearing his answer, she knew one of them had to speak. "So I'll see you back at my place?"

Aidan looked at her with hard eyes and shook his head. "I don't think so. Why don't I call you tomorrow?"

"Why? Because of what happened inside?" He didn't respond. "I think we need to talk about it."

"I don't," he said firmly and turned toward his truck.

"Hey, I'm talking to you, damn it!" She stormed after him and got right in his face. "If you're angry at me, then say it. Don't just walk away and pout because you didn't get your way!"

"I'm not going off to pout," he said, his rage barely contained. "I just don't feel like talking right now."

"Bullshit."

"Excuse me?"

"You heard me. I said bullshit. I think you have a lot to say right now, but you're going to go off alone and try to work it out on your own because that's what you do. You don't let anyone else in because then you might actually be like the rest of us. And you think you're so superior, that you don't need anyone, that you're the only one with the answers. And to that I say bullshit."

"You want to talk?" he asked loudly.

"Yeah, I do," she said, crossing her arms over her chest.

"Fine, we'll talk. But not here."

"We already had plans to go back to my place," she reminded him.

His eyes were near black when he looked at her. "I'll

meet you there." And without another word, he climbed into his truck and drove away.

Fifteen minutes later, they were climbing the stairs to her apartment and the door was barely closed before Aidan spoke. "You had no right to involve yourself in that conversation tonight! None!"

"I had every right to get involved," she countered. "I was sitting right there! Your sister is crying out for help, and you all keep ignoring what she's saying! What she's asking for isn't so outrageous!"

"She's none of your concern!"

"Well then, I'm making her my concern! Like it or not, Aidan, not everyone has to agree with you and your decisions!"

"Oh, I get that. You've always been up front about when you agree and disagree with me, but that's business. I won't tolerate it with my family."

"You won't *tolerate* it?" she mocked. "So basically, I'm good enough to sleep with and it's even okay for you to let me be around your precious family, but I'm not allowed to have an opinion of them? What exactly are we doing here, Aidan? I thought we were in a relationship."

"We are," he said with frustration. "But my family is off-limits!"

"For how long?"

"What?"

"You heard me. How long?" When he didn't respond, she stepped closer and continued. "We've been involved for a couple of months now, and you're telling me that even though I've gotten to know most of your family, they're off-limits to me. What happens a couple of months down the road? Will they still be off-limits? How about six months? A year? When will you deem me worthy of being a part of your family?"

"Is that what you want? Are you so desperate to cling to my family because you don't have one of your own?" he demanded.

A slap in the face would have hurt less. "Wow," she whispered. "I can't even believe you went there."

"I'm just saying…it seems odd that you want to be so involved in someone else's family. You don't know us and you don't know what you're talking about where we're concerned. I know what's best for them. I've helped raise each and every one of my siblings. You don't know anything about it and I want you to stay away from them."

Everything in Zoe went cold. She knew he had issues where his family was concerned; she even thought she understood them by now. But this? This she couldn't understand. This hard, cold, and callous attitude was more than she could bear. She looked up and saw Aidan staring at her expectantly.

"I wasn't trying to cling to your family, Aidan," she said, even though she felt as if she was going to be sick. "They're a part of you and that's why I wanted to be with them. I fell in love with you and it was a natural progression to fall in love with them too. They're all amazing." Tears began to well in her eyes and she quickly swiped them away. "But I can see that it's something you really don't want. So I'll respect your wishes. I won't get involved." She gave another sad laugh. "With any of you."

Doing her best to force her legs to work, Zoe

walked over to the door and held it open. "I think you should go."

Aidan held his ground for a long moment, just staring at her. "Zoe… I…"

She held up a hand to stop him. "No, you *really* need to go." There was a brief moment where she thought he was going to argue, but then he simply nodded and walked toward her. He stopped when he was right in front of her, his expression blank. "Good-bye, Aidan."

Once he was down the stairs and she heard the door close, she sank to the floor. There was nothing left inside of her. This was the last loss she could handle. And although she didn't think it was possible, there were still enough tears left inside her to give in to one final cry.

"I fell in love with you…"

The words were on a continuous loop in Aidan's head as he drove around. He was too wound up to go home and yet didn't know where to go or what to do with himself. How the hell had the night gone downhill so fast? One minute everyone was having a good time, just talking and laughing and the next…?

Why couldn't Zoe just listen to him? Why couldn't she just understand that he obviously knew his family better than she did and that things would be better for everyone if she just stayed out of it? It wasn't difficult. If she had, he wouldn't be driving around right now; he'd be in bed with her, kissing her and making love to her, like he had thought about all damn day.

Now what did he have?

Flashing red lights appeared in his rearview mirror and he couldn't believe his luck—it looked as if he was getting pulled over. "You have got to be kidding me," he muttered, parking his car on the side of the road. A minute later, Bobby Hannigan was at his side.

"Hey, Aidan. Where's the fire?"

"What are you talking about?" he snapped. If it were any other cop, he'd just hand over his license and whatnot, but seeing Bobby right now irritated the hell out of him.

"You were pretty much doing double the speed limit. What's going on?"

"How is that even possible?" Aidan took a look around and finally realized where he was. "That's only because the speed limit is twenty; it's not hard to do double and still feel like you're crawling."

Bobby chuckled. "Be that as it may, you were speeding. Is everything all right at home? Your dad okay? Darcy?"

Aidan threw his head back against the headrest and closed his eyes. "Just give me the damn ticket."

Bobby stood silently next to the car for a minute. "Maybe you're heading toward a hot date. Word around town is that you're dating the sexy decorator." He waggled his eyebrows and almost fell on his ass when Aidan slammed the truck door open.

"Dude, what the hell?"

Aidan felt nothing but rage. "Don't… Just don't call her that, damn it! She has a name!"

Bobby looked at him curiously. "Okay, okay…relax. Sorry. Word around town is that you're dating *Zoe*. There. Happy?"

No. No he wasn't. "We're not dating," he mumbled and leaned against the truck.

"Wow, the grapevine is losing its touch."

"No…it just happened."

Again, Bobby studied him. "You okay?"

Aidan just glared at him. "Never better. Are you going to give me the ticket or not?"

"I'll let you off with a warning this time. Just…slow it down a bit, okay?"

"Yeah, whatever." Climbing back into the truck, he drove off. Slowly. And headed home. There was nowhere else for him to go.

Not anymore.

Chapter 12

"WHAT IN THE *HELL* DID YOU DO?" THESE WERE Quinn's first words when Aidan opened the door.

"What are you doing here? It's after midnight," Aidan said. Even though he wasn't asleep, he still felt tired and worn out.

"I've been on the phone for so damn long I feel like a teenage girl," Quinn said, sitting down on the sofa. "I've talked to Dad, Darcy, Hugh, and Anna. Seriously, man, what did you do?"

Figuring his brother wasn't leaving anytime soon, Aidan shut the door and joined him on the couch. "I went to dinner at Dad's like I always do. Why? What have you heard?"

"Don't be a smart-ass. I'm tired and I've got to be up before the sun. I'm here because I'm worried about you. Now what happened?"

Aidan let out a sigh and then relayed the events of the evening, including what happened at Zoe's. "I don't even know what happened," he said honestly, finding that it felt good to finally get all of it off his chest. "I just…snapped."

"Well, we all knew it was coming."

Aidan glared at his brother. "Oh really? All of you?"

Quinn nodded. "Dude, you're my brother and I love you, but you are a royal pain in the ass."

"Did you draw the short straw? Is that how I ended up with you here to cheer me up?"

"I hate to break it to you, but I'm not here to cheer you up." When Aidan just stared at him, Quinn smirked. "And for the record, there was no drawing of straws because no one wanted to come here. I just decided to be nice."

"Great. My day just keeps getting better and better," he mumbled and rested his head back against the couch.

"Here's the thing, you have been everyone's rock for, like…ever. Even before Mom died, you always made sure that you made time for all of us and you were always there when we needed you. And I believe I can speak for all of us when I say we both appreciated it and took advantage of it."

"What? That's crazy. No one took advantage—"

"We did. All the time. Hell, you made it easy. None of us ever had to make a serious decision. Why? Because you were there to make it for us. None of us had to work hard at getting jobs. Why? Because you always knew a guy who knew a guy who knew a guy who would hire us. You helped with homework, job interviews, house hunting… I mean…how the hell did you do it all?"

"I don't know. I just did." Aidan shrugged.

"Well, stop it."

"Excuse me?"

"I said to stop it. We're all grown-ups—well, Darcy is almost a grown-up—and it's time for us to handle our own stuff."

"Yeah, but—"

"But nothing," Quinn interrupted. "Look, I know that I would not be where I am today without you there cheering me on and pointing me in the right direction. And you can ask Hugh, Riley, Owen, and someday you'll even be able to ask Darcy; they'll all tell you the same thing. But there comes a time when you need to back off and focus on your own life. We all thought you were finally doing that with Zoe."

"Why is everyone harping on that? It's not like I never dated before!"

"Yeah, yeah…you dated. A random, one-time event every now and then. You never got seriously involved. I thought that's where you and Zoe were at. We all did. And we were thrilled. How could you've messed that up?"

Aidan sighed with irritation, stood up, and began to pace. "Everything was changing," he finally said. "I could tell everyone was treating me differently and I knew it was because of Zoe and…I didn't like it. I didn't want anything to change. Why couldn't it all stay the same while I was with Zoe? Why did everyone feel the need to freak out?"

Quinn chuckled. "The only one freaking out was you." When Aidan made to defend himself, Quinn cut him off. "You were totally different around her. You seemed happy and content. You were more relaxed than I'd ever seen you, and yet you acted like an ass every time she interacted with anyone else. Like that lunch…"

"Okay, enough with the lunch!" Aidan yelled. "I get it. I was a jerk! It just seemed weird to see Zoe hanging out with Anna and then you and I were there and it was like a double date and it just… Okay, it freaked me out! Sue me!"

"You just never got comfortable with her being around us, and I don't know why. She's great. We all love her and the last I checked, we're not all that bad either. So what gives?"

Aidan shrugged again. "I don't know. I like things the way they are. I like the dynamics the way they are. Other than Darcy's recent obsession with going to school out of state, there are no surprises. Life is… simple. Neat. Uncomplicated."

"Life's not neat, Aidan, not if you're actually living. Sometimes things go wrong and life gets loud and messy and complicated. I believe some people even call that 'interesting.'" He laughed but noticed Aidan hadn't joined in. "Seriously, what's wrong with things being a little…unorderly?"

As much as Aidan didn't want to get into this any deeper, he figured he might as well unload it all. "Do you remember our lives before Mom died?"

Quinn looked at him oddly. "Yeah. Of course. Why?"

"What do you remember?"

He shrugged. "I don't know. Everything was just…normal."

"Do you ever remember Mom and Dad having a fight? Do you ever remember there being any chaos in the house?"

"There were eight of us living in the house, Aidan. Of course there was chaos." When his brother just continued to stare, Quinn caught on. "Okay. No. We were up at the same time every day, seven days a week. Ate the same meals: Monday was meat loaf, Tuesdays we had spaghetti…" He chuckled. "We took the same vacation every year—Myrtle Beach for five days not including the day it took to drive there and the day to drive back because we made them stop so damn much. We had the same meals on the holidays. What about it?"

"That's what I want," Aidan said.

"Why?" Quinn asked, clearly perplexed. "Why would you want that? I mean, it was all fine and good when we were growing up, but you do realize why it was like that, don't you?"

"What do you mean?"

"For crying out loud, Aidan, our mother was a stay-at-home mom and Dad worked like a beast. She wanted things to be peaceful when Dad was home. Having a structured routine helped keep the peace. We took the same vacation because it was all they could afford with all of us kids. It wasn't like that by choice. It's just the way it was. God, Dad used to talk about wanting to go on vacation to New York or Florida but we couldn't do it. It wasn't in the budget."

Aidan was perplexed. "How do you know this? How did I *not* know this?"

"You didn't want to know. You were content. After Mom died, I was still living at home, and sometimes late at night, Dad and I would sit up and talk. He used to tell me how he felt bad that he didn't give Mom more, that he spent so much time working and how…" Quinn paused and tried to get past the lump in his throat. "How they had always planned on having time to travel together. But they never did."

In all the years their mother had been gone, none of them really talked about what it would have been like if she were still alive. Aidan sat back down on the couch. "She would have loved Hugh's resort in California," Aidan said. "I think she would have gotten a kick out of spotting the celebrities."

Quinn laughed. "Remember all of the tabloid magazines she used to buy?"

"She used to make Dad crazy with all of her Hollywood stories," he said as he felt some of the tension leave his body. "Just think of what she would have done with Riley. She just might be up on stage with him!"

"Nah, she never liked rock music. She would have made an awesome manager though." They sat silently for a few minutes, each lost in their own versions of what could have been. "All I'm saying, Aidan, is that you shouldn't romanticize the past so much. Your future doesn't have to look like their past. You've got a successful business and a great place to live, and you did a great job helping to raise all of us. Go and do something for yourself. Go and work things out with Zoe."

He shook his head. "I can't," he said gruffly. "You have no idea the things I said to her tonight. I'm pretty ashamed of myself."

"So tell her you're sorry. Tell her you're a jackass; she'll believe you," Quinn said as he elbowed Aidan in the ribs.

"It's not that easy. She's been through so much and all I've done is add to it. She deserves someone who'll put her first and treat her like she's the most important thing in the world."

Quinn studied his brother for a long time. "And you don't think you're that guy?"

"Maybe someday. But right now, I don't even know how I can face her after the way I behaved tonight."

"Aidan, she worked with you before you started dating. She knows how you can be. In a day or two I'm sure you'll both be fine."

There was no way he was going to argue this right

now. It was too late, both time-wise and where Zoe was concerned.

He was too late.

~~~

"I don't think I understand."

Martha looked Zoe in the eye, and Zoe did her best to keep from shaking too much.

"I'm asking you to take me off the Shaughnessy job," Zoe repeated. "I can't work for Aidan anymore. There are plenty of other designers on staff who can do the job. I've got all of my files and everything is laid out for them. All they have to do is follow the plans, which have already been approved by Aidan, and they won't have a problem."

Martha looked over the rim of her glasses at Zoe and frowned. "I'd ask why but unfortunately the gossip mill works quickly in this town."

Zoe blushed.. "It was wrong to get involved with a client, and I am so sorry that I put the reputation of your firm on the line because of gossip. It wasn't my intention. I would completely understand if you asked for my resignation."

With a roll of her eyes Martha sat up straighter in her seat. "Please, if I were twenty years younger, I would have played the cougar and jumped Aidan Shaughnessy myself," she said with a girlish laugh. "I know his father is quite the handsome devil too, but the man never goes out and socializes. It's a damn shame." Zoe's eyes went wide at the comment. "Oh, knock it off. I may be getting old but I'm not dead yet. I can appreciate good-looking men and the Shaughnessys are good-looking times five!"

It was hard to stop the small smile from crossing her lips. "That they are."

"Okay, so you don't want to work with Aidan for obvious reasons," Martha stated, getting back to business. "I can't just okay that request without speaking to him first. If he agrees to another designer taking over, then we'll be fine. But if he doesn't, then I'm afraid you'll have to tough it out."

"Believe me," Zoe said sadly, "he's not going to argue it."

"That remains to be seen. In the meantime, why don't you take the rest of the day off? I'll call you after I've spoken with Aidan."

"Thank you." Not that she wanted the day off since all that managed to do was give her time alone to think. Still, she seriously didn't want to work on anything Aidan related.

It felt weird to be standing in the parking lot at ten in the morning with nothing to do. It was a beautiful day out and after a few minutes to contemplate it, Zoe decided to face at least one of her demons and go to the beach.

Traffic through town was relatively light and it was easy to find a place to park. Leaving everything except her keys in the car, she walked out onto the sand, kicked off her shoes, and moved closer to the shore before sitting down.

The sun felt wonderful on her skin and the sand beneath her toes still gave her the thrill it always had. But looking around, she didn't have the peace she'd had a month ago. She thought of her mom and wondered what her advice would be. "I wish you were here with me," she said softly. "I feel completely defeated and alone and…I honestly don't know what to do with myself here."

Waves continued to crash along the shore as she sat down, just watching and thinking. "This was supposed to be my big adventure, my new beginning. But nothing has gone right since I got here." With a shrug, she drew circles in the sand. "I like my job but everything else is a mess. The house is gone, Aidan is gone, and I'm not making friends here as easily as I thought."

There was a depressing thought. "Maybe I need to go home." She looked up at the sky. "I gave it a go and although I know you didn't raise me to be a quitter, I also know you didn't raise me to keep fighting a losing battle. I came, I saw… I failed. We all can't be winners, right?"

Zoe had no idea how long she actually sat in the sand. When she finally got up to leave, there were more people milling about and her stomach was growling. Her first instinct was to go to the pub to see Anna and grab some lunch. But Anna was semi-family to the Shaughnessys and she didn't think that would be appropriate. She was going to miss her friend.

Walking back to her car, Zoe looked back one more time at the ocean and sighed. So many hopes and dreams, and most of them were gone. On her way back to her apartment, she went through a drive-through and grabbed herself the most obnoxious burger she could find plus fries and a milkshake. What good was going through a hellish time in your life if you couldn't curl up with junk food?

Doing her best to juggle the large bag of food, the

drink, her purse, and her keys, Zoe didn't notice Anna standing at her front door until she was practically tripping over her. "Oh! Holy crap, Anna, you scared me!"

Anna raised her eyebrows at her and then looked at the bag. "Seriously, we have fabulous food at the pub, and you're cheating on me with fast-food burgers? I'm crushed."

Chuckling, Zoe unlocked the door and walked up the stairs and opened that door too. It was a given that Anna was behind her. Placing her food down on the kitchen island, along with the myriad of other things, she turned and faced her. "So what brings you here?"

"Knock it off. I talked to Quinn Friday night and kept waiting for you to call me, but you didn't," she said, looking sad and offended. "Then I went to your office and Martha said she'd given you the day off. I had someone cover my shift at the pub and I've been sitting outside your door for an hour. How are you? Why didn't you call me?"

Ugh…where did she even begin? With a fortifying breath—Zoe figured Anna wouldn't appreciate being lied to—she just blurted out the truth. "It's over between us. Aidan doesn't want me to have anything to do with his family. You're like family to him, so that's why I didn't call you. Sorry."

"Wow," Anna said, reaching into the takeout bag and helping herself to some fries. "I don't know which part of that statement bothers me more."

"What do you mean?"

"The fact that it's over between you and Aidan or that he told you to stay away from his family. That's just… Wow."

"Tell me about it." Zoe pulled up one of the bar stools and took her lunch out of the bag. "Grab a knife and split this thing with me, you know, before I have to ask you to leave."

"Shut up. I'm not going anywhere," Anna said, knife in hand, evil grin on her face. "Aidan's not the boss of me."

They broke into a fit of giggles. "I don't want to make any more trouble than I already did."

"Um…excuse me? How did *you* make any trouble? The way I see it, Darcy pitched a fit on a topic she knows gets everyone riled up, and she chose to do it with an audience in hopes of getting her father and brother to cave. You were an innocent bystander, my friend, who happened to get manipulated by a teenager."

"Nice of you to say, but not quite. I defended her. Not that it made any difference, but I just don't agree with the way they shelter her."

"Most of us don't," Anna said and then moaned with delight at the first bite of her share of the burger. "I know I shouldn't like this so much, but I do."

"Junk-food therapy. Trust me, it's a good thing." Zoe finished her bite. "When you say 'most,' do you mean the remaining Shaughnessys or others who dare to have an opinion?"

"The latter. I get that they're protective of her; she's the only girl in a sea of men over there, but they don't realize she's growing up. My mom and my dad have both tried to talk to Ian, and I've talked to all of them, but they don't want to listen. If they don't watch themselves, they're going to see her on a *Girls Gone Wild* video and then wonder why."

"That's what I was trying to tell Aidan the other night, but he just wouldn't get it."

"They're stubborn like that."

Zoe was just about to make a comment when her phone rang. When she saw Martha's name and number on the screen, her heart stopped. This was it. She was about to find out just how through with Aidan she really was.

Picking the phone up, she stepped away from Anna and took the call and listened carefully to Martha's words. Two minutes later, she was sitting back at the island, shaking and on the verge of tears.

"What is it? What's happened?" Anna asked frantically.

"He let me leave," she said quietly.

Anna looked at her oddly. "What are you talking about?"

"That was my boss. I asked to be taken off of Aidan's job and she said she would have to talk to him about it first. I put up a fuss, saying that he wouldn't want to keep me on as his decorator, but in the back of my mind, I really thought that he would, that maybe he'd had time to calm down and would try to...I don't know...not let me leave." Unable to help herself, she choked back a sob. "But he did. He told Martha he was fine with her sending somebody else." Everything inside of her hurt as she finally let herself give in and cry.

Anna's arms immediately went around her. "I'm so sorry, Zoe, so, so sorry. I don't even know what to say!"

"There's nothing you can say," she said when she finally caught her breath and sat up from Anna's embrace. "I can't stay here. I thought I could, but I just can't."

"What are you going to do?"

"I think I'm going to go back to Arizona," she said solemnly. She hadn't realized it until just that moment.

"Don't make any rash decisions," Anna pleaded. "I know it all looks bad right now, but it's going to get better. I promise."

Zoe shook her head. "I've been thinking about it all weekend, and this phone call was the final confirmation. I never should have moved here."

"That's not true! Moving here was something you always wanted to do! Not here specifically, but you wanted to live on the coast. Why not try another city? There are plenty of options on the East Coast, and then we can still hang out!"

"You know that I love you, Anna, but…it's just too hard. I don't want to have to look over my shoulder and wonder if I'm going to run into Aidan, or any of the Shaughnessys for that matter." She sighed wearily. "It's for the best."

"For whom?" Anna asked.

Good question, Zoe thought. *Good question*.

—⁂—

Saturday afternoon, Zoe sat in Anna's house and smiled. "I think we did a great job."

Anna sat beside her, beaming. "I agree. I can't believe we did all this."

Bobby stood in the middle of the room and looked at the two women. "Um, excuse me, but I seem to recall being the guy who did all of the heavy lifting and moved all of the furniture. Do you think that *maybe* you can acknowledge that?"

They both laughed and Anna stood up and hugged her brother. "Yes, yes, we couldn't have done it without you. You're our hero."

Zoe couldn't help but join in and walked over to make it a group hug. "There's no way we could have done it without you."

"That's better," Bobby said with a laugh and hugged both women tightly before stepping away. "Please tell me there is beer in the fridge."

Anna nodded and shoved him in the right direction before facing Zoe. "So how did Martha take the news of your desertion?"

"Better than I thought. She understood and promised there would always be a place for me with the firm if I ever wanted to come back."

"I hate this, you know," Anna said and took the beer that Bobby was handing to her. "I still think it's a wee bit drastic to go all the way back to Arizona."

"I've got a lot of friends there and I've spoken to the woman who bought my firm and I'll probably go work for her to start off with. It's exhausting moving across country, so it will be nice not to have to job search in the middle of it all."

"Won't you reconsider, Zoe? Please?" Anna pleaded.

"I have to agree with Anna, Zoe. You shouldn't have to move across the country. The Shaughnessys are a big family, but I really don't think you'd have trouble avoiding them. Aidan's a creature of habit, and now that you know his schedule, you'll know how to avoid him."

"You're sweet, Bobby, but it's not that simple. In the almost four months I've been here, I've had to deal with far too much. Between Aidan and the house…"

"But you have that great apartment now!" Anna said. "It's amazing and you've done so much work to it to make it your own; it just doesn't seem fair."

It wasn't, but Zoe wasn't about to get into that. "You can always come and visit me," she finally said. "I've already started packing. Not that there's much since the whole house-dropping-in-the-ocean thing. But still, I'm making progress. I may leave some of the basics behind for the next tenant. You know, paying it forward and all that."

Anna's eyes filled with tears. "Damn you," she muttered and pulled Zoe in for another hug. "And damn Aidan for causing this."

"It's not all his fault, Anna," Zoe said, amazing herself by defending him. "Let's not talk about this anymore. It is what it is. Let's focus on how amazing this place looks. You picked some beautiful colors and all of those candles are the perfect touch."

"Yeah, just in time for the next tropical storm," Bobby said, taking a pull of his beer.

"What storm?" Zoe asked.

"It's not going to be much of anything. More of a rain event than anything, but still, this place is prone to losing power so the candles will come in handy."

"I got them because they make for romantic lighting," Anna corrected.

"Please, I don't want to think about you and romantic lighting. Any man who comes near you, I'm going to have to kill."

Anna laughed. "Yeah…okay. You keep thinking that."

"Anyway," Zoe interrupted with a laugh, "when is this rain event supposed to happen?"

"Wow, you really don't watch any television, do you?" Bobby asked with a grin.

"Nope, not since my house made the news. I kind of avoid it like the plague."

"Understandable," he said, nodding his head and still chuckling. "It's actually going to roll·in tonight. I'm surprised it hasn't started raining yet. But it's gonna rain all night and all day tomorrow."

"So weird," Zoe said. "This weather makes me crazy. It's sunny and dry in Arizona. We didn't have this constant stream of storm threats like you have here."

"Keeps it lively," Bobby said with a wink.

"I hate you!"

"Oh yeah? Join the club!" Aidan felt as if his head was about to explode. It was a Saturday afternoon and he was at his father's house, hanging out with his sister while his father was out on an emergency inspection.

"I don't care!" she screeched. "Why do you have to be such a jerk?"

"Why do you have to be such a damn brat?" he yelled back. It was the first time he'd ever really yelled at her and by the look on her face, she was just as shocked as he felt.

"I am so tired of all of you! Zoe was exactly what this family needed, what I needed! You have Hugh and Quinn and Riley and Owen, and I have nobody! There was finally a female in this family and you made her go away!"

"She wasn't family, Darce," Aidan said, trying to calm down. "We were just dating. She wasn't going to be your sister or anything." That wasn't true. Aidan had seriously thought about a future with Zoe—before he'd acted like a major-league jackass. Unfortunately, he wasn't going to give his sister that kind of ammunition.

"I'm sick of all of you! Has it ever occurred to you that I might need a female to talk to? That it might be helpful every once in a while to speak to an adult woman who isn't my guidance counselor or a teacher?"

Actually, it hadn't. "We're not perfect, Darcy. We've all done the best we could."

"Well, your best sucks," she said and flopped on the couch and crossed her arms over her chest. "I have been begging all of you for years, but you all thought you knew better. And you know what? You don't! I can't talk to any of you because you refuse to listen!"

How did his father live like this day in and day out? "Don't you ever get tired of whining?"

Darcy jumped to her feet. "Don't you ever get tired of being an asshole?"

That was it. He'd hit his limit. "You know what? You can sit here and whine all you damn want, but I am *not* going to have you talk to me like that! You talk about wanting to be treated like a grown-up and yet you're acting like a baby right now! You want to go to a party tonight? Well, forget it. Not gonna happen. You can sit up in your room and scream and cry and call me every damn name in the book. But in the end, you'll still be sitting in your room. There's a storm moving in, and I know for damn sure that Dad did not say you could go."

Darcy glared at him and silently cursed him to hell. She wouldn't give him the pleasure of seeing her cry. Instead, she spun around and walked calmly to her room. Once her door was closed and locked, she began to formulate a plan.

"Who does he think he's kidding?" she murmured, pulling a change of clothes out of her closet. "That was an Oscar-worthy performance and now he'll sit down there and not bother to check on me for hours. So stupid." Stuffing the clothes into a satchel, she grabbed her phone from her nightstand and called her best friend Chrissy. When she answered, Darcy said, "I'll be there, but I need you to pick me up down the block."

Fifteen minutes later, she shimmied out her bedroom window and gave the house a one-fingered salute. "Screw you, Aidan."

"So this is a tropical storm," Zoe said later that night as she looked out her window. Seemed like just rain and wind to her, nothing to get in a huff about. Turning away from the window, she looked around the apartment. There were boxes everywhere and it was depressing. Her Chinese takeout had gone cold and she was bored out of her mind.

There was only so much packing she could do in one night, and the thought of turning on the television was equally unappealing. "Maybe I should read," she murmured and went in search of her Kindle. "I could read about other people's lives and how they all get their happily ever afters. Only in books do those things exist." But still, she curled up on the sofa and indulged just for the sake of something to do.

When her phone rang later on, Zoe was amazed to see how late it was. Almost eleven. "At this rate, I can go to bed and call it a day." The phone rang again and reminded her why she couldn't go to sleep just yet. The number wasn't familiar but she answered anyway. "Hello?"

"Zoe?" a small voice said on the other end.

"Darcy? Is that you?"

"Can you come and get me?" The reception was bad and her voice kept fading in and out. "…party… people drinking…"

"Sweetheart, where are you? What's going on? Have you called your father?"

"I…I can't…Aidan…fight…doesn't know…"

Her words were all broken up and Zoe had no idea what to do. "Okay, okay, text me the address because I can barely hear you and I'll be there soon, all right?" The line went dead and for a minute Zoe feared that Darcy hadn't heard her words. But a minute later her phone beeped with an incoming text and she sighed with relief.

Zoe really didn't want to get involved, but she didn't want Darcy to be stranded someplace. With nothing left to do, she called Aidan. He may not like it, but it was his family and his problem to deal with.

Just like he wanted.

The call went directly to voice mail and Zoe cursed. Of course there was a possibility that he really was on the other line or that his phone was off, but she couldn't help but be annoyed at the thought that maybe he was purposely not answering her call. Not leaving a message, she dialed Ian's number. The answering machine picked up, and this time she decided to leave a message. Where the heck were they?

"Ian, it's Zoe. I just got a call from Darcy and I'm

really concerned for her. I'm going to go pick her up. The weather's really bad and I was hoping to reach you or Aidan, but I can't seem to get either of you on the phone. I just wanted you to know that I'm going to get her and I'll bring her home as soon as I can, okay? Um…okay. Bye."

Five minutes later, she wondered what the hell she had been thinking. The storm was pretty fierce and even with her windshield wipers on full blast, it was hard to see. The GPS on her phone was guiding her to the address, but it was slow-moving on the roads at best. "I need to get my head examined," she muttered. "This is so not my problem."

And she could keep saying it, but the reality was, she felt bad for Darcy and there was no way she was going to leave her in a potentially dangerous situation. Aidan could be as pissed as he wanted to be, but Zoe knew she wouldn't be able to live with herself if anything happened to Darcy and she hadn't done anything to prevent it.

Turning down the road the GPS directed her to, Zoe noted all of the cars lining it and the number of teenagers walking in the rain. Didn't these kids have parents?

Her car was moving at a slow crawl as she maneuvered between the parked cars and the teens. Visibility was next to nil, but she heaved a sigh of relief when the road opened up again. Looking out the side window, Zoe strained to see a house number on a mailbox. She had no idea just exactly where this house was. Her car moved slightly to the left and the next thing she knew, there were headlights coming right for her.

She felt a moment of panic, and then everything

seemed to happen in slow motion. Frantically, she tried to accelerate and move out of the way, but the oncoming car was swerving all over the road and before she knew what was happening, the force of the impact caused her head to smash on the steering wheel and everything went black.

—•—

"Ohmigod, ohmigod, ohmigod," Darcy yelled as she desperately tried to pull open the door to Zoe's car. "*Zoe!*" She pounded on the window. "Zoe, please wake up! Please!" Sirens blared in the distance and people were trying to pull her away from the car, but Darcy was nearly hysterical.

The police car showed up first and she almost sagged to the ground at the sight of Bobby Hannigan. "*Bobby!*" she screamed. "Zoe's in there! You've got to get her out!"

He was completely in work mode, and he had his partner take Darcy aside while he figured out what had happened. It looked like the other car had hit Zoe's. The kid who'd been driving seemed okay, a little banged up and more than a little drunk, but at least he was all right. Zoe, on the other hand, wasn't moving. "Shit," he muttered and tried to open her smashed-in driver-side door.

Another round of sirens blared and Bobby knew backup was here to help. He gave the fire and rescue crew a rundown of the situation and then stepped aside and walked over to Darcy. "Are you hurt?" he asked her.

She shook her head furiously.

"Why didn't you call your father or your brother?" he asked, even though he had a sneaking suspicion what she was going to say.

"I…I…" she stammered. "I wasn't supposed to be here. I wanted to leave but everyone was drinking. I called Zoe and she was coming to get me and now…" She broke down in tears.

Bobby took pity on her and pulled her into his embrace before pulling out his phone. "I have to call your dad, Darce," he said solemnly. "You were at a party with underage drinking and you know he's going to have a fit."

She nodded. "I know. I know." She looked beyond him to what was going on with Zoe's car. "Are they going to get her out? Is she going to be okay?"

"I don't know, kiddo. I honestly don't know. They'll get her out and get her to the hospital, but I have no idea what kind of injuries she has." He looked over and saw that the paramedics were carefully removing her from the car and had her stabilized on a board.

"Can I ride with her?" Darcy asked. "Please?"

Indecision warred within him but in the end, he hauled her over to the ambulance. "Take her too. They're together," he said to the paramedic and stood back as they helped Darcy inside and quickly pulled away. Bobby looked at the phone in his hands and quickly put a call in to Ian Shaughnessy before taking care of the rest of the scene.

~~~

Darcy was pacing in the emergency room an hour later when her father and Aidan came rushing through the door. She ran into her father's arms and burst into tears. "I'm sorry!" she sobbed. "I'm so sorry!"

Ian held on tight to his daughter, almost falling to his knees with relief that she was all right. "You're okay?" he finally asked. "Are you hurt? When Bobby called and said you were on your way to the hospital…" He choked back a sob. "He told me you were fine, but I thought…I thought something had happened to you. I didn't even let him tell me what had happened." He cupped her face in his hands, his eyes welling with tears. "You scared the hell out of me, young lady. Don't you know that I would die if something happened to you?" Before she could answer, Ian pulled her in close again.

And just held her.

Beside them, Aidan was trying to decide whether to hug his sister or throttle her. He was beyond relieved that she was all right, but she had easily scared about ten years off his life. "We were out looking for you," he snapped. "When I realized you weren't in your room, I called Dad and we've been driving around for hours trying to find you. Why didn't you call?"

"What happened?" Ian asked, still refusing to let his daughter go. "How did you end up here?"

Tears were streaming down Darcy's cheeks. "I wanted to come home. I really did. But everyone had been drinking and the storm was getting worse so…" She looked nervously at Aidan and then back to her father. "I called Zoe to come and get me."

"*What?!*" Aidan yelled. Moving his father aside, he took his sister by the shoulders and shook her. "What happened?" He had seen the missed call from Zoe on his phone and now he felt like crap for ignoring it and not calling her back.

Darcy was nearly hysterical and had to try to catch her breath before she could speak. "I…I…"

Bobby Hannigan walked in at that moment and came up to them. "Hey, Aidan. Ian." He turned to Darcy. "Any word on Zoe yet?"

Aidan's eyes were wild as he looked from his sister to Bobby and back again. "What happened to Zoe? Where is she?"

"The…the doctors haven't come out yet. I…I told the nurses I was waiting, but no one's come out yet," Darcy said, her voice shaking.

"I'll go see what I can find," Bobby said as he walked away.

"Aidan," Darcy began, "I'm…I'm sorry. I shouldn't have left. I know it was wrong and…"

Inside, Aidan was seething with rage, but as much as he wanted to direct it all at Darcy right now, he knew that wasn't going to help the situation at all. "I'm really disappointed in you," he said instead. "How… Why didn't you call me?"

"I really thought I'd be able to sneak back in without you knowing. Zoe was coming for me and…I guess I didn't think beyond that." Tears welled up in her eyes again as her lip trembled. "I didn't think anything would happen to Zoe."

Aidan had to force himself to mentally count to ten before speaking again. Taking a deep breath, he asked, "What happened to Zoe?"

"I…I'm not sure. I rode in the ambulance with her, but no one would tell me anything."

He cursed under his breath and turned away, torn between wanting to shake his sister and wanting to force his way into the triage area and see for himself that Zoe was all right.

"I said I was sorry, Aidan," she cried. "I didn't mean for Zoe to get hurt!"

That's just it, Darce, he thought angrily, *you didn't think at all.* He turned and walked away and then strode back to her. His eyes bore into her and he knew she was already beating herself up for all of this. His yelling at her wasn't going to change the situation. If anything, he'd just make it worse. Unfortunately, his brain and his mouth weren't working together. "You better hope—"

"That's enough, Aidan," Ian said, effectively cutting Aidan off as he led Darcy, who was sobbing uncontrollably again, to one of the sofas in the waiting area.

Aidan paced back and forth for what seemed like forever until Bobby came back over. "Well? What did they say?"

"She's got a concussion and some bruised ribs. Luckily her air bag deployed and saved her from anything worse. It looks like she hit the steering wheel before it went off, and then hit her head on the door when the kid hit her." He paused and shook his head. "I gotta be honest with you, I'm surprised it's not worse. Her car was a mess."

He couldn't even think about it. It was all too much. "Are they keeping her here?"

Bobby nodded. "Overnight at least. She's awake and I'm going to go back and talk to her. Do you want to go with me?"

More than anything, Aidan wanted to, but he shook

his head. "No. No, you talk to her. I don't think she needs or wants to see me right now." Before he could change his mind, he took a step back. "Is it all right if we take Darcy home?"

"Yeah, sure. If I need to get any information from her, I'll come by the house tomorrow and do it if that's okay."

"Sure. Yeah, that's fine." He shook Bobby's hand and walked over to where his father and Darcy were sitting. They were sitting close together and while Darcy was still crying, it wasn't nearly as intense as it had been a few minutes ago.

Taking a minute, Aidan thought about everything that had led them to this moment. For months he had been so intent on keeping Zoe away from his family because of her changing the dynamics. But had she? Not really. If anything, she'd made things…better. Then he thought about himself and his family and what they'd all done— particularly to Zoe.

And then he cursed and was forced to see things for the way they really were: maybe he should have reversed the whole concern thing. He'd been so wrapped up in protecting his family from Zoe that he'd failed to protect Zoe from all of them.

Well, damn.

With a quick look over his shoulder, he gave serious thought to going back and just seeing her. Just one look so he could be certain she was okay. But he couldn't. The thought of seeing her injured and knowing he hadn't been able to help her was too much for him to bear. "C'mon. Let's go home," he said, his voice void of emotion.

"I want to see Zoe," Darcy wailed.

"Maybe tomorrow, sweetheart," Ian said quietly, holding her close.

"I need to make sure she's okay. I want to make sure she doesn't hate me!"

"Tomorrow, Darce," he said.

The three of them walked toward the exit when Ian stopped in his tracks.

"What is it? What's the matter, Dad?" Darcy asked.

Ian pointed to the solarium just inside the doorway.

"What? What are we looking at?"

Father and son looked at each other. "Well, I'll be," Ian said with wonder.

In the middle of the lush greenery and flowers stood a single daisy.

Chapter 13

"You are the worst patient ever."

"Technically, I'm not your patient," Zoe said. "But if we're going to go there, what kind of nurse eats all of the cookies without offering the patient any?"

Anna looked sheepish. "Okay, fine. I'm a bad nurse."

"And in case you haven't noticed, I don't really need a nurse. I need some Advil for this headache, but other than that, I'm fine. It's been a week. I'm good."

"Are you sure? Because it looks to me like you're still favoring your ribs."

Zoe rolled her eyes. "Tell you what. Let me smash a car into you and tell me how you feel a week later. How's that?"

"Sarcasm really doesn't suit you," she said with a smirk.

"Yeah, well…it's all I've got right now."

"Oh, come on. You know you've got more than that. Aidan has already fired three of the decorators Martha sent to replace you. You can't tell me you didn't feel the least bit gratified by Martha telling the whole town that 'Zoe is the only person in the business who was able to tame big, bad Aidan Shaughnessy,'" Anna said, putting on Martha's voice. "Admit it."

Zoe gave a wicked little smile. "All right. That did make me feel good." It felt better than good, actually. Not the getting more people fired part—that was all on

Aidan—but there was nothing like your boss praising you in public.

"And you're going out to dinner with me and Bobby tomorrow night." She gave a cocky smile. "And let me tell you, people for miles around will be jealous."

"Seriously? I think you overestimate the Hannigan appeal."

"So snarky," Anna said with a sigh.

"Yeah, yeah…I'm a mean girl. I know."

"How did it go with Ian and Darcy yesterday? I heard they came by to visit."

Zoe couldn't help but smile. "Darcy has called me at least three times a day to check on me and texts me almost hourly. She'd been wanting to come over for a while now but yesterday was the first time that Ian allowed it."

"I wonder why," Anna said.

With a shrug, Zoe said, "I think he was embarrassed and he feels bad about what happened and wanted to make sure that I really wanted them to come over."

"Oh, like you'd hold a grudge," Anna said, standing up to get them both something to drink.

"It wasn't her fault. It could have happened anywhere. It just sucks that it happened the way it did."

"You're far too forgiving." Sitting back down, Anna handed Zoe a bottle of water. "You know that I love the Shaughnessys and how I sympathize with Darcy, but what she did was wrong. I practically had to tie Quinn down to keep him from going over there."

"Like you would have minded that," Zoe said with a sly grin.

"Wait…what?" The blush flaming Anna's cheeks

did not help her innocent declarations. "What are you talking about?"

"You know, we've spent an awful lot of time putting me and Aidan under the microscope, but I think we can put that to rest and maybe focus on you and Quinn. Admit it, you would not have minded tying him up… and keeping him there."

"You're crazy," she protested but couldn't look Zoe in the eye.

"I don't get it. What are you waiting for?"

Anna finally raised her gaze to meet Zoe's. "We've been friends since we were six. He doesn't see me as a woman; he sees me as his friend, his buddy, his pal. Look at me! I dress in jeans and T-shirts. Whenever I put on a dress, he's the first one to make fun of me. It's my own fault for crushing on him, the big jerk."

"Yeah, well…I guess the jerkiness is genetic."

"Hmm…maybe," Anna said and finished off her water. A quick glance at her watch showed that it was time to go. "I've got the dinner shift at the pub so I have to go. Do you need anything?"

Zoe waved her off. "Seriously, I'm good. Have a good night and I'll see you and Bobby tomorrow night, okay?"

"Sounds good."

<center>~~~</center>

Best laid plans and all… Zoe thought.

"So…Anna got called in to work," Bobby said apologetically as he stood in the doorway of Zoe's apartment. "It's just going to be you and me. I hope you're okay with that."

It was a bit strange to Zoe but…

"She's going to try to join us for dessert if she can get someone to cover for her. They're just shorthanded and I really did want to take you out before you left. You've been a great friend to Anna and she is positively gaga over what you did to the house for her."

Zoe couldn't help but smile. "Are you sure? We can just get some takeout and hang out. There's no need to go out if you don't want to."

"Are you kidding me? This place has the best steaks in the area. I've been waiting all week for tonight."

She laughed. "I enjoy a good steak too. Let me just grab my purse and we can go."

It took about twenty minutes to get to the restaurant, and Zoe was glad she had dressed up a bit. Her little black dress and heels were the perfect outfit for such a place. It looked like an old Southern plantation home from the outside, but once you walked through the front doors, it was a magnificent restaurant. "This is amazing," she said to Bobby as they walked in.

"I'm not usually one for dressing up for dinner and dancing and all that, but the food here is just incredible. I know Anna's disappointed to be missing it."

"Maybe we should bring her something if she doesn't make it," Zoe suggested.

"Sounds like a plan to me," Bobby said as he held out a chair for her at their table.

"Thank you." It was surprising to realize just how much she and Bobby Hannigan had in common. They talked about current events and movies and books while they looked at the menu, and Zoe was almost sorry she hadn't taken the time to get to know him better before now.

"Are you all ready for the move?" he asked after the waitress had taken their orders.

"I think so. I was going to get one of those pods that you pack up yourself and they move it for you, but there was no place to put the pod by the apartment. Since I don't have any furniture to move and my car is totaled, I'm going to just rent a truck myself and do the drive on my own."

"Damn, Zoe, that's a lot of driving to do by yourself. Plus, it's not really safe to do it on your own. Isn't there another option?"

"It's not a big deal, really. I'm not in a rush to get back to Arizona, so I can take my time and do it safely."

"*Oh my God!* I can't believe you're here!"

Zoe looked up to see Darcy practically running across the restaurant to get to her. Zoe jumped up to hug her and almost got knocked to the ground with Darcy's enthusiasm.

"Hey! What are you doing here?"

"It's my birthday!" she said proudly. "Eighteen. Finally!" She looked over her shoulder. "All of my brothers are here to celebrate—even Riley came home from his tour!—and we're here for dinner because it's my favorite restaurant. What are you doing here?"

"I'm…I'm having dinner with Bobby," she said, her voice trembling only slightly.

Bobby stepped up beside her and put an arm around her waist, which Zoe did not expect.

"Sort of a going-away thing," Bobby said. "You know that Zoe's leaving next week, right?"

Darcy nodded sadly. "I really wish that you weren't."

Zoe was just about to comment when Ian walked over

with the rest of the Shaughnessys behind him. He hugged her and asked how she was feeling before introducing her to the sons she hadn't met before. "This is my son Hugh, the world traveler. We managed to steal him away from his fancy hotels to bring him home for dinner."

"Hi," Zoe said shyly. Even though he was younger, he was bigger than Aidan and much more polished. But when he smiled, well…she could only imagine there was a trail of women who would do anything to have him smile at them like that. "Nice to meet you."

"Same here," he said, taking her hand in his. "I hear you helped Darcy out last week. I can't thank you enough. Not many people would go out in a storm like that."

Zoe blushed. "She's a friend and she needed help. It wasn't a big deal."

"I'm not so sure about that," he said and then turned to Bobby. "Bobby Hannigan! How the hell are you, Mr. Big-Time-City-Cop?" They shook hands and laughed.

"Knock it off. Although I believe that's a better title than when you were home last time and called me Opie." They laughed and then Ian stepped forward again.

"And this is my son Riley. I don't suppose he needs more of an introduction than that."

Rather than shake Zoe's hand, Riley Shaughnessy reached out and lifted her hand to his lips and kissed it. "It's a pleasure to finally meet you, Zoe," he said softly.

The giggle that escaped her was almost embarrassing. She was only human. "It's nice to meet you too," she managed to say.

"Good to see you, Bobby," Riley said without releasing Zoe's hand.

"Same here, Riley. Let me know how long you're going to be in town, so I'll know if we need extra hands on deck to keep you safe from rabid fans."

They laughed until Quinn stepped forward. "I thought Anna was going to be with you? Where is she?"

Bobby looked at Quinn with annoyance. "She's at work. She got called in at the last minute."

"Oh," he said with a frown.

"Mr. Shaughnessy?" A petite blond waitress walked over and addressed Ian. "Your table is ready if you'd like to follow me."

Everyone said good-bye except for Aidan, who had stayed back and watched. His chest actually ached and he'd felt himself fill with rage when Bobby had stood up and put his arm around Zoe like he had every right to. That was why he stood back; beating the crap out of a cop, not to mention a friend, in the middle of a restaurant was not a good idea. Didn't mean he wasn't tempted.

Once they had all walked away, Zoe and Bobby sat back down. "Okay…where were we?" Bobby asked as he nervously looked around, certain that daggers were being shot at his back.

"My driving to Arizona alone." *Damn it! Why would you bring that up again?* she cursed herself. "I'll be fine. I can drive it conservatively in about four days. I have GPS and AAA and it will be good, like an adventure."

"Like staying in your house during the storm was going to be an adventure?"

"That's just the cop in you talking."

"Doesn't mean that I'm not right."

Well, damn. This was not the pleasant conversation she had been hoping for. "Okay, enough about me. Tell me about you. Other than being a cop and being Anna's brother." She stopped and decided to change the direction. "What's the deal with you and Quinn? You seemed tense when he was here a minute ago."

"What do you mean?"

Zoe shot him a pointed gaze before arching a brow at him. "Really?"

Bobby swiped a hand down his face and slouched in his chair. "I'm not blind," he said. "I know Anna has this…crush on him." He rolled his eyes like he couldn't even believe it. "She does everything for him—goes with him to parties and events when he needs a date, cooks for him, brings him food when he's working late, and he does nothing for her. Sometimes I just wish he'd step out of line, law-wise, just so I can get my hands on him."

"Hmm… Does Anna know you feel like this?"

He shook his head. "I usually play dumb, but I notice these things and I'm logging it all away for the right time. All he needs to do is just make one mistake and I'm going to be all over him like white on rice."

They were saved from continuing this particular conversation when their salads arrived. Deciding that a more neutral topic of conversation was in order, Zoe talked a lot about the differences in food between coastal North Carolina and back home in Arizona. They continued that discussion through dinner, when they expanded it to include all of the places Bobby had visited in his travels up and down the East Coast.

Once dinner was completed, he stood and held out a hand to her. "Want to dance?"

Zoe's eyes went wide at the question. Did she? No

one had ever taken her dancing before. Her ribs were
still sore, but she knew they weren't going to be doing
anything wild here in the classy restaurant and decided
to throw caution to the wind. "Sure. Why not?" Putting
her hand in Bobby's, they walked out to the dance floor
and joined several other couples who were slow dancing
to the bluesy jazz group that was playing.

"This is nice," she said after a few minutes.

"Yeah, it is. I normally only come here with Anna,
and believe me, we don't dance with each other. That
would be weird."

Zoe laughed. "Well, if it's any consolation, you're a
very good dancer." They smiled at one another and just
swayed to the music and enjoyed what was being played
until Zoe felt a buzz against her hip. She jumped back
and then chuckled when Bobby reached for his phone.

"Sorry," he said softly as he put the phone to his ear
and frowned. "I'm so sorry, Zoe, but I've got to go.
It's an emergency, police business, and…" He looked
at her, then his watch and then for their waitress. "I…
damn it…"

"Okay, look, I understand. You've got to go. I don't
want to endanger anyone because you were delayed
with getting me home. Go. I'll be fine."

"No, no…I brought you here and I should at
least pay…"

"May I cut in?" Zoe turned to see Hugh Shaughnessy
standing behind her with that killer smile on his face.

"Oh, well, actually, I think we have to leave," Zoe
said apologetically. "Bobby just got a police call. I'm
going to call a cab so he can go." She turned to Bobby.
"Go. Really. It's okay."

"I'm so sorry, Zoe. I'll take care of the check and… Really, I can drop you off. We just need to go and—"

"There's no time. Stop worrying about me and just go."

"I'll make sure she gets home okay, Bobby," Hugh said.

Bobby shook Hugh's hand before he darted across the room.

"So, how about that dance?" Hugh asked.

The last thing Zoe wanted was for anyone to think that her pseudo-date had run out on her, and on top of that, she certainly didn't want to be here dancing with one of Aidan's brothers. "It's okay, Hugh. I really should call a cab."

"Oh, come on. I've heard so much about you that I really want to just take a few minutes and talk to you. C'mon, Zoe. One dance and I'll call the cab myself, if you'd like."

That smile of his did her in. *They were lethal, this family,* she thought. Stepping into his loose embrace, they began to sway to the music.

"Darcy has not stopped talking about you in weeks."

"She's a great girl. I imagine it's not easy being the only one in such a large family of boys."

"She holds her own. We tend to forget that she's never had an adult woman around to help her with, you know, girl things. The fact that you made some curtains and pillows for her room made her feel like some sort of princess. It was a big wake-up call for all of us that she isn't a tomboy." He looked down at her and smiled. "So thank you. For everything."

Zoe felt herself blush. "It really wasn't a big deal. It's

what I do for a living, and just the fact that she was so excited about it made it all worthwhile."

"Well, you've made a big impression on her. And that was before you came to her rescue the night of the party."

Zoe looked down at her feet. "Some rescue. I ended up making things worse for her."

Hugh reached down and tucked a finger under Zoe's chin to make her look up at him. "Hey, you ended up risking your life for her and got hurt in the process. I hate that it happened like that, but you have no idea the lesson you taught her. So again, thank you."

"May I have the next dance?" They looked over to see Riley standing there, that famous sexy grin he was known for spreading across his face. Zoe could see the family resemblance, but he was more of a hipster than the rest of them.

"Be my guest," Hugh said and kissed Zoe on the cheek. "Thank you for the dance. It was a pleasure meeting you."

"So, how are you feeling?" Riley asked when they finally settled in to the music. "I hear you got a bit banged up saving Darcy from herself."

Zoe's head was spinning by the time Riley took her in his arms and spun her around the dance floor. Not that she didn't appreciate everyone's concern, but she was getting tired of telling the same story. "I'm fine, I'm fine. Luckily the kid wasn't going that fast. But what about you?" She looked around the room. "How is it that one of the biggest rock stars in the world is dancing in the middle of a crowded restaurant and no one is bothering him?"

He laughed, a full and throaty sound coming from him. "I'm old news around here. This is probably the only place I can come to without getting into too much trouble. It's kind of nice."

"How often do you come home?"

"Not as often as I should," he said with a shrug. "With everything that's happened lately, it's sort of come to light how much we all need to reevaluate our lives. Darcy's growing up, and it's about time that Dad got out and started socializing and doing something more than just being a dad."

"I'm sure he doesn't mind that role at all."

"Maybe. But we can all help out, especially once Darcy goes off to school. He'll have empty-nest syndrome or something."

Zoe's eyes went wide. "Does that…does that mean that she's going to school out of state?"

Riley chuckled. "It means that we're more open to the possibility. I think that's all she really wanted, you know? She just wanted to know that she was allowed to choose. She may stay close to home or she could move across the country, but either way, she has a choice."

Zoe almost sagged with relief. "I'm so glad. That's awesome." The music came to an end and the band announced they were going to take a short break. "Thanks for the dance, Riley. And it was really nice meeting you." She held out a hand to shake his and giggled again when he kissed her hand instead. "I'd better call that cab."

"Don't be silly. Come and join us. They're getting ready to bring out the cake. Darcy would love it, and we'll take you home. It took three cars to get us all here, so I'm sure that we can fit you in one of them to get home."

She shook her head firmly. "Sorry. No. I need to get going."

"Please stay," he said softly, a slow smile crossing his lips.

"Really…I…I can't. Thank you for the offer and please wish Darcy a happy birthday for me, but I have to go." Rushing off the dance floor, Zoe got back to the table and fumbled for her purse.

"Can I get you anything else?" The waitress appeared next to the table as Zoe was collecting her things.

"Actually, I need to call for a cab," Zoe whispered.

"Follow me," the waitress said. "We have a list of cab companies up by the podium."

Well, that's a relief, Zoe thought. She'd figured the restaurant would keep a list of trustworthy cabs for their clientele. "Thank you."

After making the call, she sat in the lobby and waited. When she looked at her watch and saw it would be at least another ten minutes, she decided to run to the ladies room to kill some time. She washed her hands and checked her hair and makeup and tried to ignore the sadness in her eyes. She'd had a lovely dinner with a friend and had finally gone dancing—and had three incredibly handsome dance partners including one of the biggest rock stars in the world—and yet all she wanted to do was go home, put on her pajamas, curl up in a ball, and cry.

Forcing the negative thoughts away for the time being, she stepped out of the ladies room and the maître d' announced that her cab was waiting. She thanked him and walked outside and looked around.

And saw Aidan standing between her and the cab.

"Hi," he said.

She couldn't have spoken even if she'd wanted to. Her mouth had gone completely dry, and she was shaking like a leaf. With a simple nod of her head, Zoe figured she conveyed her greeting. She cautiously stepped forward and hoped she'd be able to simply walk around him, get in the cab, and leave.

"I hear Bobby got called away."

"Mm-hm," she said and did her best to keep her eyes on the cab. Just a few more feet...

"Riley said he invited you to join us. There's more than enough room at the table and Darcy would have loved it. Why didn't you?"

Was he serious? She halted in her tracks and turned to face him. "You did *not* really just ask that question."

"Actually," he said mildly, "I believe I did."

"You... I just..." She let out shriek of frustration. "Look, you told me to stay away from your family and I have. I was respecting your wishes. Now if you'll excuse me, I'm sure the meter is already running."

"Tell the driver he can leave. I'll take you home," he said, placing his hands in his pockets.

"Why?" she asked and it was almost a sob. "Damn it, Aidan, what are you doing out here?"

"Bobby should have taken you home. What kind of man leaves a woman at a restaurant to call a cab to take her home?"

"It was *police business* and I didn't want to hold him up," she said. "There was no time for him to drive me home and get to whatever emergency it was that they needed him for. So if you'll excuse me, *again,* my cab is waiting."

"I'll take you home."

Zoe was two steps away, her hand reaching for the door handle when he said it, and she slowly turned around and faced him. It took almost a full minute before she could force herself to respond. And it was with a laugh, a near-hysterical laugh. "You're kidding, right?"

He shook his head. "Mmm…no."

"I don't think so." She turned to open the cab door when he reached out and gently grasped one of her wrists to stop her. Unable to help herself, Zoe swung around and shoved his hand off her, but the twisting motion hurt her ribs and made her to cry out in pain.

"Damn you, Aidan. Just…just leave me alone!" Wrapping one arm around her middle, she once again turned toward the cab but Aidan stepped in front of her and put his arm around her waist and just held it there.

"Why?" she asked, cursing the tremble in her voice. "Why couldn't you just stay inside and leave me alone?"

He took a deep breath, his eyes searching hers. "Please let me drive you home, Zoe," he said quietly. "Please."

She was too tired to argue and now she was mildly in pain. "Fine." She sighed and stepped back as he leaned into the cab and paid the driver and sent him on his way. A minute later he quietly led her to his truck. He helped her to climb in before walking around and settling in behind the wheel. "What about your family? Won't they wonder where you went?"

"Maybe," he replied and left it at that.

They drove the entire way to her apartment in silence. It was the most awkward twenty minutes of Zoe's life, and she sagged with relief when her building came into view. Aidan did a U-turn so she would be climbing out right by her door. He came to a stop and Zoe's hand immediately went to the door handle so she could make a quick escape.

But Aidan was quicker.

As soon as her feet hit the pavement, he was there in front of her. He guided her away from the truck and closed the door. "Are you okay?" he asked.

"I'm fine," she said, refusing to make eye contact with him. "Thank you for the ride home. I appreciate it." It killed her to even have to say it. She would have appreciated it more if he had let her take the cab home like she had planned, but there was no point in splitting hairs about it now.

"Can I…" he began and then cleared his voice. "I would like to take you out for coffee sometime, if that's all right with you."

This time she did look up at him. "I'm moving back to Arizona next week. I have a lot to do before I go."

"Oh," he said quietly. "I didn't realize that was actually happening."

She nodded. "It is." Looking over toward her door, she struggled for something to say. "So…yeah. Thanks again for the ride and…take care of yourself." Not wanting to engage in any more conversation, she turned toward the door and looked up to her windows and froze.

"What's the matter?" Aidan asked, noticing the direction of Zoe's stare.

"I turned off all the lights when I left," she said distractedly. "I'm sure of it." Turning to look at him, she pointed at the window. "I'm not crazy, right? There's light coming from my apartment."

Aidan stepped up behind her and looked up. "There's definitely a light on up there." He shrugged. "You probably just forgot one."

She turned around with annoyance. "I did not forget to turn off the lights, Aidan. I'm positive of it." Reaching into her purse, she pulled out her phone.

"What are you doing?"

"If someone broke in, I'm going to call the police."

"Zoe, you don't know that someone broke in. C'mon. I'll go upstairs with you and if someone broke in, I'll wait with you until the cops come, okay?"

She was more willing to take a risk with a burglar than she was with him, but it was obvious he wasn't going to just leave. "Fine. Here." She handed him her keys and let him go inside first. They made it through the main floor door and then walked up the stairs to the second door. "Wait," Zoe whispered as he was about to put the key in the lock. "Do you hear that?"

"Hear what?"

"Open the door," she said quickly. "There's noise coming from inside. Voices. Like the TV or the radio or something."

Aidan opened the door and stepped aside as Zoe rushed by him.

And stopped in her tracks.

"What the...? How...?" Turning, she looked at him. "I don't understand." The entire room was bathed in candlelight and there was soft music coming from the stereo that she had sworn she'd packed already. "Who would do this?"

Quietly, Aidan closed the door behind him, walked up behind her, took her purse from her hands, and put it on the nearest table along with her phone. Zoe was still standing there, lost in confusion, when he came up behind her and slowly wrapped his arms around her waist.

And began to sway to the music.

She stiffened in his arms before slowly turning her head around to look at him. The question was stuck in her throat at the expression on his face. Her eyes went wide as he maneuvered them until she was facing him and they were actually dancing to the slow music playing in the corner.

"Why?" she whispered, her gaze looking less guarded as it washed over his face.

Aidan gripped her tighter, bringing her closer to him. "It occurred to me that I never did give you that candlelight," he said quietly, his blue eyes watching hers. "Or took you dancing. I should have."

A shaky sigh escaped before she could stop it. "Oh." With a sigh, she melted against him, luxuriating in the feel of being in his arms. Part of her argued that she should be mad at him and not make this easy, but another part—the part that was all girly and glowing from this romantic gesture—told her to shut up and just enjoy being close to him again.

Zoe lost track of time and had no idea how long they just swayed to the music. Aidan's hand was splayed across her lower back and every once in a while, she'd feel him kiss her gently on her temple. Looking around the room, she finally allowed herself to take in the scene—there were close to a hundred white candles scattered around the room along with bouquets of flowers, tons of them.

The music finally stopped playing, and she lifted her head from his shoulder and looked at him, really looked at him. "This was pretty romantic of you," she said softly, a hint of a smile on her lips.

"Well, I can't take all of the credit," he said, smiling down at her, still swaying even though the music had stopped.

"No?"

He shook his head. "Someone gave me the idea about the candles a while ago. I just didn't listen."

"Silly man."

"I can see that now." Taking a fortifying breath, Aidan placed both of his hands on Zoe's hips and put some distance between them. "I'm so sorry, Zoe. For everything." He looked down at the ground before looking at her again. "I have no excuse for the way I behaved. I know I hurt you and I was wrong. Tell me I'm not too late. Tell me I haven't ruined everything."

Her mind was racing. It was sensual sensory overload—the candles, the flowers…Aidan… Deep down, Zoe knew she didn't really want to leave. It was the thought of being close to Aidan and not being able to be with him that was making her run. But the thought of trusting him again…trusting *them* again… It wasn't as easy a decision as she would have thought.

A sense of panic overcame Aidan. He knew he was taking a risk with this tonight, but he'd needed to get his head together before approaching her. Never in a million years had he imagined that Zoe would move back to Arizona. Maybe he'd rushed into this or maybe he didn't act fast enough; all he knew was that her leaving and not being with him wasn't an option.

"What…what about your family?"

He shook his head. "They all love you. I panicked. For so long, it's only been us—me, my dad, my brothers, and Darcy. I didn't know how to react when someone else was added to the equation. I was… I'm not good with change. But I've been spending a lot of time by myself thinking and…I can finally see that change can be a good thing."

"I used to think so too," she said quietly. "But all the things I tried to change didn't work out so well."

"I know and I'm sorry. I take the blame for a lot of that. I know I can't change the past or the things I said, but…I want you to know that if I could, I would."

"Aidan…"

"I'm not perfect, Zoe. There are going to be times when I mess up and I say stupid things, but…I don't want you to go. Please. You once asked me what would happen a couple of months from now and six months from now and a year from now. I didn't have an answer then…or at least I thought I didn't. The truth is, the answer to all of those is that I want to be with you. Don't leave me." He rested his forehead against hers. "Please don't leave me."

"I…I…I'm already packed," she said lamely, still trying to process his words.

"So unpack," he countered.

"I've reserved the truck."

"Cancel the reservation."

Her mind scrambled to function, to say something he couldn't debate or argue. "I have a job waiting for me back in Arizona," she said, looking up at him dazedly.

"You have a job waiting for you here. Seriously, tell Martha to stop sending me incompetent people. There's only one designer I want to work with," he said with a sexy grin.

She couldn't help the smile that started to spread across her face. "I've given my notice here with the apartment, and Lisa's already rented it out. I'm homeless."

"Live with me," he said, his tone and his expression serious.

"The last time I was homeless you pretty much ran screaming from the building to make sure I understood that you weren't going to live with me. What's changed?"

"I'm not scared anymore. I love you."

Zoe's eyes went wide at his admission.

"I can't seem to remember a time when I wasn't in love with you." He shook his head. "I should have said it to you sooner. Hell, I should have said and done a lot of things sooner. And that day? That day when I told you we wouldn't be living together, I was scared, Zoe. So damn scared because my feelings for you were overwhelming. If I had been honest with myself, I would have said that I wanted to stay with you, that I didn't want you to find another place to live because you belonged with me."

"But—"

"I know I'm asking a lot of you. I'm asking you to forgive all of the things I said and the things I did, but if you'll just give me a chance to make it up to you, I promise to be a better man and to put you first."

"Wow." She sighed as everything inside of her melted. "That's some declaration."

"It's the truth." He skimmed a hand down her cheek, in awe of how soft her skin was.

"I don't need you to put me first, Aidan. I just need for you to not shut me out. That's all I really wanted." Zoe mimicked his pose and reached up to touch his face, caress his cheek and the strong line of his jaw. "And you don't need to be a better man. I think you're pretty amazing just as you are. Flaws and all. I don't need perfection." She paused. "Just promise me you're going to listen when I talk and try to realize that you don't have to take care of everyone. Let someone take care of you once in a while."

"Will you stay?" He hated how needy he sounded, how shaky his voice was, but he had to know that this was leading somewhere, somewhere he had put all of his hopes into.

For a minute, Zoe pretended to think about it. "So you're saying that I can unpack and cancel my moving truck…" Aidan nodded. "And that I have a job here and a place to live…" Again, Aidan nodded. "I don't know… It feels like I'm missing something." She was teasing him of course, but gasped when he dropped to one knee in front of her.

Reaching into his pocket, he pulled out a small black velvet box and opened it. "How about this?" he said softly. "This ring belonged to my mother. My father kept it and hoped someday one of his sons would give it to the woman he's going to marry. I love you, Zoe. I love to laugh with you, I love to work with you, and I even love to fight with you. You turned my whole world upside down and helped to put things into perspective. I don't want to live another day without you. Will you do me the honor of being my wife?"

Tears instantly sprang to Zoe's eyes as she sank down to her knees in front of him. "Aidan," she whispered, looking at him and then the ring. "I never thought… I didn't believe…"

"What? That I love you?" he asked and watched as she nodded. "Sweetheart, I promise you that I will make sure you know every day for the rest of your life that I love you and that you are everything to me." Taking her left hand in his, he held it and looked Zoe in the eyes. "Will you? Will you marry me?"

Unable to speak, Zoe nodded as tears began to freely flow. "Oh, Aidan…" She looked down at her hand. "It's beautiful. I love it." And then she looked up at him. "And I love you."

He almost sagged with relief. "For a minute there I was wondering if you were ever going to say it," he said with a lopsided grin.

"I do, Aidan. I love you."

With that, Aidan leaned forward, closing the distance between them, lowered Zoe to the floor, and finally kissed her. Her touch was so familiar, so comforting, it was like coming home. He kissed her until he almost couldn't breathe and even then, he only lifted his head long enough to take a breath.

"I've missed you so much," Zoe said when they finally broke apart.

"I've missed you too. I haven't been able to function at all without you."

She giggled. "So I heard."

Aidan made a face. "What's that supposed to mean?"

"Martha filled me in on what's been going on at the job site."

"You're a tough act to follow," he said, smiling down at her.

"Aidan?"

"Hmm?"

"I really hate to kill this romantic moment, but the floor is killing me," she said and then broke out in laughter. "Could we maybe move this to the couch or…" She didn't get to finish because he reached over and carefully scooped her up into his arms and walked toward her bed. "Oh, I like this plan much better."

"Occasionally I have good ideas," he said with a grin as he placed her down on the bed.

"Can I ask you something?" He nodded. "How did you manage to pull this off?"

For a minute, he hesitated. "I kind of had some help."

"Oh really," she said as she got comfortable on the bed. "From whom?"

"Pretty much everyone," he said with a grin. "Anna helped me with the candles and the flowers, and Bobby came back here and set it all up."

"How did he get… Wait a minute! Are you saying there wasn't any police emergency? That he made me look like an idiot whose date left her for no reason?"

"Well…I wouldn't say that. There was an emergency. It just wasn't police related."

"I really should be mad right now," she said with a fake pout. "A man of the law breaking and entering…I mean…really."

"Desperate times call for desperate measures," Aidan said as he kicked off his shoes. "Don't be mad. I wanted everything to be perfect when we got here. I wanted to surprise you."

She couldn't help but smile at him. "That you defi-nitely did." As she looked around the apartment, a sigh of contentment escaped her lips. "I love it. All of it."

"I'm glad."

On the bedside table was a vase filled with flowers. Zoe sat up and looked at them, reached out and touched some of the petals, and smiled—first at the arrangement and then at him. "Thank you for bringing happy flowers here tonight." Leaning forward, she inhaled the sweet fragrance. "They may not smell as nice as the roses, but they always make me smile."

Aidan smiled down at her and nodded. "Me too," he said, coming down beside her on the bed. "Me too."

Epilogue

Three months later

"I WANT YOU TO LOOK AROUND THIS HOUSE AND TELL me everything you see that's wrong."

The words were very familiar to Zoe. "Everything?"

Aidan turned and faced her, crossing his large arms across his chest and nodding. "I want you to start at the front door and walk through the entire house and tell me what's wrong."

Just as she had done once before, Zoe walked to the front door of the house and stood in the entryway. "Do your landlords want you to do something with the house before they sell it?"

"What makes you think this house is for sale?" he asked from across the room.

"C'mon, Aidan, it's completely empty. It's like one of your model homes. It doesn't look like anyone's ever lived here."

"They haven't."

Zoe walked over to him and put her hands on her hips. "Okay, you're not making any sense here. Why would someone buy a house and then never live in it?"

"I'll answer that after you do what I've asked you to do."

Rolling her eyes, Zoe walked back to the front door and opened it and then closed it. "The front door needs to be replaced. The property is beautiful and you'd want a door that allows you to look outside. This builder's-grade door is a boring stock item. It shouldn't even be here."

Aidan smiled as he watched her walk into the main living area and Zoe returned it. "And the white walls? Really? I would think on a custom house like this, color should have been discussed and put up on the walls as soon as the primer was dry."

"What colors would you pick?"

Zoe walked around the room; there were so many windows and the stone fireplace was to die for, she thought, touching all of the walls and trim. "The floors are even more beautiful than the ones in the first model home we did," she said absently as she crouched down to touch them. "The finish is darker, but they are just magnificent."

Standing, she looked around the room and started picturing it finished. "Write this down," she said and started calling out a list of all of the things she pictured for the room. It was coming to her faster than Aidan could type it into the tablet and she knew it and yet couldn't seem to stop herself. The vision was so clear and she could picture how it would look that it was almost overwhelming. "Are we staging it for sale? Is that what's going on?"

Aidan held up a hand to signify that he needed a minute to finish putting his notes in. When he looked up at her, he asked, "What about the walls? The trim? The doorways? Is everything level? Is everything plumb?"

Zoe carefully circled around and nodded. "I believe it is. Whoever the finishers were on this house, they did a fantastic job. You should use them on some of the homes you're doing now."

With a serene smile, he took her by the hand and led her up the stairs to the master bedroom. There were blinds on the windows and a king-size bed in the middle. Zoe turned and looked at him quizzically. "I thought you said no one's lived here."

"No one has." He nodded toward her feet. "Take off your shoes and feel this carpet. What do you think of it?"

It was an odd question, she thought, but did as he asked. "Oh…my…God…" she groaned. "This has got to be the cushiest carpet I've ever walked on. Wow." She curled her toes into it and purred with delight. "We have got to find out where they got this carpet because I am definitely going to want to install this in our place."

Leaning against one wall, Aidan said, "Okay, what about in here. Tell me what's wrong with this room."

"This carpet makes up for everything," she said but still walked around and looked and touched. "The white walls, obviously."

"Obviously," he agreed.

"It's a great size, the windows are fabulous, and although I'm not a huge fan of blinds, these are high quality and I believe we can work with them." With a half turn, she continued. "The bed is a good size for this room, and I think something with a massive headboard would look amazing. Normally a room this size could pull off a four-poster bed, but I'd rather feature the tray ceiling than the bed." And a minute later, a design came to mind and she had Aidan take notes again.

Five minutes later, she collapsed on the bed and looked over at Aidan and smiled. "Sometimes creativity can be exhausting." Aidan went and stretched out beside her and kissed her. "Easy there," she said against his lips. "No fooling around in a client's home."

"It's okay. I know the owners," he replied and reached for the top button of her blouse.

She swatted his hand away with a laugh. "Well, I don't," she said, trying to sit up. "I still feel weird about the whole model home thing. I'm not fooling around on someone's unused bed. That's just wrong."

Aidan pulled her back down and went directly to her buttons, and when she went to move his hands away again, he pinned them above her head. "What if I told you that we had permission to do it?"

She frowned and then made a face. "Eww…that's just…that's just wrong, Aidan. You told the owners we were going to do it in their house? Major ick factor."

"What if I told you that…*we* own this house? Technically then, you do know the owners and that would remove the ick factor." He waggled his eyebrows at her. "What do you say, Red? You up for christening the new house?"

"This is really our house? Like yours and mine?" Aidan nodded. "How…? When…?"

He shrugged. "I built the house over a year ago but couldn't make myself finish it. That's why I made the place over the garage, so I could come here and work on it and have a place to crash. Nothing felt…right. I already had a place in town by my dad, and this was just sort of a project for me that I knew I'd move in to someday." He picked up one of her hands and kissed her palm. "Turns out I'm ready for someday."

Her eyes softened at his words. "Me too." But then

in a swift move, she managed to roll away from him and off the bed.

"Hey!" He laughed. "What about christening the new house?"

"Oh, we'll get to that," she promised. "But first, I need to see the rest of it! Please! Can I?"

In that moment, he would give her anything she wanted.

"Is that a garden outside? I don't remember seeing it the last time we were here." Zoe peered out the window toward the back of the house.

Aidan shook his head. "I haven't gotten around to it," he said as he looked out the window over Zoe's shoulder. There was a patch of wildflowers off in the distance.

"You see what's out there, don't you?"

He did and he wrapped his arms around Zoe's waist and held her close. He had shared with her his theory on the daisies, and it just made the moment that much more perfect for him.

There were daisies in the field.

And he knew that his someday was ready to begin.

KEEP READING FOR AN EXCERPT FROM

Return *to* You

IN THE MONTGOMERY BROTHERS SERIES

THERE'S NOTHING LIKE A GOOD CHALLENGE TO PUT A LITTLE pep in your step and to get the heart pumping. In the last several years, William Montgomery had put a lot of pep in his step, and his heart had never felt better. Who knew matchmaking could be so rewarding? Getting his three sons married to their perfect matches had certainly been a challenge, but it was nothing compared to the one before him right now.

"Are we sure about this?" he asked cautiously as he scanned the file he held in his hands. William absolutely adored his role as the family matchmaker, but this particular situation was a little more sensitive. One look at his nephew, and he saw that it wasn't being taken lightly on his end either.

Ryder Montgomery nodded. "Believe me, it wasn't easy to get even that much information out of him. Luckily, James gets chatty after a couple shots of tequila."

William chuckled and flipped through more pages. "It seems to me like you're onto something here, but I want to be sure before we move forward. Have you talked to any of your other siblings? Anyone willing to give us a hand with this?"

"Actually, there's someone here I think can help." Ryder stood and walked to his uncle's office door and opened it. "Her name came up in the conversation at the wedding, and it didn't take much to track her down." He motioned to someone in the reception area and then stepped aside. "Uncle William, this is Jen Lawson."

William stood and welcomed their visitor with a smile. "Thank you for being willing to meet with us. Please, have a seat."

"I have to admit that I feel a little overwhelmed by all of this," Jen said as she sat down. "When your nephew contacted me, I thought he was crazy."

Another small chuckle escaped before William could help it. He looked over at Ryder and smiled. "Well, we Montgomerys tend to be a little unorthodox at times." His expression turned serious as he leaned forward on his desk. "My family means the world to me. In a million years, I never would have imagined Ryder coming to me with such a request. As of late, most of my nieces and nephews seem to run in the opposite direction when they see me coming. I'm sure he's mentioned my recent hobby…"

"You mean the whole matchmaking thing?" she said with a saucy grin.

William looked at the woman and smiled broadly before turning to his nephew. "I like her," he said. "I think she's going to be an asset to this whole thing."

"What exactly are you planning?" she asked.

"It's been a little over ten years," William began, "and this conversation Ryder had at my son Mac's wedding was the first time James even mentioned what happened back then. He's distanced himself from his family and is leading a very solitary life. I can't bear to see it, and I think it's gone on long enough."

Ryder pulled up a chair and finally sat back down. "He's my brother, but to be honest, I had no idea exactly what had happened. We were close growing up, but once we hit our teens…well, things changed. Back then, he was rebellious. He and my dad fought all the time and were always at each other's throats. Then he finally left and went to live with some distant relatives of my mother's. I'm ashamed to admit this, but I was too self-absorbed to pay much attention to what was going on. Apparently my parents had some kind of inkling of what had happened at the time, but they kept his secret for him. None of us had a clue."

Jen looked between the two of them and leaned back in her seat. "I still can't believe that James is from such an affluent family." She shook her head in disbelief. "I mean, back then, when we all knew him, he was working as a landscaper, had no car, and seemed to be dirt poor. I think that speaks highly of his character—especially knowing what I know now—but why would someone purposely make their life more difficult when they didn't have to?"

"I think he found having the Montgomery name to be more of a burden than a blessing," Ryder said. "It's opened a lot of doors for us, but my brother wanted to get by on his own merits and not because of his name.

On top of that, my father was grooming all of us for corporate careers. That was never James's style. I think he felt that he had to take drastic measures to be who he wanted to be."

"That's one of the drawbacks of being from a big family," William said with a sigh. "There's a lot of pressure on the Montgomery men to continue the family traditions in the business. James wanted to make his own way. As long as he lived at home, that wasn't possible. My brother Robert was not pleased that James moved so far away—in spite of their differences. Unfortunately, he had no choice but to let him make his own mistakes."

"I still can't believe all he went through," Ryder said. "I don't know if there was anything I could've done at the time, but I hate the thought of him going through it all alone."

"It was worse to be there living it with them, with Selena and James," she said sadly. "I never felt so helpless in my life."

All three grew silent for a long moment before William straightened in his chair. "And that's why we're doing what we're doing. Enough time has passed. This situation should never have gotten to this point, and I think between the three of us, we can rectify it." He stared intently at the woman before him. "I need to know that you are fully committed to this. You are going to be the most directly involved, and you're going to need to keep your story straight in order for it all to work out."

She gave a small smile. "Actually, your timing couldn't be better. When I get back home, it seems I will have a legit reason to get in touch with James. Selena is going to be the problem."

William wanted to probe into the woman's predicament, but right now his nephew's future and happiness were on the line. "Do you keep in touch with her? With Selena?"

She nodded. "We talk at least once a week, but she hasn't come home in…well…" She shrugged her shoulders and looked at the two Montgomery men. "A long time."

Clapping his hands together, William said, with a wicked grin, "Well then, it's about time Miss Selena Ainsley received an offer to come home that's too good to refuse." Standing, he reached over his desk to shake her delicate hand. "Ryder will fill you in on all the details, and if there's anything else you need from me, please feel free to contact me. Anytime. Day or night." Reaching down, he found a business card and then wrote on the back of it. "That's my personal phone number on the back. I expect to hear from you periodically to keep me up to date."

"I wish I had your confidence, sir," Jen said hesitantly as she took the card from him. "I'm afraid too much time has gone by, that maybe it won't all work out."

"I have an excellent track record, my dear. My sons were all stubborn and convinced they didn't need any help with their lives, and now? They're all married with children on the way. Which reminds me." He turned to Ryder and grinned. "How is Casey doing?"

Ryder smiled at the mention of his wife. "She's finally done with the morning sickness and is getting her energy back. I have to remind her to take it easy most days. All in all, we are both beyond excited for this baby's arrival." He turned to the woman. "And don't let my uncle fool you; he'll try to take credit for my marriage too, but I was already on a mission to win Casey back."

"You can tell yourself that all you want, Ryder, but you and I both know that if it hadn't been for me, there wouldn't have been a wedding for you to work with Casey on."

Ryder rolled his eyes and couldn't help but smile at his uncle. "I was already in the area and had no idea about the wedding when I walked over to Casey's beach house. Sorry, old man, but this match is firmly on me."

William winked at his female guest. "I'm four for four, no matter what my nephew says."

She chuckled. "With a track record like that, I don't think James and Selena stand a chance."

"Atta girl!" William bellowed with characteristic gusto. "I knew we'd win you over. I look forward to hearing from you in the very near future." And with that, he excused himself and fairly skipped out of his office.

William smiled and nodded to his assistant Rose on his way out. "If you need me, you can reach me on my cell. I think I'm going to take my lovely wife out for a celebratory lunch."

Rose was used to her boss's cheery moods and his multiple excuses for celebrating. "What are we celebrating today, sir?"

"Another successful match."

Yes, there was nothing like a challenge to put a little pep in your step, and if this challenge turned out the way he thought it would, William Montgomery's feet weren't going to touch the ground for a long time.

Chapter 1

"I DON'T UNDERSTAND. I THOUGHT THIS WAS A DONE DEAL. There wasn't enough interest or funds to make it happen, so I just thought we were through," Selena Ainsley said over the phone.

"So did all of us," Jen continued, "but it seems like someone has stepped forward and is providing the funds to cover the cost of the entire reunion. All we need now is a person who is able to pull together an event of this magnitude on short notice. You know, the kind of woman who is super organized, great with delegating and numbers, and who maybe, perhaps, does this for a living. Sound familiar?"

"You can't be serious," Selena said with more humor than disbelief.

"As a heart attack."

"Jen, as much as I would love to help out, there is no way that I can get away for the length of time it would take to put together something like this reunion. You need to find someone local who can handle all the particulars. It's too much to manage from six hundred miles away." She could have added that Jen should probably look for someone who actually wanted the job and the chance to go to the reunion, because that certainly wasn't her.

"Oh, please," Jen said with a snort of mock derision. "You know as well as I do that you can delegate a lot of the particulars. We have a venue, and you can speak to the catering staff anytime you need to, even from six hundred miles away. I'm sure with all of your connections you can organize the invitations and activities and whatever else is needed for this reunion. C'mon, say yes."

Selena was torn. Ordinarily, this was the type of job she loved: big venue, short notice, and a bit of challenge. The problem wasn't the job, per se; it was the location. It had been years since she had gone back to the small Long Island town where she had grown up, and just the thought of returning there now made Selena break out in a cold sweat.

If it were anybody else calling, she would have had no problem telling them no. But this was Jen. Her best friend. Her confidante. Her conscience.

Dammit.

"Don't do this to me, Jen," she began.

"Do what? Offer you a fabulous challenge? I know you thrive on this sort of thing. Everything is essentially paid for; the donor wrote us a huge check. It's a no-brainer. Basically, all you have to do is talk to a few people and show up. You can do this kind of thing in your sleep."

"Then I'm sure you or someone else can handle it. Seriously, I don't have that kind of time—"

"Okay, look," Jen interrupted. "I think I've been more than understanding. You moved away and never came back, and I never pushed you to. I come and visit you, and I love seeing you, but I'm beginning to feel like this friendship is a bit one-sided."

"That's not fair—"

"Not finished!" Jen snapped and instantly felt bad about her tone. "I'm not saying you weren't within your rights; however, it's been like…forever. Enough is enough. The thought of our ten-year reunion without you is just not even within my realm of comprehension. You were student body president, Selena. Everyone will expect to see you there. And on top of that, I'm your best friend and…well, to be honest with you, things haven't been going so great for me lately, and I could really use a little time with you." Jen knew it was hitting below the belt using her private issues to flush Selena out, but desperate times called for desperate measures.

"What's going on?" Selena asked, concern lacing her voice.

"Remember that guy I told you about? Todd?"

"Vaguely."

Jen would have felt annoyed at her friend's lack of memory, but Todd had been nothing but a blip on the radar. "Well, he's kind of been stalking me. It's starting to freak me out."

"What? Oh my gosh! Jen! Are you okay? Have you gone to the police?"

"I have, and basically there isn't a whole lot they can do because he's not threatening me or anything like that. It's just harassment."

"Like what?"

"He calls a *lot*. I run into him everywhere. Honestly, it's kind of creepy."

"What does he say when you answer the phone or see him?"

"Basically, he's pleasant."

"And…" Selena prompted.

"Until I say that I don't want to see him again; then he tends to get a little mean."

"But he hasn't threatened you?"

"No," Jen said with a sigh. "Like I said, I went to the cops and filed a report, but unless he threatens me, there's nothing they can do. Their hands are tied and so are mine."

"Have you thought about changing your phone number?"

"About a dozen times a day."

"Then why haven't you?"

"Because I keep thinking he'll stop and just go away. I hate having to disrupt my life because this loser can't take no for an answer."

"Jen, you have to do something. If he continues to have access to you, then he wins."

"I'm finally at a place where I feel like my life is going well: I own my own little house, my job is good… If I could just get rid of this creep, life would be perfect. Plus, it wouldn't hurt if my best friend would come to our ten-year reunion that we planned together."

Selena laughed. "Cheap shot, Jen."

"I'm not above begging."

"I just don't think—"

"Then don't think," Jen said quickly.

"But what if—?"

"You won't."

"How can you be sure, Jen?"

It was times like this that Jen hated the physical distance between them because all she wanted to do was to wrap her arms around her best friend and hug her. "Selena, you are a grown woman. You own a successful business, and you never turn away from a challenge. Except this one. It's time to own it and face it."

Selena's gut clenched. "What if people, you know, bring it up?"

"So what! It happened, Selena, and all of the denial in the world isn't going to change it. I'm not trying to trivialize it, but there it is. And believe it or not, everyone has moved on with their lives. I'm sure the topic of you and James Montgomery isn't something everyone we know is dying to talk about. People have gotten married, had kids, gotten great jobs, and some have crazy stalkers in their lives… It's not all about you, you know." The last was said with a smirk that Selena could detect even over the phone.

It was hard to say which emotion was the stronger one at the moment. Hearing James's name out loud for the first time in years knocked all of the breath out of her and left her shaking, but Jen's teasing tone helped lighten the mood almost immediately. Perhaps she was the only one who remembered or even thought about her past relationship with James. Clearly he hadn't, since he'd never bothered to look her up. Maybe it was time to put some old ghosts to rest and go back to her childhood home and see her friends.

"*If* I say yes," she began, but Jen's whoop of delight stopped her and had her laughing. When they finally calmed down, Selena continued, "If I say yes, then I'll need you to email all of the information to me right away so I can get started. What kind of time frame are we looking at?"

"Eight weeks," Jen answered and prayed that she wasn't cutting things too short.

Selena did a mental check of her calendar and all that would have to be accomplished in order for her to pull this off. "It's going to be tight, Jen, but if you promise to help me and get a committee together quickly, I think we can have one heck of a ten-year reunion."

"I've already got the committee lined up and the email is drafted. I was just waiting for you to say yes."

"Mighty confident, weren't you?"

"Hopeful. And yes, there is a difference."

"Only you could talk me into this, Jen. You know that, right?"

"That's what I was counting on," she said and let out her first relaxed breath of the entire conversation. "So when do you think you'll actually come up here?"

That is a good question, Selena thought to herself. "I should be able to do the bulk of it all from here, but I'll come up a couple of days beforehand, to make sure everything's in place."

"A couple of days? *A couple of days*?" Jen cried. "I pour my heart out to you about everything that I'm going through, and you can't even spare me a little extra time? That's just cold."

Selena pinched the bridge of her nose and counted to ten to wait out her friend's audition for most dramatic phone conversation. Finally, she relented. "Fine. I'll block out two weeks of time to come up there. A week before and a week after. How's that?"

"Is there any way I can convince you to stay longer?" Jen asked.

"No."

"Fine," she said with a sigh. "Two weeks, but I would prefer that it be more time before the reunion."

"Why?"

"Because that means you'll get here sooner. You have no idea how much it means to me that you're finally coming home, Selena."

She wasn't going home, Selena reminded herself; she was just going back to a place she used to live to visit a friend. Her home was in North Carolina now. She wanted to remind Jen of that fact, but the emotion in her friend's voice was enough for Selena to avoid trying to back out again. "I really am sorry I've stayed away so long, Jen. I never realized I was hurting you."

"I understand why you have, but I miss you."

"Well, by the end of those two weeks, you are going to be sick of me. I'm staying with you, right?"

"As if I'd let you stay anyplace else! I will do my best to make my guest room a place you'll never want to leave!"

"Ease up there, Sparky," Selena said with a laugh. "I have a business that needs me and employees who depend on me here in North Carolina. I'm giving you two weeks, but then it's back home for me."

"Fine, fine, fine," Jen said dismissively, "be that way. All I'm saying is that maybe it won't take another reunion to make you come back again."

"One trip at a time, Jen. One trip at a time."

About the Author

New York Times and *USA Today* bestselling author Samantha Chase released her debut novel, *Jordan's Return*, in November 2011. Although she waited until she was in her forties to publish for the first time, writing has been a lifelong passion. Her motivation was her students: teaching creative writing to elementary-age students all the way up through high school, and encouraging those students to follow their writing dreams gave Samantha the confidence to take that step as well.

When she's not working on a new story, Samantha spends her time reading contemporary romances, blogging, playing way too many games of Scrabble or solitaire on Facebook, and spending time with her husband of more than twenty years and their two sons in North Carolina.

Return to You

The Montgomery Brothers

by Samantha Chase

New York Times and *USA Today* bestselling author

———

She will never forget their past…

He can't stop thinking about their future…

James Montgomery has achieved everything he'd hoped for in life…except marrying the girl of his dreams. After a terrible accident, Selena Ainsley left ten years ago. She took his heart with her, and she's never coming back. But it's becoming harder and harder for him to forget their precious time together, and James can't help but wonder what he would do if they could ever meet again.

———

What readers are saying about Samantha Chase:

"Samantha Chase really knows how to tell a story."

"Perfect romance! Love it, love it, love it!"

For more Samantha Chase, visit:

www.sourcebooks.com

Meant for You

The Montgomery Brothers

by Samantha Chase

New York Times and *USA Today* bestselling author

———

She dares to dream...

Summer Montgomery wants to be taken seriously almost as much as she wants her brother's best friend, Ethan. But with a long résumé of seemingly random career choices and a protective brother on watch, those things are nothing more than pipe dreams...

Does he dare to try?

Ethan Reed would like nothing more than to live by his own rules. Not wanting to disappoint his best friend Zach, or any of the Montgomerys, Ethan's had to push aside his long-denied feelings for Summer. But it only takes one night away from watchful eyes to make impossible dreams come true...

———

What readers say about the Montgomery Brothers series:

"The Montgomery brothers are perfect romance!"

"Great story line, strong characters—a great read."

For more Samantha Chase, visit:

www.sourcebooks.com

Not So New In Town

Harmony Homecomings

by Michele Summers

—◁◇▷—

You can't go back, and you can't stand still…

Lucy Doolan is a marketing genius. She can sell rain to a frog and snow to a polar bear. Newly single and unemployed, she's lured back to her hometown of Harmony, North Carolina, to help out her pregnant evil stepsister…only to find her former crush, heartthrob Brogan Reese, has returned too, to open a new business in town. To add insult to injury, he's still hot.

If the thunder don't get you, then the lightning will…

Brogan never noticed Lucy much when they were young, but seventeen people have recommended her to help him. She's got his attention now. With her sweet personality, brilliant imagination, and penchant for doing the completely unpredictable, Brogan is finding a whole lot of excuses to spend his days—and nights—with Lucy.

—◁◇▷—

Praise for *Find My Way Home*:

"A lot of emotion and off-the-charts sexual tension." —*RT Book Reviews*

For more Michele Summers, visit:

www.sourcebooks.com

I'll Stand By You

by Sharon Sala

New York Times and *USA Today* bestselling author

—◦◦◦—

When no one ever takes your side...

Dori Grant is no stranger to hardship. As a young single mother in the gossip-fueled town of Blessings, Georgia, she's weathered the storm of small-town disapproval most of her life. But when Dori loses everything within the span of an evening, she realizes she has no choice but to turn to her neighbors.

All you need is one person in your corner

Everyone says the Pine boys are no good, but Johnny Pine has been proving the gossips wrong ever since his mother died and he took over raising his brothers. His heart goes out to the young mother and child abandoned by the good people of Blessings. Maybe he can be the one to change all that...

—◦◦◦—

Praise for *The Curl Up and Dye*:

"A delight...I couldn't put it down." —*Fresh Fiction*

"One of those rare treats." —*RT Book Reviews*

"Engaging, heartwarming, funny, sassy, and just plain good." —*Peeking Between the Pages*

For more Sharon Sala, visit:

www.sourcebooks.com